A Mind of Smoke

Rebecca Maeve Hartwell

Content Warnings
WARNING: CONTAINS SPOILERS!!!

Depicted (on the page):
Adult language; explicit and vulgar in every sense. I write adult characters who use adult language doing adult things. Fully explicit/adult sex scenes. Confrontation with abuser. Death (adult humans only). Violence, gore, injury. Alcohol and substance consumption. One use of the 'N' word. Mistaken cheating that didn't actually happen.

Mentioned (NOT on the page):
Mention/descriptions of rape, sexual coercion, non-con, etc. in backstory (Zero non-con depicted). Mention/descriptions of abuse in backstory. Mention/descriptions of cheating in backstory. Mention of abortion in backstory and in the abstract. Acid attacks (mention, not depicted). Word use: Amputation, decapitation.

Bonus Material

To claim your free eBook copy of the prequel novella for the Unlocked series, A *Life of Stone*, scan the code below or visit: www.rebeccamaevehartwell.com/a-life-of-sto ne

A Life of Stone

CHAPTER ONE

A ngie picked her way through the maze of bodies, doing her best to look lazily pleased and like she wasn't a little grossed out by the orgy that had devolved across the floor of the main hall of the mansion. She pulled the skirt of her long, silver silk dress out of the way as a threesome rolled off their velvet cushions to the thick, crimson carpet, not even noticing that they nearly collided with their hostess. *Why would they?* Angie mused, glancing over the sprawling mass to the other end of the gilt hall to where their guests who were still upright were just as inebriated, and indulging equally debauched delights in gluttony, gossip, and intoxication. It was the winter solstice and Saturnalia week was in full swing. Everyone seemed to think that since they had bread, they might as well also play at circuses.

She turned away with a swish of silk when someone reached for her, finally spotting the reason for them hosting at all. The familiar shaven head of Noah Byrne rose over the rest, grinning lazily as he shifted around with his partners. Angie swallowed, wishing she could avert her gaze, but knowing it would spoil her act. The orgy had been planned meticulously to lure the Supreme

Justice of the English Court out into the open with his guard down, and she had to take advantage of it working. She hadn't seen him since the blackmail banquet they'd hosted two-and-a-half months ago and didn't know when she would again.

Angie mentally checked that her aura, swirling around her like a cloud of smoke, only expressed the serene arousal she wanted it to and approached. "Hello, Lord Justice, I'm so glad to see you."

Noah stood, the faint fog of tan magic surrounding him going as rigid as his anatomy. "Hey," he said in a rough voice, and Angie took in his wine-soaked complexion. "Thank you. You too."

Angie plastered an admiring smile across her face, brushing her fingers down his bare arm, and tried not to think about her previous encounters with the large Celt. She handed him the untouched drink in her other hand, which he downed in one. "I hope you're having a good time, and I don't mean to interrupt, but I wondered if we could have a word?" An honest twist of darker smoke in her aura threatened to betray the urgency in what she hoped to get from Noah, but she soothed it.

"Sure, when I'm done here," Noah said, gesturing just behind him where three women and another man were tugging at him to rejoin them. "Unless..." His gaze turned hungry, and he reached for her hand. "Would you join us?"

In a snap, Angie's aura was peppered with orange sparks, and she repressed her revulsion, snatching her hand back out of Noah's reach. "No, I wish I could, but

I shouldn't," Angie said with a show of disappointment, dropping her shoulders. She fought the urge to will her magic into a shield around her against the man before her, who pouted.

"Are you sure?" Noah said in his lilting accent, but another voice behind him cut him off.

"Hey, Angie," Casey said, appearing from behind her, his usual exuberance far more subdued than normal. "Have a minute?"

Angie's stomach dropped. "Yeah, for sure." She led Casey by the sleeve of his iridescent beetle-green suit to the edge of the party by one wall. She stopped when she was reasonably sure they weren't going to be overheard, and hardened her Fire aura into shields for the rest. "What are you doing here? If you're caught..."

Casey looked startled, his expressive white-blond brows drawing with concern. "Wait, what? I thought I was still in good standing with the Court. Just not very active. I've still been receiving my allowance, which I've been sharing out with you-know-who..."

"Oh," Angie breathed, the knot in her gut loosening with pleased relief. "Sorry, I thought you were, you know, over that line." Casey shook his head, looking shell-shocked. "I'm sorry. What did you want to talk to me about?"

Casey ruffled his messy blond hair with a slender, tattooed hand. "Nothing. I was just getting you away from Noah. I don't miss those days."

Angie hid her frustration at having been interrupted in the face of her friend's good intentions. Her brain glitched about what he meant about 'those days' before remembering that he was trans and had experienced her side of creepy or demanding men in the past. "Oh, right. Thank you."

Casey relaxed. "No problem. I remember you telling me he wasn't good at taking no for an answer, and I don't want you having any reasons to run away or disappear again." Casey's voice broke, and he covered it by clearing his throat. He looked away, his cheeks touched with pink, and he frowned at something behind Angie.

She turned to see Marissa slowly and intently reaching for Daniel's bare hand, and felt her aura click over from smoke to flames. She opened her mouth to angrily shout at them to stop, but the immature, over-possessiveness of her instinctual reaction caught up with her just in time, and she snapped it shut. Through the crowd, Angie saw Marissa pull back when her fingers were an inch away, laughing, and Daniel dropped his hand, too, saying something sly or teasing in reply with a lopsided smile.

"Catch you later?" Angie asked Casey, her attention fully distracted.

"Yeah, no problem. See you soon."

Angie shot him a tight, apologetic smile, and he gave her a reassuring nod before moving away toward the far end of the hall. She could feel the flush in her cheeks but ignored it, mindful of her posture and gait as she slipped her way through the crowd to Daniel.

He was standing in the heart of the throng, dressed in black from head to toe, a gold watch, tie pin, and rings the only exceptions. His wide, expressive mouth stretched into a smile when she spotted him, making his perfect teeth, sharp nose, and angular jaw more pronounced. His dark eyes beneath his low brows, half-hidden in the chandelier light, were unreadable, even with the pale yellow light of his aura twining placidly around him.

She kissed Daniel when she reached him. "There you are," he said in his rich accent with endearing, honest delight, and Angie smiled too when Marisa's lips pursed. They had a mission, she reminded herself. He was just playing his part. He was her Daniel. Beneath his public personas, he was the real Daniel she knew him to be. Angie returned the smile he gave her, draping an arm around his waist and leaning into him with the same besotted air as their disrobed guests a dozen paces away.

Beside Daniel stood Jonathan, his metallic copper suit an oddly close match to his tan, weathered face, but beautifully accented by his black hair and beard, and the rich, deep blue of his Water aura, which he had draped around his shoulders as a classical mantle. She couldn't help but compare the two very different ways her lover and dearest friend, brothers in their own right, existed, lingering on Daniel. She still wasn't used to his short, sandy-gray beard or shorter light brown hair that barely brushed his ears, but at least he seemed familiar to her again, after her long banishment.

Marissa gave Angie a small nod of greeting, seeming derailed from whatever she'd been saying. "Never mind," she said. Angie didn't look away from the older patrician, taking in her long, thick black hair coiled atop her head, and the way the satin ribbon of her blood-red aura wove in and out of her brown skin, exactly as she'd seen it the first time they'd met. "It sounds like the loophole in your skin curse isn't one you fully understand, so I won't press."

Angie's stomach lurched, her aura roiling over itself from gray to black smoke that smelled of cedar and hot metal. "Enjoy the party," she said blandly. Adding, with more edge, "Make yourself at home." Angie shifted around between Marissa and Daniel to face him fully as the other woman moved away with Jonathan, the tension in her shoulders easing.

"What did you tell her about the loophole in the skin curse I found?" Angie asked when she stopped feeling the faint tingle of Marissa's blood-red aura through her own.

Daniel arched a brow. "Everything I could. That you said it was a matter of adjustment, and that beyond that, I have no idea how I am able to touch you, and only you, with my bare skin without you passing out."

The party seemed to quiet with the demons in her heart telling her to lash out against the whole spectacle and everyone in it. "Okay." Daniel was watching her to say more, but she didn't feel like explaining her momentary intense jealousy at the mere thought of Marissa finding her loophole.

Angie kissed him fully, tasting the sweet and tart on his lips. She felt his hands wrapping behind her back, his pale yellow aura of light twining through hers, and she wished briefly that they could safely participate in the hedonism they had contrived to lure out the English Supreme Justice.

Angie pulled away, remembering their purpose, and licked her lips as the delicate scent of rosewood smoke leaked from her aura. "I made my approach but got interrupted." She and Daniel shared a loaded look.

"We have to try again," Daniel said, his lips barely moving, and Angie glanced over his shoulder to make sure his obscuring shields were active and as formidable as ever. "We can't let the English lock get rebuilt and lose everything you unlocked by breaking it. Not if we want to stand a chance of freeing all the other languages from the same exploitation and repression. To do all of that, we need an in, and for that, we need Noah Byrne."

Just as Angie stepped away with a sigh to return to her unsavory task of convincing or seducing a man she'd once called her friend, a commotion at the grand door to the hall made them both turn.

Milton Cartwright strode in among his usual collection of devotees and sycophants, even more vibrantly magnanimous than normal, his fuchsia magic billowing around him as he accepted congratulations. "I've been appointed to the Council!" he crowed to the whole room before Angie could wonder why. His eyes were locked on Daniel beside her, his round face beneath his halo of white-blond hair twisted with sadistic satisfaction. His Transvaalian accent was as clipped and subtle as always, and touched many terrible memories for Angie, making her aura shrink in toward her skin before she could soothe it.

"Fuck," Daniel muttered. "I thought, for once, we might get out ahead of that bastard."

Angie let a long breath hiss through her nose as anxiety teased up in her chest. The other patricians around Milton, a churning mass of every color of aura imaginable, seemed to be the usual assortment of kiss-asses, with a smattering of people desperate to just be near enough to feel a part of those circles. They were making a beeline for Angie and Daniel over and through the front half of the room strewn with writhing bodies, and Daniel held his arm out to Angie.

"I suppose we must change tack."

She rested her hand in the crook of his elbow, and when his aura fluttered cold, she gave it a squeeze. "Might as well, since he's here. Let's try."

"Welcome," Angie said as the group approached and came to a stop before her. Several auras nearby flared and Angie braced, but none instigated. "That certainly is news, *Councilor*," she said with a small curtsey, and beside her, Daniel bowed a degree. "May we speak privately to offer our congratulations properly?"

Milton's piggy eyes flashed warily, and he waved one hand, the other absently petting the maroon velvet of his suit over his belly. "No need. I have nothing to hide." He puffed out his chest, his double chin quivering, and Angie smiled wickedly, fighting the urge to roll her eyes at his defensiveness. He'd chosen to come to them.

"Oh, but you do," Daniel said. "Remember? Our little secrets around your stint as Supreme Justice?"

Several people turned to Cartwright questioningly, and his posture sagged, his face hardening. "Please give us a minute," he called to his posse, and they slowly dispersed away from the three, muttering as they went, in a rustle of costly fabric and jeweled chains.

"We have a favor to ask of you," Angie said, and Milton's eyes narrowed. "Several, in fact." She took a step closer, Daniel beside her, and blinked away the stench of cigar smoke clinging to him that made her eyes water. It was different when the smoke wasn't her own magic.

"You will help me become the next Councilor," Daniel said, "now that your admission has been rammed through. I would ask a more popular or powerful Councilor instead, but you are apparently the only one vain, pompous, and possibly stupid enough to reveal your identity to the masses."

Angie admired the way Daniel's Caledonian accent added weight and music to the words he spoke and did her best to follow his lead without mocking him or embarrassing herself. "Secondly, you will aid Supreme Justice Noah Byrne in making sure that Daniel is assigned a recruit this year. We wish to do our part in shaping the newest generation of patricians to uphold our great and ancient system."

Cartwright's complexion darkened by shades as she and Daniel spoke. "Blackmail is illegal," he spluttered quietly. "I will not have demands made of me, a Senator and Councilor."

"You want to talk about illegality?" Daniel replied, pulling Angie one elegant stride closer to Milton. "Then perhaps I can make sure you are given no choice but to talk to the Court, Senate, and Council about your extremely illegal misuse of the English Focal Nucleus for three ceremonies, implanting orders to benefit you alone, rather than all patricians as was your office. Or about your even more illegal siphoning off of English magic for your own use when the governing bodies of the patrician Empire were already strained in their own allocations to maintain order?"

"Careful, Fawl. You don't want to push me over the edge. Damage my reputation enough, and I'll have nothing left to lose. You don't want to see what I'd do then."

"Really? Because I don't think you would have anything left to hurt me with, be that friends, magic, or breath in your lungs, if everyone found out about how your catalyzing moment, from which your sponsor saved you, was killing two people in cold blood."

The color drained from Milton's face, and Angie smiled. They'd already told him that they knew about his misuses of his former office. The older elements of his past were newly discovered by Daniel and relayed to her.

"I am a Councilor now," Milton spluttered, the fluctuations in his aura giving away his dismay at the conversation not going as he'd hoped. "I am above you, and you will show me respect! I won't stand here listening to vague, wild guesses from you, a traitor, and your bitch." His attention turned to Angie. "The hypocrisy of a Fire aura trying to make me feel bad for my actions is laughable. All you people ever do is cause destruction. I should never have let you be recruited. I should have let you die like you were supposed to."

Angie didn't expect the jab at the reputation for Fire auras to be destructive to sting, but it did, and Daniel responded for her.

"The Nkosis'. In Johannesburg."

Milton fell back a step, which Daniel followed, holding the invasive closeness between them. "Oh yes, we know about that too. Tell me. Did you just kill that man so that there was someone in the world more miserable than you? It seems so scrying back on it. And when your sponsor snatched you up, saving you from your fated death on the weapon of his widow, did you enjoy watching her bleed out slowly, the gun in your hand, as much as it looks like you did?"

"You can't... you can't know about that. We erased it."

"Ah yes," Angie purred. "Your sponsor helped you dump the bodies and used her magic to shield and obscure the event. But that wasn't good enough for you, was it? That ugly, bullied, worthless nobody you were at twenty-eight? No. You had to use the two things you had—matches for the smokes you could steal and a bottle of cheap rum—and burn the whole neighborhood down. Over three hundred dead. Men, women, and children. Because you and your sponsor both knew those were deaths you would need to pay for with your own, unlike any of the deaths you have spent so long trying to punish Daniel for. You fucking hypocrite. And if anyone found out, you wouldn't get a trial from your peers. You'd be stripped of every scrap you never should have gotten as a patrician and banished as unceremoniously as you deserve. I might be the Fire aura, but you're the monster."

Milton was watching Angie wide-eyed, and she didn't hide how good it felt to finally, fully, put Milton in his place as he stammered, "You both know…"

"Yes," Daniel said, loud enough for a few people nearby, all other people who had been at their blackmail feast, to hear. "And if anything happens to one of us, the other ruins your life. We promise."

"And it goes without saying that once you have suffered in the gutters long enough for killing the person we loved most in the world, we promise to the other every day that you will die by the hand of the survivor." The words weren't planned, and Angie felt Daniel's emotions soar and drop through his aura where it overlapped with hers, honed by closeness and time. They didn't have to be planned. She'd spent seventeen months fighting to survive in the banishment the old man before her had thrown her into. Nearly a year and a half for that promise to seep into her bones if she returned and found Daniel wasn't waiting for her.

Angie saw Daniel's Adam's-apple bob several times before he could speak, his voice not quite as firm as it had been a minute before. "That's right. And everyone knows that no one, not even you, are a match for the two of us together."

"Maybe not," Milton said, just quiet enough to sound menacing. "But you have set the rules of this game, and I can play it just as well. You should both be dead. You," he nodded at Daniel, "should have died when Shan tried to kill you. I wish every day she'd succeeded, and maybe it's time someone finished the job. And you," he turned to Angie, "should have been dead a dozen ways by now. I will find your weakness, and when I do, neither of your threats will mean a damn thing."

Without warning, a tall, slender man with steel-gray hair and a look of terrified shock appeared between them to many gasps and exclamations. "Anthony?" All three said in unison.

"You aren't welcome here," a voice among the onlookers called. "Thief. Traitor. Attempted murderer."

Anthony swore, ducking his head. "Sorry. I didn't realize…" The moment he saw Milton, he tried to back away so fast he knocked into Angie and fell over. He scrambled back to his feet but hit a solid wall of fuchsia magic. Angie watched as his panic teased up his navy-blue aura into a fractured pattern that totally obscured him in patches, fully open in others. She took two steps along the curve of the shield Milton had trapped him in, clearly trying to Voyage away but unable to, whimpering.

"You ungrateful bastard," Milton shouted, and Angie saw several people outside the pink dome scowl, clearly confused as Jonathan pushed his way to the other side of the shield, placing a hand on it and scouring it with his ice-blue eyes and azure aura. When Cartwright spoke again, his first few words seemed to warp in her mind before clarifying again.

"You fucking traitor. I should kill you for running away from me. For betraying me. I gave you everything. I gave you magic, although you refused to see it. I gave you purpose, wealth, all of it! And you repay my kindnesses by informing me that I never really loved you, leaving to blab to the whole fucking patrician community that I performed unlawful banishments?"

Cartwright took a step toward his cowering ex-husband, and Angie stepped directly in between them, bringing up a shield of fire. Cartwright looked ready to claw her with his bare hands and Angie sent a thin thread of her aura to the edge of his shield, which was trapping them all in, to test the viability of shoving him back and breaking them all out to run. It was solid.

"It's true then!" Cartwright squealed, almost unhinged, looking between Anthony and Angie defending him. "You did run to them! The traitors in our midst! Giving them our secrets! I should have killed you that night, like I promised you I would. I should have chased you down and finished the job. You ungrateful, useless coward! When the end comes, don't think I'll show pity and bring you along. You will be left to die with the rest."

Daniel blocked Milton when he shifted to follow Anthony as he circled around behind Angie, wildly looking for a way out. The poor man looked ready to crawl out of his own skin. As Angie watched, she saw something that made her wonder if she was suddenly and mysteriously drunk. Anthony took a step that seemed to jitter forward through space, like the whole world moved backward around him. Angie blinked, but his next step did the same, and he passed through the barrier of Milton's shield like it was nothing, Voyaging away and disappearing with his third step.

"Milton!" Noah Byrne called from outside the shield, and all three turned to look. He had pulled on a pair of pants and his expression was stricken. The faces of everyone else watching and listening ranged from shock to disgust to open delight. Angie turned back just in time to see horror dawn in Milton's eyes as he dropped the orchid-pink shield. Jonathan lowered his hands, which a few people marked, including Noah, who added, "We could hear you. Every word. That's... that's so not what you told everyone happened around him disappearing."

No sooner had Noah finished speaking than the jeering began. Angie caught Jonathan's eye, pointing at him subtly with a *was that thanks to you?* Look. He nodded with a small smile and Angie felt a glow in her chest. She really had missed him in her banishment and was so glad to have him back in her life.

"You," Milton snarled, advancing on Jonathan, clearly having seen his interaction with Angie. He was stopped in his tracks as someone threw a cushion at him, his ruddy complexion darkening.

Daniel quickly intervened. "Doctor Crowther only exposed your words at my orders, Cartwright. He acts for his family as you act for yourself. Now. Don't forget the favor I asked from you."

Milton just puffed for a long moment as people hurled a cacophony of insults and harmless objects at him, calling him a liar. "You won't take from me what I've fought for," he eventually said, fully focused on Daniel. "You won't send me back to my suffering before magic saved me."

His words struck a deep, unsettling chord within Angie that left her reeling. She could have said the same from the depth of soul to explain what she was fighting for in heading off the new English Court lock.

Without waiting for a reply, Milton turned on his heel to whisper in the unwilling ear of Marissa, who looked horrified to have any contact with him under the circumstances.

"Wait," Angie said as Noah tried to scatter with Jonathan and the rest away from the irate Milton, turning her attention away. "We need to talk."

"Happy to," Noah said, looking anything but. "In fact, there are a few things I have to say."

Angie raised a hand when he drew breath to go on. "Save it. As far as I can recall, all our conversations in the last two years have been limited to a few topics, none of which I am interested in rehashing. I don't want to hear your pickup lines, your attempts to gaslight me, to hear you boast, or be accused of being nothing more than Daniel's puppet." Noah looked like a gasping fish, clearly unprepared for Angie to preempt whichever topic he'd been intending to resuscitate, and Angie let her vicious delight show. "No. I'm going to pick the topic. You remember that little dinner party we hosted two months ago? Remember the first course?"

The Celt went pale beneath his bushy beard at the veiled mention of their blackmail and threats to keep themselves safe after Angie's return. "Yes?"

"Well, we now have a favor to ask in exchange for staying quiet and uninvolved with what keeps happening to your plebeian girlfriends when you get bored with them or they dump you. Daniel wants to be assigned a recruit for this year's conference. That gives you exactly three months to pull whatever strings you have to."

"Now hang on," Noah protested, his posture shifting as if he'd rather fight than cave to their demands. Angie readied herself to defend, realizing they may have misstepped, but Milton turned to Noah, away from a dazed-looking Marissa, and the Supreme Justice stilled.

"No, it's alright. Do as they ask. Give him his recruit." Angie just blinked in surprise. Noah nodded, wilting, his lips pressed tight with a scowl. Angie felt a small rise of warmth in Daniel's aura beside her communicating his pride in her and took a deep breath. She wanted to feel triumphant, but if Milton was handing them what they needed, it must be a trap.

She gathered herself, bitter that they'd had to stray so far from their original tactic and desperate for the night to be over. "Good. And don't make me follow up with you on this. I have no patience for you left."

Milton made for the exit, stepping on various body parts of the patricians littering the cushions, carpets, and low couches who were either too intoxicated or distracted to have been disturbed by the dramatic but contained display. Marissa followed in his wake, her dark red aura messy and unreadable.

Angie moved to follow him, determined to make him stay until she gave him permission to leave, playing her part in the drama he always created.

"No, let him go," Daniel said, grabbing Angie's arm.

When she turned back, Angie felt a million miles away from the man holding her back. He was calculating. She was a fighter. She couldn't reconcile the two in her mind for a heart-dropping breath. Angie let go of her instinct and the way it prepared her body with adrenaline, and Daniel released his grip, looking for something to fill the awkward space between them.

"What the hell was that?" she asked, glancing around at the people who were all giving them a wide berth. "How did Anthony get out of the shield?"

"Don't know. Phase-walking, maybe? I had no idea he could do that. The skill was thought to have died out." Daniel scratched his short beard, his eyes worried as he scanned the crowd. "From the look on his face, I don't think Anthony knew he had that skill before just now either."

Angie was shocked. "How could he not know?"

Daniel looked at her, some of his worry melting into gentle amusement. "Do you know if you can phase-walk?"

"No, but I've never tried—oh."

Daniel smiled as Jonathan joined them. "No. That's the thing. People don't try to do things they don't know are an option. And even then, just as a person's aura as a whole is catalyzed by their experiences in life, so can individual skills be. Anthony may not have been a natural phase-walker before he needed to be tonight. It's just part of magic being intention and willpower."

Angie thought about how useful the skill would have been running through half-worlds for an eternity, and her pulse shot up. She searched for a different topic to change to as a drunkard nearby crashed into a golem crafted from a marble statue and sent its tray of glasses shattering across the floor.

Jonathan spared her. "This was good, despite not going to plan. We'll lie low now, and only start poking those bears again if we don't see progress by the Senate meeting at the end of February."

Angie only half-listened to Daniel's pleased reply, wondering why Milton's mention of life before magic had thrown her so off balance, and yet she'd felt so divorced from them. She'd left her life of suffering among other downtrodden humans behind nearly three years past. So why didn't she feel happier, or safer, or more healed when she looked at her life at large? *I should have gotten there by now. Whoever I am these days.* The thought nudged at something buried deep inside her. As old demons that whispered to her that she was a failure, fucking everything up, and might as well call it all quits reared their ugly heads, she shoved them right back down.

There would be time for that when she was done saving the world. *Stay focused. Get into the English Court's conference. Sabotage the solstice ceremony to stop them from rebuilding a Focal Nucleus that had been used to steal magic from anyone they disapproved of for thousands of years, using it to their own ends to run a global Empire that crushed the masses beneath their boot.*

Once their own continued powers were safe, they'd free the rest of the world. Make sure everyone being locked away from accessing their own power were freed so they could use it to force justice on everyone who had hurt them their whole lives. The grander thoughts finally brought Angie comfort, and she paused to process why.

The small wins weren't doing it for her anymore.

It's time for the bad guys to fucking finish losing.

CHAPTER TWO

T he clock on the temple tower behind Angie struck five, and she took a deep breath, shifting on the sweeping concrete and wood bench, and tugged down one sleeve of her fine wool coat against the cold. London in late February was gray and damp and smelled of cigarette smoke and stale beer. Construction work on a building a few blocks away competed with the sound of traffic and bustling people, and Angie tried to ignore it all. She let her eyes drift over the ever-shifting mass of smartly dressed people swarming around the artistic, raised planters in the open clearing of the courtyard among the forest of skyscrapers in the patrician quarter.

The Senate meeting Daniel was attending in the nearest monstrosity of steel and glass was scheduled to end at five, but Angie didn't expect them to be that prompt. Her finger strayed to her coat pocket, and she smiled. That morning, it had carried several fat envelopes of cash, employment paperwork she could alter and forge as needed, and keys to decent apartments. She and Daniel had spent most of the day going to visit the last of the women he had collected to testify against their common abuser just over a year ago, giving them each a chance at a new life, carefully carved out from their allowances from the English Court and favors extracted from Senator Utley, who oversaw the plebeian housing authorities in the English-speaking territories.

Angie tucked her hand back under her arm to warm her fingers, relishing the weight that now felt lifted from her shoulders, knowing she had finally finished doing something, anything, to make up for not being there for them through the trials to bring their abuser to justice. She closed her eyes, attempting to shift her boredom of waiting into some sense of peace among the bustling city life she hadn't yet readjusted to after so long in the wild on her own. It was strange to think of how connected everyone and everything was.

A bar of iron on the back of the bench pressed into the muscles along her spine, and thoughts of her life before magic, working in a Vasilis Corp. foundry, flashed through her mind. Everyone there, from the lowest worker to the foreman, to Mr. Vasilis himself, were just puppets to the Empire, and through that the patricians. *Did they even know how much was at stake and in play so far outside their understanding? What would happen to them when the facade of the Empire crumbled...*

"Angelica?" a familiar and uncertain voice asked a few feet away, and Angie's eyes flew open. Before her stood a tall young man, a few years older than her, with dark blue eyes and black hair, dressed in a suit a size too big for him.

"Holy shit," Angie said, standing quickly and trying to process. "Garrett. I haven't seen you since high school graduation. What are you doing in London?" Her hands and feet grew colder, and she found it hard to look him in the eyes. Did he know she'd cried through the last six months of high school because he'd dumped her?

The young man blinked, hefting his briefcase. "I was invited, all expenses paid, to interview at Augustus Investments." He nodded at the Suardo Building just past Angie. She blinked. Augustus Investments was the fake cover company for the Senate's London meetings, according to Daniel. "But look at you," Garett added, looking Angie up and down with an unreadable expression that made her uncomfortable. "You're a patrician now? How did you pull that off? Or are you just faking it with knockoffs?"

Angie opened her mouth, trying to come up with an answer, and felt Daniel's aura brush hers from behind. She turned to find him still a dozen paces away, his eyes locked on Garrett. He was dressed smartly in a navy shirt and black suit, his gray coat swaying in the cold wind that approached with him. He walked tensely but gracefully, his gold-handled cane tapping lightly on the stained paving slabs for show. He slid an arm around Angie's waist when he reached her side, and Angie's chest warmed in an instant, feeling it spread across her face and relax her shoulders.

"Everything alright?" Daniel asked, and Angie could hear the bracing stress in his voice. Garrett looked shocked, his eyes darting between them, before his expression soured and he retreated half a step.

"I'm fine," Angie said, her voice light and happy. "Just ran into someone from my hometown. Daniel, this is my ex from way back, Garrett. Garrett, this is my partner, Daniel Fawl." Daniel extended a hand gloved in black leather, and Garett shook it hesitantly. "How did the meeting go?" Angie wanted to ask more specifically about further details on the new Focal Nucleus, the lock of patrician power, which they would be trying to head off in the summer, but held back in front of a plebeian witness.

Angie turned to Daniel, and he gave her a meaningful look before tipping his head as his gaze slid past her. Angie followed to see what he was looking at, and found two London centurions approaching, hands on the weapons on their hips. Angie's breath caught, and her jaw clenched. She looked quickly at Daniel, trying to read him, but he just scowled out from under his low brows and gave her a small squeeze.

"Papers," the taller of the two centurions said, holding out a hand.

"Sorry?" Angie said, and the other centurion shifted his grip on his gun.

"It's alright," Daniel said, releasing Angie's waist to fish around in the large pocket of his coat. "I have our passports here." Angie watched him pull out their passports, likely summoned into his pocket a moment before, and handed them over. Nearby, Garrett fished his out of his breast pocket, looking pale. People walking by rubber-necked nervously as they passed, many patting their pockets or ducking their heads as they quickened their pace.

The taller centurion opened Angie's passport first. "You're from the Americas?" he asked, and Angie nodded. "Well," he sneered, "you'll need to return to your home province in the next ninety days, and register with the population office there, or face forceful deportation." Angie took her passport back from him with a twisting drop in her stomach. *What the hell was happening?*

When the centurion opened Daniel's passport, his entire demeanor changed. "I'm sorry, sir," he said quickly, glancing between the open document and Daniel's clothing and cane. "I should have realized. Patricians aren't affected by these new policies, of course." He handed the passport back to Daniel, looking Angie up and down. "Please just be sure that your papers are kept up to date and on your person, accurately reflecting your station or sponsorship status."

"Thank you, officers," Daniel said, gripping Angie's elbow and turning her away with a tight smile to the centurions. "We will." He pulled her away a dozen paces, and they stopped as the centurions checked Garrett's visas, informing him that he would also have to return to his home province.

She turned away to Daniel, hissing, "What the hell was that?"

Daniel blew a breath out through his teeth. "Well, you weren't around after your Victume Ceremony to get your papers updated like usual, or any of the other ways recruits are officially made full patricians, legally speaking. My passport shows my status, and apparently you can get the benefit of the doubt off that, for now. We can alter your papers as needed shortly."

Angie looked back at the centurions, still speaking with Garett, and he darted her a glance over his shoulder. For half a second, old bitterness blossomed into triumph in her chest, seeing the blatant regret and envy on his face.

"And why were our papers checked at all? What happened in the meeting?"

"Nothing good." Daniel pulled a hand down his worried face. "They passed several bills by the narrow majority we haven't gotten leverage over. They've decided to implement mass deportation of anyone living outside of their native province, and end border crossing of any kind. They want full segregation of languages and are going to start shuttering all social and public services for or with plebeian citizenship." Angie swallowed hard, and Daniel saw pinching the bridge of his nose. "It's bad. None of this bodes well for anyone. And based on this," he gestured to the centurions moving away from Garrett to approach the next little group of people trying to hurry by, "they already had everything lined up to be implemented at a go sign they wasted no time in giving to everyone already on the street."

"What can we do?" Angie asked. *Just kill the people giving the orders*, a small voice in her mind said, and she shoved it away.

Daniel shrugged, looking defeated. "Nothing today. We need people in the Imperial branches who could warn us when things like this start filtering into preparation stages, so we aren't blindsided and can get out ahead of them. That's not something we can make happen today."

Angie sighed, closing her eyes for a long moment, trying to dispel the sinking feeling in her gut. When she opened them again, Daniel's expression had softened a little, and he held out an arm to her. "Let's just go home," he said, and Angie wearily hooked her hand through his elbow, and let him lead her toward the alley bordering the temple to Hephaestus at the edge of the square.

As they stepped into the cloistered solitude to Voyage home to their cottage, the hair on the back of Angie's neck stood on end. She subtly pulled Daniel's arm forward when he slowed to check that they were unobserved, and his aura juddered warm and cool against her cheeks. He gave her a questioning glance, and Angie kept her gaze fixed firmly on the far end of the alley. "We're being followed."

"You're sure?"

Angie didn't answer and felt tension line her shoulders. Security cameras Daniel could deal with. Less so a stalker, especially when his relevant skills were carefully guarded secrets.

Daniel paused when they reached the street at the far end and moved to her other side. He pulled out his cell phone, sneaking the arm holding his cane around her back and pulling her close. Quick as a flash, he raised the phone high in front of them, kissed Angie on the cheek, making her grin, and snapped a photo. Angie was still processing what he'd just done when he brought the phone down, looking at the selfie displayed on the screen. Up in the corner of the picture, back down the alley behind them, were unmistakably Garret's legs.

Daniel's jaw clenched, but Angie didn't notice. Her eyes were locked on the selfie until the phone disappeared back into his pocket. That was probably the only photograph of her from the last four years of her life. The only picture in existence of her and Daniel together. Angie's chest heaved, and she touched the silver key through her scarf, trying to haul her mind away from the deep reaction to those thoughts she couldn't begin to sort through.

Angie looked around the bustling central-London street. They couldn't just go Voyaging away in front of plebeian witnesses, let alone on camera, with tension around the growing awareness of uncontacted recruits dying messily across the English-speaking world. She carefully kept her aura blank, and turned to Daniel, instinctively hoping that he would have a solution to the pickle they were in.

"Listen," Daniel said, his gloved thumb rubbing Angie's side in a way that made her melt. "I'm feeling too drained after today to trust my shielding or other abilities we might use to Voyage away safely. Why don't we just get the train home? We can get first-class seats, and can also grab something to eat at the station. We should be able to lose our tail between here and Minerva Station by cab, and that takes the stress off trying to find somewhere discreet."

Daniel was clearly confident and familiar with the idea, and Angie realized it might be a glimpse into his life before magic. The thought pleased her, and her eyes stopped stinging and crinkled as she considered.

"Yeah, alright. That sounds nice."

CHAPTER THREE

Angie turned away from the pastry kiosk in the packed rush-hour train station, searching for Daniel in the fading evening light filtering through the glass ceiling. She spotted him near the ticket booths, and when she caught his eye, he pointed to two seats together in the rows of chairs bolted to the polished floor, and Angie lifted her box of scones in acknowledgement.

Angie wove and shoved her way through the lines of people waiting for different kiosks or platforms, doing her best to tune it all out. When she glanced up to get her bearings to where Daniel had indicated to meet her, she saw someone doing what she was; trying to push their way through the throng, clearly intent on getting to Daniel. The woman was just the pretty side of average, maybe a decade older than Angie, with thick, brown hair cut in a short bob. The flow of people Daniel was navigating with ease seemed to be conspiring against her, and the closer Angie got to intercepting Daniel at the seats, the further behind the other woman fell.

When Angie reached Daniel, she opened her mouth to warn him, but before she could, Daniel pulled her in and kissed her deeply. Angie's mind went blank, and she nearly dropped her paper box of pastries. When he released her, Angie's mouth was twisted wide to one side, and she blinked at his answering lopsided grin, bemused. "What was that for?"

"Just feeling extra lucky to have you here, with me, and not anywhere else, with anyone else." Daniel gestured for Angie to sit before settling beside her. Angie let her aura warm a little and fill with cedar and rosewood smoke to caress him.

Her thoughts flitted back over the unexpected encounter with Garrett, who had been her first real heartbreak so many years ago. "Me too. Oh!" She leaned forward, scanning for the woman who had been following Daniel.

"What's up?"

Angie spotted the woman a dozen yards away, her face flushed and buried in her phone. When she caught Angie looking at her, she blushed a shade darker and turned her back, lifting her phone to her ear. Angie did a double blink, pressing her sight into the magical spectrum to confirm that the woman's aura was the washed-out ghostly color of a plebeian, and decided she must have thought Daniel was someone else she knew, and was embarrassed by the mistake. "Never mind. Here, I got us scones with cream and jam."

Daniel happily tugged off his gloves and took one from her when she unpacked the box, using the plastic knife to spread the toppings on. "Oh," he said in an undertone, setting the knife back in the box on his lap and passing her their passports. "While we're eating, see if you can use that gift of alteration of yours to get your passport updated. It's subtle enough magic that no one will notice."

Angie took them from him, tucking them between her legs while she got her own scone situated on a paper napkin, before laying them open on her lap side by side, and checking that the person beside her was snoring gently and that others along the bench were all thoroughly distracted and not paying her any attention. She looked at them both for a long minute, taking note of all the subtle differences, while Daniel stared at his phone. It didn't take much to change the color of the lining of her passport from dark blue to Imperial purple, and to shift the watermarks and holographic inlays to match those in Daniel's passport, indicating patrician status, which plebeians thought was just the ultimate wealthy class in the split legal distinctions around such things.

"What are you doing?" Angie asked when she'd finished, tucking her updated passport into the breast pocket of her coat, and Daniel's into his, before nibbling at the last of her pastry and crumpling the napkin into a ball. She still hadn't fully recovered her mindset around food from her banishment. Her instinct had been to wolf it down as quickly as possible and get as many more as she could immediately upon finishing.

"Sorting out our transport from the local station to the cottage. I'm pulling some strings with Marissa, who's head enforcer at the conference again this coming spring, to send over one of the conference cars with a driver golem they use for shuttle people in, in case we hit more Voyaging snags in Chippenham."

"Ah." Angie watched a solo centurion walking away from the ticket booths, scanning the crowd, and felt her stomach clench when his eyes landed on her and didn't leave. "Heads-up," she muttered. Daniel quickly followed her gaze and stiffened, just as the electric lights in the station flickered on in the growing dusk.

"I'm looking for a Miss Forester," the centurion said when he got over to them, his accent half Britannian, half American. Angie took the most noticeable deep breath she could, holding it as she handed her passport over. The centurion took it with one dark hand. He opened it, looking between the picture and Angie. "You confirm that you are Angelica Forester, from the Americas, born the twenty-ninth of June?"

Angie just nodded, trying to push away the old paranoia about just such an encounter that had been a constant theme in her life after escaping the American Tegesta peninsula, reminding herself that the ex-centurion she'd run from was now safely behind bars. The centurion just turned away without a word. Angie and Daniel both watched as he took them back to the ticket booth, and spent a few minutes talking to the clerk, and, for a minute that made Angie squirm, into his cell phone.

"Thank you, miss," he said when he finally returned, handing her back her passport with a dark smile. "You're all set. Have a nice day."

"Thank you," Angie replied. "May I ask what the trouble is?"

The centurion just puffed himself up, casually hooking a thumb on his gun belt with a cocky smirk. "Official

Imperial business. Just trust us to do our jobs, and don't worry your pretty little head about it."

Angie's lip curled the moment he turned away, and she blew out a long breath as she watched him move to check someone else's papers. "Power-tripping bastard," she muttered, tucking her passport away.

Daniel rubbed her shoulder, and she tried to let it soothe her. "It was nothing. Just part of the new citizenship policies. They probably just had you flagged as a patrician with outdated documents to double check. I'm only surprised that they didn't question how you got them updated in the last few hours."

The speakers overhead squawked, announcing that their train was arriving, and would be unloading before outbound boarding and departure, and Angie and Daniel both stood, looking at the scrolling announcement boards to see which platform. An odd spot of movement caught Angie's eye, and she glanced down to the ticket booths beneath the boards in time to see the woman who had been following Daniel earlier turn away from watching them with a smile, hurriedly purchasing a ticket from the clerk.

Daniel started moving away toward their platform and Angie followed, glancing ahead to the security line with metal detectors people were queued to get processed through. "Will they let you on the train with your cane?" she asked, thinking back to the first time they'd ever taken public transport together, flying from Boston to London.

"Of course," Daniel replied, smirking. He jauntily flipped his cane up onto his shoulder. "Even if it's against the rules."

As she had done in Heathrow airport the first time she'd ever set foot in the grand city in which she now stood, Angie pressed her vision into the auric spectrum, and saw tendrils of Daniel's clear aura wrapped around the cane, reaching out to touch the mind of anyone who might try to take it from him and convince them not to notice it.

And, as it had nearly three years ago, the sight made her squirm.

CHAPTER FOUR

D aniel just stared out the window at the rushing lights and great swathes of darkness, letting the first half hour of their journey pass in a rush. It felt so ordinary to be riding the evening train out of the city. Granted, not in sparsely populated first class, and not London, rather than Glasgow, but still.

He turned his dark phone over and over in his hands beneath the small table between him and Angie, lost in thought. He missed ordinary, to the point where he tried not to think about it, lest he noticed the pain in the longing to be free of everything extraordinary about his life. He couldn't remember who had first called the different parts he had to play for different people his masks, but he could hear the word in his mind in a dozen different voices. His, Angie's, Milton's, Jonathan's, Dawn's... Each of them describing his pretend selves, like the one they liked to see was him without a mask. Political dark horse, old friend, mole for the resistance, lover... *Were any of them truer than the rest?* The thought jarred him out of his reverie, and he looked around for something to anchor him.

Across from him, Angie was staring, frowning slightly, down the aisle of the car, as she had been doing since they'd left the station. When she caught him watching her, she shifted, looking right back at whatever she'd been staring at. "Hey," she said softly, "I think a woman has been following us since we got to Minerva Station."

Daniel raised a brow. "Is it possible your ex following us just put you on edge for that sort of thing?"

"Yes," Angie replied, her aura leaking the faintest hint of cedar smoke into the air, "which is why I didn't mention it until now. She keeps looking up at me, and she was definitely trying to follow you through the crowd earlier. I think she only got a ticket for this train when we gave away which one we were getting onto. I thought she might have recognized you from somewhere."

"Where is she sitting?"

"Opposite side from us, aisle, facing me. Cream-colored coat, with short, brown hair. The conductor is just getting to her now."

Daniel cracked his neck and stretched his arms up. He then stood casually into the aisle, stretching his back, then twisting side to side. When he turned in the direction Angie had been staring and saw who the conductor was speaking to about her ticket, his heart dropped into his stomach. He sat back down quickly, his chest growing tight as he felt yet another mask, another version he had been, and shed, and preserved to put back on again if he ever had to force itself over his face, thoughts, and emotions.

"Tonya. My ex-wife."

Angie's mouth fell open, and she quickly shut it, her eyes wide. Daniel looked back out the window, unconsciously seeking the calm sense of ordinary he'd lost himself in not five minutes ago, and gingerly scooted over to the window seat, just to be a foot and a half more shielded from his past. Angie followed suit, and Daniel rubbed his hairline, hiding his eyes.

"Can I help?" Angie asked softly. Her voice sounded gentle and cautious, but even without looking, Daniel knew her posture was relaxed and confident.

"No, it's fine. Just a shock, is all. And after everything else today." He dropped his shaking hands to his lap, looking up over the top of Angie's head. "It's fine."

"Does she know about magic? Should we make contact with her, or ignore and ditch her?"

"No," Daniel answered quickly. "She doesn't know. And... I don't know."

They sat in silence for a long minute. Little by little, Daniel felt the initial numbness of the shock wear off, replaced by an upset he didn't know what to do with, trying to lash out of control with his roiling aura. Across the plastic train table, Angie's posture inched down toward pity by corresponding degrees.

"She's the one you mentioned, isn't she?" Angie eventually asked, breaking the rumbling wash of the train and other people chatting quietly nearby. "The first time I tried to tell you about my experiences with abuse, after my stress test, when you said you could relate, but—"

"But fucked it up," Daniel finished for her. "Yeah." He didn't look away from the window, and neither spoke again for a long minute. Daniel replayed the memories of Angie trying to open up to him about her abuse, and how he'd put his foot in his mouth, telling her that her definitions didn't count. And of finally confessing to her, weeks later, that the reason he had was because if he let himself accept definitions of abuse that didn't include physical injury, he'd have to admit things about his ex-wife and his past he didn't want to.

"Do you want to talk about it?" Angie asked, and Daniel shrugged half-heartedly.

"Like what? I haven't seen or spoken to her in... Gods. At least a decade. At this point, does it matter that she left me when I was at my lowest point so far in my life, or that she sold nearly all of my possessions when she did so to fund her own new life? Ten, eleven, twelve years on, I shouldn't care anymore that she'd throw tantrums when I didn't give her expensive gifts, or kids, or a nice house." Daniel felt his voice pitch up and took several long breaths to calm himself. He'd never said any of it out loud before. Not to someone who, he knew, would hear all of it as the abuse it was. "I don't see what good it would do to talk about the gaslighting, cheating, shaming me in bed, or screaming at me one day for working too much to spend time with her, and for not working enough to make the kind of money she wanted to spend the next." Daniel sniffed, rubbing the back of one hand under his nose, and cleared his throat gruffly, finally turning back to Angie. "I think the saying about 'the best revenge is a life well lived' has to be true at this point."

He waited for Angie to say something, but she just watched him. When she looked away, for a moment he thought he saw anger twist her face before fading. "Maybe for normal exes, like Garrett. But even they deserve to have their noses rubbed in it. And abusers aren't normal exes. Any advice that tries to lump them all in together is bullshit."

Daniel reached inside himself for something to say but came up empty. Angie was clearly so far away inside her own head, her own emotions and past, he doubted he could reach her. He knew she was right. Maybe he just couldn't shed the masks he wore for the people who hurt him like she could. Maybe he didn't want to.

Angie sighed. "So. What do you say the chances are that each of us encountering exes on the same day is an accident or coincidence?"

Daniel gathered himself, setting his jaw, and nodded. "You're right. Slim to none. We'd best stay on our toes."

CHAPTER FIVE

D aniel released his hold on his aura a bit as they stood on the platform outside the Chippenham station in the dark, waiting for the car to pick them up. Angie had pointed out when they arrived that they could just walk into town until they had enough privacy to Voyage, but Daniel had declined. He'd said it was to make a show of using the favor they'd asked Marissa for, and in case there was still extra scrutiny on them around the new citizenship document-checking, but the truth was that he simply wanted normalcy, and a bit more time to decide what to do about the ghost from his past.

He glanced over Angie beside him to where Tonya was still hovering under the awning of the ticket window, trying to pretend she wasn't watching or following them, and saw two centurions—an old man, and a young woman—approach her. A train horn blared, and he didn't catch what they said, the words lost into the cold, damp, February night laced with the smells of exhaust, wet dogs, and the lingering plastic smell of the first-class upholstery.

Angie noticed he was distracted and turned to watch with him just as the older centurion grasped Tonya firmly by one arm, steering her back into the station, and Daniel's self-control snapped. His aura whipped out from him in layers of hot and cold, all dripping with moisture, and he strode toward the minor scuffle, Angie close behind.

"Good evening, officers. I apologize for any misunderstanding. This woman is under my sponsorship. If you would please release her." All three of the people before him gaped for a long moment, not least of all his ex-wife, who was giving him a look like he'd somehow betrayed her.

"I'm sorry, sir," the female centurion said, pursing her lips. "But this woman says that she does not have shelter here for the night, nor could she provide a satisfactory explanation for why she came here. She doesn't have any identifying documents on her, which means we must detain her until those documents are provided."

"Besides," the older centurion huffed, "only patricians can sponsor people like you're saying, and I've seen too many fakers with a bit of cash to take you at your word."

Daniel tugged on his gloves and withdrew his passport, holding it out under the meager light from a dim lamp high overhead on the side of the building. He studiously looked only at the old man as he took the document from him, closely inspecting the gloss of the paper, watermarks, and more, and bending the little booklet inside out to check the binding. He could feel the older woman's attention boring into him, but tried to focus instead on the smooth, smoky warmth of Angie's aura just behind him.

"Very well, sir," the centurion eventually said, curtly nodding at his companion, and both disappeared back into the station as a light mist began to fall.

Left with no alternative, Daniel finally turned his full attention to the painfully familiar face before him as Angie shifted forward to his side, wrapping a hand around his bicep. He waited for her to say anything, for her to thank him, or explain, or apologize, but she just stared at the two of them.

"Tonya," Daniel eventually said to break the awkward silence, "let me introduce you to my partner, Angie Forester. Angie, this is Tonya…"

"Fawl-Davies," Tony replied, extending a hand to Angie, which she let drop when Angie's only response was a twist in her lip, quickly covered by a tight smile.

"I know. Daniel has told me plenty about you." Angie looked up at Daniel, and he silently asked her to play along. Angie sighed, visibly relaxing, and smiled more genuinely. Daniel felt his chest brighten with the simple delight of the unspoken communication with her he had missed so dearly for so long, but his heart nearly stopped when Angie spoke again. "They mentioned you don't have somewhere to stay tonight. Our house isn't far. You'd be welcome to our guest room."

Tonya looked as shocked as Daniel felt, and he almost took the risk on a witnessed glitch to stop time and ask Angie what in the name of Mars she was doing. But before he could, the faintest whiff of rosewood and pine smoke, sexy and purposeful, made him grin. Angie was offering him exactly the revenge he'd said he wanted, despite her disagreement with him on it. A car honked its horn politely a dozen yards away and Daniel turned to see a sleek black car pulled up, the uniformed chauffeur barely visible in the driver's seat.

"Yes, please join us," Daniel said with a smile, gesturing at the car.

Tonya smiled nervously back. "Thank you. If you really don't mind, I will."

So much for being careful.

"So," Tonya asked once they had all settled into the car, Angie and Daniel in the back seat, and Tonya in the front, ignoring the driver completely and twisting to see them. "What do you do for a living these days?" He reached for the dome light in the car and switched it on as they pulled away.

Daniel fought the urge to roll his eyes. No inquiry after his health, no addressing of the fact that she stalked them from London, or inquiry after when he noticed her, or why he came to her aid, or how he'd fared after their last meeting. She just wanted to know if he was worth getting something out of. Typical.

"I went into politics and education," Daniel said confidently, and caught the faintest expression of impressed surprise from Angie. Not technically a lie. "What about you?"

Tonya's look of greedy delight faltered slightly. "Oh, you know. Being me, living my best life."

Daniel bit his cheek to keep from laughing. "Which means?"

Tonya sat up straighter, caressing the lapel of her cream leather coat. "I'm an influencer. I do exposure for luxury brands in exchange for products, discounts, and cash payments."

One of Angie's brows shot up so high it looked like it might leave her face altogether. Daniel laughed and covered it with a cough when Tonya gave him a wounded look. He didn't need Angie's instinct in the matter to know it was a blatant lie. "And the Davies of your new name?" he asked, trying to keep a straight face.

"The ex-husband after you." Tonya turned to embarrassed scorn on Angie, blatantly sizing up her freckled skin, just fading back to pale from tan, the white scars scattered across her face and hands, and the long, curly, auburn hair swept up off her face. "And what about you? What do you do?"

Angie grinned, her gray-green eyes sparkling. "A bit of this, a bit of that. Used to work in textiles, then ironwork. These days I'm an unemployed fighter."

Her answer threw Daniel off, and he missed Tonya's huff of disapproving amusement trying to figure out why. All of it was technically correct. And yet he couldn't find anything of Angie, the actual woman, in those words.

"So, education," Tonya said, turning her attention back to Daniel. "Does that mean you went back to school? Are you Doctor Fawl now?"

"No," Daniel replied, resting a casual gloved hand on Angie's knee, enjoying the way Tonya marked the gesture. "Just Mr. Fawl."

"Or Senator," Angie added with a smirk, and Tonya's eyes went wide.

Daniel grinned. "Oh, right. Or Senator."

CHAPTER SIX

A ngie was just settling into bed, listening to Daniel finishing up in the bathroom of their cottage, when there was a timid knock on their bedroom door. Angie rolled her eyes, flopping down for a moment to master her patience. After an awkward late dinner filled with Tonya alternating between unsettling silences, grilling them both about their lives, and dropping not-so-subtle hints that Daniel should gift her with a similarly comfortable life for being his ex-wife, Angie hadn't been too subtle in rushing to get the other woman set up in the guest room and saying good night.

"I've got it," Daniel said from the door to the washroom, and Angie looked up gratefully to find him dressed in nothing but a pair of loose flannel pants, his toothbrush still in one hand. "One minute," he called out to the hall before disappearing back into the bathroom.

Angie bit her lip, her aura leaking rosewood smoke which she didn't try to contain, remembering how to play such games. She tiptoed across the room to open the window paned with antique glass, letting in the cool night air with its aroma of wet grass, and the sounds of dripping moisture from the roof. She snuck back into bed as Daniel finished brushing his teeth, pulling off her short nightgown and tossing it under the bed before snuggling down beneath the down comforter in its linen and silk cover.

Daniel crossed the carpeted floor to the door, lifting the little latch and opening it onto the dark hallway. Tonya opened her mouth to say something the moment she was visible, but stopped dead at the sight of Daniel, half-naked, standing in the doorway, his lean physique brushed with soft light that highlighted his toned muscles. Angie admired the view herself for a moment before pretending not to pay the other woman any attention, stretching and turning in a way that exposed her naked arms, shoulders, and chest just down to the limits of indecency.

When Angie returned her attention to the door, Tonya looked away, coloring. Her eyes dropped to Daniel's tattoos and stuck there.

"Did you need something?" Daniel asked, subtly flexing as he lifted one hand to rub the back of his neck, giving her a better look at the spiked, circular sigil inked to the inside of his wrist.

"Um, yeah. The light in my room. I can't seem to find the switch." Tonya clearly had a hard time tearing her eyes away, and stepped back from the doorway, holding an arm out as if telling Daniel to lead the way, but he ignored her.

"Ah, yeah, sorry, I should have warned you. The people who refurbished this cottage for the previous owner mostly did an excellent job, but that one's a little weird, as they had to avoid damaging the original sixteenth-century woodwork. It's right behind the door. Chest height, same color as the wall. I promise you can't miss it if you know where to look."

Tonya just hovered, clearly waiting for something more. "Well, good night!" Daniel said cheerily, closing the door swiftly, and Angie chuckled. He rolled his eyes as he turned back to her, and froze when Angie stretched again, this time exposing herself fully. She watched with delicious satisfaction as Daniel's breath sped up, and the soft fabric at the front of his flannel pants tightened.

"She's only staying one night," Angie teased to reassure both of them. She let go of her aura, using the smell of rosewood smoke to communicate her intentions to him, and let the duvet slip down further.

Daniel smiled, his dark eyes dilating. "We can make sure of that." He prowled forward, and in him Angie saw the feline predator which had both excited and scared her when they'd first met, and realized as her mouth went dry that the effect hadn't dulled that much over the years.

When he reached her, Daniel didn't join her on the bed as she expected, but simply stood over her, his gaze raking down her exposed body. Angie lay still, posed for him, waiting to see what he intended. The bed was tall, and when Daniel snugged his thighs up to the edge of the mattress, his fingertips were just long enough to trail delicately along her skin. The sight of him standing tall over her, his arm stretched to touch her, and the faint tingle of his skin which she'd learned to adjust to sent thrills down her limbs and made her cheeks heat.

Quick as a flash, Daniel scooped her up, setting her on her feet beside the bed, and released her. Angie grinned, double-blinking to see the oil-slick layers of golden light surrounding him and was taken by surprise when he moved into her. Not slow or gentle, but also not reaching to touch her with either hand. Purposeful and swift, Angie backed away instinctively until she was backed against the wooden-slat door to the room by the beautiful, lithe, hungry man before her.

Her smoke flowed through her freely, and she swallowed as she heated between her legs, shifting her feet apart on the carpeted floor to encourage the sensation.

Daniel looked down, lacing his fingers with hers, and brought both of her hands up over her head, pressing them into the door. He moved his body closer until she was pinned against the door, his breath on her neck, and Angie's own breath quickened. He shifted both of her hands into one of his, and Angie watched his free hand slide down the door, pulling away the threads of magic that warded it against unwanted sounds getting out or in, dissolving back into his aura. "Let's make sure she wants to leave in the morning."

Angie realized what he was doing, and a moan fell from her lips. Daniel bumped his body into hers, his erection nudging between her thighs, and the door he had her pinned to rattled slightly. "Yes," Angie said, practically panting, and Daniel's mouth met hers in a deep, hard kiss.

His free hand trailed down the side of her ribcage, and Angie's knees nearly buckled.

"I am going to touch you however I want to make that bitch out there as jealous as possible," Daniel growled, and Angie felt herself melt as his hand found the inside of her hip, caressing the pressure point there that made her mind go blank. "If you ask me to stop, I will, but I want to take you like I have something to prove. Is that alright?"

"Yes," Angie breathed, and his mouth closed around her throat, pressing into her pulse.

He didn't wait to trace his delicate, tingly hand up over her stomach to tease her breasts, gripping the base of her skull as he kissed her deeply once more, and to trail it back down, down to the front her hips, circling down to where she was dripping for him.

When his fingers found her wetness, halfway down her thigh, he moaned into Angie's mouth, and her knees finally gave out. Daniel caught her only a few inches down by her wrists and her cunt. Angie stopped breathing.

As he pulled her back up, his fingers slipped inside her, and she hissed through her teeth, desperately underwhelmed by the small degree of satisfaction compared to her need for him. Daniel tipped the side of his face against hers, his eyes closed, and Angie squirmed. "Are you ready?"

"Yes," Angie said.

"Again," Daniel said, pulling his fingers out of her to shed his pants, letting his erection brush against her.

"Yes. Please." Angie didn't hide the note of pleading in her voice.

Daniel hauled her leg up to wrap around his hip, releasing it to hold it in place with his forearm as he reached down around to guide his cock to press against Angie's hot opening. In two strokes he entered her, and Angie jerked, her eyes closing as she flexed around him involuntarily, pulling him deeper inside.

The door rattled faintly as Daniel braced against it, Angie's wrists still pinned against it over her head, and Angie swore quietly at the way his rock-hard shaft twitched inside her. "I'm not going to last long," he grunted, making Angie bite her lip. "I need you to tell me when you're close."

Angie just nodded, the side of her face brushing his. She bucked her hips against him, the only movement under her control, and felt the muscle in Daniel's angular jaw clench as he matched the motion.

He wrapped his free arm around her back, and she clung to him with the leg wrapped around his hip as he drove into her deep and slow, setting a rhythm that made the door thump in its frame in time. After a minute, Angie tried, without thinking, to pull her arms free to touch him more, but he tightened his grip, leaning back enough to watch her. "No," he panted. "I am taking you."

"Fuck," Angie muttered as he held her gaze, keeping her pinned to the door, and started slowly increasing his speed. Almost immediately, Angie felt herself start to build, the faint tingle from his skin being taken over by another kind as she tightened around him. Her eyes closed and her head tipped back.

"Tell me," he reminded her, his voice tight.

"Now," Angie panted, and it was his turn to swear.

His pace and depth didn't alter in the slightest as Angie built, hanging her weight from his hand on her wrists, and her thigh clamped to his hips, and she finally fell down the tumbling currents and screamed her pleasure as she was lost to it.

Daniel slammed into her, harder and faster, and in a dozen strokes he shuddered against her, his moans shaking as he spilled into her, his hand on her wrist gripping so hard her fingers went cold.

"Daniel," she gasped as he finally stilled. "My hands."

He released her instantly, catching her under the arm with one hand, and slowly, carefully lowering her shaking leg from around him with the other. "You okay?" he asked through a panting smile, and Angie mirrored him, nodding.

"Yeah. Better than okay. Great." She laughed weakly as Daniel pulled her into an embrace, listening to his heart thundering in his chest.

"Good," he said after a minute, sweeping her up and carrying her off toward the bathroom to clean up, and pressing a kiss to her forehead that oozed golden light into his aura as it spun around them. "Me too."

CHAPTER SEVEN

"Are you sure you won't stay longer?" Daniel asked, trying to balance his tone between teasing and sarcastic. He poured more syrup on his pancakes while Tonya gave him an accusing glare from across the table in the pale, clear morning light bathing the gleaming white and copper kitchen.

"No, thank you. I need to get back to London." She glanced at Angie, sitting at the kitchen table between them, before poking at her breakfast with her fork. "I got what I came for. Now I know you were lying about everything that came between us. I just hope you'll consider me whenever you get bored and decide to cheat on your newer, prettier, younger plaything here like you did on me all those years ago."

Daniel's pancakes turned to ash in his mouth. Beside him, Angie's smoky aura barely twitched, but she wouldn't meet his eyes. "I didn't cheat on you," Daniel said, trying to hide his edge of anger. "And I never lied. Circumstances just change."

Tonya scoffed, and Daniel felt himself slipping back into sickening old patterns around playing, balancing, and soothing her moods. "I can see that," she said, looking greedily around at the understated but expensively furnished cottage. "But we both know that people don't."

Daniel's patience broke, and he tossed his napkin onto the table, throwing his weight back in his chair and crossing his arms. "Then what the hell are you doing here?"

Tonya looked openly shocked and offended, and it was Daniel's turn to scoff. "Why did you follow me out here from London? Why are you pretending you didn't? If you don't believe people can change, then why did you think we would have anything real to say to each other, or that we could even get along for a full day, if you clearly remember how we left things?"

Tonya opened her mouth to reply, her freckled nose scrunched, but Daniel raised a hand dotted with thick gold rings to silence her. "Never mind. I already know the answer. You don't believe people change, and you're here now, because *you* don't change. That's the answer. You've never wanted to believe people might change for the better, because that excuses you from ever trying. You're here because, like you have since we met, you're hoping you can get something out of me."

"If that's how you feel, then I'll just go and get out of your hair," Tonya snapped.

"Great," Daniel replied, letting himself lean into his distant role of a powerful and detached Senator. "Go pack, and I'll take you back to the station."

Tonya got up with an indignant huff. Neither Daniel nor Angie looked at her, and after an awkward moment of her clearly waiting for someone to stop her, she stormed out and down the hall toward the stairs.

The moment Daniel heard the click of the guest room door upstairs, Angie turned to him, her expression dark and fearful. "Did you cheat on her? Was she... were you in love with her, whoever she was? What happened to her? Was it Marissa?"

Daniel raised a hand, trying to calm the bright sparks building in Angie's burning plastic smoke. "No, I didn't cheat. My marriage with Tonya had been declining for a while, and I didn't hook up with anyone else until after she kicked me out, and told me it was all over, and that she would be divorcing me."

Angie only relaxed a little, still eyeing him warily. "So, it *definitely* wasn't cheating?"

"Correct, to both." Angie relaxed fully with a small smile. "And," Daniel added, bracing himself against a secret he knew he didn't need to keep from her, but which had been buried so deep, for so long, that he had to remind himself that shame had never been a reason to keep it. Only safety. "*He* was not Marissa. And yes, at one time, I think I was in love with him. Nothing happened to him. We just... didn't last as lovers. That was also a long time ago now."

The smoke swirling around Angie shifted to thin wisps of silver as her frown blossomed into a slightly shocked smile. "Oh. I—I didn't know. I'm sorry I assumed..."

Daniel shook his head, leaning to rub her shoulder affectionately, not looking at her as he felt his face heat a little, hoping his beard covered most of it. "Not to worry. I'm pretty sure you're the only person I've ever told. Me being bi doesn't come up much, now or ever. I never felt the need to tell you. There's no reason you would have known."

Angie nodded and stood to clear the table, the corners of her mouth still twitching up, blinking more than usual bemusedly. "Okay. Well... thanks for telling me. It's nice getting to know more about you. Even now."

As she turned away, Daniel took a deep breath, something deep and subtle in his chest easing. It was nice being known more, too.

The drive to the station was silent, which suited Daniel fine. At least that meant he wouldn't have to explain why the enchantedly lifelike golem driver was mute.

When they got to the station, the place was almost empty, a few cuckoos and doves the only notes among the rumble of traffic and trains in the distance. Tonya hovered by the ticket counter, clearly expecting Daniel to buy her ticket for her, and he shooed her away with a twenty-pound note. "I've got this. Go buy us both coffees. Cream and three sugars for me."

When she returned with the coffees, Daniel intercepted her just outside the doors into the station, pulling out the ticket he'd bought for her. "Here," he said, handing it over, carefully placed on a neat wad of several thousand pounds in cash.

Tonya's eyes lit up, and she took it quickly, slipping it into her pocket. "I knew you'd have a little something for me," she cooed. "And I know I can count on you when this little gift runs out—" She fell silent, her smile falling away when Daniel stepped in close with a snarl, backing her against the brick wall.

"That's not free. That is a payment for you never, ever, crossing my path again." Daniel tilted his head with a warning look when Tonya's expression turned cunning and simpering, baring his teeth. "I know you were abusive to me," he hissed, and saying the words out loud sent a thrill down his spine. "Emotional, psychological, and financial abuse at a minimum. Don't," he warned as Tonya tried to speak again, and she shrank back. "Just don't. If you even think about telling me otherwise like you did every single week of our marriage, if you speak one word trying to twist, and cover, and convince me I'm misremembering or crazy for saying so, then I will take the money back, and instruct the plebeian government to strip you of everything and stick you in some rotting hole of a prison for the rest of your life."

Tonya mouthed the empty air, and Daniel felt an overwhelming surge of relief and satisfaction. "Good. Finally, you've shut up and listened. Now," he said, backing up a step and shaking himself. "If you want my advice, once you get home, you'll lie low. There's a storm coming as the patricians hurtle towards total fascism, and your best chance of weathering it is to fade as far into nonexistence as possible."

"You don't want to end things like this," Tonya whined, and Daniel had to turn away from all the memories that flooded him with the familiarity of it. He started walking back to the car, but Tonya called after him. "I'm moving back to Boston in a week. Who knows when you'll ever see me again—"

"Never," Daniel shouted, whirling with a whipping cyclone of dry wind, and shoved Tonya back against the wall with a gloved hand on her shoulder. "I will never see you again. Not in a year, or a decade, or on my deathbed. This was not a first re-meeting start of knowing each other again. This is an end. This is closure. And you want to know something? I can say that as an absolute statement. If I ever see you again, I will leave before you can speak to me. If I ever hear from you again, I will block you without listening or reading."

As he turned away for the last time, Tonya drew breath and Daniel snatched it from her lungs with his aura without looking. His heart pounded in his ears, and he reined in his expressive aura, wrestling it back down into a slight breeze that ruffled his hair. He barely felt his sleek black cellphone buzz once in his pocket and didn't reach for it.

He only truly started breathing again when he was enclosed back in the car, out of sight of the breathless Tonya. "Drive back to my home," he instructed the golem driver, taking several deep breaths and blindly watching the charming tableau of the Britannian Cotswolds out of the window. Once his head felt a little clearer, he pulled out his phone, glancing at the text message from Noah Byrne displayed over his lock screen image.

You have been assigned a recruit. Come for details tomorrow, 7 A.M. Address will be sent an hour earlier.

Chapter Eight

Daniel arrived at the appointed address at five minutes to seven in the car he had decided to keep an
extra day and was shocked to find himself outside of a
sickeningly familiar grand estate. A huge, centuries-old
house that might better be called a castle. Milton's home,
which he had burgled not quite two years ago.

Daniel swore under his breath. After only a moment
of hesitation, he stepped out of the door the golem was
holding open for him and took a deep breath. He was
dressed up in their winter best, without his cane as his
knee wasn't paining him that day, and yet he felt a chill to
his bones. Whatever Noah and Milton were playing at, he
certainly wouldn't like it.

He knocked and was ushered by another golem, this
one the standard stock of a spruced-up store mannequin,
past the spider web wards at the front door which Daniel
remembered snagging an identifying scrap of his aura
that had almost gotten him caught on his previous visit.
He let it keep his magical finger print this time. He was
invited this time.

As he was shown through the house, he considered
calling Angie to join him. On his own, Milton might try

something dangerous or deadly. He dismissed the idea, knowing he needed a recruit to mold and use. That he needed to just play along until the chips finished falling one way or the other.

When the golem opened a carved ebony door on the ground floor and stepped aside, Daniel strode into the cluttered office, giving the man seated behind the heavy, gilt-edge desk a curt nod. "Councilor Cartwright."

Milton Cartwright sneered. "Senator Fawl."

Cartwright's office in his home was precise in every detail to how it had been on the conference site when the Councilor had merely been the Supreme Justice, and Daniel begrudgingly admitted to himself that the magic to lift and move a whole room and its contents from one building to another was impressive. It still smelled of cigar smoke and poppies, and was stuffed with paintings, statues, bookcases, and glass curio shelves holding ancient trinkets, including the golden astrolabe Milton occasionally favored for fidgeting with.

"I thought I would be assigned my new recruit by the Supreme Justice of the English Court, Noah Byrne. Why did he direct me here instead?"

"Because he asked me to handle your assignment, and I am happy to help a friend. He apparently doesn't want to be in the same room with you if he can help it, and I must say, I fully understand that feeling."

Daniel didn't wait to be invited and settled himself on the stiff-backed chair opposite the plump, jowled man folding his hands across his stomach. Milton looked deeply tired, and much older than the last time Daniel had seen him. He raised a stubby hand to scratch his cheek, dotted with white stubble and age spots, and Daniel mastered his expression away from contempt.

Instead, he let a serpentine smile twist across his wide mouth, and tutted disapprovingly, looking the Councilor up and down, then looking over the messy desk strewn with papers, crumbs, empty mugs, and other detritus. "My my. How far you've fallen. And yet," Daniel cocked his head, enjoying Milton's glower, "how far you still have left to fall."

"If I have fallen behind in any way, it's because of all the stress put on me by your threats against my person, everything you have burdened me with in the favors you hide those threats behind, and how much I have been inspired to push myself to greater heights to make sure you pay, sooner than later, no matter the cost to my personal comfort. Not to mention you turning my husband against me and brainwashing him to help the terrorist friends you claim not to have," Milton snapped.

"You have a recruit for me?" Daniel chuckled.

Milton sighed through his nose, a muscle feathering in his jaw. He reached into his desk, pulling out a folder, and spun it across the desk to Daniel. "Thirty-four-year-old male. American, Elemental aura. Easy recruit, as our new Seer says the two of you are already acquainted on good terms. His contact moment is in two weeks, March 7th, in Oregon. Same place you grabbed Angie, ironically enough. Seems to be a dangerous street to visit."

Daniel blinked. *It couldn't be that easy. Not from Milton Cartwright, or from Noah Byrne.* "Really?" Daniel said involuntarily, a deeply suspicious, warm relief and hope-fulness spreading through his veins. He reached for the dossier as Milton replied with a tight smile that didn't reach his hard, calculating eyes.

Daniel flipped it open, ready for his hopefulness to fall, but found himself biting back a smile. "Seth Laufey. Another Fire aura."

This was perfect. Better than he could have hoped for. Seth would be an easy recruit, after spending so, so many long hours together in the legal matter of getting Angie's abuser put away, which had been Daniel's pet project for nearly two years. And not only did Daniel now have experience sponsoring a Fire aura, but Angie could help a great deal in speeding up his training, and if Angie's Fire aura had allowed her to break a Focal Nucleus in the past, having another to stop the new one being locked into place was a stroke of luck that made Daniel want to whoop with triumph.

He reined in the deep yellow, warm currents of his aura lazily shifting the papers in the desk before him, and casually closed the folder, braced for the other shoe to drop. He schooled his face into polite dismissal and slowed his breath that might betray his excitement. "Thank you, Councilor. I'm sure he will make an excellent addition to the Victume Ceremony, and its crucial func-tion of restoring much-needed order to our community and jurisdictions. I accept the duties of sponsoring and overseeing his initial education and preparation. Good morning." Daniel stood to rise, his mind already spinning with telling the good news to Jonathan, Angie, and Dawn.

"Good morning," Milton replied. Daniel strode to the door. "Oh, before you go, I have made progress to share with you on one of the tasks you've set for me." Daniel stopped with his hand on the latch and turned. "The Latin Language Court is throwing a party. A dead language, of course, but the official language of the Empire, alongside English." Daniel blinked. He'd never thought about whether or not Latin still had a living Court. "You should come, as everyone who's anyone will be there. Bring your bitch, and, if a week and a half is enough to stabilize him, your new recruit. As usual, I'll text you the details."

"Thank you for the invitation." Daniel gave Milton a curt bow of his head, biting back a smile, and saw himself out. Nothing could have prepared him for how perfect this assignment was, and he couldn't wait to share the good news. Time to strategize their approach.

CHAPTER NINE

For once, Angie wished she had a phone—despite how infrequently she would use it, and her long-held paranoia around carrying one as an unintended tracking device. It shouldn't have taken more than a few seconds for Daniel to send up his mental Voyaging beacon for her once he reached the location given to find his new recruit, and yet Angie stood, anxiously waiting, for more than a minute in the front room of their cottage before it came.

She let the magic yank her toward the signal like a rope around her middle and landed just behind a tall fence twined densely with shrubbery, bordering a familiar park. The onslaught of sound from the rioters and centurions and the scratch of metal was instant and intense.

"What the hell?" Angie asked, her eyes wide, as Daniel shielded her with his body. One of his hands was braced against the wrought-iron railing of the fence. The other leaned on his cane which had changed shape to heavy, strong, and plain, the sharp tip digging into the grass they stood on.

"Sorry. I'm pretty sure I was spotted Voyaging in, which may have escalated things a bit. It took me a minute to find anywhere private enough to risk your arrival, and me blocking this corner from sight was part of it." He lifted his head and pushed back from the fence gently, scanning around over Angie's head, and behind him, every muscle lined with tension. "Here." He discreetly summoned Angie's sturdy dark blue jacket, his brown leather one, and two bandanas. He handed one to her with her coat and pulled on his own, tucking the other into the back pocket of his jeans.

She stepped away from the shielded alcove herself as she pulled on her jacket, taking stock of the situation. She was standing in the exact spot where Daniel had first introduced himself to her, having just saved her from a mad gunman as he tried to rescue her from her own blossoming powers and a fated death to a centurion's bullet.

The park she could see fully was dappled by the trees in the afternoon light, and the tent city of homeless people that had been there since Angie had first moved there was burning. The fleeing residents were being attacked and rounded up by local centurions and civilian loyalists, mercilessly being beaten and hauled off toward waiting trucks, screaming as they were torn from their loved ones. Angie swore. The Empire hadn't taken military and labor slaves like that since the decade following the global unification.

She followed Daniel to the edge of the fence which opened onto the street, where the conflict seemed to be centered around the entrance to a new construction job site where an old building had been torn down. Angie tried to remember what had been there when she'd lived in her car on these familiar Oregon streets. *Had it been the library?*

"Have you spotted him?" Angie asked, tying the bandana across her mouth and nose.

Beside her, Daniel shook his head. "No. But we know exactly what we're looking for. We know his face, and his magic, which should help." He glanced behind him at the homeless people getting dragged off, and Angie scanned the clashing blue-clad protestors and legionnaires before them. "Split up? We still have fifteen minutes before he's due."

"Sounds good," Angie said, and stepped away toward the skeletal five-story building, looking abandoned, dripping with iron chains, stacks of rebar, and tools. Her old foundry was probably helping to build it. Who but the Empire could afford new construction these days?

A minute later, she was in the thick of it.

"Fuck the Empire!" a nearby teenager screamed at the legionnaire attempting to corner her with a riot shield. "They don't need a new prison when we all need food, homes, and medicine!"

Angie moved closer, and with a moment of close concentration, willed her aura to stuff the soldier's lungs with the most acrid, sludgy smoke she could manage. As the man fell, coughing, and the teenager ducked out and ran, Angie smiled.

There was some activity down at the far end of the street where the capitol building stood, and Angie did a double take. A mixed group of local centurions and

Imperial legionnaires were raising a flag on the tall pole built into the sidewalk below the steps. One bearing the symbols of the cult of Mars, a shield with two crossed spears, which had become the de facto symbol for every branch of the government that forced the people into submission. The red and gold eagle of the Imperial flag lay trampled at their feet.

A brush of air behind her made Angie duck, her adrenaline spiking. She dove to the ground, grabbing up a crowbar one of the protestors had likely abandoned, and whirled, not seeing who or what in the chaos had narrowly missed her. She briefly considered bringing up her shields, but decided against it. No need to add to the panic.

Angie shifted to one side, reading the currents and movements in the crowd, keeping her back to the protestors as much as she could. Her wary attention stayed anchored on the legionnaires. A flash of red hair caught her eye but disappeared almost as fast, and Angie surged toward it. "Seth Laufey!" she called out over the din of chanting, commands, and cries of distress or pain. "Seth! Wait up!"

A hefty man rammed into Angie from the side—she didn't see why—and sent her sprawling to the asphalt road. The crowbar skittered out of sight among the sea of churning legs, and the sides of her balled fist she broke her fall with were scraped raw in an instant.

In a flash, Angie was mentally running from demons again, fleeing through half-worlds as she desperately clung to the meager tools and supplies she had gathered,

the loss of which might mean her death in the next unpredictable encounter, terrified that every scrape might
become infected and weaken her. She gasped as the wind
that had been knocked out of her rushed back into her
lungs, bringing the sensory overload of her deeply human
surroundings back to her awareness with it.

Angie scrambled to her feet and found Seth Laufey only
a foot away in front of her, his back to her. Angie lunged
forward, catching his shoulder, and when he turned it
was to swing at her with a strong, fast blow she was barely
able to deflect with one forearm. "Seth, wait. I'm not here
to hurt you, I'm here to help," she panted from beneath
her bandana.

Seth didn't even pause. Another calculated swing of
his pale fist, his bright orange hair tousled and falling
over his eyes. Angie did her best to defend herself as he
slowly pushed her back and felt her panic swell when her
back hit the very solid brick wall of the building beside
the construction site. "No wait." She was just about to
take the risk of exposing her magic to a whole street of
riled-up plebeians when Daniel's gold-ringed hand appeared on Seth's shoulder, spinning him around, and both
men froze.

"Fawl?"

"Yeah," Daniel said, releasing Seth's shoulder and deftly
using his cane to redirect a legionnaire hauling off a
cuffed protester who had been on course to collide with
them. "Sorry we couldn't have done this under better
circumstances." He shifted around to stand by Angie, who
pulled down her bandana, watching Seth closely. Daniel

glanced at his gold watch. "But we need to leave now. If you don't, you will die in about ten minutes, and we need you. Will you come with us, quickly, so we can explain further?"

Seth's unlocked, but not yet awakened Fire aura billowed around him, and Angie couldn't help but smile watching it and the sweat-sheened flush of his skin. It made her think back to how she must have looked to Daniel when he'd first laid eyes on her. She watched his expressive, black smoke aura and his expression, swaying slightly under all the déjà vu, and something darker, some distant memory, nagged at the back of her mind.

"No, thanks." Seth said, turning away, but Daniel stopped him with a few words.

"We are patricians."

Seth turned back, and his face had transformed. His hard scowl had been replaced with a look of utter delight and adoration, and he looked between Daniel and Angie, clearly trying to confirm which 'we' Daniel had meant. Angie breathed a sigh of relief and tried to focus all her attention on the welcome eagerness in every inch of Seth's being.

"All three of us," Daniel added in a silken tone, holding out a gloved hand, and shifting his body toward the nearest path away from the chaos surrounding them. "If you accept our offer."

CHAPTER TEN

A ngie kept her head down as Daniel guided the three of them to the hotel room they had already checked into and prepped before going to get Seth. She had cleaned and bandaged her scraped hands while Daniel had answered Seth's many questions. Seth's background as a lawyer in the expert grilling he'd given Daniel on every possible aspect of magic and the patricians he could think of. She kept her mouth shut and her eyes averted to avoid signaling which of Daniel's answers were lies.

"I knew there had to be some truth in the rumors," Seth said, smiling. He was sitting on the edge of one of the two beds opposite Daniel, and pushed up from leaning his elbows on his knees. He scratched his head, clearly starting to run out of questions to ask. "It's just beyond what I expected that not only there *have* been lots of magical explosions across the Americas, but that the patricians were covering them up because they are all magic too."

"Yeah, it's not just wealth and privilege," Daniel replied. "Though obviously those two things are intricately con- nected with the magic, and all of those with the patricians being, essentially, the ruling class behind the emperor and everything below him in the plebeian world."

"Can I see?" Seth asked, and Daniel turned to look at Angie.

She smiled and stepped forward. After considering what might most entice Seth from what little she knew of him, she concentrated and created a fistful of dancing flames in her palm. "I'm a Fire aura, like you. I can also alter things," she said, releasing the flames and grabbing the hem of her shirt, changing it from white to black, "and I can teleport by magic." She Voyaged to the other side of the room, behind Seth, and Daniel grinned at her, making Seth whip around to stare, looking impressed. "There's a lot more. But as Daniel said, there's no telling what skills you will naturally have or be able to learn until you try."

"I'm ready," Seth said quickly, turning back to Daniel, and both he and Angie smiled as she moved back to where she'd been settled, watching, in the chair by the desk near the door.

"Are you sure?" Angie asked, feeling the faintest twist in her gut. "Just to be clear," she added, glancing at Daniel, who was giving her a questioning look, "do you freely and clearly consent to having your magical powers awakened, and to all that entails? Including possible physical changes, committing to close supervision until after the summer solstice, and seeing through the three-month-long conference in Britannia where your powers will be trained and tested, no matter what that might bring? To leave your current life behind, possibly forever, and commit to being a dedicated member of the Patrician Order?"

"Yes," Seth replied confidently, his bright blue eyes excited.

Angie watched Daniel rub his nose. She didn't have to ask to know what he was feeling at that moment. How differently her introduction to magic could have been if he'd simply been as blunt with her. If he'd given her the chance to consent to all of it, instead of being blindsided. If he could have afforded to take that risk of her potentially saying no.

"One last question, actually," Seth said as Daniel stood and gestured for Seth to lie down. "If you are a patrician, like I suspected, and even more committed to running the Empire than the emperor himself, then why did you spend so much time, energy, and money getting a centurion, and public servant to the Empire, locked up for private, individual crimes that had no bearing on his job or who and what he served?"

Angie saw Daniel's aura of light dim briefly and suspected the words were quite familiar to him from Seth's legal defense of her abuser. She felt her stomach twist with the repeated reminder of how they knew Seth and pushed it away. Like Daniel had pointed out several times over the last week, Seth was just doing his job, and taking her abuser's money, only to ultimately fail, which she should be happy for.

"It was a personal vendetta," Daniel replied, his face a dark and unreadable mask. "A well-earned one, I might add." He glanced at Angie, and she gave him a small, sad smile.

"Ah," Seth said, looking between them. "I see."

Angie excused herself to the bathroom as Daniel got himself and Seth settled and explained what was about to happen, needing a moment of privacy. Staring into her own eyes in the mirror, she whispered the word she needed to hear. "We need this. We need a recruit to stop things getting worse, or going back to how things were. He's not perfect as a person, but he's way better than we hoped for practically. I can set my own doubts and worries aside for four months. That's nothing. Then we can all go our separate ways."

When Angie reemerged, Seth was already unconscious, Daniel's bare hands on his forehead and chest. He glanced up at her briefly, his eyes unfocused as his aura twined through Seth's, and she felt herself heat unexpectedly as Daniel turned away, in a manner that had nothing to do with her magic. She settled back down in her chair to watch, trying to cool off. Had she ever told him how very intimate her dreams had turned while he had been awakening her powers in a similar hotel room all that time ago? Had he somehow noticed?

She wasn't sure she wanted to tell him if she hadn't already, thinking back to how immature she'd been back then, and how taboo he had felt when she'd thought he was twenty years older than her as he looked, not just ten, and had known him to be prepared to attack her, violate her consent in rescuing her, and the rest.

She also knew that thinking back over those memories bled rosewood smoke into her aura.

When Daniel was finished, he didn't linger, standing and turning to Angie with a knowing, amused, hungry look in his eyes. "You too?" he asked, and Angie blushed.

"Yeah. Back then, were you also... um... interested?"

Daniel grinned, but before he could reply Seth sat bolt upright, his eyes wide, and yelled a noiseless burst of anger. "Oh shit, he's one of those," Daniel muttered, spinning back to Seth and visibly bracing for whatever odd behavior came from the predictable befuddlement of awakening and summoned one glove to put on, leaving his other hand bare.

Quick as a flash, Seth launched himself off the bed, right at Angie. "Agitator bitch!" he screamed as Daniel caught him around the middle, looking shocked. Seth kept lunging at her, raising a fist over his head as insane glee twisted his pale face into a grotesque mask of delight. "I'll kill you, you traitor to the Empire, you ungrateful—" Daniel took enough air from Seth's lungs to steal his words, but not stop his flailing.

What Angie saw, staring at Seth's expression, wasn't just déjà vu, but an intense memory. "I know you. In the protest where I met Daniel. You swung a baseball bat at a woman's head. You probably killed her..."

Seth let out another wordless yell, and Daniel had to tighten his grip, both arms wrapped around Seth's waist to stop him from reaching Angie, unable to let go with one hand to touch Seth's skin. Angie's mind was reeling.

"You were here three years ago, and now... you told Daniel you lived a town over when we grabbed you... Why did my abuser hire you as his lawyer? If you live here in Oregon, and he was living and being prosecuted three thousand miles away on the Tegesta peninsula?"

"I got special dispensation." Seth laughed maniacally. "Since I was already actively working for him in that capacity. He'd hired me to track down some bitch who'd run away with his unborn child, who he'd gotten word was working near me." Seth's eyes were locked on Angie's, and all she could see in them was fanaticism. "That was you, wasn't it? You're Angelica Forester. I can't wait to tell him exactly where you are. What a perfect gift to celebrate his early release tomorrow."

Angie's heart leapt into her throat, and she reached for her silver key necklace, trying to anchor herself into it as her emotions and magic screamed out of control into a tumbling mess of soot, smoke, ash, and sparks that shrank in toward her skin like it wanted to press her into nothingness, until she had to deactivate her auric vision with a double blink to see the two men clearly. "Tomorrow? He's out tomorrow?"

"Yes. We got help from our own patrician sponsors. Once he gets his hands on you, you are going straight to hell. Now that I have been blessed with powers I never even dreamt of, I will reshape this world into a glorious Eden, with no place for—"

Daniel gave a great heave and pulled Seth upright into his chest, and butted his forehead into the back of Seth's neck. Daniel dropped him in a heartbeat and Seth crumpled to the floor, Daniel standing panting over him.

"Angie," he said, stepping over his unconscious recruit, and Angie flung herself into his arms, shaking.

"You said he was sentenced to forty years. But he's out tomorrow. Daniel," she pulled her face out of his shoulder, casting around like her abuser might be spying on them from a corner, or come bursting in through the dead-bolted door. "The centurions in London, checking my papers. And him," Angie glanced at Seth, "he knows me, and *him*. He was paid to find me by *him*. He can't...when he wakes up..." Angie's voice was pitching up with every word frantically, and Daniel pulled her back into his chest, kissing and stroking her hair.

"I won't let him get to you. I promise. I can handle this." Angie relaxed a bit, pulling her mind back from the brink of hysteria buried in her memories with the version of her that had escaped. When her breathing had slowed a little, Daniel half-released her, and Angie nodded that she was doing better.

Daniel knelt by Seth's side, and Angie glimpsed a tendril of his aura wrapping itself around Seth's skull, undoubtedly altering the contents, before she turned away and scanned the room to make sure they weren't leaving anything behind. When Daniel stood away, leaving Seth in a crumpled heap on the floor, Angie nodded her thanks, turning to the door. "Good, thank you. Let's go."

Only when she reached the door and clicked the dead-bolt open did she realize Daniel hadn't followed. She turned back to find him standing stock-still where she'd left him.

His brows were knit, wincing. "Angie, I'm sorry. We can't just abandon this recruitment. By all means, go if you have to, stay away from the conference so you don't have to see him, but I can't walk away." Angie's chest heaved, and she searched him for the joke, or the lie. "I took your name from his memory, and his client's. I made him forget what that job he was hired for was, or exactly how he ended up working on the Tegesta peninsula. He won't, can't, betray you to your abuser or anyone else."

Angie's thoughts were a jumble. "No, you have to undo the awakening. Put him back to sleep. We... we have to dump him back where we found him and never go any-where near him ever again!" She gestured at him help-lessly, feeling her anger rise that Daniel wasn't under-standing. "He's just like the fucking monster he defended and has helped release back into the world! He's just as bad! I could forgive him for defending an abuser, rapist, groomer, and the rest, but this? Everything he just said? You can't possibly still argue that he's just doing his job, or whatever."

"Angie, I hear you," Daniel said, his hands, one gloved and one not, raised in supplication. "But think of what is at stake. We need a new recruit to get us on the inside of the Victume Ceremony so that we can head off the new English lock. We need to do that to buy ourselves more time to stabilize the global situation before helping all the other languages free themselves too. We need to play along with our roles in the patrician Court so that we are in a position to chase down and end banishment being held over our heads, and those of everyone we care about."

Angie felt disgusted to her core. She studied the man before her and saw only a stranger. "No, you don't hear me," she said, her voice shaking as her hands did. "And you don't see me. Or know me. If you did, you would be leaving with me. You would be *doing* something about everything he just said. We just got cornered, and you are arguing in favor of sitting down and waiting for the killing blow."

Daniel looked hurt, and Angie saw the faintest hardening of his aura around him, like he was considering shielding against her. "Angie, you know I'm not. I'm just saying we need to be smart. Look, he's going to be unconscious for half a day. If you need me to leave with you for a little while to cool off, I can, but—"

"Nah, fuck that," Angie said, shaking her head and turning away as raw emotion hauled down her whole being. "You can do whatever you want, but I'm not waiting for him to find me."

Angie Voyaged to the prison she'd gone to see the outside of once before, when she'd needed the reassurance of knowing the man who haunted her nightmares was truly locked away. A thought lit her mental Voyaging beacon to Daniel alone, but he didn't appear. *Fine, then. On my own.*

She took her bearings and Voyaged again into the front office. It was empty, the lights off, and Angie conjured flames from the tip of her finger to see by, locating and rifling through the sheet-metal filing cabinet along one wall.

When she found what she was looking for, she took note of the cell number her target was assigned. She looked around the dark office, spotting the large maps on one wall, and located the corresponding cell on the second floor at the far end of the prison. She put the file away and oriented herself, feeling her heart and mind settle down into a dark, familiar focus that made the scars peppering her skin itch and tingle. She Voyaged.

The cell was small but clean, with a sink, toilet, and a single cot the only furnishings. A small, orange spark on the cot was the only light, and Angie stalked over to it, kicking the metal leg of the bed as she conjured a handful of fire.

The man sat up, startled, the cigarette falling to the floor. He was a bear of a man, easily twice Angie's mass, and she braced for whatever reaction she would feel to seeing his short blond hair and clean-shaven, handsome face only a few feet away again, but compared to the utter shock on his face, she felt nothing.

One of his hands reached for her as if disbelieving she was really there, but a lick of flames jerked it back.

"You're awake? Good." Angie grabbed the collar of his orange jumpsuit and hauled him to his feet, her face splitting into a lupine smile as she braced to Voyage away with him. "I don't want you thinking this is a dream."

CHAPTER ELEVEN

D aniel followed Angie's beacon as soon as he'd hauled Seth onto the bed, jotted down a note explaining their absence should he wake, and done what he could to leave the room fireproofed and shielded, raising his own shields just before he Voyaged.

He landed in a dark field of short grass, near the edge of an aspen forest. There were no lights from cars or buildings in sight, only the full moon high overhead illuminating the emptiness. A hundred feet ahead, Angie threw a large man Daniel instantly recognized to the ground, looming over him, her aura an almost still sphere of crackling yellow and white fire. They had clearly arrived only seconds before him, and the bear of a man in the prison jumpsuit stayed down, visibly disoriented.

"Angie," Daniel called out to her, but when she looked up at him, her mask of rage utterly hid the woman inside.

"Stay out of this," she called back, and Daniel raised his hands. He swallowed his own worries and emotions, blowing out a long breath.

As he watched Angie Voyage away, returning thirty seconds later with an armful of iron chains, he layered clear, glowing, enormous shields around the space, their intentions carefully honed. She clearly needed space to do whatever she needed to, and he could at least hold that space for her. No one would pass in or out but her. Anything that happened within would be theirs alone to know. As Angie welded the chains around the wrists of the cowering man at her feet with her intense heat, melting the other ends into a small patch of rocks among the grass beneath him, the night air stilled utterly, the only motions the occasional cricket or firefly.

"This ends here, tonight," Angie barked at the man, and Daniel braced himself for what she'd do next, quietly relieved she hadn't just dropped him off a cliff, and to his surprise, she Voyaged away.

When she returned, she was clinging tight to a sleep-befuddled Vicky. The shorter woman rubbed her eyes, her lime-green aura swaying uncertainly. "Stay here," Angie said, reaching out to grab Vicky's chin and stop her from seeing the man in orange who was silently investigating the chains holding him knelt to the ground quite yet. "I'm going to get the others, and you're the only other adept among us. When I bring them, just tell them this is all a dream, and do what you can to keep them quiet and ready. They know and trust you. They've barely met me." Vicky nodded, frowning, and Angie Voyaged away again.

Daniel watched as, one by one, Angie brought all nine women who he had gotten to testify against their common abuser, and three he'd asked but had declined for various reasons. As each landed, Angie barely waiting for their feet to touch down before leaving again, Vicky would catch their arm, reassure them in a whisper Daniel couldn't hear. They settled into a loose ring around the man on the ground, every single one tensing and calming when they recognized him, then saw he was shackled.

For his part, the prisoner watched each arrival indirectly, his focus caught more by the repeated appearance and disappearance of Angie, seeming unaware of Daniel standing back behind the ring of wronged and wary women. When she'd brought the last, she let Vicky do her thing, calming the woman into place in the circle, pacing around the prisoner in a wide arc.

The man sat up cross-legged, watching her, his chained hands resting casually in his lap and his expression shrewd. "So," he said like it was his first move in a chess game, his easy, placid charm as familiar to Daniel as he was sure it was to the rest. "Witches are real, like the gossip rags have been saying. I wonder how much of a reward I'd get for turning you in. And, if it's real, I'd guess the patricians have a hefty bounty out on monsters like you, for one reason or another." Daniel could see no hint of the monster he had glimpsed in the man who had lunged for Angie after his sentencing, but he knew everyone watching knew it was there, waiting.

"Aw, how nostalgic." Angie sneered, still pacing, and several of the other women risked weak smiles as they took in her confidence and tone. "Just like the good old days. Stating how clearly you know me. Citing external support to your angle. Then casually twisting it into a threat you hope will throw me off balance. Toss in the insult designed to lessen and undermine me, and there we have it. You in a nutshell. The thing is," Angie squatted down in front of the man, just out of reach, "this time, I'm not still stuck deep in your mind games. The conditioning has worn off. I'm no longer permanently bruised by your words and actions enough for little jabs like that to sting."

The prisoner stayed silent, his eyes just boring into Angie, and eventually she stood, her lip curling. "Oh right. When we start talking back, you just refuse to acknowledge us." Daniel watched her aura flare and swirl briefly, betraying that his second move had gotten under her skin. "Very well. Let's see if you're less of a coward with a weapon in your hand." The man smiled, and Daniel wondered if that had been the response he had hoped for or set up, carefully maintaining the stillness within his shield against his buffet of emotions.

Angie Voyaged away, and when she returned, she held a long piece of thick rebar in each hand. "You were always so good at violence," she said, the steel in her fists glowing orange as she started another lap around the man sitting on the ground. "For twenty years, your entire identity that wasn't work or women has revolved around being the best at pretending to kill others."

The twelve women watching were all silent, seeming to hold their breaths. "When one club, or job, or arena would kick you out for being a fucking predator, you'd always manage to find a new one with fresh prey." The rebar in her fists glowed nearly white hot, and as Daniel watched, they both shifted and reshaped under Angie's touch into two swords with long handles. "Fine, then. Let's settle this once and for all in the language you speak best." The swords turned to dull silver as she pulled the heat back out of them, tossing one on the grass beside her. "Or are you as much of a coward as I think?"

The man just lifted his manacled wrists with a glint in his eyes and Angie stepped forward, holding her sword tip to his throat, to press a spark of heat into the links of the chain, breaking them away. The prisoner lunged at her, hands grasping for her as his face contorted in fury. Every woman watching stepped back as one, and the man froze as blood pearled on his neck at the tip of Angie's sword. She raised a hand, and the onlookers stepped back. She backed away, not even blinking as she watched for his next move. "See? Coward. Just like I said. Or will you fight me like your equal and prove otherwise?"

The man sunk back to his haunches, all emotion sliding back beneath his easy, charming smile. He looked around at everyone watching him, finally noticing Daniel. His lips parted, but Daniel deepened his scowl, matching the faces of the women showing the man in their midst no pity or remorse, and the prisoner turned back away.

"Oh, but longsword was never your weapon of choice, was it?" Angie asked condescendingly. She bent and picked up the second sword, once more heating and altering it into a gilded spear with three sharp points. "You were always partial to the trident in your gladiator days, weren't you? Just like the one you tried to brand me with for life?" Angie tossed the cooling weapon back at his feet, but the former gladiator barely glanced at it. "The only things I left with of yours when I escaped were that fucking tattoo, a scar I hated just as much, and pain." Angie pulled aside the neckline of her shirt, exposing the clear, unmarked skin over her heart where a gladiator shield had once been inked, seemingly pinned to her flesh with a tattooed golden trident. "You never had any claim to me, or the seed you raped into me."

Daniel's heart constricted, and he closed his eyes momentarily, the defiant pain in Angie's words making the sight of a dozen others he knew must feel the same nearly unbearable.

"Fight me," Angie demanded, twisting the sword she held with a flick of her wrist, dancing in at him and back away. She moved to flank him, circling behind, and Daniel got a glimpse of the bright embers glowing in her eyes even the plebeians present would be able to see. "Stand up and fight me!" Streamers of fire shed from her skin like kerosine, scorching the grass and making one of the onlookers flinch. "You rapist, serial abuser, cheating, lying, groomer piece of shit—"

The prisoner moved with surprising speed, snatching up the trident and spun on one knee to stab it mercilessly through where Angie's rib cage had been a half second before she dodged to one side, his face hard and set. Angie's teeth glowed in the moonlight as she grinned, not even lifting her sword, but gesturing to the watching women to expand the circle a bit larger.

"I saved you, you ungrateful bitch," the prisoner snarled, pointing around the circle with his weapon.

"Liar," Angie barked, but he ignored her.

Each woman held his accusing, patronizing glare, despite how hard it clearly was for some. "I saved all of you in one way or another. From your parents, from shitty jobs, from exes who beat your asses. Or," he turned his attention back to Angie, "from whole mods intent on raping and robbing you in Hindustan."

With the last syllable he lunged at Angie again, and this time she met him, redirecting the blow with her sword and striking for his head, which he blocked with the shaft of his trident in the nick of time. Vicky shouted her approval and delight, and the other eleven women quickly joined in as Angie swung low for his hip, grabbing the tines of his trident with her off-hand and pushing it down as her blade scraped the gold plating off the steel trident and she brought the hilt up with a twist of her shoulder under her ex's jaw, launching her full weight off the ground with the blow.

The man in orange staggered back.

"Is that all you've got?" Angie asked over the cheers and jeers of the onlookers, and a brief eddy of wind passed over them before Daniel was able to rein it back into stillness. She dripped fire that refused to harm her magically fireproofed clothing, her bare arms roped with lean muscle and covered with scars. Her balance was stable but agile, and Daniel looked on in awe of the strong, beautiful, ruthless woman who stood in Angie's skin, and looked out from the glowing eyes of the woman he had known before her banishment.

"Make him finally pay!" one of the watching women, Amy, shouted out, and Angie lay into the bear of a man with a relentless volley of blows, each landing with a ring of metal and she in turn blocked those he delivered, limited by his weapon of choice to stabbing. When they stepped apart, both breathing hard, Daniel strained his eyes to see if there was blood. Angie had a cut along her cheek, but otherwise seemed unharmed, while the burly man was covered in nicks, and had a long gash down the outside of his thigh that was oozing into his jumpsuit.

"You know," the man said, gingerly dabbing at a split lip from Angie's pommel, "this sure doesn't seem like you've really moved on like you say. Maybe, beneath all this childish frustration, you're still just a little obsessed with me..."

In the time it took Daniel to blink, Angie had her sword to the man's throat, his trident on the ground. "Not even a little," she hissed. She backed away, her chest heaving, allowing him to retrieve his weapon, having proven her point that she was toying with him in their sparring. She was the cat. He was the mouse. He attacked her again, less frenzied than before, and between each exchange Angie seemed to speak not to her opponent, or to the witnesses, but to herself, shouting what had been too quiet for too long.

"You broke me. You ruined me. Everyone warned me away from you, but I didn't listen. I should have. So I listened the next time I was warned away from someone, and I nearly lost him for it." Daniel realized with a pang that she meant him, and heard every other reference she wove between the words she actually spoke. "Do you have any idea how much it hurt that you never showed me off? Never even mentioned me in public? I lived with you, I loved you, and yet you took Amy to your publicity appearances. You showed off Sharron on your social media. It's been five fucking years since I first named how much that hurt, and I still feel that wound so keenly, even when there are actually good reasons for secrecy."

"Fuck you, that's not my fault," the blond man huffed, recovering from a lunge that nearly sent him to the ground.

"Lie!" Angie shouted. "And you know it. I can hear it in your voice. I can see it in your body. You lied to me so. Many. Times, I learned how to *always* tell without even meaning to. I'll bet they could all say the same." Angie gestured out at the onlookers, and most of them nodded. Angie launched another attack, punctuating her sentences with blows. "You say you rescued me. But that's bullshit. You were the biggest thing I ever needed rescuing from. And I got myself out. Alone, by myself." Angie's eyes flicked to Daniel's for a moment, and away before he could offer her whatever she was looking for in him. "That story of yours fucked me up so bad that when someone really did rescue me, when someone actually pulled me out of my misery, I was so distrustful of it I nearly threw the wonderful things he offered me, like love, and comfort, and safety, all away."

Angie had built in intensity with each of the last dozen exchanges, and with the last, the man fell hard to the ground, his trident skittering away as Angie slammed a knee into the base of his neck. The onlookers were silent, and as Daniel looked around, he saw matching, shining smiles of pride, relief, and hungry satisfaction on every face.

Their abuser, rapist, and groomer was wheezing, and Daniel suspected one of his lungs had collapsed. His handsome face was bruised and mangled by Angie's hilt, his whole body cut and bleeding from her blade still stained with it.

"Will you ask for forgiveness now?" Angie said, breathing hard, but clearly not too badly hurt. "Will you admit any of the ways you abused us if I spare you?"

The bear of a man slowly raised his hands toward his head, smiling, but remained silent. Disgust flickered across all the watching faces but one as Angie smiled. "I thought so."

Angie brought her sword around, raising it in both hands above the pounding pulse in her rapist's throat. Her voice dropped to a whisper that rang in the still night air as she lifted the sword to bring it down. "The best thing people like you can ever do for the world is die."

Before he realized what he was doing, Daniel dashed forward, extending his arm between Angie and her target as his aura removed all the oxygen within his shields just for a second before restoring it, blowing out her flames back to smoke so thick he had to deactivate his auric vision to see her. All he could think about was the weight of every life he had ever taken that never went away. Angie screamed at him with pure rage, lowering her sword to a different angle, shoving his arm away with her other hand, but Daniel gripped it firmly. "Please. Angie."

Angie swayed, and for a breath Daniel saw all the true pain, loss, bitterness, suffering, and trauma beneath the mask of anger crack and gush from her being in a cold ripple of stale cigarette smoke and the smell of wet ash. Angie looked away, dropping her sword to the grass, and pulled her hand away, covering her face as it contorted. Daniel watched, his heart in his throat, as Angie's back silently shuddered several times as all the other onlookers quietly moved forward to gather close around, Daniel becoming part of their circle.

Angie was still crouched on top of the prisoner's wheezing chest, and when she quickly scrubbed her face, dropping her hands to reveal that she was still trying to find her composure, she eased up a little. "I knew who I was before you," she told the beaten face below her, his eyes locked on hers, unreadable. "I had dreams, and hope, and could *rest* before you." She bowed her head, pressing her eyes closed, her voice growing tight. "You took away who I was. You took away my ability to ever again love or trust as completely as I loved and trusted you." She turned her head away from Daniel, still bowed, and his heart utterly broke for her. "You broke everything I was, had and wanted."

Angie hauled herself to her feet, wiping the back of her wrist under her nose and turning in a full circle, holding each person's gaze, before returning her attention to the man on the ground. She bent, picking up the chains from where they had fallen, and welded them around the prisoner's wrists with her fingertips without resistance. "I should kill you right here and now," she said, kneeling over him, "just to make sure you never do it again to anyone else. Just like I should have done the day I escaped and left you bleeding on the floor because you could never believe a woman half your age could ever be your equal, let alone your better. I should have stopped you before you got to Vicky, and all those after her. I should stop you now." Angie looked at Daniel, clearly collecting herself. "But it appears the man I love now thinks I should show you mercy. And unlike you, he's proven to me that I should trust him."

Angie stood. "If you ever cross my path again, or theirs, I will kill you. If you ever even think about contacting me, or them. I will kill you. Do you understand?"

"Yes," he mumbled through swollen lips and broken teeth, and Angie kicked him hard in the side one last time for good measure, and Daniel didn't even think about disapproving. One by one, each of the other women there did the same, some turning to heel kick him, and Vicky chose to give him a good thump across the stomach with the shaft of his trident, making him groan.

As each one took their parting shot, Daniel reached a delicate tendril into their minds, soothing them into a dreamlike state, making sure they'd remember the events of the night as nothing more than vivid dreams.

Angie looked at Daniel, her whole body and face sagging and trembling, and he realized she was silently asking him what to do next. "Take them home," he told her gently, collecting tendrils of his bright yellow aura to help get the prisoner up into a fireman's carry. "I'll take care of this."

Angie held out her hand to Shannon, who took it sleepily, and they Voyaged away. Daniel hoisted the large man, knowing full well he was getting his bodily fluids all over him in doing so, and took two unsteady steps forward, stopping time and Voyaging away to the prison he had visited once with Angie. Setting the prisoner down just outside the front gate, Daniel secured the chains binding his wrists to a lamp post, making sure that the bear of a man was utterly unmissable by at least three of the guards that stood in sight, still as statues.

He retreated to the shadowed safety of a nearby stand of trees, and restarted time, using his shields for an extra layer of invisibility. It took three seconds for the sirens to start blaring. Daniel watched with satisfaction as a whole platoon of auxiliaries, marshaled by two legionnaires, descended on the battered inmate, guns all pointed at him, all shouting. When a stretcher came out, Daniel turned away to Voyage back to the field where he'd left Angie, eager to comfort her in whatever way she needed to go back to being her normal self.

He allowed himself a small smile as he set his intentions carefully and took two steps forward, disappearing from the hill by the prison, and appearing in the field where Angie and Vicky were grabbing the last two plebeian witnesses.

A prisoner of the Empire was ineligible for early release if they attempted to escape, or succeeded. No exceptions. They might even get their sentences doubled.

CHAPTER TWELVE

A ngie mostly kept to herself for the next week and a half. Daniel was kept busy getting Seth's training started, and it had given her time to process and replay everything that had been dredged up from her past.

When they arrived together at the Latin Council party which they'd been preparing for for nearly a month, hosted in the capital of Rome, Angie was surprised and thrown off to see just how utterly nonexclusive it was. Daniel had made it sound to her like some secret, previously unknown pocket of power in the heart of the Empire which Milton had invited them to as a high-value bargaining move to buy their favor. In reality, as Angie and Daniel stepped onto the mosaic floor of the immense circular temple, its vaulted ceiling stretching far overhead, Angie found herself simply overwhelmed with people, and mostly faces she already knew, at that.

Daniel's glowering annoyance beside her told Angie he was feeling much the same. He guided them toward the columned hallway off to one side that opened out into the gardens, glowing with old-fashioned lamplight in the gathering dusk, stopping when they were in a good place to observe. Angie leaned into him, too weary from lack of sleep and emotional exhaustion she couldn't seem to shake to find the willpower to smile her way through yet another decadent party.

"Do we have to?" she mumbled into his soft silk suit, and he wrapped his arms tight around her. She breathed in his calming scent of beeswax and frankincense, and let her attention spiral down to how the rise and fall of his breath gently rocked her head. "I'm sorry. I know it's been over a week. I know I should have been able to move on by now. I don't know why I haven't."

Daniel caressed her cheek with his bare hand, his expression kind. "If you need to go, you can. But if you think you can handle it, it would help to stay for an hour or so, and make as much of a memorable impression as we can in that time. We are so close to catching up with our enemies at the very top. We just have to push a little bit more."

Angie nodded, taking a deep breath. She stretched her face, feeling the caking texture of the heavy makeup she had worn to cover her exhaustion, but which she was deeply unused to. She looked around at the glorious filigree marble work and inlaid tile patterns, the great white pillars around the perimeter of the room and out along the covered walkway into the gardens adorned with heavy gold drapes creating a thousand hidden alcoves. "If we have to be here, at least it seems like a cool place to explore."

Daniel gave her a squeeze, releasing her to lace his fingers with hers. "Then let's do that."

They hadn't made it more than three steps when Milton Cartwright stopped them, dressed rather garishly in a turquoise suit, with his fuchsia aura crafted into a toga over it. "Hello!" he greeted them with suspiciously high spirits, and Angie avoided looking at him directly. She didn't think she could hide her anger that he had probably been the patrician sponsor that helped her abuser get early release and didn't want to give him the satisfaction. "Was your new recruit not able to join us? I was looking forward to meeting him!"

"No," Daniel said pleasantly, the only hint of his suspicion buried deep in his eyes. "He still had a few plebeian matters to wrap up, and I gauged him as being well able to keep his powers contained for a few hours. He has my cell number if needed."

"Ah, I see. What a pity. I did think you'd bring him to such an *exclusive* event to help convince him to stay." The Councilor put a great deal of emphasis on the word and Angie finally looked at him. His smile was affable, but his eyes held an edge that Angie assumed meant he'd purposefully invited everyone he could, just to make the invitation feel less special for Angie and Daniel. She looked around the room, and sure enough, most of the patricians she didn't recognize looked distinctly put out. She assumed those were the usually exclusive crowd whose party Cartwright had hijacked.

As she watched, an elderly Hindustani man lifted a glass of champagne laced with orchid-pink magic to his lips, and Angie shuddered. She'd once partaken of Milton's specially intoxicating wine. She hoped it didn't linger after consumption. Just past him, Marissa Hayward caught her eye, and Angie inwardly groaned.

"Is there food?" she cut in with a tight smile before the two men could continue their subtle sparring and didn't wait for an answer before pulling Daniel away toward the gardens. "Sorry."

They passed little huddles of people nestled into the nooks and crannies at the edge of the room, passing out toward the gardens. Daniel just squeezed her hand.

A large group of people, filling the width of the hallway approached, heading back in the way Angie and Daniel had come, and Daniel twisted the arm holding Angie's hand behind his back, guiding her into his wake where she wouldn't be jostled. She smiled politely and was instantly distracted when she overheard what one of the passing patricians was saying.

"...rumors about the Council gathering all the banishment keys from the Senate and Courts that still have them, taking inventory for some big move they've started prepping. I'm just worried that when Ragnarök—"

Angie tried to twist and see who had spoken, but the group was too dense. "Did you hear that?" Angie asked Daniel, and he shook his head, looking bewildered as she stepped back out beside him. "Never mind. I'll tell you later." Angie quickly ran through it again in her mind, trying to make sure she'd remember the snippet accurately.

Twenty minutes passed pleasantly, and Angie relaxed into the beautifully crafted gardens she and Daniel explored, finding delight in randomly stumbling across heavy-laden tables of drinks and treats, or stunning pieces of classical sculpture. When they encountered their third table of food, Angie realized they were quite alone, and picked up a candied raspberry, turning to Daniel with a wicked grin.

Stepping in close to him, she pressed the fruit to his lips. Daniel blinked, then he took it from her, his tongue grazing the fingers she let linger on his skin. He shifted even closer and kissed her, the taste sweet and light between them. A bird cooed in a tree high overhead in the cool Roman evening, and Angie kept kissing Daniel, tracing a hand up the side of his mahogany-red suit, so dark it was almost black. She felt his arm around her shoulders flex in response.

He pulled away, giving her a skeptical but intrigued look. "Here?"

Angie bit her lip, scanning all around them. "Well. Maybe not right here. But over there?" She nodded to a statue of Venus nearby, standing before a secluded cluster of cypress and juniper trees. Daniel grinned his approval, and Angie tugged him over, both watching around for any witnesses.

"Can I at least shield us?" Daniel asked and Angie laughed.

"I'm going to. Two is better than one."

Daniel descended on her mouth, devouring her, and Angie returned his fervor, swooning a little when Daniel's hand cradled the back of her head, dipping her over his thigh, making her helpless in his arms. When he righted her, Angie's head spun and her cheeks heated.

Daniel licked his lips, tracing down the side of Angie's face, his eyes locked on the sight. Angie watched him, sneaking a hand inside his jacket, popping open the single button to press her palm against his abdomen through his shirt. It felt like it used to with him, at that moment. Like he was someone she didn't quite know but was eager to explore, his dark, laser focus on her utterly seductive.

Angie brought her other hand up to caress his neck and jaw, dropping the hand against the point of his throat just above the knot of his gold brocade tie before lifting again to comb through his hair and grip firm to the base of his skull.

Daniel returned his mouth to hers, his hands cupping and massaging her breast and behind, gently pulling them apart in the way that made her insides come to life.

She trailed the hand on his stomach down over the front of his slacks and found him already at half-mast beneath the fine fabric. She unbuckled his black leather belt and unfastened his pants, sliding her fingers up under the edge of his shirt and down the smooth skin of his stomach until she could grasp his shaft, smiling as she continued to kiss him when she felt how much more he'd stiffened in the minute it had taken her to reach it.

Daniel tugged up the skirts of her long, deep green tulle dress until one hand could slip beneath, and Angie moaned when his fingers slid inside her panties. He massaged her clit in time with her grip on his cock inside his pants, extending every few strokes to pull his finger along her heated labia, making her squirm. When he sank into her, it stole her whole attention and her own hand stilled, all thought lost to the sensation of his fingers beckoning against the front of her insides.

"More, please," he whispered to her against her still, gaping mouth.

"Oh, sorry," she whispered back, cracking her eyes to find him grinning at her, and kissed him as she resumed stroking his cock from the base to the tip, circling the pre-cum there with her thumb.

Angie worked steadily, half-distracted by Daniel's ministrations on her, gauging his status by his little sounds and the subtle shifts in his body, just as she communicated to him in kind. It wasn't long before she was trembling, the palm of Daniel's hand grinding small circles against her clit as his fingers worked inside her. As her excitement grew, her pace on him sped up until he, too, was panting, his abdomen bent forward and his eyes screwed shut.

Angie let her mind go blank, falling wholly into the sensations Daniel was wringing from her, and came hard, convulsing around his fingers. The pleasure hauled her under, only dragged back with Daniel's hand wrapped on top of hers around his cock, clamping her grip back down and picking back up her pace that had faltered with her climax. She watched his face, grimacing with concentration, for the thirty seconds he used her hand for his own pleasure before he shuddered with release, not sure if it was hot, or she should apologize for him needing to step in to achieve his own pleasure.

When his convulsions had passed, he opened his eyes and released Angie's hand, smiling lazily at her, and her worries melted away. He withdrew his fingers from her, which made Angie groan in protest, and a wave of his hand cleared away the mess that had stained both of their clothing. "Thanks," he mumbled, and Angie grinned, kissing him even as she cleaned away the lipstick she'd left all over his mouth.

"My pleasure."

They quickly put their clothes to rights and dropped their shields, stepping out from their secluded spot. The area beyond was still blessedly empty. At least, until Marissa Hayward stepped into view, her long black gown with a high collar decorated with a beaded gold star across her ample chest whose rays dripped all the way to the hem.

"There you are," she exclaimed. "I've done two whole laps of this place looking for you. Do you have a minute?" Angie nodded and hoped she didn't look too odd with most of her lipstick gone as Daniel graciously spread his hands wide. "Wonderful, thank you." Marissa looked all around, her demeanor slipping, and Angie saw a blood-red shield shimmer up all around them. "I… Goodness, I don't know how to say this. I… I want to defect."

Angie's face utterly failed to disguise her disbelieving surprise. In a heartbeat, Daniel's much stronger shields snapped up around Marissa's, and Angie added hers for good measure. Daniel's aura snapped warm and tropical, spinning yellow light around them, the happiness in the display at odds with his skeptical expression, which Marissa seemed to mark as closely as Angie.

"Look," the raven-haired woman said, her usual superiority greatly subdued. "I was just made the Minister of Communication for the Empire." Angie gasped, and Daniel's careful composure cracked. "I thought it would be a position of true service to the whole Empire, but... the things I've seen there in only a few days. I see it now. The propaganda briefings, the guides for spin jobs and cover-ups... it's opened my eyes. I've been wrestling with it for days now, and I just don't think I can keep ignoring the truth of the Patrician Order's control of the globe I've now seen." She looked imploringly between Angie and Daniel, who exchanged a bewildered look.

Daniel pinched the bridge of his nose, likely trying to buy himself some time to process. "Congratulations, Marissa, on the appointment. I can't think of anyone more deserving of that esteemed position. And I am sorry to hear that it has been so distressing to you." Daniel inhaled deeply, clearly choosing his words carefully. "You were my first recruit, my friend, and an admired colleague. I am, of course, eager to help you in any way I can if you are in distress. You know I dipped my toes over that line of loyalty to the Court, by my own admittance, before we met, but I hope you can appreciate that this is a very delicate matter."

Marissa nodded, looking both relieved and chastened. "Yes, of course. Please, don't take any risks you don't have to on my account." Again, she seemed to search Angie and Daniel for what she sought, and Angie's mind just couldn't make sense of what was happening. Her aura was nervously leaking oak smoke and the scent of struck matches, and the moment she noticed she shut it back down under control. "I just need some direction. I've seen the true colors of the Empire now, and I feel so lost." Her face matched her words, and she reached out to grasp the shoulder of Daniel's coat familiarly. "However, you can, please, Daniel. I need guidance from my sponsor. Please."

She turned away, her beaded dress sparkling in the half-light from a gas lantern nearby, pausing and staring at it for a long moment before picking up a sopapilla dusted with powdered sugar and disappearing back down the garden path, her shield disintegrating in her wake.

"Is she genuine?" Angie asked.

Daniel shrugged. "It seems so. But we do have to consider the alternatives. Like her just trying to get out from under our leverage over her, or the possibility that she intends to be a double agent."

Angie blew out a long breath and closed her eyes, wishing for the hundredth time that her life was less complicated. "Is this worth meeting with them in-person to discuss?" Angie asked under her breath with a meaningful look.

Daniel caressed her arm, giving it a comforting squeeze and reaching into his pocket for his phone, letting go of her to unfold his reading glasses and balance them on his nose. "Yeah. I think so. I'll see if they're free tomorrow."

Chapter Thirteen

"So yeah," Daniel said, looking around the little collection of picnic tables at Dawn, Jonathan, Angie, and the rest of the gathered listeners. "That's everything Marissa said about her desire to defect and why I think we can't afford to not try to use her. Which is why I asked for this meeting."

The little village green of the rebellion compound was flooded by the bright, late-morning light of the clearing in the massive redwood trees that bordered the property, making the scene laid out around him vibrant.

Dawn shrugged, toying with one of her long, blue-dyed braids as she rested her elbow on her knees, perched on the top of one table, her heavy boots on the bench. "It's not like we can turn down having the propaganda minister on our side," she said, addressing the whole crowd of outcast adepts.

"Which is why we should be cautious," Angie said. "Daniel and I said as much out loud, outside the Senate meeting back in February. We were shielded, but if someone on their side still managed to hear... It's just too perfect to not be a trap."

"I agree," Jonathan said, twisting the gold wedding band on his finger absently. "But even if it's not, she's most useful to us on the inside of the patrician structure. We shouldn't take any risks we don't have to with everything else on our plate. Recruiting unlocked and uncontacted English adepts is finally tapering off, but that's just opening the way for other vital preparations for whatever comes next." Jonathan nodded at Anthony Shupee, quiet and subdued, standing at the back of the crowd. "Everyone here has been training up on any and every skill that might be needed or useful, like phase-walking, healing, and more."

"And," Mahina said, "we're having to put more and more magic and time into dealing with the new deportation threats if we're found, or when we go out, since many of the people here never got official patrician papers, or had theirs revoked."

"I can help with that," Angie piped up, and the beautiful, plump Hawaiian woman gave her a grateful nod.

"That being said," Jonathan. "If Marissa does become our spy in the Empire, there are certain skills she should hone to be as productive as possible. Like seeing if she can pick up listening skills like mine. The problem is, how do we communicate with her, teach her, and get info back without putting us all at risk of exposure if she proves false." He pulled a hand down his weathered face. "Complicated by the fact that I was informed this morning that the English Court is asking me to step in as a Judge again last-minute, since one of their newly recruited puppet Judges was very old and sadly passed away last week."

Daniel's aura buffeted cold as his stomach flipped. "One day before the conference opens? Speaking of likely set-ups..."

"How's that going to work with your family?" Dawn frowned. "I know you've already been stressed about the growing unrest around more magic exposure in your area. And will you be able to keep Hannah's unlocked powers repressed, being away so much for duties at the conference?"

Daniel's face contorted. He opened his mouth to verify that he'd really just heard that his best friend's wife was one of the people Angie had accidentally unlocked when she'd broken the Focal Nucleus at Stonehenge nearly three years ago and Jonathan had been hiding that from him but stopped himself. No one else nearby looked surprised in the slightest, not even Angie, and Daniel bit back his hurt at being the last to know, silently admitting he probably wouldn't have reacted well to being told directly and couldn't blame Jonathan for choosing not to.

"I'll figure it out. It's the kids I'm mostly worried about. We're thinking about pulling them out of school, maybe even moving. Though we're not sure where would be safer."

"So you accepted?" Daniel asked, feeling wounded and frustrated that his friend would even consider taking such risks. "Why? It's almost certainly a trap, which I know you are too smart to not see. This is probably another setup from Cartwright, through Byrne, hoping we attempt to repeat Angie's appearance at Stonehenge, *which we are*, and that he can make us fail and catch us in the process this time."

"I know," Jonathan admitted, his bright blue eyes as piercingly observant as always. "I'm sorry, Dan. I know this adds stress to you. But I can't pass up the opportunity to help what is going to be the most stressed batch of new recruits in living memory deal with the incredible amount of pressure they will be under around everything the Court has at stake in getting a new Focal Nucleus put in place. No one else in the English Court has the credentials or experience that I do to help how I can." Daniel shook his head in defeat, dropping it to stare at his clasped hands and heard Jonathan sigh, his tone shifting even deeper into reassuring and kind. "Plus, this means I will be closer and in a better position to help you, and make sure you, too, are safe and supported through the high-stress ordeal."

"Right. Fine. Thanks," Daniel said, sitting up and rubbing the end of his nose, eager for someone to change the topic.

"Besides," Jonathan added, clearly not yet satisfied, "as much as I hope and pray otherwise, the chances of us reaching a nonforceful redirecting of the patrician systems are looking slimmer every month. I'd rather be in the thick of things if and when everything slips over that edge, in the hopes of minimizing the polarization or damage."

Angie perked up next to him. "If you're ready to admit that now, then why are we still not considering that the best defense is a good offense?"

Jonathan shook his head. "I'm not saying hope is lost. Not even close. And even if it was, how would we still be on the right side of history if we went around murdering people we don't like? That's not good, just, moral, or right."

"But people like Cartwright have killed, would be killing right now if he wouldn't get punished for it, and will kill us the moment he can in a way that benefits him—"

"So anyone who has taken a life deserves to die?" Daniel asked rather pointedly, addressing Angie.

"No! It's more complicated than that. Never mind." She sagged, looking away.

He did too, trying not to think about the thin lines of reasoning that allowed him to justify the deaths he'd caused under orders or accidentally. Some days, they felt more like self-serving lies of logic and morality.

No one spoke for a stretched breath of awkward silence until Angie threw her hands up in defeat. "If the most we are aiming for is mitigation, stalling, and nonaction like that, then why are we even bothering?"

Daniel's mind flashed back to the almost identical conversation they'd had, standing atop the cliffs nearby immediately after Angie's return from banishment, and resentment that she still hadn't moved on from her stubborn stance in the last five months soured the breakfast he'd eaten a few hours earlier. "Because," Daniel snapped, losing his patience, "if we don't do anything, or overplay our hand and get shoved out of a position to stand up for ourselves, then we *all* get our magic repressed again. Siphoning away to be used to harm us in the most painful, weakening, helpless way you can imagine, just like millions of other outcasts like us in every other language on the planet are still dealing with everything single day."

"And looking after the plebeians, who are much less empowered and much less well-informed than we are, as is our duty in our position," Jonathan added in a much kinder tone.

Dawn nodded. "And, for ourselves as much as them, it's vital we end the massive wealth disparity of the patricians. If we can get into the Council and learn how they prevent resource production through magic, even without the restrictions of an individual language Focal Nucleus, then we can make sure no one has to go hungry, unhoused, or without the medicine they need ever again."

"And I don't know about you," Casey said quietly from his seat across the circle between the dark-haired Demitria and Olivia, "but I really don't want to lose a friend to banishment ever again, and it sounds like Dawn and them don't either, which is why they are doing what they're doing, and giving us all the directions they are." Angie dropped her gaze as her freckled cheeks colored.

Daniel's annoyance softened. "So yeah. Angie, just trust us for a few months more. Keep your distance from Seth if you feel the need to, but understand that he is our plan. He's our next move, and it's not a bad one."

"I wouldn't go that far," Dawn said, thankfully shifting the attention back to her. "The Victume Ceremony will be very heavily warded against Voyaging or Skipping in as always. We still haven't figured out how we're going to deal with the fact that he seems very unlikely to sympathize with our cause, so may not do what we want, and that the very first thing they are going the do the moment Stonehenge starts waking up is restrict the magic of anyone and everyone but the Supreme Justice to sort through later, to head off the exact sort of thing we are hoping to do. By the time the site is open enough for us to infect the new lock, or rip it out altogether, none of us will have enough power."

Daniel cleared his throat, his mouth twisting to one side with apprehension. "I've actually had an idea about the first point. We might just try to use Seth to help one of us Voyage in through the wards without him even knowing."

"How?" Dawn asked, blinking rapidly as her eyes narrowed.

"We plant an aura-bonded token on him before he enters the circle."

Dawn's eyes went wide, and several jaws among the onlookers dropped. Absolute silence reigned for a long moment.

"How have we never thought of using that before?" Dawn whispered, looking stunned. Daniel just shrugged, feeling more than a little pleased with himself, the light of his aura almost matching Dawn's gold magic.

"And what about me for the second part?" a timid voice in the crowd asked, and all eyes turned to the small, beautiful Hellenic woman standing close to her fiancé. Demitria squirmed under the sudden attention from everyone, and Nikolaos wrapped a comforting arm around her shoulders. When she spoke, as usual, the translation magic she used meant the way her lips moved didn't match the sounds that came out. "You said my magic is too old to be repressed by the Greek language Court. Couldn't I do it, if Niko and I did the token bonds thing, and I took Seth's place when the lock was ready?"

When Daniel glanced at Dawn, unexpected, solid hope warming him further, he found her grinning. "Great idea. We'll pursue that." Her aura shifted subtly in an unusual way, and beside him, Angie frowned.

"It's okay," he whispered to her, fighting the urge to roll his eyes. "That just means she'd already thought of it, maybe was even already counting on it, but was waiting for the other person to volunteer, so it seems like their idea."

"Still," Dawn said, cracking her neck and standing from her perch on the picnic table, "I'd rather not keep all our eggs in one basket around any of this. If folks have backup plans, I'm all ears."

"Actually, I do," Angie said, raising one hand, the other reaching for her silver key necklace, and Daniel stopped breathing. Her eyes were glassy, and she flinched as if she wasn't sure she actually wanted to say what she was about to. "We know what worked the first time. We could try to find more of the same demons, one we could bring with us in an object like I did and have that as a doomsday option in case the new lock gets fully integrated, and we need to destroy it. When I did it, I was already feeling the magic repression, so we know that wouldn't cripple that contingency."

Daniel's breath became fast and shallow. "No. No, that's insane. Those demons, their world, we shouldn't go anywhere near them. They killed a fully trained, powerful patrician, and very nearly killed me."

"I know, but I have more experience dealing with demons and half-worlds now than anyone alive," Angie said reassuringly. "And back then, you didn't have these." She fished in her pocket, pulling out the large, heavy copper coin with the anti-possession sigil Jonathan had carved into one side.

"I've been doing more research about that," Jonathan said before Daniel could object further. "That ancient book we grabbed for you to read leading up to your first Victume Ceremony has what I think are references to that practice of 'hosting', which was in the act of being outlawed at the time, about a thousand years ago."

"No," Daniel barked, his aura lashing fully out of his control, his hands balling into fists as his shields overhead fluctuated. "That would be sending lambs to slaughter, both trying to collect a new demon, and trying to use one if you succeed." He could barely see past the fog of panic clouding his vision. "It wouldn't be a Victume Ceremony, a maintenance ritual, but a victim ceremony. Sacrificial blood on the altar stone."

"Fine," Jonathan said, appearing at Daniel's side and gripping his shoulder firmly through his coat. "We won't pursue that. We'll stick to what we've been building toward and hope for the best. Dan, take a deep breath." His expression was worried, his voice soothing, and Daniel did as he was told.

Beside him, Angie's aura was thick and silver, leaking mugwort and mahogany smoke, and Daniel didn't have the capacity to decipher it as she and Jonathan shared a meaningful look.

Everyone looked around when Dawn bolted for the edge of the green everyone was gathered on, intercepting a teenage girl with a mountain of coiled brown hair and a juddering aura of pumpkin-orange magic. "Léa, you shouldn't be here," Dawn said, trying to hustle the young woman away, but Léa clearly wasn't having it.

"None of it has come true yet!" she shrieked, batting Dawn's hands away to stumble forward to the center of the crowd. She turned in a full circle, her fingers picking at the deep brown skin on her arm. Her disheveled appearance and erratic movements reminded Daniel strongly of Ophelia in a production of Hamlet he'd once seen at the Globe Theater in London. "An angel of flame and chaos will bring an end to order. Water will stand against the Empire and fall. Demons shall let the angel pass, leading them to the broken door. The Angel in the Forest. Two are one, one is two, all is nothing." Léa muttered in a strange voice, her eyes touched with orange, making Daniel's blood run cold. "No... I'd hoped we weren't on this path... The angel... we need her..."

"I thought we agreed not to push her gift anymore as she deteriorates," Jonathan said in his 'disappointed dad' voice, skirting around and reaching for Léa, whose eyes snapped to him, full of magic and insanity. As Jonathan gently turned her away from the body at her feet, she yanked her arm free.

"How will you lose your water? And where will you find your spirit..." Léa's demeanor switched from defiant to pleading in a blink, and she clawed at Jonathan, clinging to his shirt as her voice twisted high with emotion. "Please. The ghosts. Unlike the others. Please. Reflections in glass, held in copper. Tell me you know."

Jonathan frowned, his eyes darting between the teenager's. "I do. It's okay. Let go of the Sight. It's hurting you. Let go."

Daniel watched as Jonathan moved Léa away, wondering if Jonathan really understood the Seer's words, or was just pretending to in order to soothe her. He glanced at Nikolaos, his arm still wrapped around Demitria, who peered up at him with open, deep concern. His expression was worried under his curly mop of black hair as he watched Dawn, Olivia, and Jonathan soothe Léa and bustle her away. They turned away, and Daniel felt the clear solidity of the path before him falter. The madness of a true Seer would take him, too, if all the languages were unlocked, including his native Greek. Even if they won, some would lose.

"The lasts are starting," Léa's voice rang out, her words echoing off the front of the common house building nearby. "The last times for everything. Don't let go."

CHAPTER FOURTEEN

T he Grand Hall of the English Patrician Court, at the heart of their conference site, was as impressively opulent as ever. Angie led Seth in through the enormous doors, each panel inlaid with inches-deep burnished brass carvings, glad he showed no signs of remembering the night of his awakening or remembered her in any context other than as Daniel's partner he rarely saw.

He followed her inside, the glittering chandeliers shining in his eyes as he looked around at the delicate filigree moldings, jewel-encrusted ornaments, and rich oil paintings hung between crimson velvet drapes and mirrored panels, walking up the sweeping staircase of polished marble to the second floor.

Angie could remember how much the light had seemed to sparkle and dance off every glittering surface the first time Daniel had escorted her through those doors. Now the light seemed to bend around her, leaving her shimmering gold gown and great spiked diadem of silver and diamonds half in the shadow of her smoke as they climbed their way toward the ornate vaulted ceiling to circle the room along the raised balcony.

As she trailed her fingers along the banister, Angie willed the chain holding the silver key pendant at her neck to expand out and down, creating a web that filled the open back of her dress. Just like the first time. Maybe for the last time.

"When will Senator Fawl be joining us?" Seth asked, not hiding his boredom at being stuck with her for the time being.

"Soon," she replied as they reached the far end of the balcony where the other staircase was. "As he said. He had some preparation for his arrival to see to." Angie stopped to assess the throng below shrewdly. The clusters of people chatting were larger than normal. Not natural conversational groups of two to five, but distinct cliques segregating themselves away from the rest. Lord and Lady Braithwaite were chatting to Jonathan, Jasper Rose, and Barbara Collins, and Angie marked them to retreat to later when her primary roles in the ensuing pageantry were done. First, she had a job to do in ensuring Seth's indulgent introduction to the darker side of the patrician Court was memorable.

A hush fell over the crowd as the air in the hall suddenly grew thin and cold, and Angie struggled to fill her lungs and not panic at the sensation. When the unnatural stillness had utterly consumed all else, Daniel appeared, alone, framed in the massive doorway out into the darkness of the spring equinox night, and the air rushed back in, rich, fresh, and warm, with a ferocity that sent patricians gasping and clutching their finery as they stepped back.

Angie hadn't known exactly what to expect, and what she saw sent her heart thumping madly and made her mouth go dry. Beside her, Seth's face opened in a look of utter, devoted admiration.

Stepping over the threshold, leaning lightly on his gold-handled cane in one gloved hand, Daniel looked as Angie had never seen him before, dressed in full Imperial legionnaire dress uniform. The spotless, flattering suit was buttoned high to the neck and belted at Daniel's slim waist, the deepest purple fabric decorated with gold braid at the seams. Thick gold cords draped around one shoulder, and the Imperial Eagle was embroidered over his heart. On the other side of his chest, he had pinned the medal he had kept in the safe in his Boston home since Angie had first peeked inside, the blood-red ribbon and gold coin bearing the rod of Asclepius standing out formidably. From his white leather belt hung a simple holster bearing the handgun he had kept from his military service as a decorated soldier and medic.

As Daniel walked forward into the room, each step careful and measured, Angie moved to the stairs and descended, unable to tear her eyes away from him. His expression was set and unreadable, his impeccable posture stiffer than normal, and she couldn't explain why the sight of him in military uniform, that medal on his chest and that pistol on his hip so excited and frightened her.

The gathered patricians had retreated to give Daniel a wide berth, and he stopped in the dead-center of the room, turning with practiced precision in a full circle. He didn't say a word, but Angie saw how he made careful direct eye contact with every Senator present, lingering on those they'd shortlisted as their guesses at Council members, including the once certain element of Milton Cartwright, standing with Marissa Hayward off to one side. Each met his gaze defiantly, but most slumped slightly as he looked away, taking in his palpable presence and his overt demonstration of loyalty and service to the Empire above all else.

When he had finished his rotation, Angie was waiting for him, and when he walked forward to take her hand, bowing low to press a kiss to the back, it felt like she was meeting him for the first time.

***

"Come, meet three of our current Judges, and well-respected former Judges," Daniel said to Seth a few minutes later once the room had largely returned to normal and Angie followed in their wake, happy, for once, to be utterly lost in the shadow cast by her shining companion.

Jonathan gave them a beaming smile of pride as they approached, and Jasper Rose, Lord Braithwaite, and Lady Braithwaite were pleasant enough as Daniel introduced Seth around to them all. The new recruit's gaze lingered on Jasper Rose, likely trying to figure out their gender, but their attention was pulled away when Marissa Hayward joined them.

She looked truly stunning, her light brown skin smooth and glowing against her revealing black and gold dress, the blood-red ribbon of her aura wound around and through both and through her long, thick, beautifully styled hair. She pressed a glass of rich red wine into his hand, toasting him with her own. "To a hell of an impression," she said, and threw her head back, nearly draining the glass in one.

Daniel gave her his darkest grin and did the same, making Angie fight not to frown as she assessed the older woman's actions. "Thank you," he said. "Let me introduce you to my new recruit. Marissa, this is Seth Laufey. Seth, this is Judge Heyward, my first recruit, who is now the head of the enforcers on the English Court." Seth eyed her a little warily as he shook her hand, clearly not quite sure what to make of her. "Oh, also," Daniel added as Seth withdrew his hand, subtly wiping it on the leg of his trousers, "she was just given the incredibly high honor of being made the Communications Minister for the Empire. You won't see her on television any time soon, but every word you'll hear there or on your radio goes through her first."

Seth's whole demeanor changed in an instant, and Angie moved away half a step as a visceral reaction of disgust snaked through her. "It's a great honor to meet you," he said, bowing deeply. When he straightened, he was grinning, looking between Daniel and Marissa as if mentally pairing them to whatever ideal Marissa had suddenly become part of in his head. "You must be quite powerful and popular to be given such a position. I hope that I can give Senator Fawl as much reason to be proud of me as you clearly have."

"Aren't you charming," Marissa said, giving Seth an amused smile, and Daniel a beaming one. "Well, if you find yourself looking for something to do after the Victume

Ceremony, I could always use dedicated, enthusiastic patricians in my department. One as good-looking as you, I would just *have* to put in front of the cameras as well." Seth beamed, and Daniel put a proud and admiring hand on Marissa's shoulder.

As Angie stood there, ignored, she felt as utterly alone as she had just after Shan had died, leaving her to her banishment alone.

CHAPTER FIFTEEN

An hour later Angie was grabbing some lemon bars off the golem-carried trays of food circulating through the guests, unconsciously intending to take Daniel his favorite treat to ease her disconnection and discomfort with how much he was drinking with Marissa when a rough hand on her arm made her drop them. She whirled around, her flames crackling up as she prepared to admonish whoever it was, finding Milton Cartwright standing before her. *Perfect. Spares me the trouble of finding him*, she thought. His hands were raised, but his expression was hard.

"What do you want?" she spat, stepping out of the way as a weathered golem bent with the sound of grinding stone to clean away the dropped sweet.

"You don't belong here," Milton hissed, his piggy eyes bulging. "I thought, since only Fawl asked for a recruit, you had the sense to stay away from the conference and all of its functions. These are my halls, not yours."

"Excuse me?" Angie asked in the most dangerous tone she could manage, turning her attention more intention-ally to keep the yellow flames of her aura from relaxing back into smoke. "Need I remind you what's in your best interest around myself and Daniel?"

Milton seemed to reconsider even approaching her several times, the gears almost visibly turning in his head as he clearly tried to decide whether he was angry, scared, or simpering. "Look," he said eventually. "I need you two to ease up. If you want me to get him into the Council, or do anything else you've asked of me, you have to help me regain face." He looked around, as if making sure no one was listening. "Just hand Anthony back over to me. Let me make an example of him. Get him to support the version of events I told everyone to get them back on my side. Just bring him back to me, and I'll do the rest. You don't even have to get your hands dirty."

Angie was so shocked by the request that she just stared, utterly disgusted, until the golem straightened to move away and jarred her out of it. "That is *abhorrent*," Angie said, putting as much emphasis behind the word as she could. "You think I would hand him back over to you, after the way you treated him the whole time you were together? I'm sure I don't know even a fraction of it but I do know that you abused the shit out of him when you were claiming to love him as your husband. I can only imagine what you have in mind to torture or brainwash him into obeying you now that you openly hate him." Angie reached for her necklace, sinking as much of her excess rage into it as she could. "I have zero tolerance for abuse. After trying to get me out of your way with my own abuser twice now, I can't believe you'd even think of asking that of me."

Milton looked half taken aback, half pleased. "And here I thought you bleeding-heart, leftist agitators preached tolerance—"

"I will not be held to a higher standard than my abusers in fighting them," Angie snarled. "And if you think you can plead or wheedle your way out of doing what you have agreed to for us, then I'm going to remind you of your place." Angie poked a finger into Milton's doughy chest. Two people nearby glanced in their direction, but quickly paled and scurried further away. "We have another favor, a new one, to ask of you. We've heard rumors that the Council is gathering up all the banishment keys. We want you to show us where they are all kept. Understand?"

Milton was grinding his teeth, looking ready to pop a fuse, and Angie readied her flames, ready to fight off his mental manipulations and befuddlement, or face down one of his illusions, thinking back with fond darkness to every time she had done so in the past.

She wasn't braced for the fist that slammed into her face, snapping her head back and making stars dance in her vision. Angie's flames roared out from her of their own accord as she fought to keep the radius limited, charring a ten-foot circle of the hardwood floor around her feet to solid black. "Fuck you!" Angie shouted at Cartwright, who seemed to have not thought through his next move, looking at his hand, when he and everyone else froze.

Angie cast around, finding Daniel a dozen yards away, standing between the frozen Marissa and Seth. "No," she shouted, and he frowned, befuddled by too much wine Marissa kept pressing into his hands. "Restart time!" Angie pushed her magic out from her to encompass Cartwright, unthinkingly trying to haul him back into her time stream with her, but he barely started moving at one-tenth normal speed.

"You sure?" Daniel said, and Angie bared her teeth. "Yes, of course. Or have you forgotten that you have a part to play in this, too?" Realization and embarrassment slowly dawn on Daniel's face. When he nodded, Angie took a deep breath, taking back up her posture and facial expression as precisely as she could.

Time restarted with a jolt, and Angie caught Milton's fist as it once more swung for her, redirecting it as she fanned her harmless flames into touring gouts. Everyone nearby scrambled away, Marissa pulling Daniel back by his arm as Seth watched with glee, her flames reflected in his blue eyes.

As Milton turned, physically attacking her in ways she was not prepared for, Angie did her best to scan the onlookers, carefully assessing who was angered by her seemingly predictable outburst, and who was rooting for her. Granted, she hadn't planned on Milton not sticking to his M.O. of testing his magical strength, but his physical attack worked just as well for the testing demonstration Daniel and Angie had planned to see who else might be interested in defecting.

"You are nothing. You will remember your place!" Cartwright yelled, throwing his full weight into a lunge at her, his hands outstretched.

Angie realized she couldn't keep him under control and watch the onlookers. "No! You will remember yours! Johannesburg. The Nkosis. Your little deviations as Supreme Justice..."

Her words had the desired effect, and Milton stopped in his tracks, his hands still balled into fists, huffing as he dropped his voice. "I have my own sources, and Seers, you know."

Angie wondered if he meant Sakshi, the Seer who had helped her reach the Norns, feeling a pang of guilt that they had had no luck in finding her during Angie's banishment, assuming she was dead and giving up after a full year. "As do I," she said, letting that bitterness deepen her voice. "Or have you forgotten that I have the fates themselves under my command? I'm the only one who decides my fate. And yours, now."

The threat utterly took the wind out of Milton's sails, and his whole being sagged as he shifted his weight awkwardly from one foot to the other for a long moment, before sullenly flagging down a golem and taking the champagne from it, the whole room resuming their buzz of sound as they read the signal that the increasingly commonplace altercation was over.

Angie looked around for Daniel, hoping they could leave now and discuss what reactions of note he'd spotted, but didn't find him where she'd last seen him. She was at the back of the hall and started making her way back toward the doors at the front, scanning for him between each shifting gap between people. When she spotted him far ahead near the doors, being steered and half-supported by Marissa, her stomach dropped.

Angie tried to use the phase-walking skill she'd taken a few lessons on from Anthony, but it didn't work. Instead, she Voyaged to land just in front of them. "Move," Daniel said, his words bizarrely slurred, and Angie's face contorted.

"What, so you can leave with her? I don't think so. What the hell is wrong with you?"

Daniel just gave her a disgusted grimace, draining the last of his merlot. Angie frowned, checking the wine Daniel was downing for any sign of Milton's fuchsia influence, but saw only red.

"Enough of this. You're too drunk to be making any kind of choices for yourself. I'm taking you home," Angie said, reaching out to grab his hand and pull him away from Marissa.

The moment Angie's fingers brushed his skin, a nauseating vibration overwhelmed her. The buzz filled her head, drowning out all thought and blurring her vision. Every inch of her skin crawled, and she collapsed as her vision faded into blackness.

Chapter Sixteen

D aniel cradled an ice pack to his aching head in one hand, his eyes zoned out on Angie, who was passed out on the infirmary bed he sat on the edge of. He sat up when she stirred, her eyes slowly blinking open, looking disoriented. "Hey," he said, and she smiled lazily, her eyes drifting back closed again before opening with a snap.

"Hey," she said in an accusing tone, sitting bolt upright and clutching her own head as it undoubtedly pounded. "What the fuck was that? Why..." Angie's eyes became bright, and Daniel felt the corners of his mouth drag down. Her voice dropped to barely a whisper, desperately searching Daniel's face. "Why did I pass out when I touched your skin? What happened next?"

Jonathan spoke up from the corner, quiet enough to be respectful of the hangovers of the other two people in the room. "We don't know why his curse affected you this time. Maybe it was all the wine. But I can confidently report that you dropping like a stone must have sobered Dan up a good chunk. By the time I was able to shove my way over, he was trying to pick you up and shoving others away, saying he had to get you home. I helped him carry you down here, since he was way too drunk to Voyage and refused to let go of you. Lady Braithwaite came with us and was able to sober him up the rest of the way with some foul-smelling concoction she enchanted."

"And, unfortunately," Lady Braithwaite's posh Britannian accent said from the doorway as she walked in, carrying a small silver tray she set down on the small table by the door, "this is far from the first time an opening ball has ended in the infirmary, and won't be the last. Take these," she said, handing Angie and Daniel each a glass of water, then a bottle of pills, careful not to touch Daniel's bare hands.

Daniel obeyed, turning to Jonathan. "Hey, would you be willing to bunk at my cottage on site here tonight? Seth was drinking a fair bit, too, and shouldn't be left on his own."

Jonathan nodded, hauling himself out of the chair and pulling a hand down his dark beard. "Sure. Anything I should know?"

"Not really. The kitchen's stocked. Be warned that the top stair squeaks, if you're trying to be quiet. And I've set the wards to let the four of us in as a default, plus Seth."

"Nice to know I could see to medical emergencies without bother," Lady Braithwaite said, taking the empty glass from Angie.

"Of course," Daniel replied. "You can't do much for me, but I don't want my recruits to ever be at risk. Besides, I trust you completely after you managed to stop that demon from killing me outright and got it confined to my knee." Lady Braithwaite rolled her eyes and took Daniel's glass as he opened the top few buttons of his uniform, which he wished he'd thought to do so much earlier.

"Can we go?" Daniel asked the head healer, and she nodded, her mane of salt-and-pepper hair bouncing.

"If you like. Those tablets should work very quickly for the aftereffects of wine for you, and your skin curse for her. Other than that, just hydrate, eat, and get a good night's sleep."

When Angie and Daniel got back to the front stoop of their cottage, unable to Voyage right in through the paranoid wards, he unlocked the front door, stepping aside to let Angie pass.

"So," Angie said, standing in the front room of their cottage, still dressed in her gold and silver finery.

"So," Daniel echoed, undoing a few more buttons on his stuffy uniform. "Talk?"

Angie pressed her eyes closed, looking pale. "Yeah." She turned toward the stairs. "But not in these clothes."

Once Daniel and Angie had changed into comfortable house clothes, they went back downstairs, where Daniel got them both cold glasses of water from the fridge, and Angie scrounged up potato chips and chocolate hobnobs from a cupboard. Angie turned off all but the soft light over the stove, and they settled down at the kitchen table side by side. Daniel kept his head down, extracting a hobnob for himself while Angie popped open the bag of chips, looking as enthusiastic about the conversation that had to happen as he felt.

"I don't know why I was leaving, or where, or had specifically chosen to leave with Marissa," Daniel said to end the looming silence, and was pleased to see Angie's shoulders immediately relax.

"I didn't really think you did," she said, eating a chip. "I just... I don't know. I don't think I've ever seen you actually drunk before. And the way Marissa was acting..."

"No, I know. It's alright. I know you have—" he almost said 'issues' but corrected himself. "I know you have a lot of horrible experiences around getting cheated on and lousy partners, and I put you in a really tough spot."

Angie nodded, eating more chips, and Daniel finished his biscuit and drank some water, his hangover fading. She glanced at him sidelong, and Daniel found he couldn't read her expression. "I'm sorry I have to ask, but could you just please tell me out loud if we, you and I, are okay or not?"

Daniel half-smiled, suddenly feeling nervous. "Yes. We are. I mean, as far as I know. I can't speak for you." Out of habit, he pulled out his phone, setting it face up on the table like his state of anxiety could be eased by the arrival of an expected call.

It was Angie's turn to give him a reassuring, half-hearted smile. "Yeah, we're fine, I hope. Except for..."

Her gaze dropped to Daniel's hands, and he drew a long, steadying breath. He set aside his snacks and Angie did the same, both shifting to face each other more. Daniel held out his hand, but as Angie reached to take it, he snatched it back, a thousand deep, old fears and thoughts of self-loathing crashing over him like a tidal wave.

Angie looked up at him, hurt and worried, withdrawing her own hand, and he shook his head. "I just don't want you passing out again right away," he said, knowing full well Angie would know it was a lie. He took another deep breath, holding out his forearm to her instead. "Maybe we should try over a layer of fabric first?"

Angie wrapped her fingers around his arm on the outside of this thin, long-sleeved t-shirt, her eyes scrunching shut and her brows furrowing. Her breath started to rise. Daniel's mirrored hers out of anxiety before she pulled away, shaking out her fingers like her hand had gone to sleep.

Her eyes were wide, and her voice cracked when she spoke. "It's just as bad as when we first met." Daniel's heart dropped to his toes. His mind started spinning through every possible suggestion he could make as his aura buffeted thick and cold around him. "It's okay," Angie added quickly. "Let me try something."

Daniel hauled his Air aura back under control, and Angie held out a tentative hand. He let her take his arm again, wrapping all ten of her fingers around it. He double-blinked to watch her aura, and she apparently noticed.

"Please don't. I don't want to feel self-conscious about what my aura's doing while I try this."

Daniel double-blinked again, deactivating that spectrum of his vision, shame at being reprimanded scurrying through his gut which he tried to not hold on to. *She wasn't mad. She'd just asked for a layer of privacy,* he reprimanded himself.

Angie closed her eyes, and Daniel watched her face slowly relax, shifting her grip on his arm slightly. She stayed just like that, her long, loose auburn curls falling across her freckled face, the smell of paper and beeswax candles leaking into the air, until his shoulder ached from the position he'd set his arm in for her. When she sighed, releasing her hands and blinking as she sat back from her hunched posture, he rolled his shoulder to ease it, wishing he could tell from his side if she had succeeded.

Angie gave him a tight smile, not meeting his eyes, as she took a long swig from her glass of water. "I made progress. I think my own thoughts are getting in the way." She shook her head, pulling more hair to hide her face from Daniel, although he suspected she did so unconsciously. "Maybe I should talk to Jonathan and see if he can do anything to help or has suggestions as a therapist."

Just then Daniel's phone buzzed once and lit up on the table, both adepts looking at it. It was a text from Jonathan saying Seth was tucked in and he was going to bed himself. "Sorry." Daniel reached to turn the screen back off, but Angie stopped his hand.

Her ocean-green eyes were fixed on the phone screen. As Daniel withdrew his hand, concerned, she reached over and swiped up on the text alert, clearing it away from in front of his lock screen image. "The selfie you took of us," Angie whispered, her voice tight, and Daniel nodded, nudging the phone so she could see it better. Angie looked up at him, her face full of emotion, seeming to struggle to find more words.

She grabbed Daniel's hand, her brimming eyes not leaving his, and gave it a squeeze. Daniel squeezed back, relieved, before he realized what had just happened and his aura again lashed out. He looked down at where Angie's hand was holding his, then back to her face to see if she was feeling any ill effects.

Angie let out a barked laugh that sucked in as a sob when she inhaled, and Daniel pulled her to her feet, wrapping her in his arms and pressing his face into the warm, rose-scented skin of her neck as he cried with overwhelming relief, and Angie echoed him.

CHAPTER SEVENTEEN

Daniel didn't lose his deep sense of relief over Angie being able to touch him still as they found and settled into their routine over the next few weeks. Every afternoon in a lull between overseeing different aspects of Seth's magical education and experimentation, as well as the coaching he taught on auric shaping and control to all thirty-five new recruits, Angie would Voyage in to visit for an hour, often bringing little treats, he would visit her at their cottage not too far from the conference site, or they would go somewhere together.

On one such afternoon, Angie and Daniel were cuddling on the white leather sofa in the living room of his cottage at the conference site, Daniel scrolling news sites on his phone while Angie dozed on his chest. The front door opened, and Daniel looked up, giving Seth a welcoming smile when he stepped out of the little vestibule and pressed his phone to his lips to signal quiet.

Seth's eyes dropped to Angie, and contempt flitted across his face. "Sorry," he said at his normal volume and Angie stirred, giving him a small wave. "I didn't realize she'd still be here." He shed his coat and shoes and headed for the two little offices at the back of the house, overlooking the stream below. "You should have been there," he called to Daniel as he went. "It was fun. And Marissa asked after you."

Angie squirmed and sat up, her drowsy happiness wiped away in an instant. Daniel tossed his phone aside and pulled her back down, kissing along her hairline until she giggled. "I'd don't want to be anywhere but here," he whispered, and Angie grinned at him.

Unexpectedly, Daniel felt a directed Voyaging beacon in his mind, and judging by the way Angie's face went rigid, so did she.

"Why is Milton Cartwright sending up a beacon?" Angie asked. "Could this be about any of the favors we've asked of him?"

Daniel shrugged as they both sat up, shaking off their lazy comfort. "I guess there's only one way to find out." They both stood and Daniel summoned his suit jacket from the kitchen and scooped back up his phone. "Just be ready to Voyage again quickly if it's a trap."

Angie snorted, twisting her long hair up into a bun. "Don't worry about me, Mister Not-a-natural-Voyager. I'm more worried about you. Should just one of us go, in case we need to be rescued?"

Daniel shook his head. "No. I have this gut feeling he's going to try something if he can get either of us on our own in a bad situation. Best to stick together."

As they stepped out the front door into the rain, he called behind him, "Seth, we've been summoned away. Don't burn the place down while we're gone, and if you need anything, call Doctor Crowther."

When Daniel and Angie landed beside Milton, Daniel looked around quickly to take stock, finding that they stood in an unimpressive, long, windowless basement of some sort, stacked high with crates and boxes. He sent out tendrils of his aura in every direction, carried on eddies of wind, and relaxed a fraction when he was satisfied that the only wards and magic in the space were run-of-the-mill protections against anyone breaking in.

Milton grunted his meager welcome, turning and walking away toward the far end of the space, and Daniel caught Angie's arm to hold her back, following Milton at a good distance. "Can you tell where we are?" he whispered to her, bending close to her ear, glad he didn't need his cane that day and could do so gracefully. "I can't get any sort of bearings."

"No," Angie replied. "I think some of the wards around this place are designed to disorient visitors. I don't think I'd be able to get back here without an anchor."

Ahead, Milton stopped by a safe door, a little wider and taller than a normal house door, but not by much, and waited for them to catch up. He sniffed, grinding his teeth before eventually sighing. "You asked that I show you where the banishment keys are being kept as they are collected. Here it is."

Daniel just arched a brow and Cartwright waved a pudgy hand, shifting to position himself in front of the door. "Yeah, yeah. I know. Not good enough." Daniel watched as Milton sent a wisp of his magic out into the lock and the huge, spoked wheel on the front turned on its own. When it stilled, Milton grabbed onto it and hauled, pulling the door open wide, and Daniel braced himself to try to get a quick count of how many keys were shelved in the safe, and any details he could quickly memorize about any of them.

When he saw inside, his aura went as stale as the damp, cool air that rushed out to greet them. A massive cavern, at least a mile long and a hundred feet tall stretched out beyond the entrance, every wall to the very top hung with keys on little hooks. Sconces filled with eternal, magical fire glittered off each trinket, turning them into a wallpaper of silver, gold, copper, bronze, and more as it stretched into the distance. Beside him, Angie's aura became a mix of every shade of gray, white, black, blue, and purple imaginable, her mouth hanging open.

Daniel took a step forward, mesmerized, and Milton threw his weight into the door. Thinking fast, Daniel wrapped his arm around Angie's back hiding his hand from Milton and summoned the fancy pen from the safe in his Boston home, seeped in the deep blue magic of Jonathan Crowther, and with a flick of his wrist, banished out ahead, into the depths of the key vault cavern just before the door slammed shut with a pneumatic sigh.

"No," Milton said irritably. "You asked to see, and I've shown you. To let you so much as set a toe over the threshold is more than my life is worth—forget my reputation. I had to do too much already to even learn where this place was and how to get it myself from the only two people, now besides me, who knew."

Daniel clenched his jaw, letting out an audible breath through his nose. Angie beside him looked like a child who'd just been handed candy, only to have it snatched away before she could eat any. He touched her cheek with a tendril of warm air and saw the subtle shift in her that showed she understood that he had something to tell her when they were alone.

"Not good enough," Daniel said sternly, mostly to not make it seem like he was agreeing too readily. "We want more than a glimpse. Give us a tour. Show us the records..."

"No," Milton snapped back, his face flushing. "I won't let you blackmail me anymore. I will fulfill what I've already promised to the letter, and nothing more. If you push me further, I'll take the consequences of my past being known in order to expose yours."

Daniel scoffed. "You've been trying and failing to for twelve years. What makes you think—"

"Not yours," Milton interrupted with an impish smile. "Hers."

Daniel's immediate instinct was to step defensively in front of Angie but held himself back. "We all know she has nothing in her past that could possibly compare."

Milton ignored him, turning his full attention to Angie. "You think you can hold accidental deaths over my head? Well, I can do the same." He moved forward until he was uncomfortably close, ratcheting up Daniel's defensive instinct. "Do you by any chance remember a certain adventure, shall we say, early in your life as an awakened patrician, when you beat three would-be muggers to a pulp at a gas station in Nevada? Yes? Well, two of them died from the wounds you inflicted on them."

Angie's aura flared briefly, then guttered into black and purple smoke that shrank in toward her skin. "I was defending myself. And I didn't keep swinging once they were down. That's not the same as two hundred innocents you knew might die, setting that fire... right?" She turned to Daniel, her eyes desperately seeking reassurance, but his mind was thousands of miles away as Milton replied.

"I guess we'll see how—"

"I knew I saw your magic infecting their minds," Daniel interrupted, barely noticing that he did so. "I saw the fuchsia magic around their heads, but it disappeared when they lost consciousness, and I chalked it up to the light through the pink plastic awning." Daniel pulled Angie closer to his side, his aura teasing out of his control. "You set her up. You were trying to get her to lose control around those gas pumps and blow us both up."

"Bit slow on the uptake, I have to say," Milton sneered. "But that's old news. What say you?" he asked Angie directly. "Are we agreed? You keep my secrets in exchange for my help in the matters already agreed to, and I'll keep yours for a favor or two of my own."

Angie's aura twisted and billowed, pulling ever closer to her skin, leaking the heavy stench of burning plastic, hair, and rubber. When she spoke, her voice was a mew, her shoulders hunching forward as she wrapped her arms around her stomach. "Yes. We are agreed."

"Good," Milton breathed through his teeth. "First, I want the truth. Are you, by yourself or both of you together, agitators, traitors, or seditionists?"

Angie shook her head, shrinking a bit more. "No, I'm not. I've only ever fought for myself or Daniel." Daniel was too thrown off by the turn of events, mentally scrambling to catch up, to do more than gape stupidly.

Milton huffed with a wave of his hand, his lip curling. "Fine. Keep lying. I won't waste my breath." Angie opened her mouth to reply, but Milton plowed ahead. "This is the second thing I ask from you." He tilted his head, leaning in closer, and Angie leaned away, dropping her arms. "When you hear the call for Ragnarök raised, assuming you aren't already the cause for it, lay waste. Burn everything down, and don't come looking for me through the smoke. Do you agree, in order to keep your magic, your place of wealth, and a place at Fawl's side?"

Daniel watched helplessly as Angie tried and failed to speak several times, clear disgust, fear, and sorrow chasing each other across her elfin features. She bit her lips tight, and a tear rolled down her cheek as she took a shaking breath. "Yes. I'll do as you ask."

"She will do no such thing," Daniel growled, grabbing Angie by the arm and pulling her away from the gloating Councilor who just chuckled and tucked a thumb into the pocket of his waistcoat, looking Angie up and down with satisfaction.

"Oh, I think she will."

Daniel shook his head in disgust, making a mental note to track down the third mugger to bring before the Senate as proof of Milton's mental manipulations, but as he turned away, the thought slipped from his mind and disappeared. Beside him, Angie looked puzzled for a moment, but her defeated sorrow replaced it quickly, and Daniel Voyaged them away to their cottage near Chippenham.

"Angie, I'm so sorry," Daniel said immediately, turning to her, prepared to comfort and console her, but the Angie standing before him was utterly expressionless and collected, eying him warily.

"I'm fine," she said, her light, thin mahogany smoke aura nearly invisible around her and perfectly placid. "You were the one who taught me auric control. Could you not tell I was faking?"

Daniel stared at her, stunned. "Faking? You mean, you don't actually—I mean, it doesn't really bother you that..."

Angie shook her head, looking at him like it should have been obvious, and that it was weirding her out a little that he hadn't been able to tell. He scrambled to replay the last few minutes in his mind, but she really had seemed utterly genuine in her upset, in every centimeter of her body and aura. Had he really gotten so bad at reading her? Had she really changed so much since he'd been able to practically read her every thought, back before...

"I guess your control really did get better during your banishment," Daniel offered weakly, struggling to let go of the emotions he couldn't identify coiling themselves behind his breastbone, feeling utterly naked as he faced her in his confusion and disorientation.

Angie just kept looking at him like he was a stranger, eventually shaking her head and turning away. "I guess so."

CHAPTER EIGHTEEN

D aniel slipped his phone back into his pocket, turning his attention to the obsidian Threshold sitting in the center of the empty conference room overlooking the heart of London through a full glass wall. They had tried several times in the last few days to get Jonathan to Voyage to the aura-bonded token of his which Daniel had left in the key vault, but to no avail. They'd set it aside, deciding they'd need to wait for a better opportunity, when Daniel had received his summons to the Council.

He stepped forward, right up to the undulating surface of the magic within the Threshold. It was clear, holding no identifying color, and Daniel found it unsettling. Bringing up his shields, preparing his mental beacons, and bracing himself, Daniel stepped through cane-first.

The Council world was empty. And, against all the odds, didn't seem to be a trap. Daniel stood on a black-pebbled beach in the cool, still predawn of a very different landscape. A circle of seven obsidian thrones rose from the wide beach against the backdrop of a smooth obsidian cliff, reaching several hundred feet straight up toward the overcast skies. Behind the Threshold through which Daniel had stepped, stretched a completely still ocean, the waving pattern of gray water and white foam along the shore unmoving. Daniel checked that he hadn't stopped time accidentally, but no.

Daniel took several long minutes exploring the space, glad he'd gotten there early. He only needed to pass through the center of the circle of thrones once to feel the deep current of power that ran through the center, Stronger than Stonehenge, which was held harmless, half a dimension off, by its own Focal Nucleus at the center. When he'd seen what there was to see, he planted himself by the astounding obsidian cliff to wait for the other Councilors to arrive.

He tried to let go of the anxiety twisting his gut, his eyes resting without seeing on the dark depths of the stone before him. Eventually, curiosity and boredom got the better of him, and Daniel faced the cliffside fully, letting his magic tip into the mindset of a basic Seer, as was one of his natural skills.

He tried to ask the scrying magic to show him something simple, what Angie and Jonathan were currently up to, but his mind hadn't been clear enough for careful, accurate scrying in weeks. Even as he tried to hold his thoughts steady, they slipped back into his memories, playing out the scene from his first naïve attempt to find the Council world, and all that it had cost those long years ago. As the images played out in life-size before him, like he was there, separated from the events only by a layer of glass, he lost himself fully to the experience as Dawn's old sponsor spoke the prophecy that had shaped his whole life since then... *An Angel of Fire and Chaos... Fawl's fall... Beware the flame...*

"Someone is eager, I see."

Daniel startled out of his vision, unsure how long he'd been under, his chest bursting with the old emotions experienced fresh once more. "Yes," he said, clearing his throat, and turned to give Milton Cartwright a terse nod. "For my first meeting, I'd hate to be late."

Milton swaggered to one of the thrones and seated himself, giving Daniel a sneering smile. "What, no parties? No celebration, jubilation, or triumph?" he looked away idly over the still ocean. "I thought after how hard you've grifted to get here, you'd at least bother to look pleased."

The comment unexpectedly stung, and Daniel frowned. Why didn't he feel any of those things? Questions for later. Much later.

"You know," Milton mused as Daniel walked to the edge of the circle, resting both hands on the top of his cane. "I could probably just tell the Councilor about all of your blackmail to get you off my back, if I ever wanted you out."

"As you wish." Daniel shrugged, his mind still elsewhere. "But remember that we'd go together. A little blackmail isn't much compared to cold-blooded murder in your unlocking moment, which will have you stripped of even your patrician status, and all those deaths immediately after." Milton tensed, and Daniel saw the Councilor's bright pink magic spread out like a mist around them, undoubtedly a meager attempt at obscuring the last thirty seconds from history.

Daniel chuckled. "Don't worry, I took precautions before speaking. I don't want anyone else splitting your attention by using the same leverage against you."

The Threshold down the beach rippled, and the front of a body was outlined as it pressed against the other side of the membrane, before it broke and they stepped through. Just as Daniel had seen when he was first interviewed about possibly taking the Council seat Cartwright had ultimately won, they were magically obscured. They seemed genderless, colorless, faceless, and ageless, and they greeted Daniel with a raised hand, their voice layered with a dozen accents and pitches. "Hello! And, I suspect, let me be the first to properly welcome you to your first Council meeting!"

Daniel smiled darkly at the veiled jab at Cartwright and limped forward to shake the Councilor's hand. "Thank you very much. It's an honor to be here."

"Please, take a seat anywhere you like. They aren't assigned. Some of us here serve different roles than others, but we are all equal."

Daniel appreciatively accepted, sitting and stretching his aching knee as other Councilors, disguised like the first, started appearing through the gate. "How do you do that?"

The first Councilor who had arrived smiled, although the effect was unnerving when Daniel couldn't truly comprehend their face. "Don't worry, we'll cover all of that for you today. Its magic tied to this place, so it's not dependent on anyone's skill. Because of that, more senior members always know who is brought in after them, but not the other way around. It's for the best." They gave Cartwright a disapproving look, which he, still unobscured, ignored.

So much for all being equal, Daniel thought.

—◦✦◦—

As promised, much was explained to Daniel over the next hour. When he had learned to successfully pull the layer of magic straight from the Focal Nucleus over himself as the others did, Cartwright had reluctantly joined him, grumbling about the magic making him queasy. Daniel suspected he just wasn't done gloating about his appointment, and anonymity ill-suited that.

He resisted the urge to jump right into needling them all about the restriction of resource magic, collecting the keys to the locked banishment half-world, and the rest. Over the next hour it became easier as he was overwhelmed with explanations about everything from the disguise and the importance of not telling people he was a Councilor, to an explanation that the world they stood in was a safe, uninhabited half-world, to details on their ongoing project to close down dead and dying language Courts, consolidating their powers into Latin for their own use.

Daniel had perked up around the last, fascinated as the Councilor who did most of the talking explained that the place where they stood was, in fact the Latin Focal Nucleus, which had been moved there and frozen in time at the height of the first Roman Empire to ensure that it would never fade, giving the highest levels of patrician governance the means to ensure that they never fell far, and were always able to rebuild. Daniel's fingers itched in his lap to excitedly text his friends the exhilarating news but he held still.

His thoughts stayed stuck on the matter as the conversation moved away into recent concerning issues with the Spanish Decuria expressing a desire to leave the Senate over some interpersonal tiffs, and he was jarred out of his contemplations by a Councilor that hadn't spoken yet.

"You don't seem to be fully present with us, Councilor Fawl. I hope that your Senate seat, your new recruit, and your personal life aren't too much to balance with your new, ultimate commitment here?"

Daniel's pulse shot up, and he quickly apologized, wondering if they could see his embarrassment through the obscuring magic. "No, of course not." He quickly settled himself back into the caricature of himself that had been invited to join the most exclusive order of power in existence, ignoring the soul-deep discomfort that soured his blood.

"Good. Because the question is no longer if Ragnarök will happen, but when. And when it does, we will need your help."

The other Councilor went back to their concerns about the Spanish Decuria, and Daniel was careful to maintain an outward appearance of focused attention. But inside, he wondered when he would be trusted enough to ask more about the one word that kept tumbling over and over in his head.

Ragnarök.

Chapter Nineteen

A ngie stared at her hands, disappointed, sitting across from Daniel at the farmhouse table in his cottage on the conference site, the last crumbs of the blueberry crisp she'd brought staining the plates before them. "That's all you were able to pick up? That's not much more than I overheard at the Latin Court party."

"Yeah. Just that Ragnarök is some event they expect will happen, sounds like sooner than later. That the Council is in charge, in some way, or that we at least have roles to play." Daniel shook his head. "I'll press more when I can, but I... I just felt like I couldn't at the time. Like they thought I already knew, and that asking would be the wrong call. I tried scrying around the word, but there's too much clutter in mythology and modern plebeian use of the word in video games and such."

Angie laced her hands and propped her forefingers against her lips, biting back repeated urges to do something to them before they did something to everyone else. She closed her eyes, but before she could think of what to say next, Jonathan's Voyaging beacon materialized in her mind just as Daniel's phone buzzed, and they flew open again.

Daniel quickly checked it, paling slightly as he turned it to show her the text that simply read 'SOS. *Come in braced but quiet. No magic.*'

Angie's gut dropped. "Not again…" she whispered, shoving her chair back and standing in unison with Daniel, sparing some attention to her aura to smooth it. She was starting to get jumpy about unexpected beacon summons interrupting their rare moments of comfort together. "Want to bet Milton's behind this summons, too?"

"I knew he wouldn't let me have an untainted win. At least it's a friend summoning us this time," Daniel said, not looking remotely comforted himself. "You're the natural. Go ahead, aiming for somewhere near him that's obscured, and I'll aim for you."

Angie grabbed her jacket while Daniel did the same before she did as instructed, landing in the hallway of an expensive apartment complex just around the corner from what sounded like a residential raid. She sent up her Voyaging beacon to Daniel and he appeared a yard away. They shared a glance, and Angie readied her magic invisibly, trusting that Daniel was doing the same.

When they rounded the corner of the hallway, their target was immediately apparent. Two armed centurions stood at attention on either side of one apartment door, other doors along the corridor cracked open as neighbors peered out nervously.

"Leave them alone," Jonathan's deep voice boomed from the open apartment, and Angie surged forward,

Daniel beside her, her attention darting between the two guards in the hallway as they both brought up their guns.

"We're patricians," Daniel announced, doing a better job than Angie of acting the part. Neither centurion so much as blinked. Angie stopped short of their weapons, her insides sinking at the realization that the bullies before her didn't care. "And I am a Senator," Daniel snarled, pulling out his passport with a bare hand and flipping it open to the second page, bearing the intricate, holographic seal of his status.

The two centurions seemed to silently check with each other before slowly lowering their weapons and stepping apart a foot, disdain and resistance written in every motion.

Angie shoved past them into the huge, beautifully furnished apartment. The moment she did, she saw why they'd been summoned. A dozen men in body armor vests were hauling apart two adults and two children, all of whom were shouting and crying. "We are complying!" Jonathan shouted, his ice-blue eyes wild with distress as the girl cried out when a soldier wrenched her shoulder.

"Not enough," the one elite legionnaire in the room, set apart by his smart gray uniform, replied with a sneer. "I have been ordered to make sure that each of you is returned to your home provinces ahead of the rest. You to Wyoming, your wife to Idaho, and your children to a local shelter since they were born here." The legionnaire spotted Angie then, and his face twisted. "Get out," he ordered, pointing a finger to the door, as the men he was commanding turned to see. "Or do you want to be next?"

Jonathan's eyes met hers, pleading and scared, but before Angie could say anything, Daniel spoke from behind her in a low, persuasive growl. "Civilians. Close your eyes, cover your ears, and hold your breath."

Angie felt the faint brush of his aura as it passed her, carrying the magical suggestions to make them impossible to ignore, and watched the woman and both children immediately obey as the soldiers holding them released their arms to reach for their weapons. She caught Jonathan suck in a breath and hold it, his eyes locked on Daniel, and followed suit just in time.

All the oxygen left the room, and likely a portion of the hall outside, in a whoosh. The soldiers all began gasping, but many continued to draw their weapons, clearly well-trained to act without needing to think. Daniel was a blur as he darted forward, brushing the hand of the nearest man with his bare fingers, already reaching for the next before the first hit the ground, unconscious. Two guns were fired, but neither found their mark as Daniel got to the last man, the legionnaire, dropping him like a stone. Angie rocked as the air rushed back into the room, and she gasped down a grateful breath, quickly turning on the spot to make sure all assailants were out cold.

Jonathan lunged for the woman and two children, tenderly pulling their hands away from their heads and reassuring them. "It's alright. It's over. You can open your eyes and breathe again. It's okay."

Nearby, Daniel was kneeling near the legionnaire, and Angie double-blinked to see a tendril of his aura wrapped around and into the man's head, making her skin crawl as it always did. "He'll think it was some form of topical chemical weapon, administered through a pin prick," Daniel said to the room at large, standing. "They'll just have to figure out their own plausible explanation for the vacuum."

"You," the woman in Jonathan's arms said, also fussing over the stunned and wide-eyed children, looking at Daniel. "You," she said again, her voice rising as she stood, her hands balled into fists at her side. She was tall and slender, with brown hair and eyes, deep parentheses carved around her mouth, and slightly hunched posture.

"Me. Hello, Hannah," Daniel replied coolly, only the continued gusts of his agitated aura betraying his stress. "We need to go. Now. Pack a bag. Quickly. Only things you can't buy or replace. You have one minute."

Angie just nodded sternly when Hannah turned to look at her, her expression shifting between anger and something unreadable. She jogged across the apartment to what Angie assumed was the bedroom and disappeared inside.

"Why don't we just Voyage out?" Angie asked when the door clicked.

Jonathan flinched. "Hannah's going to be mad enough about me still being in touch with magic folks as it is. If we can avoid adding to that, I'd prefer it. This is a mess. Besides, I can't carry them all to Voyage at once, and I couldn't leave two behind to deal with all the soldiers who would have been freaking out over the magic." He looked overwhelmed and scared as he soothed his two small children, and Angie didn't press.

"I'm so sorry, Jon," Daniel said, pulling leather gloves from his pocket and pulling them on, kneeling beside his friend and gently rubbing the back of the young boy, a year or two older than his sister. "I shouldn't have mentioned your family in front of Milton when you let the party hear him, just to cover our asses. I shouldn't have given him more reason to target you all."

Angie joined them, giving the girl a small, uncertain smile when she peered up from her father's shoulder. "Mentioning your family once to Milton at the winter solstice doesn't explain this," she said, giving Jonathan's shoulder a squeeze. "You're still a Judge, and a patrician, and should be immune. Do you have any proof Milton is behind this we could use against him? Were you called back here, or did he somehow know you'd be here?"

"I wasn't called," Jonathan replied, picking up the girl as he stood, the boy clinging tight to his leg. "It was just lucky. I don't know what might have happened if I wasn't." His weathered, tan face was haunted beneath his dark beard, and his voice was strained.

Hannah appeared a moment later, a backpack slung over one shoulder, and jogged back to throw her arms around Jonathan's shoulders and around their daughter. "I have the family album and worship book, the baby things we saved, and my grandmother's wedding veil. Anything else I should grab?"

Jonathan shook his head, disentangling her arms to grab the boy's hand, pulling them toward the door to the apartment, stepping over the prone soldiers. "No. If we think of more, I can hire someone to sneak back in and grab them if we don't get looted."

Only then did Angie remember that Jonathan hid his magic from his family and blinked. She followed closely as they left the apartment, down the hall and two flights of stairs, wondering if he'd just Voyage back himself for their other belongings once they were all safe.

As they reached the front of the lobby, a loud crack, muffled by the heavy doors out onto the street, made them slow. "Is there another way out?" Daniel asked, his angular face lined with tension, and Jonathan nodded. He handed the girl off to Hanna, picking up the boy, and they all jogged back the way they'd come, then around a corner down a service passage, to a door marked as an emergency fire exit only.

Daniel pushed past Angie to throw his shoulder into it, and they burst out into an alleyway reeking of garbage and urine, the door locking shut audibly behind them. "Come on. We need to hire a car to get us away to some-where we can regroup."

No sooner did they make it to the street than a tide of people crashed into them, jostling them away down the road before Angie could even process, the flames of her aura teasing up as she carefully held them under control, one hand grabbing Daniel and the other Jonathan as the four adults and two children fought to not get sepa-rated by the current of shouting, shoving people. Angie saw Jonathan's deep blue shield bloom around them, but watched people pass through the walls of it without even noticing, and assumed the shield was more to obscure their presence and identities from prying eyes than anything else, invisible to most.

A glance over their heads showed a line of centurions and auxiliaries locked tightly side by side, marshaled on my gray-clad legionnaires, forcing the crowd down toward the end of the dead-end street, capped by the boarded-up front of a brick factory. "They're kettling the crowd," Angie shouted to her companions, trying to haul them back to the nearest edge of the crowd, hoping to find an obstacle to shelter behind and let the kettle line pass them. "Trying to trap us all to wait for the slave trucks. We need to get out." Angie's instinct was to Voyage away, but neither man was moving to, and she followed their lead.

Daniel pulled a phone from his pocket, his other arm gripping Jonathan's as Hannah sheltered from the chaos between them, all color gone from her face. "Maybe Marissa can get involved in their comms. Tell them to stand down. At least enough for us to get to privacy..."

Jonathan let go of Hannah to grab Daniel's wrist, stopping him. "No. We can't trust her that much yet. It would also betray her defection, and she probably can't even help."

A megaphone blared at the far end of the tumbling mass of limbs, and Angie flinched. "Plebeians. You are all under arrest for attempting to contravene patrician expulsion and reorganization mandates. Calm down and comply peaceably or we will escalate force."

"I'm on your side!" a muscled young man with a shaved head, wearing suspenders, shouted beside Angie, waving over the crowd at the soldiers in riot gear. "I'm only here to help take these fucking libtard illegals out, see?" The man reached out to grab Jonathan's daughter, a wild, confident grin on his face.

Without thinking, Angie clocked him in the jaw with every ounce of gladiatorial training, weight, and momentum she possessed, sending him stumbling back, clutching a bloody nose. "Move," she shouted to her companions, shaking her bruised hand and hauling her aura under control as the loyalist fell to his back beneath the trampling boots of the crowd, his screams of pain short-lived.

"There," Daniel said, pointing to a slightly sheltered alcove where one building was set further back on the street than the one beside it, and Angie shoved Jonathan's shoulder in that direction.

"Move out of my way," Jonathan bellowed to the people standing between them and their destination, his voice louder than a megaphone through his magic, and a hundred startled faces looked up, but didn't part.

Daniel glanced at his watch as they finally came to a stop as the herd of people hit the building at the end of the street.

Again, Jonathan grabbed his wrist. "No. Just hide us with me. We need to be able to act freely! Hide us now so whoever set this up can't see where we go!"

Daniel nodded, wrapping his arms around Jonathan and Angie to keep the children more sheltered at the center and closed his eyes. Angie watched his barely yellow shield shimmer up around them, not stopping any physical passage in and out, but thicker than she had ever seen it before with layers of light. When he opened his eyes again, Angie was shocked to see real strain in them. She'd assumed that his unrestricted magic didn't really have limits, and the reality unbalanced her.

Something moved out of sync with the flow of people nearby, and Angie's heart skyrocketed. She silently chastised herself, blowing out a long breath and reminding herself she was back in the true world as she scanned around, trying to find an avenue of escape.

A shot rang out and everyone dropped a few inches. They all spun to find a legionnaire in their midst, not far away, the gun still in his hand. The throng parted in front of him, eager to not get between him and his target, but when Angie, Daniel, Jonathan, Hannah, and the kids tried to do the same, the legionnaire moved, and they froze, realizing that they were the targets. He raised his gun once more, and time slowed in her perception as she realized two things simultaneously.

First, the gun was pointed directly, unmistakably, at the girl in Jonathan's arms.

Second, the clean-shaven, faintly smiling man was surrounded by the light red aura of an unlocked and awakened adept.

In the time it took Angie to blink, Jonathan's deep blue Water aura surged forward, encasing the gun and the hand that held it in ice. The legionnaire raised his other hand gloved in magic, but before he could do anything else, Jonathan's magic pummeled into the man's open mouth, surrounding him in a sphere of water that grew quickly, each layer echoed by screams from the plebeian onlookers. In a breath, it spread across the ground and around their feet, intelligent and solid, forcing people back away from them as they danced back, terrified.

Angie watched, aghast, as the legionnaire burbled once, panic stealing his composure, before he exploded from the inside in shards of frozen flesh and blood that were caught by the surface tension of the sphere. She watched as every shard dissolved into the water, and as, in the space of a dozen beats of her hammering heart, the water slumped back to Jonathan's outstretched hand, leaving nothing but a dusty-gray uniform where the patrician soldier had stood.

"Witches," someone screamed from the throng, breaking the calm of horrified murmurs from hundreds of witnesses that suddenly surged forward, fists brandished in fear, anger, and disgust.

"Yes, we are." *So much for hiding magic from Hannah or anyone else.* Angie sucked in a deep breath and blew it out between pursed lips, her arms outstretched, letting her aura spin into a fireball around the six people at the center of the attack, willing it into the visible spectrum for inepts and adepts alike. The first person to come into contact with it, a middle-aged woman, yelped in pain, yanking her blistered hand back, and Angie smiled as darkly as she could, channeling every time she'd seen Daniel wear the same mask.

She watched Daniel's shield shrink to skim the outside of her roaring display of flame as the boy and girl beside her clung to their parents in terror.

"Are we obscured?" Jonathan asked. Daniel just nodded, frowning with concentration. "Compound, now. Three of us can Voyage. We each take one." Hannah looked too scared to object as her husband gave the commands.

Angie dropped her flames, taking the girl Jonathan handed her, but Daniel hesitated. "Are you sure? Wouldn't the conference be the better—"

"Plebeians aren't allowed," Jonathan cut him off sternly, taking his son from Hannah and handing him to Daniel, "and that might put them in even greater danger."

Angie and Daniel both nodded, and as Jonathan wrapped his arms around his shaking wife, Angie held his daughter tight to her chest and Voyaged to the rebellion compound.

CHAPTER TWENTY

Angie landed in the little village green of Dawn's compound. The others arrived barely a second later, and Angie and Daniel both set down their small charges. Around them, the few people who saw their arrival called out to others and pulled out phones, looking concerned but practiced at coping with such unexpected arrivals of refugees.

"It's real. It was all real," Hannah muttered, backing away from Jonathan who wouldn't meet her gaze. Angie crouched down beside the little girl, who hesitated to return to either parent, sensing their discord. "How could you?" Hannah's face was a mask of disgusted betrayal, and she ignored her children and Angie, looking back and forth from her husband to Daniel, who rested a protective hand on the shoulder of the boy still leaning close to him.

Jonathan turned away from her without replying, kneeling and opening his arms wide. Both children ran to him, starting to cry, and Jonathan held on tight, his eyes sparkling with emotion, whispering gentle reassurances to them in a tight voice.

"You bastard," Hannah choked out. "You lied to me. All these years, you lied…" She jumped when a gentle hand gripped her shoulder, but relaxed at Mahina's kind, comforting smile.

Anthony Shupee came up behind with a bottle of water and a blanket, and Angie gave him a nod. She hadn't seen him since she'd finally conquered phase-walking through their infrequent lessons together. Angie stepped in next to Daniel, not knowing what to do next. He took her hand in his gloved one, but just as he opened his mouth to speak, something past Angie caught his attention, and something subtle shifted and hardened in his expression. "Brace yourself," he muttered, and Angie turned to see Dawn striding confidently up the path to the green, her thick gold magic clearly ready to handle whatever new crisis had landed at her doorstep.

When Hannah saw Dawn, she screamed in anger. "Her?" she shrieked, raising a hand to slap Jonathan where he still knelt with their children, but hit his shield and her face flushed. "Both of them? Magic. All of it? You lying, evil monster!" Angie recoiled from the desperate agony and distress in her words, horrified that anyone would say such things to her dearest friend. Moreover, that he might deserve it.

"I never did anything to hurt you," Jonathan said calmly, beckoning Anthony Shupee over, who handed off his burden to Casey and knelt with a kind smile by the two crying children, helping to soothe them. "I only ever kept secrets to keep you and the kids safe. So that you could have the life you chose for us."

"You're dead to me!" Hannah replied before Jonathan had truly finished speaking, and Dawn backed away, her palms raised but her expression blank as Mahina inserted herself between Hannah and the little huddle below. "I want nothing to do with you, now or ever again. I don't care why. You *lied* to me. To us. We're done. I'm taking the children and... and..."

Angie watched the horrific realization that she didn't actually know what to do next dawn across Hannah's face. Mahina gently moved her back a pace, turning her away toward the small densely packed houses that surrounded the green, expanding deeper into the redwood forest with every new addition to the haven. She pulled Hannah into a hug, and Angie saw Hannah's shoulders start to shake as she hugged Mahina back, and Angie's heart constricted with pity.

"It'll be alright," Mahina said, setting her down on one of the picnic benches nearby. She took the blanket Casey held out, draping it around her shoulders. "I know this is a lot. But you're safe here. There are other children. And adults like you, who are new to knowing about all this through their partners, or parents, or siblings. Everything will be alright. Today, just worry about getting you and your little ones settled a bit. It can all be sorted out in time."

Hannah nodded, standing, beckoning for the kids to follow her as Mahina led her away. They clung to their father, but Jonathan gently untangled their arms, handing them off to Anthony, who led them over to the women.

"No, it's okay. I'll see you soon. Go with Mom and my friends. We're safe now. I promise."

Only as the little group moved away did Angie realize Jonathan didn't stand and stepped away from Daniel to crouch beside him. As his wife and children moved out of sight, Jonathan convulsed, falling to one side, and Angie caught him.

"Jonathan," Angie said in a high-pitched voice, barely registering the large red stain spreading across the side of his shirt beneath his jacket before Daniel was beside her, his aura buffeting around them. Another breath and the first aid kit from their Boston home was in his hands, bolts and all.

Daniel hurriedly unpacked it, pulling on a pair of rubber gloves. "Healer," he called in a loud, strong voice, not looking away from his work for a second.

Dawn was across from Angie in a flash, her dark eyes wide. "I'm beaconing Olivia, but she's in Morocco. Our counterparts there asked for aid an hour ago when their compound was raided by the Arabic Court. She's probably up to her elbows."

Angie barely breathed as she cradled Jonathan, watching Daniel rip open the front of his shirt, exposing the oozing bullet wound and the finger-wide scar running down the center of Jonathan's chest Angie had seen once before when she'd tried and failed to heal him at her first conference. Her blood ran cold in her hands, and she forced her scared, retracting smoke up to heat the chilly April day around them, seeing how Jonathan was trembling.

Daniel stripped off his gloves and rings, fishing out a sterile wipe he cleaned his hands with in a quick, practiced pattern, then a package of gauze he ripped open with his teeth. Angie had to look away when Daniel stuck a finger into the hole in Jonathan's side, his hands and shirt cuffs instantly crimson. "I don't feel shrapnel, and no major arteries. I think it was a through-and-through." Jonathan clung to Angie as he shook, his eyes screwed shut, and Daniel began packing the wound with gauze. "Just hang in there. We'll get you patched up."

Ten minutes that felt like a lifetime of adrenaline later, Angie was crouched in front of Jonathan, who was sitting on the bench of a picnic table as Olivia slowly removed the last of the bloodstained gauze which Daniel collected and vanished away to some unknown disposal. Olivia had returned just as Daniel had gotten Jonathan stable, and watching Jonathan slowly stop shaking and regain his color as the Australian woman healed him had allowed Angie to breathe again.

As she watched the very last of the bullet wound at the front of Jonathan's side, just below his ribcage, vanish, Angie's eyes drifted back to the scar running down the center of his chest from his solar plexus to below his belt, wondering why it had never been healed.

He seemed to read her mind. "Gunshot wound before magic," he said simply. "They had to do exploratory surgery to find all the shrapnel. I suspect either the attack or the surgery was my catalyzing event. I've never resented it, so it survived my awakening resurrection." Angie just swallowed and nodded, standing on numb legs as Daniel and Olivia moved away to finish cleaning up the mess of Jonathan's blood across the ground. "We all have scars. The trick is just to learn how to keep living like you don't."

Angie sat beside him, Jonathan's unnervingly obser-vant eyes making it hard to miss the double meaning she heard in his words. "Yeah, well. Maybe when my scars are a decade or two old, I can also make wise quips about them."

Jonathan chuckled but stopped quickly, wincing and grabbing his side. Angie helped him pull the torn remains of his shirt and jacket back on, getting his permission with a glance before mending them with her magic. When she let go, she couldn't even tell he'd been shot. They sat in comfortable aftershock silence, watching the other people moving around them, which Angie barely noticed. Her whole attention was anchored on Jonathan's every breath and shift, every beat of his heart as she tried to push away the near loss that welled up in her chest to her throat and eyes.

"I'd miss you," Angie said, the words barely audible, and Jonathan's hand found hers, giving it a squeeze.

"I know."

She dashed a hand across her eyes as her vision blurred and took a deep breath. She mastered her expression as Daniel came over, his mask of commanding detachment a touch unnerving.

"I'm sorry." Jonathan pulled his free hand down his face, looking apologetically between them. "You shouldn't have taken the risk of coming to pull me out. I shouldn't have called you. It was foolish."

"Don't be an idiot," Daniel said, waving a hand and not meeting Jonathan's or Angie's gaze. "You're the glue holding us all together." Angie felt a brief ripple of liquid impact touch her skin, but it was gone a moment later, leaving her perfectly dry.

"Listen," Jonathan said. "If they came after my family, they'll probably be coming after yours as well."

"Doubtful," Angie replied numbly. "I haven't even exchanged a letter with them in five years. No one can get to me through them."

"Pretty much the same here," Daniel said. "Only longer. Ack." Daniel jumped and pulled out his phone. "Marissa just texted. She says she just got orders to repress any mentions of nuclear options around the growing unrest in the Middle East."

Angie's insides twisted, hearing her own heartbeat. "That's not good."

"No. Dawn!" Dawn came over, and Daniel redirected her, their words fading as they moved away for privacy. "You all need to start working on an evacuation plan to a safe half-world. Probably not even locus proxima."

"Why?"

"Long explanation for later. But everyone needs to start preparing to bring any plebeians they want to live with them here for that, or at least get them out of the cities."

Angie tried to keep the anxiety pounding through her head, drowning out much thought from sparking up her aura.

"Please keep an eye on Dan these next few days," Jonathan said softly, watching the backs of the two people his wife had clearly disapproved of him knowing. "He's in survival mode right now. When that breaks, he'll likely be in a rough way, and I can't be there for him through that anymore like you can."

Angie just nodded her assurance and leaned her forehead into Jonathan's shoulder, trying to find some spark of hope to fan instead. "If Daniel is now talking about evacuation plans to half-worlds, do you think we can stop sneaking off to search for possession demons, and let him in on it?"

Jonathan sighed. "Yeah, we should. I think we need him to make progress. He's been there before. He might help in finding what we need. I don't think my research is going to get us any further. There's a page missing from the best resource I've found on it, and none of the magic I try will restore it. Even if he wasn't open to it, it's time to get the ball rolling."

Angie found herself smiling, and it took her a moment to name why. As she scrutinized the man beside her as he was forever scrutinizing her, she saw someone who'd just given their last fuck. Less the careful ambassador, and more the determined fighter Angie had longed to see in him since her banishment. She wrapped her arms around his shoulders from the side, squeezing tight, and Jonathan's focus broke into an amused smile.

"I know I've said this already. Probably just today, but I'm glad to have you around. I look forward to getting to know you in peacetime when all of this is over. Watching your kids grow up." She waited for him to say the same back, but he just twisted toward her, returning her sideways hug. When he spoke, his voice was rough.

"I know."

Chapter Twenty-One

"They're settling in well," Angie said happily a week later when Daniel opened the front door of his and Seth's cottage. She lifted the covered dish in her hands, adding, "And I brought peach cobbler."

Daniel beamed, stepping aside to let her enter. "Grand. On both counts."

"Seth around?" Angie asked, cringing when it occurred to her that she should have asked before mentioning Daniel's family at the rebel compound.

"No, not to worry. He's out with Noah's current posse, doing something with transformation magic up at the amphitheater. And the house wards are fully up."

Angie led the way to the small dining room at the back of the cottage, and Daniel followed with plates and forks. "The only thing I still don't really get is Jonathan's relief at having a bunch of people helping him keep his wife's unlocked magic hidden from her." They sat down, filling each of their plates with the steaming cobbler. "Not the relief to have help, part. I get that. He said it was a big drain on his aura. But keeping it from her at all. I thought we were all on the side of empowering as many people as possible."

Daniel's mouth stretched wide in a grimace, poking his afternoon treat with a fork. "It's for the kids." Angie just gave him a nonplussed look, and he shifted. "It's not my place to go into detail, but Jonathan is worried that Hannah might not take the revelation that she has magic very well. He is, quite rightly, worried that she'll then try to pass along her 'gift from God', as she'd put it, to their children."

"How?" Angie asked, instinctually revolted but not sure why. Daniel just shrugged, and something else he'd just said caught in her mind. "Wait. She's monotheistic? Christian?"

"Yeah," Daniel said, clearly uncomfortable with the topic. "They both are. Mormon. One of the splinter cults that was only around for about a century before the unification. He never really mentions it and certainly doesn't preach. But she's... different."

"Are you?" Angie asked, feeling deeply conflicted, totally prepared for anything after learning something she never would have expected about Jonathan. *How could someone so kind and intelligent ascribe to an illegal cult?*

Daniel actually laughed, breaking the tension. "No. Not at all." Angie smiled, somewhat relieved, and they ate more cobbler happily, talking about conference and compound drama.

"So," Angie said, cautiously circling back around as she put the leftover cobbler in the fridge and Daniel washed the dishes with a wave of his hand. "I overheard you mention evacuating to half-worlds when we got Jonathan's family to the compound, and you've touched on it briefly a couple times since then."

Daniel stiffened, crossing his arms, and leaned against the end of the counter in the gleaming white and copper kitchen. He just nodded, giving Angie a wary look.

She stood a little straighter, keeping her tone light, and watched him in the corner of her eye as she gazed out through the window over the sink to the walking path between the two rows of cottages beyond. "If you're more open to half-world solutions now, would you consider helping Jonathan, me, and maybe a few others find the half-world with the animalistic, insubstantial demons we could collect into objects for our backup plan at the summer solstice?" Angie braced herself for the windy outburst of upset she expected in reply, but it didn't come.

Daniel's frame shrank an inch, his shoulders sagging. He scrubbed his face with one hand before tucking it once more across his chest, his eyes not leaving Angie. "Yeah. It's a good idea. And you're probably right that I might be able to help."

Happiness bloomed in Angie's chest, spreading to her face, and Daniel weakly mirrored her. "Yay! Thank you," she said, sidling up next to him to also lean against the counter, the shift in her mood making the charming, clean room around her seem brighter.

She waited to see if Daniel had immediate follow-up, but when he didn't seem to, Angie jumped right to the next burning question she'd been dying to ask him. "Hannah had a pretty big reaction to seeing you and Dawn. As far as I could tell, she was mad at Jonathan for knowing you both. What's the story there?"

The question seemed to break Daniel's exhausted shell, and he scratched the end of his sharp nose.

"Are you blushing?" Angie asked, genuinely excited, and shifted in front of him, pulling his hand away from his face. "You are, aren't you?" She laughed, and he playfully batted her away, his cheeks going even rosier.

"I am not," he protested, but the lopsided grin he was clearly fighting betrayed him. Angie braced her hands on the counter on either side of Daniel, closely trapping him, pouring herself into the happy, sweet normalcy of the moment. "Look," Daniel said, looking anywhere but directly at Angie. "It's not something I have ever talked about to an outsider, but back in the day, around and just after my own recruitment and awakening, the three of us—me, Jonathan, and Dawn—were... a thing."

"A thing?" Angie repeated with over-the-top teasing and surprise.

"Yeah," Daniel admitted, his tongue appearing briefly at the corner of his mouth as he dropped his head. "A thing. Me and Jon, Jon and Dawn, me and Dawn... Before the skin curse, obviously."

Angie half coughed, half laughed, trying her best to not picture it. "I knew Jonathan was a recruit the same year you were, but I didn't know Dawn was too."

"She wasn't," Daniel corrected. "She was a sponsor that year. She's much older than she looks." Angie watched Daniel squirm, delighting in the playful teasing and sharing, and waited for him to say whatever it was he was clearly chewing on. When he spoke, he sounded more serious. "Remember when you asked about the person my ex-wife accused me of cheating on her with? Well… It was Jonathan. And, again, not cheating."

Angie grinned. She wasn't surprised. She'd seen the closeness between Daniel and Jonathan the first time she'd seen them interact clear as day. She'd just misinterpreted it as exclusively brotherly. "I can't think of anyone else on the planet I could feel genuinely relieved to hear you name."

Daniel threw his head back and laughed. "Gods above. And here I was giving myself ulcers for years worrying you'd trash your friendship with him if I told you."

Angie held his sparkling gaze when he grinned at her, tilting her head and leaning forward until her breath brushed his neck where his beard ended. "The jury's still out on how I feel about you and Dawn, but like you say, that's well in the past." She let her lips brush his skin, and the way Daniel tensed and shuddered at the contact sent a shiver down her spine. "But the thought of you with another man is a rather hot image that's been flitting around in my brain since you told me you were bi."

"Don't get your hopes up," Daniel said a tad breathlessly, as Angie kissed her way up the side of his neck. "You're still the only person in existence I can touch."

"That's not what I meant. Don't ruin this. I want you entirely to myself," Angie teased, hiding the way her thoughts and feelings briefly guttered. "I prefer to think you actually chose me, despite the skin curse stuff, and I have some lovely mental images going."

"I did, do, choose you," Daniel said solemnly, grabbing Angie's wrist when she lifted it to caress his cheek, craning his neck to see her face. "I love you, and only you." His dark eyes were serious and gentle, beautiful in the light hitting them in the bright kitchen.

Daniel pressed a kiss to Angie's palm, making her heart flutter. He then pressed her hand over his heart, holding it in place with his own. His eyes roamed her face for a long time, his expression loving and intense. Angie's instinct told her he was building up to saying something that had been weighing on his mind, reinforced by the subtle patterns she could see in the light of his aura, and waited.

"What do you hope our future looks like?" he eventually asked.

Angie blinked several times, unprepared for the question. "I don't know," she managed, trying to turn her thoughts inward to find an answer.

"Could you try?"

Angie nodded, blowing out the anxiety that tapped at the bottom of her stomach, letting herself settle back into the beautiful, calm moment she stood in. After a time, her mind began to swirl around an answer she could grasp, and she began tentatively. "Did I ever tell you I always wanted to fly? That I dreamt about it all the time as a kid, before the world—or, at least, my world—went to shit?" Daniel looked mildly puzzled, smiling kindly and shaking his head. "Well, I did. I wanted it more than anything, but it faded until it disappeared altogether when I was too busy just surviving to the next day to dream of flying. I didn't remember it was something I wanted until I saw someone else had it, one of my first days at the conference that first year when Emilia levitated." Angie swallowed hard, and Daniel pressed her hand a little harder into his chest.

"I tried to fly, then, too, since I suddenly saw that this dream was possible. But when I tried and couldn't, I got so bitter that I shoved it away, convincing myself I'd never really wanted it. Like when I pushed you away, down by the stream, however many weeks later. Because I convinced myself that because I couldn't be openly happy with you, I'd never really wanted to be, and that not even trying would stop it from hurting."

Understanding relaxed Daniel's bearded face, and Angie smiled, feeling reassured as she pressed on. "Well, then, I got it. I got to fly the first time I left my body in the astral projection class." Angie's chest lifted with the memory. "It was amazing. It made me feel free, and like I could do anything. A literal dream come true." She kissed Daniel, and he held her lips until she pulled away. "But then I got lost in astral form. I got to fly for so long, losing myself and never able to truly land as my mind disintegrated, that it soured. It ended up connected in my mind to the embarrassing, immature belief that I could fix my life, my world, with one perfect moment at Stonehenge. So I pushed the dream aside again to survive, and make sure anyone, ever, could have a happy ending. Like," her voice got very small, "during my banishment when I couldn't dream of living to old age with you, because surviving the day took all of my attention."

Her eyes were fixed rigidly on the top button of Daniel's shirt, and he kissed her gently on the forehead. "I understand. And now?" He rubbed a thumb along Angie's side, and she melted into him, letting go of her discomfort in revisiting her past.

She shrugged, pulling her mind away from the memories that always tried to pull her under like tar. "Now... I don't know what I want. I know the dream is still there, at the center of my heart, but it feels like I wish it for past me, not whoever I am now. I don't know how I feel now, about anything. I end up gauging things more by what would bring me the least pain than by what would bring me the most joy. I just feel wrong in my own skin and know that your touch, your company, is the only thing that makes it feel right."

Daniel kissed her, full and deep, and Angie melted into him, letting the electric connection and the enticing promise of what would come next send her heart soaring. When he finally broke away, his glittering eyes crinkled by his grin, Angie bit her lip and leaned the full length of her body against his. "And what do you hope our future looks like?"

He pressed her to him with a strong hand on the small of her back, the other caressing the side of her face tenderly. "A happily ever after. And for now, I can wish it hard enough for both of us."

When his mouth again met hers, Angie closed her eyes and shifted the front of her hips against Daniel. She felt him tense and trailed her fingers up his chest to where his casual collared shirt opened, grazing along up his neck.

He did the same, only tracing down with the hand on her cheek, and Angie shivered with pleasure.

She turned her mind back to how it had been touching his soft, warm, vulnerable skin the first time they had slept together, and pulled away to watch her own hands as she slowly, carefully undid each button of his shirt, savoring the sensation—and his sensitive reactions—caressing every centimeter of him she could touch. He explored her in measure, taking his time with every pleasurable contact he made on her sides, neck, and breasts, not moving to undress her.

After a few minutes, Angie's impatience won, and she gave Daniel a teasingly pleading look as she removed the rest of his clothes. He grinned, his breath shallow, but when Angie stepped back to remove her own clothes, he stopped her. He pulled her in with one hand as the other undid her jeans, silencing her with his mouth. Angie barely had time to giggle before Daniel spun her around to push her gently over the counter, her bare ass displayed before him.

"Wards," she gasped as Daniel's fingers beckoned along the slickness between her legs, twisting over her shoulder to see his face as the thought of Seth walking in on them sent both a thrill and dread through her. He closed his eyes for a moment as he continued to play with her, making her buck. Angie couldn't tell if he'd adjusted the wards to repel any visitors, but he smiled when he opened his lust-filled eyes, and Angie relaxed into the pleasure of his ministrations.

Daniel teased her far past when she was fully ready for him, and when he finally entered her, Angie cried out, clawing at the pristine counter she was bent over. "Daniel," she groaned, gasping as he set a rhythm.

"Angie," he growled back, bracing one hand on top of hers as he bent low over her, shifting her legs apart as far as he could with one knee, her jeans still hobbling her around her thighs. When he picked up his pace, his hand on her hips shifted to her center, and all thought left Angie's mind as he found her clit with perfect, firm circles.

Time lost all meaning. She cried his name again and again as he expertly sought her pleasure, barely registering the thick clouds of rosewood smoke in her aura being stretched and ribboned by the wind of Daniel's magic twining through hers in currents of rich yellow light and his signature smell of beeswax and frankincense.

She shifted her stance subtly to change Daniel's angle and position on her clit and felt him speed up just as she crested into climax and slipped beneath the dizzying sensation. Behind her, Daniel straightened, gripping her hips as he slammed into her to her limits, and Angie almost cried out from overwhelm as her orgasm trailed off. The edge of the counter pressed into her flesh and bone with each stroke, and when she felt Daniel shake and slow, hearing his delicious climax as he came inside her, she released a silent breath of relief.

She panted, unmoving, feeling full and satisfied for a long minute, glad they no longer had to use condoms since she'd gotten her implant. *Not to mention that there was no chance he couldn't be sleeping around.* She groaned her protest as Daniel separated, and the thought slipped away. He pulled her around to face him, his gaze dropping to her hips, and frowned.

"Shit. Sorry. You okay?"

Angie nodded, rubbing at the red marks on her skin from the edge of the counter, giving him a delighted and content smile. "Yeah. Fine. Maybe a little bruised, but I don't mind." She let Daniel wrap her against his chest and didn't even think about pulling away.

This was what she wanted for her future.

Once the world is free from the Patrician Empire, a voice in her mind interjected, and she shushed it.

No. Just this, right now. Happy.

CHAPTER TWENTY-TWO

D aniel had regretted agreeing to aid in finding the possession demon world, as they had come to call it, from the moment the words had left his mouth. Standing in the midnight darkness beneath a sky filled with stars was no exception. The low scrub hill they stood at the pinnacle of held little interest, and he turned his eyes skyward, gripping the handle of his cane tightly to still his hands.

"Everything alright?" Jonathan asked, detaching himself from the others and stepping close.

"Aye, sure," Daniel said, dropping his head from the band of the Milky Way overhead with a shake. "It's all just so familiar. I can't tell you why, but the sky even looks how it did that night. Maybe it's just the way the stars are aligned this time of year."

Jonathan's usually open face got a funny look. "You think the stars have something to do with half-world navigation?"

Daniel shrugged. "No. I'm just trying to convince myself that it's a good omen, and not a very, very bad one."

The two others joined them then, Dawn blowing warm air onto her fingers, and Daniel used his aura to warm the air around them, glad to have something in his wheel-house to do, however briefly. "Are we ready to go?" Dawn asked, and everyone nodded. "Good. Again, how many layers out did you say we should aim? How many layers out did your sponsor take you?"

"Seven," Daniel said through his teeth. He'd had to scry to remember that day of his own past clearly, and the emotion in the visions still hadn't faded back into the past.

"Right. And everyone has their anti-possession sigils?"

Again, everyone nodded, and Daniel swiped a thumb over the spiked, circular tattoo on the inside of one wrist with his thumb before tapping the pocket that held the newest version of the heavy copper coins Jonathan had designed and handed out to them all. He rolled his shoulders as he looked around at the others, trying to hide his trepidation, feeling the comforting weight of the pistol in its holster beneath his leather jacket.

Angie was quiet and distant, one hand shoved into the pocket of her jeans, staring vacantly at the ground. She wore a heavy canvas jacket, not her usual blue one, belted tight at the waist, with a long, sheathed sword of her own design.

Jonathan noticed when Daniel did, asking, "Are you sure you don't want one of the updated ones?"

Angie roused, looking between them with unfocused eyes, her jaw tight. "No. I trust this one. It hasn't failed me yet and has been tested thoroughly."

"I know, but the new ones have extra tethers built in, so I can retrieve them if they get lost, and—"

"No."

Jonathan gave Daniel an exasperated look, but dropped it. Daniel reached for Angie to offer comfort from the tension lining every inch of her body, but she turned away, squaring her shoulders. "Right. Let's go Skipping."

Daniel followed her beacon when Angie Skipped away, unnerved as always by how similar it was to simply Voyaging within their own world. Dawn and Jonathan were always close behind as Angie led them out a layer at a time, barely setting foot in a half-world before moving away.

The smell of hot tar, a glimpse of hulking shapes through thick mist, a sense of shifting, tiny marbles underfoot were all Daniel had to mark each world they passed through. On the seventh, Angie stopped and waited for the others in a world of fur, squishing unnervingly underfoot, which made Daniel's skin crawl.

"Is this it?" she asked when the other three had joined her, and Daniel shook his head, uninterested in testing his voice against his unease. "Right. Then we go back and try seven layers out in another direction." She Skipped away and Daniel followed suit, wishing with every fiber of his being for it to all be over.

It took them five tries to find the right world. Daniel's knees nearly gave out when they landed in the dense forest and Angie caught his elbow, not bothering to ask if they'd found the world they sought. She watched him calmly as he spun around, his heart galloping as he tried to find comfort in the fact that there were no demons in sight.

"It's alright," she murmured. "Everything will be fine."

Daniel just nodded as his whole body began to shake. He watched Angie turn in place, her alert, spring-loaded confidence further unnerving him. Half-worlds were places to be feared. Places to be fled and forever avoided. But she looked more at home in this terrifying nightmare of dense thorns, great, twisted trees blocking out the sky, and treacherous footing than she did in their everyday lives. It was oh-so-wrong, and Daniel turned away.

"Great, we found it," Daniel said, the shaking in his chest audible in his voice even to his own ears. "Now let's drop the marker and come back with an army to get what we need."

Dawn pulled a small flashlight from her pocket, and Daniel double-blinked to see the flowing scrap of deep blue magic that saturated it. She handed it to Jonathan with a sad smile, who looked around briefly before tucking it under a massive tree root, out of sight. When he straightened, his light blue eyes scanned the little clearing, and he stiffened as his eyes passed over Angie, standing behind Daniel. Before Daniel could turn to see why, Jonathan stepped forward, quickly asking, "Hey. When your sponsor hauled you out into half-worlds, did she say why she stopped here? Could you guess?"

"No," Daniel said bitterly. "All I know is that she wasn't making a lot of sense by then, and that we were attacked the moment we got here. I don't know if she even meant to stop here, or if she just didn't have the chance to leave." Daniel rubbed the back of his neck. "Why do you ask?"

"It's nothing, really," Jonathan said, bouncing on the balls of his feet as he always did when he was wound up from too much Voyaging or Skipping. "I'm probably just seeing connections that aren't there in all the research I've been doing."

Daniel was suddenly overwhelmed with the feeling that his best friend was stalling for time, keeping secrets, or both, and his need to leave doubled. "Look, we absolutely should not be lingering here." Jonathan drew breath sharply to speak as Daniel turned to ask Angie to lead them away, but a crash in the woods behind him distracted them all.

An orange glow of roaring flames flickered through the dense branches and brambles, the sphere of fire barreling through the trees toward them, just out of sight, half-charred branches and trees falling in its wake.

In a flash Jonathan's deep blue shields surrounded them, Dawn's hands crackled with deadly golden magic, and without even thinking, Daniel stopped time. Before he could draw breath, all three acts of magic spluttered and failed, as did the flames hurtling toward them.

"Fuck," Daniel said, his panic tightening his chest. "This world warped my magic last time too." Dawn and Jonathan each grabbed one of his arms, hauling him back as whatever was coming their way slashed through the thicket, and he tripped and dropped his cane as his aching, throbbing knee gave way.

"Run!" Angie exclaimed with a brief flare of fire that blossomed around her and shed off her skin as she fought her way through the last of the briars, her face and hands scratched and bleeding. Daniel's heart threatened to pound its way out of his chest as Dawn and Jonathan hauled him to his feet. Angie ran at them full pelt, scooping up Daniel's cane in the hand not wielding her sword, and shoved it into his chest, whirling to watch the clawing, shifting mass of shadows that had followed her, her face bright and animated with excitement. "Now!"

She wrapped her arms around Daniel and hauled, and in the blink of an eye, he found himself standing on a great frozen lake. He swallowed hard, his mind grinding against itself, and Dawn and Jonathan joined them a moment later. Daniel felt like he was miles away, barely seeing the people in front of him as he fought back the urge to vomit. *They were just as he remembered. Just like the demon that had pained his every moment for years upon years. So close, so close...*

"I guess these work," Dawn said happily, tossing her copper sigil coin to Jonathan, who caught it, looking pleased.

"No!" Angie shouted, looking down at Dawn's legs, and Daniel was snapped back to his full senses with a sickening lurch as the shadow clinging to the black woman's ankles sunk deep fangs into her flesh, flowing inside.

"Dawn," all three cried as she fell, convulsing. Daniel dove to catch her head, his knees slamming into the hard ice, her dark blue braids spilling through his gloved fingers as he pulled her into his lap. Jonathan was pressing the coin back into Dawn's fingers, his eyes wide with desperation, and Angie clutched Dawn's leg, her finger wrapped tightly around the flesh the demon had sunk into.

"Do what Braithwaite did when I was possessed," Daniel instructed Jonathan, who quickly placed his hands high on Dawn's heaving chest where her dark skin was exposed. "Keep it from spreading through her body. Keep it stuck where it entered."

"Get it out!" Dawn shrieked, her voice unrecognizable with pain.

"I need somewhere to put it," Angie said, looking up from her concentration with eyes that glittered like falling embers reflected in water.

"Your necklace, it worked last time," Daniel replied, holding Dawn tight against him as she writhed, memories of experiencing exactly what she was now flitting across his vision.

Angie frowned, exasperated. "No, I need something else."

Jonathan passed the now-ineffective sigil coin to Angie, who released one hand from Dawn's leg and held the hefty coin over the shadowy bite marks.

"Quiet," Daniel tried to soothe Dawn, with a glance at Jonathan, who silently returned to his healing.

Daniel watched, rapt, as Angie bent low over Dawn's leg, her eyes closed, clearly lost deep into concentration as her lips formed the ghosts of words. This time, Daniel was braced for it when the demon expanded upward in a towering dark mass of twisting, insubstantial wings, claws, and fangs. He watched in awe as Angie smiled kindly, invitingly, holding out the thick copper coin up in the palm of her hand.

Dawn stilled as she and Jonathan both joined in staring as the great, roiling demon of smoke and shadow reached out to touch the cold surface of the metal, recoiling. Angie's expression faltered slightly, and she shifted to hold the coin between two fingers. When the demon touched it again, the coin glowed faintly with heat, and the demon sank into it without resistance, a single glob of melted copper forming at the edge of its new home before Angie dropped it to the ice where it melted in a quarter of an inch.

The silence and stillness that remained were bizarre. Daniel helped Dawn to her feet, watching her closely for any sign of distress, but she just smiled tightly, shaking herself.

"Thank you," she said to Angie tightly as Jonathan stood, pulling her into a hug.

"You're okay?" Angie asked, clearly relieved, and, when Dawn nodded, bent to retrieve the cooled coin.

"Yeah. Better than okay." Dawn and Angie shared a slow smile, both staring at the coin in Angie's fingers as she slipped it into her pocket. "In fact, we now have a real chance of staying free. Of winning everything we hope to, with a demon to use at the solstice. I'm ecstatic."

Daniel just stood leaning on his cane, grateful to be numbed by the shock of the last few minutes as horror, relief, jealousy, and admiration warred through his head and heart. The other three seemed to gather themselves quickly, and the ringing in his ears nearly drowned out Angie's words.

"Ready to follow my beacon home?"

Daniel just nodded mutely. Angie Skipped away, and he followed without hesitation. When they landed on the top of the mountain, Angie did a brief check that all three were with her before Voyaging away, and Daniel followed her blindly, landing in the little green of the rebellion compound at the same time as Dawn and Jonathan.

"We did it!" Angie crowed, lifting Daniel's hand beside her, and the onslaught of joyous, triumphant whooping and screaming that exploded from the hundreds of adepts crammed into the space, bleeding out onto every path that spiderwebbed away from it out through the buildings nearly knocked Daniel off his feet. All his apprehension, fear, and desperation were shaken away as people jostled him from all sides with congratulatory slaps on the back and grateful touches on his arms.

Daniel caught Angie's eye and held it, letting her open, vibrant happiness silence the parts of him that objected, and let himself fully embrace the unbounded delight of being alive, triumphant, and in possession of a tool that could mean everything for everyone he cared about.

He pulled Angie into a tight hug, and she returned it fiercely. Nearby, Dawn was saying something, clearly trying to get people to settle down a little, but was completely ignored. "Just two more, for now. Getting Hindi and Cantonese as well would be..."

Angie pulled away, tossing the possessed coin to Jonathan. "How's that for a backup plan?" The people around them cheered again, even louder. "Now we can really bargain and don't have to rely on finesse. We can now be certain that none of us will have our magic exploited again." Jonathan pulled Angie into a crushing hug that rocked from side to side. Daniel reactivated his auric vision, and the explosion of exuberant color that met his eyes made him smile wider than he had in years.

Jonathan released Angie, holding her shoulders as he beamed at her proudly. "You were amazing." Angie beamed back, only looking slightly put out when Jonathan asked, "Please don't hate me for asking, but could I borrow the sigil coin I gave you back for a little while? I promise you'll get it back. I just want a first iteration to compare to as I work on the next round of improvements." Angie fished it out of her pocket, handing it to Jonathan before she was pulled away by a jubilant Casey.

Jonathan slipped in into a pocket and pulled Daniel into an equally tight hug, careful to avoid any skin-on-skin contact. "We did it," Daniel said, still trying to process that all of them were still alive and unharmed, and they had successfully acquired the key they needed to the lock the Court would try to build, with the way open to get more.

Jonathan squeezed him a little tighter before letting go, his tan, weathered face full of pride and relief. "We did."

CHAPTER TWENTY-THREE

The happiness didn't last. Daniel wound his way through the densely packed throng ringing the hot spring Roman bath house of the conference site, wishing he had Jonathan's ability to dampen the blaring music. As much as he wanted to fight them, the demons of his old masks were so tempting. So familiar and safe.

A thousand candles glittered off the aquamarine water and the weathered mirrors that hung along the perimeter of the raised dais, creating the illusion of being separated from the outside world without blocking the spring-night breeze that cooled the press of intoxicated, provocatively dressed bodies.

Daniel dodged a recruit in their sixties as they rushed past to jump into the pool with a splash, making those who noticed cheer, smiling grimly as they swam to the edge and hauled themselves out, dripping. All in all, the current batch wasn't acting that much worse than normal, despite the added stress. Their sponsors, on the other hand...

Noah Byrne was nearby, well into his cups, a beautiful woman on each arm as he chatted up a third, all flushed by the wine and flattered by his easy charm. Past him,

Marissa and Seth caught his eye, waving, and Daniel fin-ished off his glass of wine—his third of the evening—to a passing golem of an ancient stone statue before weaving his way over to them, glad to have his cane. Not just for his knee that had been hurting even more since the frozen lake, but for the way the world was starting to tilt.

"Here," Marissa said with a sultry smile, handing Daniel another glass of cabernet, which he accepted, taking a sip.

"My favorite. Thank you," he lied, watching Marissa's blood-red aura pulse with satisfaction. He needed her happy and at ease if he was going to get any deeper info from her about Ragnarök as he hoped to over the course of the bacchanalian evening.

"I'll catch you later, Fawl," Seth said with a wave, moving away toward a group of his peers nearby. Daniel thrust his chin in acknowledgment, feeling his head spin even more than just a minute ago.

"Let's go sit down," Marissa cooed, and Daniel agreed, glad he didn't have to be the one to try to get her alone to ask questions.

They found their way to one of the stone benches on the other side of the mirrors in the relative dark, most of the other patricians nearby making out or fondling. "Thanks. Needed some fresh air," Daniel said, half-heart-edly fighting the way his accent slipped back into the thicker twang of his teens as his speech slurred. He set his half-drunk glass of wine aside, distaste at how much more he'd been drinking lately flitting through the back of his mind before something made him ignore it.

Marissa followed the motion, reaching across him to pick it up and pressing it back into his gloved hands. "Finish it! It's your favorite."

"No thanks. I think I've had enough."

"Not at all," Marissa countered, a hard gleam in her eyes. She wrapped her hand over the back of his, the leather of his gloves keeping his curse at bay, and guided him to drink, the dark red wine shimmering with blood-red ripples in the light of the candles. Daniel frowned as he drained the glass, Marissa finally releasing him. *Weren't the candles blocked from where they sat?* No sooner had the thought formed than it broke back apart, dissolving into the wine filling his mind, and something more that didn't want to be looked at directly or named, steering his thoughts away.

A vague sense of unease lingered, and Daniel tried to stand. "I think I should go." Marissa's gentle hand on his arm was too much to fight, and he plunked back down on the stone bench without protest.

"No, please stay. You're safe with me. I'm on your side. Remember? You are a free man tonight." Daniel nodded. Of course she was. Of course he could trust her completely. "Your ball and chain isn't due to check in on you until tomorrow evening. I can satisfy your sweet tooth until then. Just let go and enjoy yourself for once." Marissa pulled a handful of chocolates from the small purse at her waist, unwrapping one and pressing it to Daniel's lips, careful not to touch his skin with her own.

"Ragnarök," he mumbled around the sweet, and Marissa clapped her hands with delight, the gold jewelry adorning her smooth, light brown skin at her ears, throat, wrist, fingers, and waist all glittering.

"Yes! I was hoping to talk to you about that."

Daniel's chest lifted as the world spun, and he braced his arm against the bench to stop himself from leaning haphazardly as he twisted more toward Marissa. Some small voice at the back of his mind told him something was wrong, but was quickly silenced.

"I suspect you've been kept out of the loop, and I've been worrying myself into an early death that you'd be left behind. How much do you know?"

Daniel shrugged lopsidedly. "Not much."

Marissa took a deep breath. "So. Ragnarök is a dooms-day option for the patricians to deal with plebeian up-risings across the globe. The first time it was called, all the language Courts moved their centers of magic to Locus Proxima to keep them away from the plebeians. All right around the time Stonehenge was moved about four thousand years ago. Another was the black death of the Middle Ages, when the patricians used magic to protect themselves, or hid in half-worlds until it was safe to return."

Daniel's gut twisted, but he stayed silent as Marissa paused, preening her hair. She leaned in conspiratorially. "This time, they will be taking all of us through to a world they call Eden. All of us who they approve of, who stay loyal, who they give the warning to. We will be safe and happy there for three years until the next Victume Ceremony year, when the dust has settled. Then we can return to reclaim our places in this world and regain the love of the masses as we help heal the scars and rebuild in our chosen image. Oh, Daniel." She grasped his gloved hand in both of hers, pulling it close to her chest. "It will be so wonderful. No stress, no obligations. No one in our way. I know we can learn to touch each other in that time, without anything coming between us. I just know it."

Daniel tried to pull his hand away, his befuddled heart and mind protesting her words and the look of hunger on her face. "No, that's not how it'd happen…"

Marissa frowned briefly with a look of concentration, and Daniel's mind went blank, like it had been wiped clean by an outside hand. When it started working again, the thoughts flowing through it hardly seemed his own. "You have to promise to keep it a secret," Marissa said, leaning forward so that her long, thick, sleek black hair fell in curtains around her face.

Daniel nodded. *Of course he would. Why wouldn't he? It didn't even bear thinking about.*

Marissa smiled. "Good. Because I want it to just be me and you there with the others. And don't worry," she said, patting his hand as she carefully placed him back on his lap, her eyes trailing across the front of his pants. "I'll remind you of all of this when you're sober. As soon as it's safe to do so. For now, just dream of me, and Eden, and listen for the three roosters to crow."

Marissa tilted her head like she felt something at the edge of her awareness. "One last thing," she said, producing a pack of cigarettes and a lighter. "You used to smoke in your army days, didn't you? Please join me." She removed two, taking one between her lips, and holding the other out to Daniel.

"No, thank you," Daniel said, his lip curling.

"I insist," Marissa said, still holding the cigarette out to him, her eyes hard and her tone insistent. "Your warden isn't here to stop you... Call this all a trial run for what our future could be."

Daniel tried to resist, but the deep red glitter of wine coursing through his veins weakened his resolve. "Alright, just one..."

Marissa's white teeth shone against her red lips and the black butt of her cigarette as she lit them both. Daniel inhaled deeply, and barely thought at all until Angie's shocked, hurt, loud voice spoke right behind him.

"Daniel?"

The shock broke his contented stupor, and as the words and thoughts of the last few minutes slipped away, Daniel scrabbled to hold on to them, making a mental note of the details he could. *Eden. Three years. Three roosters.*

"Hey," he said, his head spinning. Marissa carefully plucked the last stub of his cigarette from his lips, and he shrugged off the gold-banded arm he hadn't noticed her drape familiarly around his shoulders. "What are you doing here?"

"Seth summoned me," she said, standing back and looking him up and down with a look of disdain that made his insides drop unpleasantly. "He was worried you were drinking too much, and that he was too drunk to get you home safely."

Daniel looked in the direction Angie jerked her head in to find Seth watching them with a wide grin from a gap between the mirrors, his red hair glowing from the candles behind him. "What does he know?" Daniel mumbled defensively.

"More than you, in that state." He watched her eyes slide to the empty wine glass on the bench beside him. "Come on. Let's get you home to sleep it off." Angie stepped forward, holding out a hand to pull Daniel to his feet, but he waved her away as the wine he'd drunk told him to.

"I'm having fun. Leave me alone. I don't need my ball and chain holding me back like you always do." Beside him, Marissa bit her painted lip, her eyes seeming to dare Angie to argue, and Daniel felt bolstered. "You aren't my warden. You can't tell me what to do."

"No. You've had more than enough of an evening. Come on." Angie grabbed Daniel's arm and pulled him to his feet, shoving his cane into his hand.

"Hang on," he tried to protest as Angie pulled him away past the little changing cubbies toward the edge of the party nearest the path that wound from the collection of buildings at the center of the conference down past the bath house to the cottages by the stream. He eventually managed to pull his arm from her grip and they stopped a dozen paces away from the nearest group of partiers.

"You reek of cigarettes and wine," Angie hissed, turning to face him closely. Daniel could see her pulse pounding in her neck and she was breathing hard, her fists clenched at her sides as thick gray shields of smoke

bloomed around them, undoubtedly to obscure whatever more she wanted to say. Her eyes glistened and
the corner of her mouth pulled down as she sniffed and
swallowed hard, leaning back away from him and looking
everywhere but his face.

The realization that she was so upset broke through
Daniel's spinning fog a bit, and he winced. "I'm sorry."

Angie just shook her head with a look of disgust. "Look
at you! Drunk almost to unconsciousness, Marissa's arms
draped around you in the orgy part of a party. You know
what? I don't care. If this is what you want to do, fine. I
won't stop you. If you want to play the clown like this, I'll
stop trying to save you from yourself. Far be it from me
to hold you back or lock you up. Go have fun. Just don't
say anything that might get people killed while you're out
of your wits."

"I didn't mean..."

"No? Because you clearly can't see right now that I only
ever want what's best for you. That I'm just trying to help
you."

Daniel's words kept coming without passing through
his mind first. "You're being stupid and childish. If you
can't handle a good time, then go home."

Her eyes looked like the deep ocean and full of pain
as her throat bobbed. "I'm sorry I'm broken and fucked
up so bad that seeing the man I love drunk off his ass
and reeking of cigarettes upsets me so bad that I wanted
to take you somewhere safe, whether you were sober
enough to know it's what you needed or not."

She crossed her arms tight across her chest, starting to turn away.

Daniel's heart dropped, more of his mind catching up to what was happening, and blurted out the first thing that came to mind to stop her from leaving him hurt and angry. "I love you."

"That's not enough," Angie half-sobbed, whirling on him with a blast of heat and the smell of exhaust. "You just said a bunch of hurtful things while doing things that might put me and the other people we care about in danger. Saying you love me isn't enough. I also need to be known and supported, and be able to trust you. Being loved is not enough."

Daniel felt bitter anger at her hypocrisy heat his blood. "You think I haven't been suffering exactly the same? I'm doing whatever I can to help us. That's why I'm even at this party, but you don't want to see that, or even ask." Daniel waved an angry hand. "You don't see me either. Just the version of me that twisted in your memory until it became someone I have never been."

Angie was unreadable as he turned away, eager to return to feeling productive, wanted, and content as he had in his conversation with Marissa, and didn't look back.

CHAPTER TWENTY-FOUR

Angie barely saw through her fog of emotions as she aimlessly walked the dark and empty conference site. Daniel's words echoed through her mind even as her thoughts resisted accepting them. The urge to keep moving in any direction pushed her forward blindly, the knuckles of her fists digging into her ribs where she'd clamped them under her arms, until she saw a light on in the window of Jonathan's office in the Tudor mansion at the heart of the conference site.

Through the beautiful garden courtyard, past the massive hawthorn tree she had once destroyed and regrown, breaking into a jog as she entered the foyer of the manor, down the hallway to the door that stood ajar, light pouring out onto the thin carpets and worn flagstone. She stopped when she reached it, trying to collect herself before stepping through, utterly unsure of what she needed or wanted, other than to stop feeling the awful way that she did.

She nudged the heavy door open with her shoulder to find Jonathan sitting at his spindly desk strewn with papers, star maps, and books around a lamp and a perpetual motion sculpture. He looked up when the door squeaked. His eyes were ringed with exhaustion, and they just stared at each other. Angie couldn't get any sound past the lump in her throat and felt herself begin to crumble under the immense force she was using to hold herself together.

"Angie," Jonathan said, launching out of his chair to hover within arm's reach, his face pale and scared.

Angie lifted a hand, cracked and flaking with ash, to her mouth. Everything inside her screamed that she was supposed to be able to carry on and power through alone. That she needed to be strong, but Jonathan's careful, gentle hands on her arms as she fell apart finally broke her resolve and she spoke what she didn't want to admit.

"I'm not okay," she sobbed, and let Jonathan catch her full weight as she flung herself into his arms, crying harder than she had in years. Sorrow, and hurt, and uncertainty barreled from her like a geyser. She briefly checked her hand over Jonathan's shoulder to make sure that the release had stopped her from turning to ash, then let it take her fully.

She didn't know how long she cried into Jonathan's chest with all she had as he swayed them gently, his arms tight around her as he stroked her hair, and promised over and over that everything would be okay. Her hands clawed his back, holding fistfuls of his shirt like she was going to lose him if he let go, no thoughts able to penetrate the primal, screaming torrent of everything she had bottled up for so long.

"I'm sorry," Angie whimpered when her sobs eventually lost strength.

Jonathan gently guided her to sit beside him on the leather therapist's couch by the window, still hugging her tightly to his side as she kept crying with a fraction of the zeal she'd started with. "Not at all. I am so happy you are finally letting it all out. It's right, and healthy, and well-earned after everything you've been through. I'm honored you came to me and are letting me be here for you."

Angie just cried for another long minute as her thoughts slowly returned, as raw and tremulous as her voice when she spoke. "I should be more okay now," she eventually said, sitting up straight and gratefully accepting the box of tissues Jonathan handed her. "I survived it all. I got stronger. I built a new life. And yet..." Angie drew a shuddering breath as the crying threatened to return to full force. "I feel just as broken, and hopeless, and hurt as ever." She blew her nose, and Jonathan waited for her to look at him before he replied.

"That's normal. I'm not saying it's anything less than how you are feeling it, but you shouldn't be adding to it by feeling you're doing anything wrong. People often feel like they should just feel better when they get out of bad situations, but that's not how trauma works. It often takes years to even get back to a balanced baseline, and many people experience their lowest points of depression after getting out."

"But I want to be happier already." Angie said, her quavering voice sounding stupid and childlike.

Jonathan smiled sadly. "I know. And you'll get there. All I'm saying right now is that feeling bad because you aren't there yet isn't going to make it happen any faster."

Angie pressed the tissue in her hands into a small ball, thinking. "It's not fair." Her chest heaved, and the crying returned in full force. Angie pushed through, her words matching the uneven pattern of her sobs. "One of the monsters that tried to destroy me could still smile his way through me beating him to a pulp like he was some sort of martyr. The other keeps getting none of the punishment he deserves, running the world at heights of power I couldn't even dream of three years ago. And I just keep not sleeping, fucking things up, wanting to fix things but getting nothing done."

Her last word was swallowed with a deep gulping sob, and it took her several more before she could speak again. "It's all too much. Everything, everyone, every-where is just another little thing that pokes at my insides, and I can't get away from enough little things to cope with the rest."

"List them," Jonathan suggested.

"Demons, and half-worlds, and coins, and keys, and hunger, thirst, and sleeping!" The words burst from Angie faster than she could think them, each one bringing a sliver of relief. She touched the silver key pendant at her throat, finding equal comfort and dismay at once more feeling a living presence within the demon she had coaxed into it when she had slipped away in the wooded half-world purring contentedly in her mind.

"What else?"

Angie laughed bitterly, gripping her thighs so hard her nails bit into her skin through the fabric of her designer slacks. "Ragnarök, whatever that is. Riots, massacres, and my papers being checked. Always feeling like something's chasing me, following me, glimpsing it in the corner of my eye when there's nothing there. Always feeling trapped or cornered, wanting to fall apart when I don't know which direction to move in, literally or figuratively. Fighting the urge to keep everything with me at all times, and the panic that swamps me when I drop or misplace anything."

Angie's shoulders hunched forward, her eyes screwed shut, and raw pain clawed down her ribcage from the inside. "Lies from people I hate that I can use, lies from people I love and can't call out." She had to stop as her breathing became too shallow and fast to think, but didn't waste a second once it eased, nearly shouting the words that so desperately needed to leave her. "Feeling like no one really sees me or understands what I went through to get home." She clamped a hand over her mouth as her sobs took over, darting a guilty glance at Jonathan before searching the room for any point of comfort that wasn't mixed with embarrassment, her eyes resting on the round, bronze-framed mirror on the wall behind the desk. "Apart from you, maybe."

She dropped the hand from her mouth as Jonathan rubbed her shoulder comfortingly, her voice dropping to a whisper. "But how can I ask anyone to see me, all of me, the real me, when I don't even know who that is?" The question surprised Angie as it fell from her lips, and she turned to Jonathan wide-eyed as the core of her distress she hadn't even known was there shocked her into stillness.

"It's okay to not know," Jonathan said, and Angie's throat closed off. "Sometimes we need the space to be nobody, to grieve everyone we used to be and accept that we can't go back to being any of them before we can figure out who we get to be next." She faced front again, waiting for his words to sink in. "Sometimes we need to finish breaking before we can start healing."

Angie felt her whole being contract, her face contorting. She held her breath until her chest stopped shaking, and scooted right up next to Jonathan, resting her head on his shoulder, squeezing his hand in silent thanks. She pressed her eyes closed, knowing she should leave Jonathan to his research or to sleep, her whole body screaming against the idea. "It's late—"

"Yes," Jonathan said before she could finish, squeezing her hand. "But I would really like to keep sitting here with you, just like this, until you are actually ready to be done."

Angie took a deep, shaking breath, nodding gratefully, and they both stared out at the room for a long, deep, comfortable minute.

She let her mind wander without direction. She was glad she wasn't alone. Seeing, smelling, and hearing Daniel at the party with Marissa hurt more than she could name. She'd still show up at their appointed rendezvous tomorrow evening to talk through it and make amends.

"I want to go home."

Jonathan's bearded chin bumped the top of her head gently. "Which home do you mean?"

Angie's gut clenched and her even breath started to rise again. "I don't know," she choked, too drained to fully cry again, or to fight the way her body tried anyway. "I don't know. I've always just called wherever I intended to sleep that night my home. But no place has ever really felt like home how other people seem to mean it."

Jonathan let her words linger for a long time in the cool air around them, scented with the aroma of wet ash and sage smoke. "I hear you, Angie. Everything you are saying, and everything you aren't."

Angie felt everything she had, and hadn't, and didn't know how to say tumble through her heart and mind in fragments of smoke, ice, and glass. She drew breath to speak several times, relaxing against Jonathan's shoulder, but let go when nothing came out.

"I know."

CHAPTER TWENTY-FIVE

D aniel remembered almost nothing of the night before. He'd woken sprawled across his familiar bed
in his cottage on site, fully dressed, and visited the conference infirmary for Lady Braithwaite's hangover tablets
before even thinking about pursuing his day.

Between escorting Seth to the astral projection class
being taught at the amphitheater and lunch in the
golem-staffed gourmet cafeteria that might better be
called a feast hall, he'd discovered a barely comprehensi-
ble note on his phone that seemed to be about Ragnarök
and spent the rest of the day connecting what dots he
could through his blackmailed Senate connections and
northern mythology, passing it all along to Dawn.

Half an hour before he expected Angie to arrive for
their weekly rendezvous over something sweet, Seth
safely occupied out of the house, Daniel found himself puttering around the cottage anxiously. He couldn't
shake a sense of foreboding, wishing his memories of
the night before weren't so foggy where they weren't
nonexistent, or that his concentration was in any fit state
to try scrying back on them.

He was tidying the last few things into cupboards and drawers, a nervous habit from living with his squirrelly Air aura, when he heard a knock on the front door. He quickly straightened himself up, checking his reflection in the dark screen of his phone, before pulling it open and giving Angie a nervous smile. "Hey! You're early."

Angie gave him a wide smile back, a pie in one hand and a bottle of wine in the other. "Hope it's not a problem. After last night, I thought I should bring an apology." She hefted the bottle of wine.

"Well, good news for you, I don't remember last night, so no apology needed." Daniel stepped aside and Angie smiled, but stopped short when the wards across the Thresholds stopped her from entering.

"What the hell?" Angie asked, frowning.

Daniel double-blinked, seeing her aura swirling around her bright red flames, and waved at the wards to let her through. "Sorry. If we argued last night, it's possible I took you out of the ward permissions. I'll fix that." Angie gave him a tight smile, stepping past him into the kitchen. "Hey," he said, frowning. "I haven't seen your flames that color before. They're usually orange and yellow, and more varied…"

"Don't worry about it," Angie said, setting down the lemon meringue pie on the counter. "And please stop looking. I don't like feeling so… scrutinized."

As if the Gods themselves had spoken, Daniel obeyed and any lingering concerns washed away. "Wine?" Daniel asked with a teasing raised brow as Angie uncorked the bottle, grabbing and pouring two glasses of the deep red liquid.

"Yeah," she said sheepishly, handing a glass to Daniel and taking a sip of her own before setting it aside to slice the pie. "I thought, after yelling at you for being drunk with other people last night, that reminding myself how much I've enjoyed getting drunk with you in the past might be a good start to the conversation."

"I don't know, I've never been that much of a drinker, and after last night, I should probably lay off when I'm not playing along with the boozers or trying to get someone else drunk..." Even as he formed the thoughts and word, and insidious intrusion in his mind shoved them back out of sight. Daniel tried to be alarmed, tried to do something about it, but again his mind wiped blank before he could act.

Daniel took a swig of the rich, dark liquid, thinking back fondly on the night in the cottage three years ago when he had drilled her in flicking little candle flames from her palm before she'd burned herself, leading to some of the hottest, if slightly self-loathing, sex of his life. "Nice choice."

Angie grinned.

The next twenty minutes disappeared into a blur of blood-red wine, utterly out of proportion with the half-bottle he consumed, but Daniel's mind seemed unable to hold on to any thoughts of concern or question as Angie plied and flirted with him. Only a glass in, he'd tried to give Angie a sloppy kiss, but she'd dodged him completely, laughing about easing back in after the argument he didn't remember. Now, with the bottle empty, Daniel reached for her again, but she stopped him with a teasing smile.

"I have a suggestion for a game."

"Yeah?" Daniel replied, leaning heavily on the edge of the table.

Angie licked her lips, looking him up and down. "How small can you shrink your shields into your skin?"

"I dunno," Daniel huffed, shrugging, the faintly lit kitchen around him swimming. "In this state, I probably couldn't do smaller than, like, this room."

Angie looked briefly disappointed, but quickly returned to her flirtatious smile. "Then put your gloves on, and we'll try second best."

Daniel frowned, vaguely wondering how'd he'd ended up in bed, naked apart from gloves she'd somehow made invisible, with Angie straddling him over a sheet but beneath the comforter covering them both. "See, isn't this hot," she whispered in his ear, her breath warm and heavy with excitement and the smell of pomegranates. "Pretending we can't touch. Like it would be with you and Marissa."

Daniel nodded, befuddled but happy, hoping Angie knew how they could proceed from there, since he really didn't have any ideas. He tried sliding a gloved hand up and down her side in a caress, but the movement was jerky and unsatisfying, his sensation muted by the invisible layer of leather.

"In fact," Angie said, her pale, freckled and scarred skin flushed with arousal and her ocean-colored eyes bright, "why don't we go all the way with the fantasy? Summon me with your beacon like you would if I was late for my visit."

"Okay," Daniel said vaguely, doing as he was told. "Can you feel it?"

"Mmhmm," Angie sighed, grinding on his lap on the other side of the sheet. "Perfect."

Daniel heard the front door downstairs open and close, and someone call his name, but was sure he hadn't a moment later.

"Then how about this next?" Angie said, and Daniel watched as her shapes and colors morphed into the spitting image of Marissa Hayward.

His excitement all but disappeared in the space of a breath. "No, I don't want... I don't like that..."

Angie-wearing-Marissa's-face before him frowned in frustration and concentration. "It's just a new illusion skill I've picked up," she reassured him, her words honeyed and irresistible. "It's hot. You don't have to lie."

Daniel's thoughts and actions were twisted utterly outside of his control. He tried to move to push her off, his emotions screaming that something was very wrong, but couldn't command his limbs or even the expression of carnal pleasure someone else was wearing on his face.

The woman astride him let out a delighted laugh that almost covered the creak of the top stair just outside the bedroom door. Her mouth fell open in ecstasy and she moaned with pleasure, bucking her hips against his through the sheet, and Daniel couldn't do more than try to complete one coherent thought before the smell of cigarettes and burning plastic blasted through the room, making him gag.

Angie stood in the doorway, her face a mask of shock and betrayal, and Daniel's brain short-circuited, ground painfully, and broke free the smallest degree from the magic puppeting him.

Above him, Marissa planted her hands above his shoulders on the mattress, her long, black hair brushing the side of his face as she twisted to give Angie in the doorway a satisfied, triumphant smile.

"No," Angie whispered, backing away, but something kept Daniel paralyzed and mute, his face blank. He watched helplessly, trying to fight it, as Angie's skin turned ashy, her eyes going dull. "You're not the man I loved. I don't know you anymore." As she turned away, a lock of her long auburn hair crumbled to the carpet on the landing as ash, and something in Daniel snapped, tearing his mind free with a blinding pain behind his eyes.

"Angie!" he roared, shoving Marissa away with his gloved hands, his head swimming as he tried to sit up. Fear and dread shot through him and the intoxication lifted from him enough to rip his gloves off and stand, pulling the sheet out from under the protesting Marissa to wrap around his waist. "Wait, Angie, no!"

He tried to stop time with a glance at the little carriage clock on the dresser, desperate to have a chance to head off the horrible misunderstanding in progress, but it juddered and glitched, some foreign presence in his mind blocking the flow of his magic.

"Wait," Marissa said breathlessly, lunging into his path with both hands raised, her expression pleading and adoring. "You have to want to find the loophole with me, don't you? That's part of it, isn't it? I had to convince you to try, and you wouldn't listen, but see me now... Please. I know doing it if you're just willing to really try, if she's no longer an option..." Her words stuttered with the attempted time-stop, and Daniel barely noticed that her existence seemed half in the world's time stream, and half in his.

"Out of my way," Daniel snarled, trying to move around her to the door, but she braced her arms against the frame, and Daniel found it a struggle to stay angry as she went on.

"I'm on your side. I'm loyal to you and you alone. Milton helped me set this all up, helped me get better at illusions, taught me the influence in the wine, but I swear. From this moment, I'll betray him. Do nothing he asked me to with it, I just needed a chance—"

"Fuck you," Daniel screamed, and felt the tendrils of magic infecting his mind, making themselves invisible to his awareness shred in an instant to the utter horror, betrayal, and terrible realization that stole his breath and stopped his heart. He ripped off his invisible leather gloves and grabbed Marissa's wrist, tearing her grip from the doorframe, and let her drop unceremoniously to the floor with a thump. He stepped over her unconscious body, holding the sheet as he descended the stairs three at a time. "Fuck. Angie, wait!"

On the bottom step a glint of silver caught his eye and Daniel skidded to a halt, snatching up the key pendant before looking up at the woman hunched double between him and the front door of the cottage, nothing visible of her skin as she folded in on herself. Pure dread coursed through him and Daniel waved a shaking hand to banish his sheet and summon a pair of trousers straight onto his body, letting go of his attempt to stop time as he crept forward on bare feet. "Angie?"

She didn't twitch, or even breathe, that he could see, and he tiptoed up behind her, his heart dropping to his toes when he glimpsed the flaking, ash-gray surface of her arm. "Angie, I'm so sorry."

His fingers grazed her arm, and as a heart-breaking scream, full of unbearable pain, loss, and anger pulverized the air in the room, Angie disintegrated to smoke, leaving nothing behind but ringing silence and the choking, ghostly smells of burning cheatgrass, sage, juniper, and flesh.

Daniel was frozen in place, his mouth hanging open. *Had she Voyaged away, or Skipped?* No sooner had the thought flitted through his mind, then it was followed by the thought, *who?*

Panic thrilled through Daniel and he stood, his breath and heartbeat rising as adrenaline coursed through him. "Angie," he gasped, turning in a circle, desperately trying to remember who Angie was.

A lemon meringue pie on the kitchen counter just through the doorway to the kitchen, beside an identical, emptied pie pan faded slowly into smoke, and Daniel gasped, every limb starting to shake. "No, no, no, no, no..." he summoned his phone to him, waking it to see his lock screen image, and watched in horror as the beautiful woman with gently curling auburn hair and freckled skin whose cheek he was kissing in the picture faded from it.

Daniel's aura ripped out from him in a tornado, utterly unrestrained, splintering the coat stand by the front door, ripping the door of a nearby cupboard that had been left ajar off its hinges, and throwing the carpet, couch, and coffee table in the living room on his other side thudding into the far wall with cracking thuds. Daniel didn't notice.

"No, no, don't fade, I'm sorry," Daniel gripped his phone so tight the plastic and metal creaked, then dropped it when he remembered the silver key in his other hand. It didn't seem to be fading, but he couldn't remember why that was a relief. He raked his fingers through his hair as a panicked, terrified sob wracked his body and he closed his eyes tight. "I won't forget. Angie. Angie. My recruit. Her fire. Her..."

Daniel lurched for his study and office at the back of the cottage overlooking the stream, tripping over his own feet and half-scrambling to get there. He clawed through a desk drawer as papers scattered from the lashing wind of his aura, grabbing the first blank sheet he found and a pen, dropping to his knees to frantically start writing, the silver key still clutched in one hand. But when his pen touched the paper, he froze.

What was her name?

"Fire," Daniel said out loud, tears blurring his vision before falling to the sheet of paper beneath him in the eye of the storm as he frantically wrote down every word that tried to fight the gaps spreading through his mind. "High desert mountain valleys. Rosewood smoke."

He barely registered the sound of someone stumbling down the stairs behind him and out the front door, slamming it behind them, as he wrote, sobbing fully against everything that was fading from him, slipping through his fingers, leaving him cold, lost, and oh so lonely.

"Freckles. Strong. Blue jacket. Silver key. Angel. Warm. Love. I won't forget, I won't..."

Chapter Twenty-Six

A ngie ripped the chain from her neck and flung it away, falling to her knees as a body hit the floor above and behind her. She collapsed into a ball between the bottom of the cottage stairs and the front door, desperately trying to hold herself together. Every bad emotion she had ever felt screamed through her so intensely it rendered her deaf, blind, and mute, unable to move or even breathe. Above, below, and around it all, grief was the strongest. *I've lost him*, tumbled over and over and over through her mind.

Her own skin beneath her fingers crumbled to ash faster the more tightly she tried to hold herself together, and when familiar, vibrating fingers brushed her arm, she gasped, and felt herself dissolve utterly from the inside out. No outburst. No attack. Just collapsing in so hard that she became nothing but her emotions, too raw and painful to remain flesh.

She screamed as she melted away into smoke, too out of control to stop or slow it, screaming over and over again with terror and loss as a gale-force wind tumbled her forward, out through the front door, sprawling on the smooth pebbled walkway, darkened and dampened by the falling Britannian mist. She was nothing but thought and emotion, and neither gave her respite as she closed her mind off to the world around her, the panic of being lost again in astral worm barely a blip in her tumultuous soul.

When did he stop loving me?

He didn't even care enough if I caught him to use a time-stop?

Or to do it somewhere they wouldn't get caught?

He did it during our special time together.

He called me there to make sure I saw.

Angie gasped, looking all around her for some relief from her own dark internal spiral, and was so shocked to find she could gasp that it broke the panic. She lifted her hands in front of her face. They were smoke-gray, not misty white. When she moved them, they barely had form, smoke and ash shedding off them in little eddies, unlike the half-translucent clear definition of her astral form.

She bent double, trying to compress herself back into solidity, the knowledge that this wasn't astral projection taking the sharpest edge off her panic. Would she starve as smoke? Die of thirst? Angie couldn't force herself to care in comparison to the frozen, debilitating realization that she had no idea what to do next. Nowhere to go. No direction to move in.

Old demons in her heart stirred and Angie cried out again as they spoke other words into her despair. She had no Daniel to return to. Nowhere to call home. No tether or token back. She didn't know who to be to survive this. Severed from reality, and utterly alone.

"I don't want to go back," Angie told herself, trying to find some comfort. But the more she let the truth of that settle into her mind, the deeper her sorrow sank until all of her agitation melted away into numbness. "I don't have anything worth going back for."

A heavy door slammed nearby and Angie spun to see Marissa retreating from the cottage, half-dressed, her face shifting too fast across a broad array of emotions for Angie to track. Bracing herself, Angie walked forward, finding that she glided weightlessly, passing right back through the front door. She didn't know why, or what she sought, but the minor detritus of devastation wasn't it.

She looked for her dark blue jacket by the splintered coat rack but didn't see it. She glanced into the kitchen where she expected to see the pie she'd brought splattered against a wall, but saw only broken dishes. She froze when she heard muffled words from Daniel's study, refusing to even turn her head.

"I've forgotten... What have I forgotten... Who was she?"

Angie fought the urge to run to Daniel to offer comfort to the clear distress in his Caledonian voice, but chastised herself. If the Daniel she loved and wished to comfort had ever existed, it wasn't the man she'd find just around the corner.

A buzz on the floor made her look down, and behind a recent text alert from Jonathan, she saw a picture of Daniel kissing the empty air, and the realization of just how far-reaching her disappearance truly was fell like a thick blanket of ash over the last spark of emotion in her soul. It settled into every crevice as her thoughts plodded out, devoid of nuance or passion, into the icy void of her new reality.

"At least if Casey forgets I exist, he can't be mad at me for leaving again." Angie wondered if she really spoke or if it was all just her imagination, but couldn't be bothered to truly care.

She searched deep inside herself for the will to fight what had happened to her, but as she drifted back out the front door, a faint aftershock of grief touched her, and she let herself go into the wind, wishing she could stop thinking or feeling altogether.

Chapter Twenty-Seven

Daniel sat with his back pressed to the desk in his office, the knobs of the drawers down the leg digging into his spine. He clutched the silver key pendant and sheet of paper to his bare chest, convulsing with sobs. He couldn't begin to understand why.

"Jonathan," he gasped, sending up an erratic mental Voyaging beacon, desperate for any help to stop feeling the way he did.

He heard the front door open not thirty seconds later. "Dan? Half the conference can feel this beacon, shut it off. What the hell is happening?" Daniel just sobbed, unable to say anything more, letting go of the Voyaging beacon. He opened his eyes to find Jonathan standing in the doorway to the little office, his face pale, and Daniel's cell phone in hand. "Dan..."

"Something's wrong, something's very, very wrong." Daniel couldn't move, his arms pulled so tight to his chest that his muscles shook from fatigue. He hauled in his out-of-control Air aura that was making Jonathan squint at him from under a raised arm, locking it down mercilessly inside in a way he knew would fester.

"I know," Jonathan said, pulling off his suit jacket and draping it over his hands, slowly and carefully easing Daniel to sit forward to drape it over his bare shoulders. "I can see that. Can you tell me anything?"

"Someone got in my head. Messing with my mind. The wine..." Daniel closed his eyes, scouring his own mind for any lingering influence with a horrified ruthlessness that left his head pounding, doubling and redoubling his mental shields. "Slow poison. I don't know how long. I was too distracted to notice..."

"Do you need me to get the sobering potion from the infirmary?"

Daniel shook his head, his chest heaving. "No. It's gone now. Marissa and Milton. They did something, got me to do something... I can't remember what it was..." Daniel desperately wanted to reach out and grab Jonathan, desperately needed comfort, but held himself back to searching his dearest friend's face for understanding. "They took something from me. From my memory. Here, look." Daniel pitched forward, frantically smoothing the sheet of paper on the floor before him. "I wrote down what I could remember."

Jonathan shifted to look at it with Daniel, frowning. "Okay. That's not much to go on. When did—" He stopped short when the front door opened.

"Hey," Seth said just out of sight. "What upset Marissa so much? I thought she was coming over to have dinner, but I just dropped by her cottage and she's in a state."

"My office," Jonathan said softly, pulling Daniel to his feet by his covered shoulders. "Drop the Voyaging out wards."

Daniel did so as Seth's red hair appeared around the corner and wasted no time in Voyaging after Jonathan.

He started pacing the moment his bare feet touched the thick, soft carpet in Jonathan's office in the Tudor manor up the hill. He pulled the suit jacket tighter around his shoulders, unwilling to let go of the silver key or paper enough to put his arms through the sleeves.

"How can I help?" Jonathan asked, standing aside, help-less worry written in every inch of his body and face. "Is there any support, or comfort, or anything else I can give you?"

Daniel's face twisted, desperately wishing he could say yes. He pressed the back of one wrist to his nose, trying to hide the drowning upset he was powerless to let go of or justify. "I don't know."

"Then just talk to me. What ties all those words on your paper together?"

"A person, I think." Daniel's mind hadn't stopped racing since the moment he'd felt like something was slipping away from him, and he could barely speak fast enough to keep up. "I don't remember their name, but I think it was a woman. I don't think I'd remember her at all if I wasn't thinking about her when she disappeared and tried to hold on. I don't know why I own three houses, least of all the one in Maui."

Daniel ground his knuckles into his sternum, searching for the touch-starved yearned that had been permanently lodged behind his breastbone for so long. "I no longer feel like it's been years and years since I had real physical contact with another person, apart from grazes that knock people out, or the ten minutes it took me to awaken Marissa and Seth as my recruits."

Jonathan smiled earnestly. "That's great, but that's impossible."

"No, it's not! Someone found the loophole, I know it. My phone," Daniel whirled to Jonathan, pointing at his pants pocket. Jonathan quickly handed him the sleek black cell and Daniel tapped the screen, clearing it and turning to show him. "See this picture? Can you imagine me, in any reality, taking this picture without someone standing there beside me? And how could I take this picture if I couldn't touch the skin of whoever I was kissing?"

Jonathan blinked rapidly, his forehead creasing deeply as he seemed to finally understand. "That's weird."

Daniel stepped even closer, some of his desperation finally easing with even the first small note of validation that he wasn't going insane.

"Why am I walking right now? When did the demon get exorcized?" Jonathan looked up at him, wide-eyed. "Who was my recruit three years ago, between Marissa and Seth? Why was I living on site three years ago if I didn't have one? And who was in first position at the Victume Ceremony that year?" Jonathan's frown deepened, and he spun around his spindly desk, flipping open a notebook and scanning a page before shaking his head, the color draining from his face. "Jon, *who broke the English Focal*

Nucleus, since we are all stressed about replacing it this year?"

The two men stared at each other for a drawn moment. Daniel's mind spun as more and more gaps bubbled up through his anguish, each one popping with another grain of reassurance. *I'm not imagining it. There's someone missing.*

"So," Jonathan managed weakly, pulling a calloused hand down his dark beard. "You're saying someone was deleted from our pasts, like she never existed?"

"No, because then there wouldn't be gaps where she did things. If she never existed, something else would have happened there, or it just wouldn't have happened."

"So, just from our memories, then?"

Daniel huffed a mirthless laugh, waving the fist still holding the sheet of paper he'd scribbled meaningless words onto. "No, because then there would still be records. Pictures, documents, clothes in the closet, something. It's like she just dissolved, erasing herself, without any purpose or meaning."

Jonathan's chest rose and fell almost in rhythm with Daniel's, and he gripped the back of his chair so hard his knuckles turned white. "This is bad. You say you think you were thinking of her when she disappeared. Do you have any idea why?"

Daniel cried again, the sheer sense of loss and shame he couldn't explain resurfacing. A small eddy of wind circled the room before he reined it back in. "I know. And... I think it was my fault." He raised a hand before Jonathan could ask why, his legs beginning to shake as he resumed pacing. "All I can remember from that moment was feeling like it was my fault, that this," he held up the little silver key necklace pendant with three interlocking rings at the handle, "was hers, and..." Daniel pressed his mind back. "Smoke. Dry grass, sagebrush, juniper, and something like burning hair."

"That's very specific..."

"I know. I was paying close attention for some reason. And it made me think of a high desert mountain valley I know in Oregon, the perfect place to test unstable magic." He looked at Jonathan with pleading eyes. "But I can't remember why I was there three years ago." Daniel's face contorted again, and his words were barely understandable. "I know I've lost her before. I know I've grieved this loss before. And I can't remember why." He bent forward, wishing he could sink through the floor into oblivion. "How do I bring her back?"

"I don't know. I can't help her, whoever she is. But I want to help you however I can," Jonathan said, stepping forward. He reached out toward Daniel's head, who jerked back, shocked and horrified, but Jonathan gave him a reassuring smile. "I'm not going to touch you. I'm just going to wash your mind of any lingering influence like you mentioned, in case that's part of what's happening."

Daniel watched as a bubble of liquid magic formed between Jonathan's palms and held his breath as it engulfed his head. It didn't feel like water on his face or hair, so Daniel tried breathing again, finding it even easier than a minute ago. He closed his eyes as the soothing magic washed over his mind, slowly, cautiously releasing his expressive aura from where he bottled it up in his center as Jonathan soothed each tendril.

When Jonathan withdrew, Daniel felt drained beyond belief, and utterly relieved by the numbness.

"Do you need to tap out? I'm sure Dawn has room for you, could keep you busy, and would like to spend some real time with you again. Your time would be almost as well-spent there, doing what practicing we can with the collected demons in preparation to keep the new lock from suppressing us again..."

Daniel shook his head, uncurling stiff fingers to shift the sheet of paper to his other hand with the key, rubbing his puffy eyes and glancing at the reassuring anti-possession tattoo at the inside of his wrist. "No. I wouldn't. I can't. But I can't stay here. Not with Marissa and Seth. She got in my head and is at least part of what happened. And Seth knows, or helped, I'm certain. He wanted this to happen." Resentment dragged down at the corners of Daniel's mouth. "You've seen the way he looks at me, like I'm some great, charismatic future dictator he adoringly wants to support on my rise to fascist power so that he can share in it." He swallowed with a hard sniff, and Jonathan passed him a box of tissues. "I can't pretend I'm that person anymore. I can't pretend I'm any of them anymore."

Jonathan didn't reply right away, looking at Daniel in the way that always made him squirm, like he could see the truth of his heart and mind better than he could. When he spoke, Daniel cringed at the inescapable truth he didn't want to acknowledge. "You're right. We have a job to do, for everyone we love. And if that goal of keeping ourselves free so that we can someday free all the languages, then maybe we need to refocus on finding and disarming the banishment keys."

"Yeah. I know." Daniel blew his nose, trying to find any sense of purpose within himself to stop the empty ringing in his heart where someone should be. "I'll stay the course. But Milton is behind this. Marissa told me. Maybe he can remember..."

"You think he did this?" Jonathan looked pale. "God. If he can do that..."

"No. Not directly. He doesn't have the power to erase someone, even as a Councilor. If he did, neither of us would be here..." He couldn't get his mind to go any further into revenge or manipulation, and hung his head, defeated. In his heart, he knew he couldn't not push ahead, but thinking about all that was at stake in making sure the patricians didn't regain their ability to strip magic away from him and his friends to use for their own ends barely dulled the edge of his panic.

"Don't worry about that right now," Jonathan said, stepping in close, and Daniel looked up into his dear, gentle face. "Just take care of yourself first for a little while. Keep your head down until you've had time to process all of this more." Jonathan lifted a hand toward Daniel's chin but quickly dropped it. "In times of great upset, or even a triggered state, which is likely if, like you say, you've lost this person before and that pattern has ingrained in your nervous system, it can be really hard to think clearly. Taking as much time and space as you can to take care of yourself is better than acting out of your dysregulation and potentially making things worse."

"Yeah, thanks." Daniel cleared his throat. For a flash, he thought about double-checking that Jonathan wasn't the person he'd been able to touch in his recent physical memory, but the wild notion passed, and his hands stayed at his side.

"Why don't you make me a copy of that list," Jonathan said, nodding at the crumpled piece of paper in Daniel's fist, "and a list of all the gaps you can think of. I'll dive into research, see if anything got missed. And, if it's alright with you, why don't I take over more of Seth's education between now and the solstice to give you more time and space to rest?"

"Yeah, of course. Thank you." Daniel replied, weary earnestness in his voice. "Take this one. I'll make a copy tomorrow."

Jonathan took the list and returned to his desk, spreading it out smooth and reading it with a determined scowl.

Daniel twisted the silver key in his fingers. His own internal voice melded with his long years of knowing Jonathan, and he didn't fight it. Maybe he did need to step back a little and just let things coast. He didn't want to be alone, so maybe it was time to accept help from friends and distance himself from enemies.

As the last thought floated through his mind, a caveat quickly followed it. Daniel pulled a hand down his face and Voyaged to his Boston home. *I swear on my life that I won't stop trying to remember. I won't be complacent if the* gaps start to fill. And if killing an enemy stands a chance of getting back what I lost, I won't hesitate.

Chapter Twenty-Eight

A ngie followed when Milton Cartwright was booed from yet another of the endless, decadent parties of the patricians. Only she fully knew why. Without physical needs and her sanity intact, what other distraction and purpose could she have but to spy? Day after day, she tried not to think about the low likelihood of ever being able to pass along what she learned to someone who could use it.

She wrapped her smoky arms around his shoulders, unseen, unheard, and unfelt, and when he Voyaged away from the antechamber of the grand colosseum, she was taken with him. They landed at the entrance to a cave ringed with frost.

Just inside the mouth stood a rudimentary Threshold built from driftwood branches. Angie watched closely as Milton took a key from his pocket and turned it in a small hole in the side of one of the upright sides of the empty doorway. A membrane of fuchsia magic filled the space like a door in a blink, stretching as Milton stepped through before snapping back into place.

Angie hesitated before following. She'd tested Skipping to half-worlds since her drastic change in existence and had found her sense for them muted almost to nothing. And the last time she'd gone through a Threshold of Milton's making... She shuddered, gathered her courage, and stepped through. The usual pressure and resistance didn't even touch her.

"Fix it!" Milton shouted as Angie arrived just in time to see him kick a whimpering pile of rags. Angie gasped when she saw who it was, but no one heard. "Getting her own magic to vanish her worked, but the rest didn't."

"Please, no," Sakshi cried, the Hindustani Seer's scarred and mutilated face twisted with pleading as she groped blindly for the wall. "Please. I can't See how. I tell you what I can, but Apollo doesn't show me everything. Please."

Milton kicked her again, the poppy smell of his magic filling the small cave. "Getting rid of the fire bitch didn't fix my reputation, and I'm honestly starting to wonder if I shouldn't have stayed in that world when it happened so I could forget the meddling whore ever existed like the rest."

The emotional numbness Angie had taken such refuge in since becoming smoke faltered as she tried to keep up with the little pieces started fitting together. Milton had a true Seer at his disposal. He took credit for Angie turning to smoke, and had known how to not forget her.

"Please, please. I told you everything you asked about them both, and how to get the raven woman to do as you wanted. Please, I'm going to die without food or water. I will die of cold. Please don't hurt me any more."

"Bah." Milton turned away, his face ruddy with anger. "It ended up being useless. Marissa lost her grip on Fawl's mind, and now he's too careful to try puppeting him myself. And his stupid little sycophant is too unpredictable to try using openly."

As he stepped away, clearly brooding, Sakshi's ruined face snapped to Angie, the acid scars across where her eyes should be flickering with the orchid-pink light from the Threshold. "I'm sorry," she whispered so quietly Angie could barely hear. "I didn't want to. I tried not to. I didn't want to die…"

"It's okay," Angie said, her face slack, not expecting Sakshi to hear.

"She never touched him," Sakshi whispered, and Angie's ephemeral insides guttered, dropped, and flared. "He never wanted her. He was controlled, lied to, forced and fighting it." In a breath, Angie's world turned upside down, and she went into freefall. "It was an illusion. You are his only love."

"Look," Cartwright said in sickly sweet tones Angie barely heard. "Here's food, water, more blankets and a source of heat." Cartwright produced each as he said them, placing boxes, jugs, and a large, glowing stone the size of a cat around Sakshi, who nervously touched each, recoiling from the heat of the stone. "Give me one more bit of information right now, and I'll even let you see." He produced a large hank of silk thread, brushing it against the back of Sakshi's hand, his expression and demeanor every bit the kindly grandfather.

"Please," Sakshi said, reaching out desperately for the thread she would be able to send her magic out through to see the world around her. "What do you want?"

"Now that Daniel Fawl is alone," Milton crooned, "he's vulnerable. By himself, he's not so powerful that I don't dare take him on. So, tell me how I can take him down. Not his network, not his cause, like I've asked in the past. Just him."

Sakshi's turquoise aura flared around her in darting, purposeful patterns. "There will be a high price for killing a Councilor. One you don't want to pay."

"I don't care," Milton said, his affable demeanor faltering.

Sakshi wrapped herself around the warm stone, clearly afraid it would be taken away. "If I don't tell you, you kill me by leaving me here with nothing. If I tell you, you are either killed yourself, or are stripped of your powers, and I am forgotten here and die."

Milton ground his teeth, clearly considering his options. Eventually he stood, dropping the skein of silk thread, his jowls shaking as he blew out a frustrated breath. "Get your strength back up. When I return, I expect you to have found an answer for me you are willing to give."

"I will find you," Angie shouted as she followed close behind Milton back toward the Threshold, her mind and heart a jumble of shock, guilt, hope, and more she couldn't separate. Sakshi nodded once, expressionless, as Angie darted ahead of the portly Transvallian back through the magical door.

Angie stepped aside as soon as they stood back in the true world. And watched, unmoving, as Milton Cartwright collapsed the magic in the Threshold and

Voyaged away. Angie reached toward the driftwood at the mouth of the empty cave, wishing with all her might that her fingers might solidify enough not to pass through. Her soul dipped and soared as she tried over and over.

If she was to warn Daniel, she would need substance. Sorting everything else around him, her new understanding, would have to wait and come in time. Eventually she gave up, gathering herself to Voyage away to every place she thought he might be. She could try to return to reality from anywhere, so it might as well be near Daniel.

She Voyaged to the rebellion compound, landing on the steps of the common house. She searched among those gathered there for Daniel, but didn't find him. She wasn't sure what she was seeking in them, but her eyes caught on a woman in the crowd, plump and pretty, a little older than Angie with mousy hair, and she found it.

Vicky was standing with Casey, both practicing reaching into the floating ball of translucent, faintly glowing threads of magic that had been built in the center of the green as a mock language lock, their brows furrowed with concentration as they willed it to change as directed by Anthony and Jonathan. Angie hadn't bothered to truly watch her when she had stood among the rest as Angie beat their common abuser. She wondered what her face had looked like then.

The thought spiraled off into others, and as Dawn passed through her from behind with one of her wives, Olivia, both carrying bottles of water, she settled on one. Like she should have done more to keep Vicky and those after her from ever going through what they did with her ex, she *had* to keep more people from dying like she almost had, like Emilia had, when she'd broken the English Focal Nucleus three years ago, not even thinking about her own survival to stop Milton Cartwright from imposing his sadistic will on her world through the lock.

One more reason on the pile. I can't let the bad guys win. We can't be the only ones losing. Angie's breath caught and sped up.

She Voyaged away to Daniel's palatial mansion in the woods of New York, searching every room. Her desperate, uncertain need grew with every moment she didn't find him. She searched his home in Boston next, then their cottage in the Cotswolds, but he was nowhere to be found.

Angie began to cry, and she threw herself down onto the tall, squishy bed in the master bedroom in the cottage, not making a dent. She didn't want to name why, but she knew. As much as the raw pain of thinking Daniel had cheated on her lingered from the days she'd believed in it, knowing the truth of what had happened was finally settling in. And even without it, she loved him. She'd never stopped loving him. If she had, even in the depths of her betrayal, it wouldn't have hurt so badly she turned to smoke and couldn't escape.

"I just want to get back," she sobbed to the empty pillow that smelled faintly of Daniel. "I just want to come home."

—❖—

Angie slept through the night for the first time since she'd become smoke. When she stirred, it was with less hollowness and more clarity than she had felt in far too long. She swung her legs over the side of the bed into the shaft of early-morning light, listening to the mourning doves and other birds chirping outside the window and gathering her thoughts.

When she Voyaged to the conference site in the Cotswolds, it wasn't Daniel she sought, despite how dearly she wanted to be near him. She found Jonathan in his office on site, seated across from Seth Laufey.

The younger man held a fistful of fire as orange as his hair, grinning as he tossed it from hand to hand. "See? I have it down perfectly now. No more mistakes. I'm a shoo-in for first position."

Across from him, Jonathan's ice-blue eyes were keenly observant but unreadable. "And how are you feeling in the aftermath of your stress test?"

Seth's flames winked out, his face twisting. "I'm fine. I told you. I don't want to talk about it. All of that is in my past, and best left there." He stood, the legs of his chair screeching against the centuries-old floor. "I was weak back then, but I'm not now. I never will be again. I am strong, and powerful, and won't let you and Mr. Fawl down. I believe that the sins must be purged from magic, just as you do. My past has no place in helping to achieve our righteous path."

Angie ducked out of his way as Seth left, closing the door sharply behind him. Jonathan still sat, leaning on his elbows, his kind face solemn. He took a long, loud breath, and returned to the papers and books on astrology, demons, and empowered objects strewn before him. Angie gave them a quick scan, spotting the ancient book he and Daniel had given her to study before her first Victume Ceremony. Her memories around it made her squirm, and she looked away.

The small, round, bronze-framed mirror on the wall over his head still didn't show even a hint of Angie's reflection, and she sighed. Being near Jonathan was as close as she could get to feeling safe, calm, and like she was home, even if he didn't know she was there. It would do.

Angie crossed to the leather therapist couch below the window, settling herself cross-legged and closing her eyes. She turned her mind inward, slowly and carefully clearing her mind, letting each flare and gutter of anxiety, loss, and apprehension slide past with the rest. Once she felt fully calm, she pulled a single, simple intention, a wish for solidity, to the front of her mind and began her long work.

The people she loved needed her. The world needed her. And if she was going to fix anything, she had to start with herself.

CHAPTER TWENTY-NINE

D aniel alternated between obsessively scrying from his Boston home on the outskirts of the increasingly militarized city, rife with roundups for Imperial labor and responding violence as civilians tried to fight back, and retreating to the tranquil house in Maui where the gaps in his memories seemed the most eager to close for several long days. He sat before the obsidian mirror as noon neared, feeling the time of power lend another layer of strength and clarity to his visions as he watched Milton Cartwright tidy away an early supper, lost in the out-of-consciousness experience.

When Milton Voyaged away to a familiar basement, Daniel's concentration almost broke. His heart sped up, and he pushed through the anti-scrying wards fighting him in his attempts to continue spying on the Councilor. The ones keeping him from seeing within were oddly weak and easily circumvented, but Daniel swore quietly when he was effectively prevented from getting any sense of where the tiled basement full of crates was.

He watched through the dark mirror as Cartwright used a scrap of magic to open the heavy door of the key vault cavern. The moment the door stood fully open, before Milton could step inside, Daniel let go of the vision to glance at the gold watch on his wrist. Time stopped with the second hand.

Standing, Daniel snugged up his tie, pulled on his navy suit jacket, and summoned his cane before gathering his concentration and taking two steps forward. Both landed on the thick carpet on his living room floor. Frowning, Daniel tried again, and again the Voyaging failed to click into place with his magic.

Daniel cursed again and closed his eyes, turning his concentration to bringing Jonathan into the time-stop with him, wherever he might be, and sending him a selective beacon. He couldn't remember if his friend had said he'd be at the conference playing his role of Judge, or at the compound trying to convince Hannah to even see him to talk, but suspected he'd enjoy a diversion from either.

"Hey, you called?"

Daniel opened his eyes with a smile. Jonathan stood a few feet away, dropping a handful of Imperial coins into his pocket and tugging down the cuffs of his shirt. "Yes. I got lucky. We have our in. Milton just opened the vaults, and I caught him in the sweet spot." Jonathan lit up. "I tried Voyaging there just now, but it seems the wards are up, or I don't have a clear enough sense of where I'm going."

"Is my bonded token still in there?"

Daniel grinned, feeling his stress ease down into confidence with the tried-and-true pattern. "Yes. That's why I called."

It was Jonathan's turn to grin, and he Voyaged away like he'd been yanked backward by a rope around his middle. A moment later Daniel felt his beacon and, taking a deep breath, tried to Voyage to it. His second step landed not on the thick carpet on his living room floor, but on gleaming tile.

Daniel mirrored Jonathan's delighted triumph, and they both stepped past the frozen Cartwright, up to the faint net of magical threads woven across the opening into the massive cave glittering with keys. Daniel ran his hands over the surface of the magic, carefully testing it and checking it for traps. "Seems safe. Though it's not like we have much choice."

Jonathan nodded, took a deep breath, held it, and stepped through. Daniel was braced for something to happen, feeling almost disappointed when nothing did. He stepped across, feeling no effects, and turned in place. "I wonder where the pen got to that it wasn't spotted and removed, but that you landed just outside in Voyaging to it."

Both men scanned the ground for a minute until Jonathan walked over to the wall right by the doorframe, crouching and reaching into a dark crevice. "Here we go," he said, standing with the pen in his fingers and a cheeky smile. "Great. Now, let's get on."

As Daniel turned his attention to the vast underground fall of keys to locked half-worlds, the daunting nature of the task before them threatened to dampen his spirits. They knew they were in search of about a dozen keys that the Council and, until recently, the Senate, used to banish people out into half-worlds so distant no one ever returned.

Except one, a little voice in his head piped up, and Daniel pulled out his phone, adding the odd belief to his ever-growing list of dots outlining the person who had been lost to the memory of the world. He just wished the hollow feeling would ease. Jonathan's hand on the shoulder of Daniel's suit jacket made him start. He hadn't seen his friend move around to his side, but the comfort was welcome, and he didn't protest.

Jonathan moved away to inspect a small stack of milk crates along a nearby wall as Daniel started scanning over the keys hung along the wall nearest the door. He tried not to let the magnitude of the cavern overwhelm him as he searched for the keys that had been used to condemn dissenters to the Empire to banishment out into the wildest half-worlds for eons.

"That's too easy," Jonathan mumbled, and Daniel tucked his phone away to go see what his friend had found. His cane tapped on the smooth stone floor of the cavern with every other step, and the last echoed off into the distance as he came to a stop. "Look," Jonathan said, tilting the wooden box he was pawing through so Daniel could see better in the dim torchlight.

Inside were a dozen stone keys, each pocked and worn by incalculable age. "You have your shields up, right?" Daniel asked nervously with a glance over his shoulder, his aura teasing up with his anxiety. "I agree. This is too easy. What do you sense from them?"

Jonathan nodded, running his limber, calloused fingers over the stone keys with a trail of his deep blue magic. "The half-worlds tied into them are all the same. Something... fiery and hard. That matches descriptions of the banishment world I found in my research a couple of years ago."

And the first-hand description I've heard. Daniel pushed the thought aside, fighting the itch to jot it down immediately. "Great. Now what?"

Jonathan plucked at one key in the tub with his fingers and magic, his brow furrowing. "We pull out the scrap of magic bound into them, and dissolve it into the air so that they can no longer access the banishment half-world, and we remove that threat hanging over all of us." The two men shared a glance, pregnant with the enormity of what it would mean for the rebellion factions across every language under the sun. "If we take them away entirely, it's more likely the loss would be noticed too soon, or that we might get tracked down."

Daniel nodded, scooting in close beside Jonathan, and did his best to copy what the other man did, teasing out the little wisps of ancient and new magic with his own, painstakingly coaxing it out of the stone it had been bound into, and forcing it to melt away into nothingness before it could return do anything else.

They got through most in a few minutes, and Daniel's mouth twisted to one side when Jonathan started bouncing slightly on the balls of his feet, glancing along the wall they were facing at all the keys like a kid told to sit still in a candy store. "Go. Explore. I'll finish these last three."

Jonathan smiled and moved away deeper into the cave right away, his azure aura thick and bright with delight.

When Daniel finished the last key, he paused for a long moment, pulling his gloves on to help with the faint lingering buzz of the magic on the pads of his fingers, looking over the small crate of now empty, boringly ordinary stone keys. When he turned back to the door of the room as Jonathan rejoined him, what he saw made his gut drop.

Milton Cartwright had moved from the position he'd been originally frozen in, and was squinting hard right at Daniel. Daniel immediately waved for Jonathan to leave, through his own shields in front of the other man.

"We both need to go," Jonathan said in a warped voice Daniel knew only he would be able to hear, but before he could agree or do anything, Milton lunged forward at full speed, throwing out a net of magic that rooted Daniel to the stone floor.

On instinct, Daniel brought his cane up, quick as a flash, willing Jonathan's old magic baked into it to change its shape to a deadly sharp point. Milton stopped barely an inch short of impaling his own throat on the skewer, his eyes beady. He bared his teeth, backing away carefully. "I've got you now," the Councilor hissed. Daniel held his triumphant gaze, desperately willing for Jonathan in the corner of his eye to get the hell out.

"Just me," Daniel said pointedly, pouring every scrap of his considerable unrestrained power into shielding even Jonathan's shields. His friend shook his head, clearly not willing to leave Daniel to his fate. Daniel gave an imperceptible shake of his own in return, and Jonathan vanished, filling Daniel with relief.

"Who else could I have caught?" Milton asked, agitated, casting around for other intruders.

Daniel swore internally, dropping his cane to lean on heavily. He shouldn't have said that. "No one. I'm just following up on that little favor between us, since I wasn't satisfied the first time." Daniel glanced at his watch, wondering how the time-stop had ceased working without him noticing. But the second hand was still. With mounting horror which Daniel tried to hide, he looked back up at the rosy-cheeked man before him. "How..."

"It's called time-stops, isn't it?" Milton said, triumph crowing in his voice. "That secret little skill of yours you've been using to do god knows what behind everyone's backs all these years?" Daniel didn't respond, but knew his silence was answer enough, and one he couldn't help but give. Milton pulled a pocket watch from his vest by its chain, confirming what Daniel already knew. "Miss Hayward put me onto it after her little encounter with you went sideways. She told me time seemed to be jumping forward around you before you knocked her out, and I pieced together the rest." Milton stepped in close, swamping Daniel with cigar smoke and the peculiar scent of poppies Daniel always associated with the older man's aura, and Daniel hastily beefed up his mental defenses, raw revulsion snaking through him. "It's a rare skill, one in several thousand, which is why I never thought of it. But now that I'm a member of the Council, you're not the only one who has learned to play with time."

Milton grabbed the lapels of Daniel's suit jacket with bold hands, jerking him forward with a sickening lurch as Daniel felt time restart. The Senator released him, and Daniel couldn't do more than gape for a long moment, trying to process that he'd just been forcefully pulled out of a time-stop of his own magic and making.

"What's more," Milton said with an evil grin, "I can now sense when you stop time. I feel it, and know that you are doing it somewhere, anywhere in our world and likely the nearest layers of half-worlds. Even better, I can sense where the time disturbance is happening. It calls me right to you." The Councilor laughed, and it was the most bone-chilling sound Daniel had ever heard. "I can pull myself into them with you. After today, likely in a matter of moments as you perceive them. I will teach all of my followers to do the same. You can't hide from me anymore."

Daniel felt the world tilting out from under him as the truth of the threat speared deep. Daniel reached for a sneer to hide behind, for something to push back with. "Don't forget who you're speaking to," he began, but the idea of trying to dredge back up the blackmail leverage he had used in the past refused to rise in the man he was at that moment, falling back away like sand through his intentions.

Milton seemed to see. "Oh, I remember." His voice was deadly soft, full of bitterness. "But your spark has gone out, hasn't it?" Daniel frowned, scrambling to hold on to the deeper meaning that didn't quite form for him between the words. "Let's see how you like a taste of your own medicine."

Daniel waited for a blow—verbal, physical, or magical—to land for several stretched, shallow breaths, and was surprised when Seth appeared a few paces away. "Hey, I got your beacon. Where are we?"

Daniel let his breath ease, almost smiling. No matter what Milton was about to try, Daniel trusted Seth's loyalty, and the conditioning he'd been feeding his recruit sense they'd met. His confidence faltered a moment later when a disguised Councilor appeared, obscured by the layers of magic they'd taught him to use at their meetings, followed quickly by the four others.

"I've caught him red-handed," Cartwright announced in a bold voice to the people gathered behind him, his sharp eyes not leaving Daniel for a moment. "This man, Daniel Fawl, as you can see for yourselves, just committed a high crime in stripping the enchantment from irreplaceable tools of the Patrician Order."

One of the disguised Councilors gasped, pushing past Cartwright and Daniel to the crate behind him, rifling through the keys with a stressed little wiggle. "No, no, no. Gods. Without banishment, there's nothing left to keep people lawful. Collecting the keys to the banishment world was supposed to keep them safe..."

"I also accuse him of undue influence on his recruit. Infecting him with treasonous, seditionist, terroristic ideology designed to undermine the right of order." Milton was clearly delighting in telling these things to Seth directly, undoubtedly hoping to hurt Daniel through the veiled threat of a sponsor's reputation and clout being a reflection of their recruits.

Seth looked horrified and torn, looking back and forth between Daniel and Milton. "No. He has never mentioned anything like that, let alone asked it of me."

Milton seemed to lose a degree of his pompous certainty, and Daniel shrewdly assessed Seth. The red-haired man didn't seem ready to throw Daniel to the wolves, and that was all he could ask for at the moment.

"These are serious charges, worthy of suspension from the Council and possibly all patrician privileges," another Councilor said gravely. "How do you plead?"

Daniel searched inside himself for the right answer. Searched for upset and strain in his aura he could call on to free himself from the magic holding him in place. He searched for black and white, but only found gray, and no aspect of himself that the man he was, with a hole still missing in his heart. Whatever the next minutes, hours, or days might bring, he would simply have to take them in stride.

He did not give an answer.

CHAPTER THIRTY

A ngie hung back, watching from a distance as Daniel stood in the shelter of a tree overhanging the Boston suburb road, the leaves speckling his skin with the headlights of cars passing through the moonless night. Usually, she spent her nights while Daniel slept spying on other corners of the globe, but he'd gone out late, and she'd followed. His face, shifting aura, and tense stillness all spoke of brooding as he watched the small, unhappy family of three through the large windows of the house across the street.

Angie recognized the woman. Thick, brown hair cut in a short bob, maybe a decade older than her. Just the pretty side of average. She turned back to Daniel, feeling fresh wounds ache, wondering why he had sought out his ex-wife, and why he seemed to have no intention of doing anything more with her than some light stalking.

Daniel hung his head, and for a moment Angie saw the disgraced Councilor he had become in the last few days, on a slope downward with no end in sight. She moved in, trying to reach out to him with her magic, her caresses, her gentle words of comfort, but he gave no indication that any were felt. That he even remembered her. The thought wrung her chest as Daniel wiped a tear from his cheek, and Angie gasped.

She looked across the street once more, finally understanding as Daniel turned away, replaying all she'd overheard him say to Jonathan in the month since she'd turned to smoke. He had a hole in his heart he couldn't name. She couldn't blame him for checking to see if someone he may have once loved fit the shape.

Her heart hurt for him as deeply as it did for herself, and she flung her arms around his shoulders, unfelt, as he turned away, and Voyaged.

The next morning, Angie was sitting on the sweeping concrete and wood benches bordering the artistic raised planters in the little clearing from the forest of glass and steel scraping the sky all around her. The square was quieter and cleaner than the first time she'd been there, no longer dominated by construction, traffic or chatter, the oppressive blanket of the ever-increasing tension and military presence weighing heavily on everything.

Jonathan sat beside her, oblivious to her presence, and Angie breathed in the clean, ocean smell of him, glad the paving stones beneath their feet no longer stank of stale beer, or the air around them of cigarette smoke. She looked up at the doors of the Suardo Building as Jonathan did, seeing Imperial-uniformed ushers haul the doors wide, a large gaggle of beautifully dressed patricians spilling out.

"Well?" Jonathan said, standing, and Angie followed in his wake as Daniel limped forward to meet him, looking dour.

"I've been removed from the Senate, effective immediately, and barred from holding patrician office ever again at any level." Angie's stomach twisted, and if her face could be seen, she knew it would show her deep pity and concern. "The good news is, because the Victume Ceremony and the solstice are in two days, they aren't stripping me of my recruit this late in the game. Though I very much doubt I'll ever be given another one."

Jonathan shifted, glancing around. "Shit. Well, listen. I got an earful from Léa this morning. She's really upset, talking about how we need to have backup plans. Or backups of ourselves, maybe. She's not very coherent, although she seems to think I have some special part to play. Is there any chance we might get me into the seat you're vacating?"

Daniel shook his head, but was cut short before he could reply. When Angie saw why, she scowled.

"Passing along the good news?" Milton Cartwright said with a sneer, sauntering up, Marissa Hayward trailing in his wake. Daniel, Jonathan, and Angie all just glowered, and Milton chuckled, stepping in close to address Daniel like there was no one else there. "You are alone now. Unprotected. A month ago, you were untouchable. Look at you now."

Daniel's careful composure cracked. "What do you know about it? What did you do?" Between the two men,

Angie saw Marissa's brow furrow as she took a step closer.

Milton ignored the questions, his attention drifting lazily right over the invisible Angie to Jonathan, looking him up and down. "And let's see how many more rats we can burn out in the coming month. Or, better yet, remove from our hallowed halls with poison set out for them to take back to the nest."

Both Daniel and Jonathan looked ready to swing, which Angie definitely was. "If that's a jab at my family," Jonathan began, but was cut off by a full belly laugh from Cartwright.

"Wouldn't dream of it," the Transvallian drawled, a stubby hand covering his infuriatingly smug smile.

As the Councilor turned away, beckoning for Marissa to follow, a tiny glint of light moved over Angie's eye, and she squinted against the glare, looking all around for the source, since it seemed to go against the direction of the late-morning sun, or any instinctually dismissible reflections off nearby buildings. She caught Cartwright pause before stepping into the limo he had just helped Marissa into, smiling, and when she followed where he was looking, her memory of blood ran cold.

"Daniel," she shrieked, trying to shove him as the sniper on the roof high above shifted his angle, and the reflected light off the scope left her awareness. She threw her full weight against his chest, panic and desperation filling her smoke with cedar and gasoline smoke, and Daniel stepped back, blinking in confusion.

A shot rang out, and Daniel reeled back, falling to his knees on the hard concrete, his cane skittering away, clutching his chest.

"No!" Angie screamed, throwing herself over him, knowing it was pointless, as Jonathan crouched down below the lip of the nearby bench, one arm shielding his wide eyes as he tried to find the source.

"Up there!" One of the patricians nearby shouted, pointing at the rooftop, and a handful of heavily armed centurions that had been patrolling the yard at the heart of the patrician quarter of London all stampeded toward the doors to the luxury apartment building the sniper had shot from.

Jonathan appeared at Angie's side, pulling Daniel up, shielding him from the known vantage point with his body. Angie was rolled aside in her smoke form, billowing and twisting back around in an instant, desperate and scared. "Dan, Dan, are you alright?"

Daniel's face was twisted with a grimace, but when he removed the hand gloved in light brown leather from his chest just above his heart, it wasn't marked with blood. A crowd of onlookers, including a pale Marissa, was gathering around close enough that Angie wasn't worried about more snipers, and she watched, stunned, as Daniel unbuttoned his shirt to reveal a slim body armor vest beneath.

Angie let out a manic sound of relief, half laugh and half sob. She pressed her ethereal hands over her mouth, her eyes not leaving Daniel's somewhat shocked face for an instant. "You're okay," Angie whispered, feeling something shift deep inside her as she processed what had just happened, and what had been miraculously avoided.

A crackle of gunfire broke the air behind her with a clatter of broken glass. "We should go," Daniel said, the last of the color draining from his complexion.

"Yep," Jonathan replied tersely, hauling Daniel to his feet, who summoned his cane back to him. "My gut says this is about to get ugly."

A body hit the ground from several stories up, making Angie turn as several people gasped. It was a woman in civilian clothes. "Stay out of our way. We are on official Imperial business," a voice shouted from inside the broken wall of glass, the soldiers moving out of sight up the staircase just inside. In unison, the other plebeian civilians on the sidewalk bubbled up in anger, screaming at the expensively dressed patricians and nearby centurions, and a few patrician adepts nearby Voyaged away, adding fear and screams of magic to the brewing conflict.

Angie didn't notice that Daniel and Jonathan were among them until they were gone, apparently deciding the cat was already out of the bag. Someone stumbled through her from the side, and Angie wished with all she had that she could bring her powers to bear. She tried for the thousandth time as the patricians fled, leaving their minions to face off with the plebeians.

As every time before, Angie felt her fire, her intention-fueled magic, try to rise, but fall short. She closed her eyes, pulling up the image of Daniel standing, clearly alive in his protective vest, and felt that part of her shift. It was all still just out of reach, but a dark little voice in her heart told her that when she reached it, there were world-ending, or world-saving, demons of flame restlessly waiting to emerge. She opened her eyes, swallowing hard, and did a quick mental tally of how she might best use the two days she had before the Victume Ceremony to figure out how to make it so Demitria wasn't going to her death.

Maybe none of them would make it out alive, but she'd be damned if she went out without a fight.

CHAPTER THIRTY-ONE

The closing ball of the English Conference was a rotten, wild imitation of what it had once aspired to be, and Daniel found himself truly hoping that it was the last. Or at least the last he'd have to attend.

A dark, glittering, mirthless circus spun around him as he made his way through the grand hall. Streamers draped from the chandeliers high overhead, paid acrobats, spinning down long waterfalls of satin. Contortionists and fire breathers were stationed on pillars around the edges of the room. Daniel held himself back from looking to see if they were enchanted plebeians, truly impressive golems, or pure illusion. On the chance it was the first, he didn't want to know.

A strange noise from the back near the mirrored wall made him turn, and he found Supreme Justice Noah Byrne sitting in court beside his mentor, Milton Cartwright, surrounded by their chosen posse of admirers and beautiful women. Milton was dribbling down the neck of a handsome young man, clearly ignoring his quarry's obvious disgust and unease, almost seeming to gain pleasure from it. Anger at yet another way Milton didn't give a shit about anyone but himself and was ready to prove it publicly made Daniel's aura lash out from him, hot and dry, and he quickly apologized to Lady Braithwaite as he passed.

The floor was covered with a mix of fluids, bodily and otherwise which Daniel tried not to think about, using his Air aura to filter out the smells of alcohol and sex. A gaggle of recruits nearby, ranging in age, at a glance, from thirty-ish to seventy, were shrieking with malicious laughter, bullying a poor, unassuming man in the middle who clearly wasn't having any fun, his dull, camo-green aura getting more agitated by the minute. Daniel hardened his expression, making a beeline for them, using his aura to take just enough air from the bully's longs to break their pattern, and taking dark delight in the act as they scattered.

"Thanks," the man said, ruffling his graying buzz-cut sheepishly.

"Go home," Daniel advised. "You've made your appearance, and your sponsor can report your position in the ceremony in the morning. Leave before things get worse." The man nodded gratefully and quickly disappeared into the crowd toward the heavy carved-brass doors.

Five minutes later, Daniel found himself not far from Noah's court, and watched with loathing as Milton Cartwright pressed a glass of bright pink punch into Seth's hand, the words he dribbled into his ear lost to the cacophony of music, chatter, and the cries of the performers. Daniel pressed his way through the throng as Milton moved away along the perimeter of the room, while Seth was momentarily distracted by one of Noah's conquests who had chosen him as her next pole to grind against.

Daniel reached him just as Seth lifted the glass to his lips, his attention fully on the pretty blonde woman dancing against him, striking the glass from his hand. It shattered across the floor, creating a brief moment of calm in the chaos as people jumped away. "Don't drink the punch that man hands you," Daniel hissed through his teeth, stepping in unnervingly close to Seth before he could protest.

"Why not?" Seth asked, his demeanor standing down from confrontational to the familiar half-bow of obsequious uncertainty.

"Look at it properly," Daniel replied, pointing at the spilled liquid across the floor with his cane. "It's toxic." He watched as Seth frowned, double-blinking several times to activate his auric vision, before realization slowly bloomed across his face. When he turned to Daniel, his face was full of the sycophant adoration that had all but disappeared since the half-world key cavern.

Daniel huffed through his nose, hoping that the way his face drew in would be mistaken as disgust of the fuchsia magic infecting the punch, and not for the way his recruit regarded him. "Be better than them. Be smarter. Keep your wits about you, and use their vices against them, instead of letting them corrupt you."

Seth nodded, his eyes wide. "I'm sorry. I lost sight of our divine quest. I know you told me to pretend I am just as sinful as the rest." Seth's voice dropped, and a thrill of unease climbed Daniel's spine. "But I promise I am true to our purpose. I haven't lost my way in bringing down all these sinners. We will still have our righteous victory. I swear."

Daniel swore he could hear Seth's desire to call him 'master' and hid the way his whole being cringed. "Good lad. Now, just be more careful."

A gentle tap on his elbow pulled Daniel's attention away, and he found Marissa Hayward at his elbow, a selection of pastries and chocolates artfully laid out on a small plate she was extending toward him. "No thanks," he said, turning away from the offered sweets. "I have no appetite these days."

Only when Marissa spoke in a small, anxious voice did Daniel really look at her face, finding her pale and shocked, still staring at the spilled enchanted wine. "You knew?"

Daniel thought fast, deciding on the truth. "I do now." He shrugged, resting both hands on the gold handle of his cane to keep them still. "I don't blame you, for what it's worth. Not really. I can see the pink in your eyes even now."

Marissa squirmed, glancing at the punch turning sticky on the floor, the cleaning golems too busy to get to it with any speed. "So you forgive me?"

Daniel huffed a mirthless grunt of laughter through his nose. "Never. I just don't care about you enough to be angry." He let his Air aura, beaten to submission by his internal bids for control these days, judder up in a cocoon of buffeting icy wind to drive home his rejection. "In fact, please consider yourself free from all debts or ties to me, as I think more space between us is well called for. The secrets I once used to ask you for favors will never pass my lips. Rest easy."

Daniel started to turn away, but Marissa grabbed the sleeve of his coat, and Daniel let his aura blister the hand that touched him with ruthless heat and cold in a concentrated coil of his magic. "You never get to touch me again," he snarled, rounding on her and backing her against a nearby table, not caring for her pain in the slightest as the anger and betrayal he felt around her slipped their leashes.

"I'm sorry," Marissa gasped, cradling her hurt hand to her ample chest. "I just, I need to tell you while you're sober. Ragnarök. I can't leave you behind, even if you hate me now. I promise I'll find a way to sneak you in before the Threshold closes. Just listen—"

"I know all about it," Daniel growled, his face inches from Marissa's. "I also know you didn't give a single fuck about my consent, experiences, wishes, or feelings when you decided you wanted to own me and did whatever you had to do to break me enough that I'd submit."

Marissa's expression turned simpering. "I've wanted you since we met. Are you really going to hate me for trying to love you?"

"You've only ever wanted possession," Daniel snapped back, his anger rising higher. "Not love. You would have been happy to have me as a mindless puppet." Daniel glanced at Noah Byrne nearby, not sure why. "That's not love."

"How do you know so much more about love than me to say so?" Marissa started, but a look from Daniel made her shrink back. The hole in his chest yawned so wide with her words he feared it would swallow him whole, and his own lashed out from him as desperate, clawing bids to not fall into the abyss where someone he loved should be.

"I don't know. But I do know you took something precious from me. And I don't care how many sweets you bring me, how many secrets or betrayals you offer, or how many times you apologize. *I. Will. Never. Forgive you for that.*"

As subtle as the memory of a dream, Daniel thought he saw the outline of a woman form from smoke at the edge of his vision, her hands pressed over her mouth below glittering eyes, but when he looked, there was nothing there. He turned back to Marissa, his outburst broken, and bowed his head as his jaw clenched. "Goodbye, Marissa. May whatever path you choose bring you less suffering than you have brought me."

He turned away, eager to put some distance between them, and as he did so blindly, he crashed right into Jasper Rose, who was a Judge on the English Court. "My apologies, Councilor," Daniel said, almost without thinking, watching the plump patrician shake a sprinkle of white wine from one of their long, thick, gray curls.

Judge Rose waved him away. "It's alright. None of this matters in the grand scheme."

Half an hour later, Daniel was nearing his breaking point of wanting to leave before the announcement of the selection for position in the Victume Ceremony. He released an audible sigh of relief when Noah Byrne wove his way up to the small podium that had been erected in front of the staircase at the far end of the hall. The performers all stilled and stepped into the shadows, and drunken cheering spread out toward the front of the hall as people realized what was happening.

"Right," Noah hiccoughed, his cheeks stained by the wine he had undoubtedly been consuming all night. "Short and sweet this year. In first position, we have Miss Bailey Johnson!" The pretty blonde woman that had been grinding on Seth earlier leapt to her feet with squeals of delight, as people cheered for the obvious nepotism pick.

Daniel was swamped with a dizzying wave of anxiety and déjà vu that made him totally miss the second position pick. Why did he feel dread mixed with desire around the announcement of the top five placements? It didn't make any sense for Either Marissa six years ago, or Seth now.

Daniel was jarred out of his thoughts when Noah announced, "Seth Laufey for third position!" to raucous cheering. Daniel took a deep breath, forcing a smile, and gave Seth a proud, unmistakable nod of approval when his recruit's beaming eyes found him through the crowd.

No sooner had he straightened than an arm reached out from the alcove behind a tapestry nearby, and Daniel found himself hauled into the claustrophobic space with an irate Milton Cartwright. "You rigged it," Milton spluttered, his jowls quivering. "You must have. I told Noah explicitly. You must have rigged it..." His words were syrupy in Daniel's ears, and he checked his mental shields, making sure it wasn't more than the Councilor not wishing to be understood by eavesdroppers.

"What. Like you did as Supreme Justice?" Daniel replied coolly, refusing to rise to the other man's anger. "Even if I could, I don't need to. My recruit should have been first position on merit alone, and his skills are above reproach." Daniel just watched as Cartwright spluttered incoherently, trying to process that the man before him had likely tried to have him taken out by a sniper the day before.

"Well, that may be," Milton said, clearly grasping for a different attack after his first one failed to sting. "But what's in it for you? You're done in the Patrician Order. No prestige through your recruit can fix that for you. After tomorrow, you might as well run back to the fucking nigger bitch who has you pussy-whipped and stay the fuck out of my affairs."

The description of Dawn caught Daniel off guard for the briefest moment, and when it cleared, he felt something click into place in his chest, pushed by defensive anger for his friend, and pulled by the sweet relief of letting go of all his masks. He leaned in close to Milton Cartwright's face, his own an open expression of confident disdain. Cartwright leaned away, clearly not prepared for Daniel to do anything other than cower as he had for a dozen such conversations in the past.

When he spoke, Daniel's voice was low and dangerous. "There was a day I took orders from her. Maybe even more recently that I'll admit. But now I only act by my own motivation. If someone else's goals align with mine, fine, but I'm done taking orders from anyone." The truth in his own words surprised and bolstered Daniel, and he felt an old, aching tightness around his ribs ease. "I don't know what you will come at me with next. What your next move is in your quest to destroy the world I once loved and the people I still do, but I will be ready, and I won't let you win. As the appointment of my recruit to third position shows, I'm not the only one falling from grace and influence, and you would do well to wake up and acknowledge that."

Milton's cheeks lost their ruddy hue, and he looked torn between stubborn anger and utter confusion as Daniel turned away, pushing the heavy brocade drapes aside with his cane. "You took something from me. And when I learn what it was, I will take from you in equal measure."

CHAPTER THIRTY-TWO

A clear, low note sounded from a ceremonial horn, and Daniel banished the fountain pen seeped in deep blue magic into Seth's trouser pocket beneath his long, white robes as the recruit turned away, grinning. Daniel held a breath of fresh, clear predawn air, waiting to see if the other man noticed as he and the other thirty-four recruits took their places among the towering monument of Stonehenge, but Seth seemed oblivious.

He released the breath, glancing around at the other sponsors and loyalist patricians gathered on the dewy grass. None seemed to be paying him any attention. Daniel pulled out his phone, glancing at the odd lock screen image as had become a habit over the last month, slipping it back into his pocket when the picture still held only him.

Jonathan strolled over to stand beside Daniel, his hands shoved in his pockets, both looking ahead at the altar stone at the center of the grove of pillars, just visible between the largest trilithon at the head of the inner horseshoe and the one beside it, across from Seth's position, as Lord Braithwaite marshaled them all into place.

"What do you think?" Jonathan said, scanning over the tense and subdued gathering.

Daniel worked his jaw, following suit and checking his shields. He watched the acting delegation to build a new English Court lock making their stately procession up the avenue to the east, past the heel stone, all smiling smugly. "No, I don't think our last-ditch attempts to leverage had any effect. My removal from office declawed us. None of them will help us."

"Perhaps it's for the best. Sometimes things have to finish breaking before they can start healing." Jonathan rocked back, blinking rapidly as his brows knit, muttering, "Sorry. Déjà vu."

When the horn sounded for a second time, Daniel watched as the rainbow auras of the thirty-five recruits all flared and joined, encapsulating the holy site and the massive power flowing within it, just as the first rays of the rising sun touched the very top of the altar stone. The geyser of magic cycling through it cascaded out in an endless loop that curved down around the outer ring of stones, back beneath the ground to cycle up again through the column of rock.

As Noah Byrne and Milton Cartwright stepped up close around the tall stone at the center of English magic, its solidity yielding to the key of the fresh, combined magic of the recruits, he braced himself. Almost immediately, Daniel felt the repression of his magic begin. Like an exhale that didn't stop, no matter how desperately he tried to breathe in—a bleeding artery of his magic that wouldn't slow, sapping his strength, color, and hope.

Beside him, Jonathan's chest heaved, but Daniel had felt it before. He breathed slowly and deeply, concentrating hard on holding on to whatever scraps of his aura he could as they were ripped away, the thumb of one gloved hand rubbing slow arcs over the other. Swallowing against the panic he couldn't hold at bay, his mind turned to Voyaging into the heart of the ceremony happening before him, but felt the membrane of the insular ritual like a brick wall to his intentions, impenetrable from the outside.

Again, Daniel fished out his phone for the comfort of the ritual, but when his eyes flicked to the screen, he did a double take and stopped breathing. When he resumed, it was all he could do to not hyperventilate. The smoky, ghostly outline of a woman was fading into the picture with excruciating slowness, her features nothing more than shades of gray.

Daniel looked at Jonathan beside him, holding out his phone. The other man also did a double take, his whole being becoming electric with energy when he saw what he was being shown. When he met Daniel's gaze, blinking rapidly, both men smiled slightly, and quickly looked around. Daniel saw a few people among the hundreds frown or tilt their heads, but most were oblivious.

Daniel banished his cane to cradle his phone in both hands, no longer feeling the sickening loss of his magic. Little by little, one excruciating minute at a time, he watched as the woman in the photo solidified by degrees, soot-thin layers of vague memories returning to him as she did.

In the edges of his awareness, the flocks of patricians were becoming more and more agitated, whispers, questions, and unease flowing past him in currents. "Incoming," Jonathan muttered, five minutes into the ceremony as the line of the sun slowly inched down the ancient stones.

Daniel looked up just in time to see a dozen patricians descending on him, many others watching but hanging back. "What's happening?" Lord Braithwaite demanded, his forest-green aura fracturing with distress. "How did you remove someone from all of our memories? Who are they? Why have we all just started remembering?"

Gripping his phone tighter, Daniel used a scrap of his newly restrained aura to blast hot and dry in their faces, pushing them back, not bothering to control his overwhelm or emotion. "I didn't do anything," Daniel said, shame and guilt twisting through him, "and I suspect you will all have your other answers at the same moment I do."

Jonathan was poised, ready to spring, barely paying attention. Daniel followed where he was looking, and slipped his phone back safely into his pocket as he watched the line of light and shadow inching down the altar stone, closer and closer to the knot of magic at the core which the governing agents were engrossed in building. When the line reached the top edge of the new Focal Nucleus lock, Jonathan Voyaged.

He landed almost on top of Seth, who reeled back, cracking his skull into the stone. Daniel quickly brought his shields back up to full strength as someone reached for him, Voyaging to join Jonathan the moment the beacon was raised. "Go. Now," he commanded Seth the moment he landed, discreetly summoning back the aura-bonded token pen that had given them their Trojan Horse access into the heart of the ceremony. Seth obeyed instantly, and Daniel smiled as the gap he left in the network of intertwined auras spluttered, clearly a weakness in the defenses.

Daniel and Jonathan both then turned their full attention to the two fully empowered patricians around the altar stones, concentrating their shields just as the first blow of barbed magic landed. Casey and Demitria landed just behind Jonathan, and Daniel quickly pulled the young man with spiky blond hair forward. "You won't have been repressed yet, as they thought you're loyal before now. Get your shields up, quick."

The three men shoved their way forward, forcing the two defending their new creation in the altar stone back. Demitria followed in their wake, small and clearly terrified, her hands tucked tight under her arms, as the remaining thirty-four recruits hung back, unsure what to do, some unable to see what was happening from their places along the outer ring.

Jonathan's shield at the forefront buckled under the attack Noah was raining down on it, but a wall of gold replaced it in an instant, and Dawn stepped forward, joining them. Daniel glanced skyward, relieved to see the delicate lattice of gold all around the monument he knew would stop Noah or Milton from beaconing in any backup as Jonathan had. Even as Daniel allowed himself a moment of relief that things were going to plan, he couldn't help but wonder how the ghost fading back into his memory bit-by-bit was going to throw it all off.

"You have no right," Noah Byrne bellowed as he and Milton continued to hurl magic at the three men now stationed defensively around the altar stone. Daniel largely ignored them, deflecting and countering each new attack, glad Casey could take the brunt of the force with his unrestricted magic, as Dawn quickly positioned Demitria behind the altar stone.

"Get them," Milton demanded, gesturing for the watching recruits to join in, but Jonathan anticipated. Daniel heard the words, "stand down, hold the line," layered on top of what the Councilor had really said, and smiled, knowing the onlookers would only have heard the latter.

Noah's attack faltered as Demitria lifted an Imperial dollar coin between her slender fingers, her whole, determined concentration on the lock of magic within the half-insubstantial stone before her as Dawn whispered last-minute guidance and encouragement in her ear. "Tell Niko I love him," Demitria said, and Daniel's heart clenched. As she plunged her fist holding the coin into the Focal Nucleus, her flesh turning to stone as her Earth aura adjusted to the torrential magic that quickly engulfed her, many things happened at once.

Daniel remembered watching another young woman doing the same three years earlier, layered with memories of processing it afterward, and threw his intention out to stop time for Demitria.

Time in the world started skipping like a broken record as a bone-chilling demonic screech rent the air, and Noah Byrne ducked and ran. The watching recruits scattered with him, and Daniel pulled off his gloves as his palms became sweaty.

Milton Cartwright snarled, dropping his attack, but Daniel didn't care. He didn't need this time-stop to be safe or a secret. "You'll pay for this," Milton said, turning away and Voyaging out of the circle as the first deadly, glasslike shard of shattering demon skewered the soil where he'd been standing a moment before. Jonathan's shields expanded to the perimeter the moment Milton was gone, all others having fled before him, and Daniel and Casey quickly matched.

Daniel felt sweet, overwhelming relief as his full auric strength returned to him as the thread of tan and orchid-pink magic that had repressed him and anyone else deemed dissidents was ripped from the altar stone and disintegrated. Daniel only got a glimpse of the shouting, churning hoard of patricians outside the monument as the first attacked their shields before he had to leap to one side, redirecting his shields, as another shard narrowly missed him.

The creature's death cries looped over and over in the early morning as the demon's explosive exposure to a foreign half-world ripped apart the new lock of English magic as it was forced from its safe home of the coin by Demitria's careful intention. As Daniel turned his full attention back to her, his heart skipped a beat. "Angie..."

The smoky outline of a woman he finally remembered, her core made of fire, was wrapped around Demitria, hugging her tightly from behind. Her elfin features beside Demitria's head, whispering to her intensely, eyes closed, were so dear and familiar to Daniel that he almost cried out. He watched in awe as Angie's whole being became blue and white flames, making the black stone Demitria had morphed into molten and alive. Demitria lifted the hand not holding the coin to grasp Angie's arm wrapped across her chest, her statuesque face etched with helpless, pained elation.

The demon in the shredding lock blasted apart with an echoing scream as Angie yanked Demitria back out of the torrential waterfall of magic flowing through the altar stone and Daniel flung himself to the ground, covering his head as the last deadly shards of dying demon speared through rock and grass, glancing off the shields of those present. When he looked up, he searched for the same pair of flames and smoke, but didn't see them.

He stood slowly, assessing any lingering danger, as Jonathan, Casey, and Dawn did the same. The air was thick with mahogany smoke, and Daniel's vision blurred with emotion. Casey had an unreadable, twisted look on his face, staring at the spot Daniel couldn't see on the other side of the resolidified altar stone, twice his width and several feet taller, and Daniel quickly moved around to see.

"Angie," he whispered. Daniel's heart felt ready to leap out of his chest with joy. Angie knelt on the ground over a shaken and groggy Demitria, surrounded by the last fading shards of the Patrician Order's attempt to once more rule and exploit English magic. Dawn let out a whoop and Jonathan was grinning from ear to ear as Daniel inched forward.

"I couldn't let what happened to me happen to you." Angie didn't look up from Demitria's face, her hands braced on the grass on either side of her, her voice tight. She stood, her back to Daniel and the others, her shoulders tight.

As Daniel reached out to Angie like she was a ghost he couldn't believe lived, he saw her skin start to shift back toward smoke, and clamped a hand around her bare arm with a thrill of panic. Angie solidified fully in an instant as the vibration of his skin got to her, her knees buckling. Daniel pulled her toward him, holding her upright as they both fell to their knees, shifting his bare hands to her sides over her shirt as her eyes fluttered.

"No, Angie," Daniel said urgently, almost drowned out by the clamor of angry patricians held at bay by his shields. "You need to wake up. Come on."

Angie swayed, half-coming to, and when her bleary eyes landed on Daniel's face, they snapped into focus. "You see me?" Her hands grabbed at his shoulders. "You can touch me? Hear me?" Her voice broke, and she swallowed hard, her eyes brimming. "You know me?"

"Yes," Daniel said, half-crying, half-laughing, as he drank in Angie's auburn hair and freckled cheeks, the smell of her smoke and the sound of her voice. "I do now. I'm sorry I didn't before."

Angie's smile stretched to mirror his own, and she sniffed. "Thanks. I'm sorry I lost control and left you."

Daniel's insides dropped with a lurch, and he released her sides, leaning away slightly as she released the shoulders of his suit jacket as they both stood. "It was all a set-up. What you saw, it was all a lie. I swear on all that I am, I swear on Jonathan—"

"I know," Angie said quickly, sobbing a laugh and covering it with a pale hand. "I heard all the confessions, saw all the proof while I was smoke."

Daniel blinked. *She had been present, observant, all the time he hadn't even remembered who she was.* Angie must have seen his churning emotions on his face, and flung herself into his arms. Daniel hugged her back tightly, careful not to touch her skin, but wishing he never had to let go. When he finally did, for the briefest flash he saw his own uncertainty around if he should try to kiss her reflected in her beautiful face, and they both stepped apart.

Daniel cleared his throat and Angie scratched the back of her neck, wincing. "What now?" Daniel asked as the escalating attacks on his shields became a strain to resist, and he felt Dawn's fail.

"I don't know," Angie replied, her whole being zeroed in on him like he was the only man alive. "We move forward, the two of us together, for today. We figure out tomorrow after that."

CHAPTER THIRTY-THREE

A ngie waited until Daniel nodded, before shifting her attention away to the chaos only fifty feet away outside the ring of stones. "Can they see in here?"

Daniel shook his head. "No."

"Is there more that needs to be done?"

It was Dawn's turn to answer as she pulled Demitria to her feet. "No, we're done. They can't unlock the space enough to try building a new lock from scratch again for another three years." Demitria smiled, her olive skin pale, as did Angie. An extra loud scream made them all turn to where a fight seemed to be starting among the gathered patricians. "Not that it seems like they'd even try..."

"Can we hear some more before we leave?" Angie asked and Jonathan nodded, looking bewildered. His layer of auric shields flickered, and a voice rose above the rest, despite the strain it clearly added to him. Angie turned in place, peering around the stone pillars, trying to find the speaker.

"English has fallen," a man with a bushy mustache and Italian accent shouted, backing away across the field toward the underground Threshold hidden beneath the nearest stand of trees. "Fallback and hold strong. The

Senate will not be taken." Among those leaving with him in a tight clump were Milton and Noah, both looking murderous, but as Seth ran up to join him, he was rebuffed.

"They Voyaged to you," the man with the mustache said, glowering. "You, specifically. You are a traitor."

"I'm not," Seth replied, the deep orange flames of his aura showing his offense. "I am loyal to my sponsor, and he is loyal to order. I don't know who that was illusioned to look like when the ceremony was invaded, but it wasn't really him. It couldn't be. He would never do that."

Milton scoffed, but was silenced. "No? Then prove it. This has pushed us over the edge. Play your part in what's to come, and we might believe you." Seth grinned as the cluster of high-ranking patricians turned away, his fire flaring brighter as he Voyaged away.

Daniel opened his mouth to speak, but the color drained from his face when Angie heard three loud rooster crows echo over the field, seeming to come from the sky at large. She didn't have to ask what it meant, feeling fresh adrenaline hit her system as Daniel beckoned them all to move.

"Ragnarök's been called. My shields are about to break, and there's no way we can finesse our way out of this one. We need to go."

⎯⊚✦⊚⎯

Jonathan folded Angie into a crushing hug as soon as they got to the little green of Dawn's compound. "I missed you," she whispered, and Jonathan squeezed her a little tighter.

"Me too. I'm sorry I forgot you. I will always be here for you, one way or another."

She didn't let go until he did, looking around to greet Casey properly as well, but he'd disappeared among the quiet, stone-faced onlookers. Daniel, who hovered close at her shoulder, glanced at his watch and Angie grabbed his wrist. "No, please don't." She swallowed. "Please don't stop time. I don't... I can't... I've been separated from reality too much recently." She knew she wasn't doing a good job of explaining the sickening lurch she felt at the thought of being moved half a degree away from existence again so soon, or the way being solid again still threatened to revert to smoke, too delicate for any more immediate shocks to her sense of reality, but Daniel seemed to understand.

"I wasn't going to. They aren't safe or secret anymore, and would bring Milton right to us." Angie's shock must have shown on her face, and Daniel frowned. "You weren't there for that?"

"No. I was with you while you were scrying, then you must have stopped time, because I blinked, and you weren't there. I didn't see you again until you came home, and I started piecing together that you'd been fired from the Council. But good," she added, looking up at the last hints of evening light fading from the Pacific coast sky. "We need time to keep moving forward if we are going to get the other language locks broken, too, as sunrise reaches each."

"No," Dawn said quickly, hundreds of watching adepts turning their attention to her. "Ragnarök's the priority. Everything has to be set aside while we deal with the more immediate threat."

"I disagree. We should strike while the iron's hot and kill two birds with one stone." Angie looked around at her friends, ignoring the strangers, as frustration warmed the aura of smoke she was itching to let loose after being dormant for so many long weeks. "We do it now, or we likely never do. We can get the holy sites we missed between Latin and English at noon in those time zones as a secondary time of power *if* we can stay a step ahead and have distractions." A few people were nodding their approval, and Angie shamelessly reached into the knowledge she'd gleaned in her smoke form, not just from Milton and his kind, but from Dawn. "Italian must be the last to fall, as it's closely tied with Latin in the half-world, closing the renewal cycle loop."

"It's a death sentence," Dawn said, shaking her head with a dismissive wave. "You can't save every single adept who puts a demon in the lock, and from what I saw, you'd have to be smoke again to do so, and it looked to me like Dan's skin curse is the only thing that pulled you out of that, so I doubt you want to risk reverting."

Angie's lips pursed, wishing it wasn't the truth. "There's more to it. Anyone can do what I did. The person just needs an external force of momentum to get them out of the flow before it's too late. When Daniel did it for me three years ago, the blast through the flow of magic also knocked my astral self out of my body, so when I felt

Demitria try to separate like that, I just used my magic to hold her together."

"Half of us have enough skill with astral traveling to do that," Jonathan said softly, his face lit with passionate interest. He looked around when he realized everyone had turned to him, shrugging. "It makes sense. The ancient book that's been our primary source for understanding how to influence the Focal Nuclei says something about 'one must become two, must become one', and this is a better explanation than any I came up with."

"Besides that," Angie added, jumping in before her point could get derailed, "it's simple. Shove a demon into the lock, force the demon out using magic, fill it with the intention for the lock to break, and let its reaction with the world that isn't its own do the rest. I've seen you all practicing that much."

"This is all a distraction," Olivia piped up nearby, the frizz of her graying orange hair under the light of the lamppost giving her a halo. "Our priority needs to be getting ourselves and our loved ones to the locked Eden world, or somewhere else safe from the devastation that is now hurtling toward us. It's the safest bet. We should reserve our energy for dealing with the loyalist patricians on the other side, in a smaller contest. We can easily overwhelm them with numbers there. They have been limited these last three years by only unlocking adepts they can be reasonably sure will fall in line with their lies and be sympathetic to their sadism. We haven't, and have several times over their numbers." Angie could see many of the listeners growing worried, nodding along.

"We should take the win of our unrestrained powers, and the continued lack of magical English patrician control over plebeian forces, and get out while the gettin's good."

"You're missing the point," Angie said, exasperated, glad when both Daniel and Jonathan gave her encouraging nods. "The goal is for this world to not get destroyed. You are arguing in favor of saving our few hundred, few thousand lives like it's morally better. I'm saying we need to push ahead now to spare *billions* from whatever genocidal calamity the Patrician Order has planned to wipe this world clean of any hope or potential of standing up to then, likely nuclear annihilation. If we try to run to the safe haven they have planned for themselves, I guarantee they see us coming, head us off, and just drop the bombs sooner."

"And they won't see us coming with your plan?" Olivia countered.

"Probably, but it doesn't matter. It takes careful balance to open and change or add to the locks. We just proved that less than a dozen can throw that balance off and destroy the locks which are stealing our magic to puppet the armies into slaughtering civilians who dare complain about the horrible state of the wider world, and Gods know what else. That leaves more than enough of us to attack the Senate and Council outright. They won't see it coming, and we'll keep them distracted while we free the powers of the other languages' dissenters, who can then help us!"

"The Senate bunkers are all in the true world, often in major cities," Dawn said, folding her arms tight across the front of her scuffed denim jacket. "Are you suggesting we start hurling magic in front of thousands of ignorant inepts, causing mass panic?"

"It wouldn't be that bad," Daniel interjected. "Awareness of magic has been slowly leaking out into the wider world for three years now. Pleb—I mean, inepts, are more open to the reveal than you might think, if not always with a positive reaction. Our departure from London the day before last proved that."

Dawn's lip curled. "Maybe, but that has been creating violence between those who believe and those who don't, which we'd be adding to."

A male voice she didn't know well made Angie turn. "There are other considerations." Nikolaos was holding Demitria close, his dark eyes under his mop of curls serious. "We're all pretty sure that I'd be a true Seer if my magic was unlocked, like Miss Renard, and we've all seen what true Sight has done to her. If the Greek language Court is broken, the gift will come to me, and I may lose my sanity, taking everything else I love with it." Demitria whimpered, burying her face into Niko's abdomen, and he wrapped his arms more protectively around her. "Every language on the planet will have people like me who will get unlocked to their poisonous gifts like Léa was when English was broken. Now she is losing herself, and she didn't even get to grow up to be an adult yet."

Angie's confident heat retreated, replaced with guilt. She was spared responding by Daniel, who asked, "Do we have any guidance from her?"

Dawn sighed, grinding the heel of a hand into her eye. "No. Léa's rarely coherent these days. Most of what she says is about immortality and the importance of backing up critical parts of a system."

Jonathan squirmed in Angie's peripheral vision, and when she looked at him, he winced. "I hate to be the one to say this, but there are more elements in play we aren't considering. Like raw resource production through magic that could mean an end to hunger, thirst, and homelessness for the rest of time, which we are still assuming is something the Council keeps locked away. Wrestling that power back away from them would mean a utopia in this world, and likely the ability to emigrate to others. But the Council will never let that go unless we force them."

Angie smiled, delighted that her best friend was finally on her side around that. "That's right. They can't be above the rest if no one is held down below them. They can't keep us too distracted, desperate, and broken to exploit and enjoy ruling over if they keep raw resource production locked away from magic's use. They can't have yachts, mansions, and VIP boxes at the colosseums if the people who build them and do all the work there could do what they love instead, because I can't imagine anyone dreams of catering to the ultra-wealthy, and they'd rather let half of us die then never be catered to again. All of that is also something we can change if we bring down their house of cards, starting at the bottom with the language Courts."

"You are underestimating them," Anthony said, and the people around him parted a little. The tall man combed his fingers through his steel-gray hair, looking uncomfortable and defeated. "They have all the resources we lack. They have the systems, armament and equipment production factories, food crops and the infrastructure to disseminate it, and prisons for an endless supply of labor."

Angie's blood flashed cold at the mention of prisons, and she forced her thoughts to stay in the present. "Exactly. We won't have another chance like this to end the corrupt, exploiting, unfair Empire. They will make sure we can't. They can and will kill us all, by starvation, overworking, and every other way they keep the masses distracted, tired, and pliable, to make sure they don't lose, and have no interest in compromise. They never have and never will, no matter what they might say to keep us docile."

"You don't get it," Anthony said, an edge of distress creeping into his voice. "Both tradition and law are on their side, not to mention the Imperial army of a hundred million soldiers, all well-armed, including nuclear options from the unification era. They have their full powers across all languages, as well as all the powers they steal from others. They are coherent, with clear power and command structures, and we," Anthony gestured around at the densely packed crowd of outcast adepts, "are a loose group of people flailing in the wind."

"He's right," Dawn said, her voice heavy. "They have had ten thousand years to prepare their plans. We are winging it. They want us to suffer, while we just want to survive, and we just aren't a match for that with this little warning or preparation around Ragnarök. They need our utter destruction to achieve their dreams just as much as the reverse and are far more willing and better equipped. They believe they are indestructible, and they are right because they always have a next step to take where they stay firmly on top. And they are right. We can't hope to match them in open battle."

"I can't believe you would say that," Jonathan said, and Angie saw that he, Daniel, and many of the onlookers wore matching expressions of horrified disbelief. "Not from you. If I couldn't see your magic, I'd think you were an imposter."

"You're right," Angie said, loud and clear, before they could get further off-topic. "We can't fight them on even footing. But right now there is a chink in their armor our little attack could pierce. That's all we need. If we take it all down in one blow, there will be nothing left standing to punish us for it."

"No," Dawn said stubbornly, and a glance over the crowd showed their disappointment and disgust. "I have a plan, and you have your orders with it. We are going after Ragnarök, not the Court."

"I don't care!" Angie's words echoed in the stunned silence that followed, but she didn't hesitate. Angie Voyaged a few feet ahead, landing nose-to-nose with Dawn, who barely flinched, teasing up the sparks in her aura with a thought. "I'm going to do this for me, and for Daniel, Jonathan, Casey, Mahina, Vicky, and everyone else who has suffered because of every huge and tiny aspect of the system the Focal Nuclei maintain and enforce. I am taking the Patrician Order down, by myself, if I have to. You can help or refuse your help. But you can't tell me or anyone else what to do."

Dawn didn't so much as blink for an unnervingly long time as she and Angie stared each other down, her gold aura pressing back against Angie's with every bit of stubborn zeal the younger woman pushed at her. "Fine," she said eventually with the ghost of a bitter smile. "We break the rest of the language Courts' locks."

CHAPTER THIRTY-FOUR

A cheer erupted from the crowd, which immediately started bustling with activity, and Angie smiled, but a glint in Dawn's eyes made her head tilt. "Did you set that all up?"

Dawn winked as she yielded a step, restoring more normal distance between them. "I needed everyone to know what they were getting into. Now it's your idea. The flashy hero. And I can conduct from your shadow, which suits me fine."

A shade of resentment clouded Angie's mind, but she pushed it away. She didn't care how or why Dawn was fully on her side. Everything Angie had said stood unchanged. "Right," Angie said, her sense of leadership faltering, but she cleared her thoughts and turned back to Daniel and Jonathan, another dozen people she recognized as prominent faces in the compound gathering close by to listen. "We're not just attacking one. We have the greater numbers, and we're going to use them."

She pushed away all the valid concerns and doubts that had been raised which tumbled through her mind, turning to Daniel. "Ragnarök is the most urgent, since it's likely a matter of hours or days before it makes us all very dead. What do we know about heading it off?"

Daniel seemed to shake himself, his angular face serious. "They'll have a five-mile radius around the gate locked from Voyaging, and, from what I've gathered, a single point of access to the Eden world in order to control who gets in. Taking control of that needs to be our priority, as we then have options around going through ourselves, keeping enough of them here that they hold off on dropping the bombs, and such."

"Well, what about phase-walking in?" Jonathan said. "We know who quite a few of the chosen loyalists who have been invited through are, so finding the rough location shouldn't be too hard."

"A small handful of us should then be able to delay them going through the gate," Dawn added. "We can defend the position, forcing them to hold off on the nukes, long enough for us to take down the shields and get more of us there to hold it long term. The trick then will be to keep them from closing the gate when they realize we're coming, but we should be able to figure something out."

"Sounds good." Angie turned to Jonathan. "I think you have more than enough possession demons collected, and it sounds like you know who has the needed skill or experience around astral stuff. Pick out a team to start hitting the holy sites as sunrise reaches them, and a second to hit western Europe at their noons. Oh also," she added as Jonathan turned away with a curt nod. "Could I please have my anti-possession coin back?" Her skin crawled at the thought of being anywhere near the demons they were all about to play with without it.

"Oh sure," Jonathan said, digging into his pocket. "Your old one is still in my office on site, but I've got plenty of spares for today." He tossed Angie a heavy copper coin, brand new and shiny, and she pushed down her disappointment.

"Thanks." As Jonathan moved away, she saw his wife Hannah by the corner of a distant building catch his eye, and Angie turned back to Dawn. "You're on manpower. We need to be hitting the holy sites with Jonathan at predictable times, and the Ragnarök stuff ASAP, but we should be hitting the Senate strongholds too as much as we can in between, as that will break the control the patricians have over the armed forces across the board, and keep them distracted from the other stuff we're doing."

"Got it," Dawn said with another infuriating wink, like she'd given Angie the words to say. "I'll also give my contacts in other language outcast groups the heads-up, so hopefully we can gain allies with each Court that falls. Give me five minutes, and we can head out." The last of the passive listeners left with her when she turned away, pulling out a battered cell phone.

Angie and Daniel were suddenly alone together in the bustling green. She turned to him and hesitated, not knowing what to say, as Daniel seemed to memorize every millimeter of her face. Her chest tightened, and when Daniel reached out she took his glove hand, and let him pull her into an embrace. She held him tightly to her, wishing she would never have to let go.

"You really know the truth? That I'd never cheat on you?" Daniel's voice rumbled through her chest. "You know I love you, and that I'm sorry I hurt you in any way, even against my will? And that I mourn you when you aren't by my side?"

Angie squeezed him in answer, hearing the fear and sorrow in his voice. "Yes, I do." Angie buried her face in Daniel's shoulder, her voice breaking. "And I love you, too." Even as she said the words that rang true to her core, some part of her mind ticked with the urgency of the world around them. She loosened her grip, shifting away to leave her hands gripping his shoulders as he held her arms. She searched his face for understanding about what it would take from both of them to survive and triumph in the coming day, and she found it. His handsome, angular face was lined with sadness, a tight muscle in his jaw twitching with his tight smile.

Angie leaned forward and Daniel bowed his head, allowing her to rest against him for a small, silent moment of connection. When they separated, Angie took a deep breath. "I want you," she said, knowing the moment would have to break. "More than anything. But we have to work to earn that. And we have to do it now." Daniel nodded, his dark eyes dropping away as he seemed to gather himself. Angie did the same, returning her attention to the people and activity around them, but tucked away the stolen moment in her heart, unwilling to let go completely.

"Right. I gave them their orders. What does that leave?"

Daniel didn't answer right away, his brows knitting. "Please tell me you'll be careful, and stay safe," he murmured, and Angie's chest tightened. She nodded with a small smile, and Daniel sighed, rolling his shoulders. "It leaves the Council. Milton is the only Councilor we know the name of to leverage, and I think I should try. Or, at least, if I can find him we may be able to follow him, or if I can keep him in this world or just distracted, there's a good chance it would delay them pulling the trigger on Ragnarök."

"Okay, sounds good." Angie wanted to reach out and grab Daniel, pulling him into an embrace and never letting go, but didn't. "I'm so sorry I left you to mourn me again," she whispered, her tight throat barely letting the words pass. "I'm so, so sorry."

Daniel nodded, his eyes bright. "I forgive you, and I'm so, so sorry too."

"What do you say?" Angie said with a weak attempt at a smile, stepping in and catching the cuff of Daniel's jacket with a finger. "We make it through the next twenty-two-ish hours, and all is forgiven." Daniel smiled, and Angie felt his attention wash over her like a warm wave of cleansing magic she hadn't known she needed until the relief of it almost made her cry.

Daniel flinched and reached into his pocket, pulling out the sleek black cell that had undoubtedly just buzzed. He frowned. "It's from Léa."

He turned the phone so Angie could read, and as she did, she felt old, familiar demons of flame, wrath, and shadow rise in her heart, ready for a fight.

'Angie. London, where your past found you. The first domino. Now.'

Chapter Thirty-Five

A few minutes later, Angie landed in an alleyway bordering a temple to Hephaestus, at the far end from the square that was their destination. "We do keep ending up back here," she muttered to Daniel beside her, watching as tendrils of his aura lashed out at the two security cameras that covered the narrow path, disabling them.

He gave her a funny look as they both sent up their beacons, and Dawn, Jonathan, and around fifty others started joining them silently, all landing in the relative sanctuary of the alley. "You mean you were here while you were smoke?" He paused, shielding Angie with his body as two people jostled past them in the tight space. "Were you here with me on Monday?"

"When someone took a shot at you. Yeah. I tried to shove you out of the way."

Daniel's answering smile was complex. "I know. I felt it, though I didn't understand what it was."

Angie dipped her head, feeling overexposed. Maybe returning to solidity would take some adjustment. As if reading her mind, Daniel flicked his wrist and her deep blue jacket, one of the few things she still had from her life before magic, appeared in his hand. Angie took it from him gratefully, shrugging it on.

"You should also have this back," Daniel said, taking something from his pocket and holding out a fist, dropping a silver key pendant on a thin chain into her waiting palm.

Angie grinned, wrapping her fingers around it, feeling the demon housed within as a vague, content, animalistic mental presence when she felt for it with her magic. A significant tool back in her arsenal. "You kept this with you? Even with..." Angie trailed off, realizing that Daniel almost certainly hadn't realized the trinket was a possessed item, and that he would more likely have destroyed it if he'd known.

"Yeah. I couldn't remember why, but I knew it was important to me."

Angie clasped the chain around her neck and pulled herself up to her fullest height as Dawn signaled that the last of the rebels expected for the excursion were present. "Right. Let's do this."

The patrician and military forces gathering to defend the English Decuria Senate Stronghold and permanent Threshold in the Suardo Building were visible before Angie even reached the end of the alley at the front of the temple. She, Daniel, and Dawn stopped just shy of being seen, still in shadow. "I think we should spread out," Angie said, less certainly than she'd hoped to, and both older adepts nodded.

"Yeah. Hit them from all sides, since it looks like they're preparing more for a single point of attack." Dawn turned around, herding two-thirds of their little band back toward the far end of the alley.

With a deep breath, Angie stepped out into the square, Daniel at her side, the rest following close behind. In three steps, the centurions and legionnaires noticed them, shouting at them to stop while some called alerts into radios strapped to their shoulders. In nine, the soldiers shifted to face the attackers more squarely across the little raised planter island of benches as they crossed the empty road, and Daniel's pale yellow shields rippled up. They walked up the short flight of stairs from the sidewalk and came to a stop in fifteen, the air thick with tension as the soldiers stopped shouting, realizing that the plebeians before them were unusual in some way.

More soldiers began arriving on foot and by truck, and Angie raised her voice to be heard. "We aren't here for you. We just want the building. Let us pass."

Several soldiers laughed snidely, and at some signal Angie didn't see or recognize, one opened fire, and they advanced. Daniel's shields held, but Angie felt his panic rise through his aura, and a stray bullet got through the gap in his concentration, narrowly missing a tall, dark-skinned woman a pace behind Angie. "Attack!" Angie called, and to her astonishment, it was Jonathan that appeared at the front of their ranks, tearing into the first line of soldiers.

She watched, agape, as Jonathan's deep blue aura sent deadly spears of ice through men and trucks alike, sending them flying with precise swings of his arm, while the liquid lapis of his aura danced around his fluid motions.

Soldiers were picked up and tossed high against nearby buildings by crashing waves, others falling where they stood as blood boiled from their mouths. Jonathan moved like a seasoned and trained fighter, a side of him Angie had never imagined, quick and grounded on his feet, not an inch of movement wasted, his weathered face set in concentration as he single-handedly held the line against dozens of well-trained well-armed Imperial soldiers.

As the soldiers' careful ranks became more jumbled, Angie spotted a condensed cloud of pink toward the back. A touch on Daniel's sleeve and a nod, and the two of them Voyaged, landing behind Milton Cartwright's back, where he cowered behind his bodyguards. A centurion nearby was more spatially aware than the Councilor and spotted them in a heartbeat, turning and shouting to his comrades.

Milton turned, his eyes wide, and squeaked in fear as Angie bared her teeth at him, unleashing her flames. "You and I have unfinished business," she snarled, and laughed darkly when the piggy little man turned, clearly trying to Voyage away, but didn't. A glance skyward at the thin net of gold magic covering the square told her why.

Angie sent a bolt of flames hurtling at the centurion who had spotted them and raised his gun at her, sending him reeling back as Daniel cracked another in the back of the head with his cane, twisting the machine gun from his grasp and banishing away somewhere as Milton scurried away, deeper into the soldiers who were starting to realize they had been flanked.

One by one, Angie and Daniel worked their way through the shouting, posturing centurions and legionnaires, Angie's flames fed and fanned by the oxygen and careful draughts of wind from Daniel's aura, his strong, lemon-yellow shields catching and deflecting every bullet that sought to take their lives. Unlike Jonathan on the other side of the flanked troop of soldiers, who was still stacking up bodies as more and more arrived in belching trucks, Angie and Daniel weren't trying to take out numbers, and didn't linger as they pursued their fleeing quarry, content to let some recover in their wake.

They caught up with Milton at the planter island, and he climbed the benches, backing away as Angie advanced on him, not even attempting to match his average magic to Angie's bolstered and enraged flames. Daniel stayed behind, guarding her back against the centurions that tried to follow. All around them, soldiers fought against magic they couldn't possibly understand but somehow took in stride, distracted from the two isolated at the center of the melee as Dawn's group descended on them from all sides. The beating roar of a helicopter joined the ruckus, and Angie ignored it.

Every dark voice inside Angie screamed with bitter triumph as she prepared to finally deliver a long-overdue blow. "You sabotaged me from the moment you brought me into your world. You have tried your best to break me, tried to force Daniel and me apart, over and over. You banished me. You tried to send me to my death, condemning me to seventeen months of horrific, lonely survival. For all that, and everything more you have done to others, I owe you."

Angie raised her hand, but Milton's aura rippled as a dark smile touched his lips. A man appeared between them, and Angie's flames went out with a whoosh. She stood frozen, unable to move, as the burly blond man gave her a charming smile that made her blood run cold.

"Hello, dear," he said, his scarred face and broken nose twisting with contempt. "Didn't expect me, did you?" He lifted the cigarette dangling in his fingers to his lips, taking a long drag. "What, no snotty quips this time?" He blew a long stream of putrid smoke into Angie's face and took another drag, waiting for an answer that didn't come.

Angie barely noticed Milton slipping away into the heart of a squad of soldiers that ushered him to the helicopter waiting in the street just out of the chaos. His words warped in Angie's ears, sliding off her as she shut down. "You will always lose. Even when you think you win, I will always be a step ahead. You gave him his magic. Now face the consequences of your choices."

"Pity," the blond ex-gladiator, ex-centurion, ex-prisoner said, flicking the butt of his cigarette away, his maroon aura dancing around him as it swelled with malevolent power. "I was looking forward to beating the insolence out of you." Before Angie could react, his large, strong hands were around her throat, squeezing, his face a sickeningly familiar mask of quiet pleasure.

The contact snapped Angie back into herself, panic unlike any she'd felt before blossoming her smoke into a cloud that filled the whole square. She tried to bring it up into flames as she struggled to breathe, the feeling of her exes' hands around her throat sending her mind tumbling into graphic flashbacks, but it wouldn't catch. She tried to swing at him, but he dodged easily, and when she tried to Voyage or Skip away, something in his rich maroon aura stopped her.

The edges of her vision faded as her lungs screamed for air, but a swift blow of her knee to his groin, and she was free from his grasp. Angie gasped down sweet, fresh air as the bear of a man on the ground beside her started to rise.

Yellow magic engulfed his head, and he fell back, writhing and clawing at his throat. Daniel pulled her to her feet, tucking her in close to his side as he backed them away. Angie felt everything that had bubbled up, cracked open, and twisted inside her shift as she got her breath back, watching her ex suffocate in turn. It all collapsed in on itself as Angie's pounding heart slowed. "Stop. Let him get up." She closed her eyes as the blond man sucked down a breath and scrambled to his feet, grounding herself in the safety of Daniel's close warmth, solidity, and shields.

"A fair fight?" the bear of a man before her said when she opened her eyes, lowering his stance an inch. "Good. I'll enjoy this even more."

"No," Angie said, the steady, calm softness in her voice surprising even her. "There's no point." She took a deep breath, raising a hand which her rapist and abuser eyed warily and stepped away from Daniel to stand on her own.

"The best thing people like you can do for the world is just die." A tendril of soot-black magic lashed out from Angie's aura where it had snaked around his side unnoticed, cracking into the back of his neck, and severing the spinal cord deep inside.

Angie watched his body slump to the ground, not knowing where to even begin sorting through everything she felt. Daniel's hand brushed her elbow, but she turned away from him toward the Suardo Building, gathering the overwhelming raw emotion coursing through her, pressing her eyes closed as she imagined collecting it all in her arms as a sun of burning memories, fears, and wounds she might finally be truly free from.

She let out a wordless shout that echoed off the spires of glass and steel surrounding her as she flung her magic and intentioned up with her arms, and watched as her fireball slammed into the top five floors of the building. It melted the structure back a good ten feet in an instant, opening the floors it hit to the open air. The sharp spells of her smoke filled the square, and Angie tried to sort out the elements. Dry grass. Desert sage brush. Juniper, and something darker, greasy, and sickening.

The building groaned and Angie saw Dawn grin, her eyes turned up at the gaping hole in not only the glass walls but the wards that had surrounded the top three floors, quickly followed by two dozen of her people as every single centurion and legionnaire scattered. Angie's aura cracked hot and bright around her, and only when she felt both Daniel's and Jonathan's auras touch hers, tentative and purposeful, did she drop her gaze back to earth.

"I'm not trying to douse your flames," Jonathan said quickly, raising his hands. "You did well. You owned them, and are in control. I'm just here if you need help winding back down."

Angie took three shuddering breaths, and her aura collapsed back into smoke. She held out her arms and Jonathan and Daniel were both holding her in an instant, Daniel safely gloved. Intense, chaotic thoughts and feelings continued to threaten to swamp her, but she let herself be comforted. It took her a minute to gather herself, but once she had, she pulled away, just as Dawn burst out through the doors of the Suardo Building.

"Done. The Senators who were here fled, and we razed their records, Threshold, and everything else touched with magic or control."

Angie smiled tightly, reaching for Daniel's gloved hand. He took hers, smiling with pure happiness and relief. "Are you okay?" he asked as Jonathan moved away, the square clearing as Dawn gave directions for who was to start pursuing the Eden Threshold, and was to start chasing language locks. His eyes searched Angie's face, and she squeezed his hand.

"I will be." A thousand more things she could say, wanted to say, hovered on the tip of her tongue, but she said none of them. She tugged Daniel's hand, and they moved to the edge of the planter island, stepping down carefully.

"What exactly was that smoke?" Daniel asked as they made for the last little cluster of people waiting for them. "I've smelled it a few times before, but can't put my finger on what it is."

Angie sorted through the elements she could, also reaching back into a few memories that matched the feeling of what she'd just done. She nodded distractedly as Dawn told them to chase down Ragnarök and stood still until she and Daniel were the only ones left. She realized the common feeling behind it was a sense of being out of control, or nearly so, and found she couldn't look Daniel in the eye with her answer.

"Wildfire."

Chapter Thirty-Six

When Angie felt Jonathan's mental beacon, she Voyaged to him immediately, aiming to land a small distance away from her friend in case he was in a bind, abandoning her directionless search for the Eden Threshold.

Nearly eight hours had passed since she had returned to flesh, and it was finally feeling permanent. German, French, Spanish, and dozens of other Courts had fallen easily and to plan, and Angie had helped with a few. Everything West of Rome was now free, their own groups of outcasts and uprisers either joining on, or staying behind to slow down the massacres of plebeians by Imperial forces happening in most major cities as tensions hit their boiling point, and the facade of civility was abandoned. Angie did a quick mental assessment. Sunrise had to be nearly done crossing the Americas. The last holy site in the south and central parts had fallen, and Jonathan had said that all the native languages in the northern part had been forcibly disbanded hundreds of years before the Imperial Unification.

She landed in a small grove of narrow, white-barked trees, the smell of willow, juniper, and sagebrush coating the dew-touched desert morning. Nostalgia and home-sickness for her childhood hit Angie like a train, and she blinked it away. A little further up the mountainside, a loud crack and a flash of light sent Angie into motion, darting up the rocky, low-scrub incline through the trees.

When she found Jonathan, Casey, and the rest of their crew, they stood in the center of a level clearing, locked in fierce battle with a larger number of expensively dressed patricians, every color of magic imaginable flying and clashing. Angie quickly beaconed for more people to come help. The open space was no more than fifty feet across, its circular boundary defined by small boulders of local stone. And through it, around it, flowed the unmistakable fountain of raw, ancient power of a language Court holy site as strong as any.

Angie sent a blistering wall of heat across the backs of the patricians nearest to her, Voyaging ahead to Jonathan on the other side of their cluster as soon as they turned, yelping. "Why is this one so much more heavily defended?" Angie asked, raising her hands as Jonathan's shoulder bumped into hers.

"I have no idea. Another group I don't know got here before us, and the fight was in full swing when we arrived. But it does explain why the others didn't have the Senate forces we expected protecting them." Jonathan's shields bowed as a woman was thrown into them, catching her and carefully setting her back on her feet with thick limbs of deep blue water. Angie sent a careening fireball toward a group of four menacing patricians who had ganged up on Casey on the other side of the stone ring, smiling when her flames didn't touch him or the trees, only eating away at the shields of, or burning, her targets.

"Is this a good time?" she shouted at Daniel when he arrived beside her, dropping an inch and shielding when the chaos hit him.

"Shit. Yeah, hold on." He Voyaged away, and the trees overhead roared with the fierce wind that whipped up. Angie didn't bother to find him in the crowd, her attention too consumed with not getting hurt and fighting back.

Angie side-stepped as a bold of sizzling green magic whizzed by, and only realized that she'd almost stepped right into the central column of bone-shredding magic when Jonathan's strong hand on her arm yanked her away, both stilling for a moment as Angie regained her balance. When he let go, Angie blasted someone over his shoulder with a choking cloud of smoke, and Jonathan grabbed something out of his pocket.

Angie didn't fully realize what was happening before Jonathan plunged his hand into the tiny lock of magic at the heart of the column. In an instant, Jonathan's shields fractured, alternating between extra thick and nonexistent by the torrent of magic flowing through him, and Angie had only a split second to determine that he was doing fine for the moment before a fresh barrage of magic from as least six patricians together drove her back, barely able to survive the strike.

Dodge. Strike. Shield. Deflect. Suffocate. Blast. Angie did everything in her power to subdue her attackers, but at least four seemed to be trained patrician enforcers, and she could barely keep up. Stress and fear started to overwhelm her, but then she remembered she wasn't trapped, and just Voyaged away to the outer edge of the circle near Casey.

A scream rent the air and everyone jumped. Angie looked up at the heart of the chaos and time seemed to slow to a crawl. A great shard of smoky, glassy, magically dying demon protruded from the center of Jonathan's chest, his white button-down shirt already stained crimson. He stumbled back a step, a misshapen copper coin falling from his fingers. In slow motion, his dark brows knit, his tan, lined, weathered face dropping to look down at himself.

"No!" The word tore itself from Angie's throat as the shard of demon flashed with fuchsia magic and Jonathan fell to his knees, lost among the battling bodies between them. Angie's own breath and heartbeat drowned out all else, the chaos surrounding her muting to a rumble.

"Retreat!" The word carried above the commotion, muffed and slow to Angie's ears as her mind refused to function, her aura a tangle of flames, sparks, smoke, soot, and ash.

"No," Angie cried again, fighting her way forward through the still-battling throng who seemed unaware of what had just happened. Between two blinks, Angie saw Milton Cartwright standing before her, his hands soaked with blood. A sharp pain sliced across her arm just above the elbow, but Angie let herself shift back to smoke, just for a moment, and the pain didn't go deeper.

"Justice is sweet, is it not?" Milton's warped, gleefully malicious voice said as Angie turned away, half returned to flesh, stumbling toward where Jonathan had fallen. "Three birds with one stone, killing Doctor Crowther. You took a life from my ranks, now we're even." A moment later, he was gone, no trace of his magic lingering with the smell of cigars and poppies.

When Angie's eyes fell on Jonathan, he was still and limp in Daniel's arms. Angie didn't even notice as she stepped through the half-quieted core of power, which solidified her fully back to flesh.

She fell to her knees still a few paces away from the two men, reality refusing to set in. All around her, both loyalists and revolutionaries were leaving in droves, having realized that the lock was broken and the moment of sunrise had passed, eager to beat each other to the next target or cut their losses. Casey seemed to have stepped into the leadership role Jonathan had left empty, shouting orders which no one hesitated to obey.

Daniel stood, hauling Jonathan's limp body up in his arms, tight to his chest. Angie turned her face up to him, unable to think or speak. Daniel's face was a twisted mask of grief, and he Voyaged away with his burden, returning almost at once, tumbling to his knees beside Angie, his helpless, shocked expression mirroring her own.

"I'm so sorry. But we have to keep moving," Casey said nearby, to her or someone else she didn't know and didn't care.

"He's okay, right? He—he just faked it to get Milton to leave?" All Angie could think, over and over, was that it couldn't be real. Her friend couldn't be gone. The world couldn't just keep turning without Jonathan in it.

Daniel's already twisted expression cracked as the last person Voyaged away, leaving them alone in the ringing silence. Tears fell down his cheeks, his eyes completely lost beneath his grief.

"No..." Angie doubled forward as she heaved, her hands clawing into the grass and dirt. Grief crept in from every inch of her skin, through every muscle and tendon to her bones, wiping anything, everything else away. She closed her eyes as her own face warped, her throat too tight to cry out. She shook as hard as the quakie leaves overhead and found she couldn't feel anything more than she already did as she began flaking to ash.

Gloved hands grabbed her shoulders tight, pulling her down to the ground in an embrace that wrapped all the way around the ball she curled into, holding her together.

Daniel's whole body gasped and shook in time with hers like they were somehow one person in their grief, and when the first racking sob of devastated loss screamed from Angie's lungs, Daniel's was just a breath behind.

Chapter Thirty-Seven

D aniel cried like the whole world had died, not just one man. Clinging to Angie, holding her together, was the only thing that held him together in turn, the gale of his winds lashing Angie's smoke and flames around them, unseen, burning him down to the bare skeleton of who he was in his grief. The last time he'd been so consumed by loss had been when Dawn had told him of Angie's banishment, and he'd believed her certainly dead. At least he could now remember that.

For a wild minute, his mind spun up a hundred ideas around how Jonathan, his dearest friend, might have faked his own death and why, but the truth couldn't be avoided. It had been a corpse he had taken to the safety of the rebel compound, laying him with the other fighters who had fallen, before rushing back to Angie's side. As Daniel named it out loud in his own mind, he collapsed the last fraction he could, and was swept under fully, crying into Angie's hair on the dirt for uncountable minutes.

As the last tears his poor eyes could produce dried on his skin, the ticking of the gold watch on his wrist grew louder and louder, filling the space which exhaustion opened in his grief with creeping urgency. Angie didn't seem as near to being drained as he was, and Daniel begrudgingly named why as his thoughts slowly regained their cohesion. He had more practice with loss. Was a decade older, and wiser, and had leaned far deeper into mastering his emotions than Angie had ever had the chance to. He had to be the one to pull Angie up and onward to make sure she didn't get caught in the world when it died because he let his grief swamp him.

"Angie," Daniel said, his voice graveled from crying. "Come on. We can't freeze like this too much longer. Sit up." He did so, his breath still shuddering, pulling her up with him. "We do have hours before the next language Court, but we may not have any time before Ragnarök. I'm so sorry, love, but we can't let billions die because we lost one dear to us."

His words clearly had an impact, and Angie wiped her face with the heels of her hands, over and over as new tears fell, holding her breath, then panting as she tried to pull herself together. "You're right. I'm sorry. I just…" Her face contorted another degree.

Daniel reached for her elbow with a gloved hand to offer comfort, but froze when he saw the tear through her jacket just above, blood from the gash in her skin beneath staining the dark blue fabric black. A wave of Daniel's hand summoned the med kit bolted to the inside of a kitchen cabinet in his Boston home, and he motioned for Angie to remove her jacket. She did so, still half-crying as Daniel swapped his leather gloves for rubber ones and cleaned the wound. He saw Angie press her magic into the jacket in her lap, and the rip in the sleeve mended as the blood disappeared, as good as new.

"Did you notice?" Daniel asked groggily, wanting to pull Angie more back to the moment, pulling the sharp cut closed with special adhesive strips. "All of your scars are gone. Returning to flesh from smoke must have acted as a second magical resurrection, like your awakening."

Angie quickly held her hands out in front of her, turning them to see as much skin as she could. "I hadn't. You're right."

Daniel gently pulled her elbow back to him, wrapping a bandage over the closed wound and giving a silent prayer to Asclepius. "A fresh slate."

Just as Angie seemed to be calming, Daniel sighing with relief, her features contracted again, fresh pain and distress lining her body and crackling in her aura. "I changed my mind. Stop time. Please. Maybe we can save him, take him to a healer..."

Daniel's heart dropped. "I can't. It would bring Milton right to us. And–" Daniel had to look away, banishing the med kit back where it had come from. "Angie, I was an army medic for years. People can't be resuscitated from that kind of injury. Not that severe. I've tried in the past... I've tried..." Daniel's voice broke, his vision swimming as he peeled off his thin rubber gloves, banishing them away too. "We can't bring him back..." Angie just closed her eyes tight, barely breathing.

I thought I'd be able to touch him again someday, Daniel thought, almost numbly. *I thought he'd still be around when the curse wore off, or we truly found how to use the loophole.* Daniel couldn't remember having ever thought about the expectation consciously before, but the background assumption he had clearly made without realizing it still cut where it had shattered from *someday* to *never*.

"It's so pointless," Angie said, almost too quietly and strained to hear. "It didn't need to be him breaking the lock. It's so stupid." She opened her eyes, brimming with tears, looking up at the trees overhead, their delicate black and white twigs, and bright green leaves illuminated by the early-morning light. "If I hadn't..."

"No," Daniel interrupted, all too familiar with the slippery slope such thoughts could tumble someone down. "That's the version of you trained by your abuser talking. You are not to blame for what other people do, or the choices of the fates. Don't listen to those poisonous thoughts." Daniel tugged back on his leather gloves, scooching back in close to Angie, ignoring the protests of his aching knee on the ground beneath him as he pulled her into his lap. He cradled her against his chest, separated from his skin by his all-black shirt, suit, and tie.

She didn't resume crying fully, but what few breaths he could feel her take were choppy, his own matching sympathetically. "You have to decide," Daniel said softly, as much to himself as to the woman in his arms. "We can crumble, and let our fates come as they will, or we can hold ourselves together for just a little while longer, with all that means. But we don't have all the time we might want or need to make this choice." Daniel glanced at his watch over Angie's shoulder. They only had two hours before the Hawaiian Court opened. A few more before Māori. And maybe none before Ragnarök began.

Angie nodded against his chest, sitting up. She scrubbed her face once more, and when her eyes turned to Daniel's, he felt strange. Like, for the first time in his life, he was one, raw, maskless man, and was being seen as nothing else. For a heartbeat, Daniel reached for a persona of himself to cover how exposed he felt, but a little voice in his mind, deep and achingly familiar, made him pause. *I can be exactly who I am and still be exactly what I need to be. Complexity is allowed.*

"Okay," Angie said, pushing herself up to stand, and reaching back down for Daniel's gloved hand, pulling him up after her. She reached for his cheek to wipe away one last tear that fell, hesitating a few inches away.

Daniel held his breath and nodded. Angie's delicate fingers wiped away the tear, and her lashes fluttered, but she didn't fall. Daniel stood still as a statue as Angie's clarity seemed to return to her with a deep, shuddering breath, and her magic flexed outward in a mass of chaotic flames. He was glad she was back. That was enough.

Angie's eyes flicked between his, and Daniel could read the way she mulled over her thoughts for a long moment before she finally spoke them. "Sometimes things have to finish breaking before they can be fixed." Daniel nodded, hearing an Echo of Jonathan's voice over the exact same words. She dropped her head, pulling her jacket back on, and clearing her throat as she pulled herself back up to her full height.

"Okay," Daniel said, summoning his cane and shoving his emotions deep down inside, out of the way, until it was safe to feel them again. "But, Angie, please remember what else he said. Make sure that we are leaving seeds in the soil as the world burns."

CHAPTER THIRTY-EIGHT

A ngie waited until the pounding, crashing buzz of Mahina's magical sound set the air all around them in the overcast, dense forest on edge before gathering her magic. Pain and loss still wrapped themselves around her chest and pressed at her eyes, but she pushed them away, reaching for the demons of anger and a very different kind of pain that never left her heart, calming as she teased them up, her thoughts clearing.

Dawn, who had just arrived, and her crew of a dozen select adepts stood at the edge of the gigantic, multicolored shields stretching high overhead and away through the trees as far as they could see, and Angie gave them a curt nod, her lips pressed tight.

Beside her, Daniel pressed a hand to the smooth surface of the magical shield. "Of course the patricians stop being selfish bastards and collaborate just to fuck us on this," he muttered, his brows furrowed with concentration. "Nope," he called out to the others. "I don't think I can crack this many layers, even with the destabilizing vibrations."

"Right," Angie said, buttoning her jacket down the front as the rumbling sound from Mahina's shell-pink aura died away. "Are we sure the Eden Threshold is in there?" Dawn just nodded, and Angie sighed. "Alright. Try phase-walking in."

Angie did her best to clear her mind, holding her natural Voyaging skill at bay. She backed up a few paces, facing the wall of shields squarely. Dawn and a couple others zipped forward like someone had pressed fast-forward on their part of the movie Angie was reluctantly part of, and Angie took a deep breath. She set her attention on a spot forty feet ahead, just on the other side of the transparent wall, and willed her magic to rush her forward through space.

In the three steps she was on the other side and choked down the nauseous bile that rose in her. It hadn't been so bad, learning and training with Anthony in the early spring, but now the way it seemed to half-dissolve her, allowing her to pass through the shields unscathed, made her nervous.

When the nausea passed, Angie grinned triumphantly with the others. She set her intentions on the center of the shields, unseen through the dense evergreen forest, but when she tried to Voyage, nothing happened. A couple of others seemed to be facing the same issue, and Angie sighed. "It looks like someone is preventing Voyaging within the shields." She turned to Dawn, covertly double-checking that it wasn't the rebellion leader doing it, but her gold aura was not among the latticework of magic they now stood within. "Suggestions?"

Dawn's teeth flashed white in her dark face with a grimace. "The aura-bonded token I planted in Marissa

Hayward's luggage is still a solid five miles away." She nodded away from the wall of shields through the dense forest. "It would take us well over an hour walking, but we can phase-walk in a few minutes, probably. The trees just make it a little tricky."

Daniel pulled out his phone, and Angie saw a small smile touch the corners of his wide, expressive mouth for a moment before he made the screen go black, peering into the dark, slightly reflective surface. He swore. "The bottleneck at the Threshold is still bad, but it looks like they know we've breached the perimeter. Some enforcers and other patricians are fanning out."

"Then what's the plan?" Anthony asked, nervously shifting his weight from foot to foot. "We don't have the time to spare walking, and we are at a disadvantage within their shields. If they see us coming and can identify us, we may never get close enough to take the Threshold before they take us out, or move up their plan to bomb us all once their own people are through."

Angie gave him a crooked smile. "Chaos." She exhaled to her limit, summoning all of her rage, pain, and desperation, and held it for a beat. When she inhaled, every leaf, needle, twig, blade of grass, and scrap of bark within the site on their side of the shields wall erupted into roaring orange flames. It felt ecstatic, and Angie's chest swelled with the glorious, raw expression and power in it.

Every person nearby ducked, covering their heads with expressions of alarm. Only when they realized that Angie's flames didn't hurt even where they touched them did they start smiling with realization. Angie extinguished the flames with a thought. The forest that had been burn-ing was barely damaged, smoking slightly.

Daniel put his phone away with a crooked smile. "Per-fect. They're sending the enforcers and guards out in every direction to find us, since it's clear we can still attack from a distance, but it seems they can't tell from what side. I'll stay here and work on the shields so we can get more people in."

Angie opened her mouth to ask Daniel to add to her plan, but he raised a hand, seeming to read her mind. Darkness fell all around them, the air within the massive dome of shields blocking out all light. A heartbeat later, a breath of air that smelled of beeswax and frankincense brushed across Angie's face, and she blinked as an odd, magical sort of light allowed her to see with perfect clar-ity despite the surrounding darkness. *Like through night vision goggles*, Angie mused, but didn't know for certain.

Angie grinned at Daniel, then turned to Mahina. "Can you give us patterned cycles of sound to work with, al-ternating flames and darkness?"

The Hawaiian woman grinned. "I can do better. I know just the song." She closed her eyes, and Angie felt her spirits lift as a dark, driving song she'd heard on the radio many times when she'd lived in her car began playing all around them, again putting Angie in mind of a movie, now with a soundtrack and everything.

When the first chorus hit, Angie brought the forest back to roaring flames with a thought, turning into it. "Let's do this."

Angie got her rhythm of phase-walking in no time at all, leaning into her delightful power and purpose to ignore her discomfort. Every twenty to thirty seconds, the lyrics in the song playing all around her on repeat gave Angie her cues to let go of her flames, traveling through the utter darkness with Daniel's auric air clinging to her face giving her night vision, before returning the forest to a roaring inferno at the next. Darkness. Fire. Darkness.

The first person she encountered skating through the forest on blades of practiced magic beneath her feet was a stocky woman she recognized from Daniel's blackmail ventures. Her eyes were wide as she felt her way forward through the dark she seemed unable to do anything about, muttering and whimpering under her breath about wishing she could just leave.

Angie positioned herself right in front of Senator Utley, ready for her next cue for flames. When it came, the forest roared to towering gouts of fire once more, and the older woman reeled back, bringing up her shields. She scrambled back from Angie so fast and with such astonished fear that she tripped over a tree root and fell, and Angie moved on, darkly delighted. *Fear meant respect, for all some might argue otherwise.*

Angie cautiously pushed her powers out to their full potential when she hit a wide stand of trees too dense to move between. For as often as her powers had fought her control in the past, sometimes winning and lashing out, encouraging her powers to expand as wide and hot as they wanted felt like breathing in a new way that was still tight and uncomfortable. She felt her solidity slip for the briefest moment as a hole opened through the copse, but when she looked at her hand, it was made of fire, not smoke. Angie pulled herself together, checked her balance, and kept phase-walking toward the center of the massive shields.

Darkness. Fire. Angie spotted a small gaggle of brightly colored auras through the trees ahead. She slowed, approaching at a normal walk. Marissa was the first to spot her. "You," the patrician said, making the other four turn.

"Me," Angie replied with a lupine smile. All five patricians facing her brought up magic, but as the last line of the chorus of the song playing all around them repeated, the young blonde woman seemed to realize what was about to happen, and crouched down into a ball. Angie released her flames on cue, handing over their little world to darkness, and phase-walked through the little group as their attempted attacks missed by a wide margin.

"It's Angie Forester, it has to be!" Noah was shouting when Angie stepped between two towering oaks and got her first glimpse of the woodland Threshold three hundred feet ahead. "The fire, the smoke, it must be." The shuffling, bottle-necked crowd between her and her ex-friend didn't notice her arrival, cowering away from the burning edge of the forest as her flames erupted on cue.

Angie was shocked to see a century of eighty auxiliaries stationed around the perimeter, but a wisp of orchid-pink magic at the temple of each made it much less of a surprise. Angie's thoughts flicked to the men who had once mugged her at a gas station, apparently under Milton Cartwright's bidding, and she pushed the distraction aside.

A cry to her left startled Angie, and when she saw that Dawn and her posse had attacked the nearest set of soldiers, Angie launched herself forward just as her flames gave way to darkness for the last time, and the music faded out. She Voyaged ahead, aiming to land as close to the unassuming woodland Threshold as she could, but was stopped short by a small dome of shields around it, barely seven feet high but a foot thick with layers and colors.

A dim umbrella of violet-purple light expanded over the clearing, illuminating what Angie could already see for the rest, and a hundred heads snapped to her. Angie swore, bringing up her shields, and slammed a fist armed with white and blue flames across the knuckles into the shield before her, having no effect.

The handful of people already within looked alarmed and ducked through the freestanding doorway, disappearing into the magic, those without hanging back. A distant roar of groaning and splintering wood grew as Angie's shields were attacked, barely holding out, and she soon had plenty of elbow room as a magically selective wind whipped up ash in the darkness, blowing it with considerable force into the eyes and lungs of the patricians around Angie and the Threshold.

A deafening crack sounded overhead as the layered, complex shields finally broke, and Angie's hands flew to her ears, her heart pounding even faster. When she lowered them she was barely in time to hear a shout of warning from Dawn, and redoubled her shields as an explosive fistful of baby-blue magic hit them, making them buckle.

Someone dressed as a plebeian or outcast adept appeared between Angie and her attacker with dozens, then hundreds more spreading all throughout the gathered patricians with their bundles, backpacks, and luggage, clearly on their way out of town. Angie smiled. Now they had a chance. Angie abandoned the shielded Threshold and threw herself at the approaching squad of soldiers with a snarl, ripping the baton from one and striking another with it, reserving her magic as the first notes of strain touched her.

It took fifteen minutes to eliminate the enchanted auxiliaries and scare off or stand down the hundreds of patricians who had gathered at the Threshold. As Angie scanned the clearing from one side for who needed her help next, the cut above her elbow throbbing from her physical altercations, as well as the magical, she again heard Noah's voice call out over the rest.

"Change it to the Council world! Cut off Eden so they can't go through, and get us access to more magic and help!"

Angie saw an ancient woman near the shielded Threshold step forward, a key in each gnarled hand. "Stop!" Angie cried, Voyaging back to the center, again stopped by the shield. She watched, helplessly, as the woman turned one key in the Threshold, collapsing the magic into empty air, and then the other, creating a new membrane of magic. She turned her ancient, papery face to Angie, and with a bitterly satisfied smile, banished the keys in a blink.

The hair on the back of Angie's neck stood on end and she side-stepped and ducked as a blast of fire shot past her. The old woman screamed as she fell to ash, and Angie turned to see Noah Byrne being backed toward her, his hands raised. When he knelt, Angie saw Seth Laufey was the reason, both hands holding threatening flames toward the Supreme Justice, his grinning face lit maniacally from below.

Angie moved around cautiously, not sure she really felt relieved when Seth made it clear that Noah was his intended target and not Angie. "You got him?" he asked, and Angie nodded, a bit thrown off, as Seth cackled off toward the trees, blasting out fists of fire at patricians and outcasts alike.

Awkward tension hung thick in the air between Angie and Noah until she jerked her chin for him to lower his hands and stand, keeping her shields up and her flames at the ready, twisting the baton she'd held onto. It still weirded her out that he looked like her friend. That she still saw kindness, affection, and charm in a man who fought against everything she believed in, and had done a terrifying job of gaslighting her about her experiences of abuse at the hands of a man she'd now killed.

The last thought decided what she wanted to do with him. "Go home," she said, her voice dripping with dismissive disdain. "Or run away to your haven, if you know where the key went. Just choose to not be here. I don't want you anywhere near me."

"Who says we're on opposite sides?" Noah said, holding out an inviting hand, his expression pleading. "Both sides have merit, and have made mistakes. Please, stop being a puppet of those terrorists and come with me. All that matters now is survival."

"Survival from your side trying to kill all of us," Angie yelled, and started bringing up her flames, ready to strike the Supreme Justice down, but still hoping she wouldn't have to as the man yielded a step. "We outnumber you three to one. The Court and Senate strongholds are falling, and we have far more people from other freed languages now than we can use. Our cause is on the right side of history. Get the *fuck* out of my sight."

Noah Voyaged away, and Angie took a deep breath in the relative peace left in his wake as the last of the chaotic altercation died down around her. Daniel approached from the side and she gave him a tight smile, trying to pull herself back to the moment. She faltered when she saw his unreadable expression and stayed quiet as he stopped only a hand's breadth away.

"The Angel in the Forest," he said softly, almost reverently, and Angie couldn't place where she'd heard the words before.

"Keep moving," Dawn said behind Daniel, and he and Angie stepped aside as she bustled in, whips of golden magic cracking at the shield around the Threshold.

"It's no longer going to the Eden half-world," Angie said, disappointed. "Some old lady changed it. To the Council world, if she did as she was told. Then she banished the keys somewhere, and Seth turned her to ash." A hundred pairs of eyes blinked at her with a wide range of expressions.

Dawn swore, pacing away a few steps, then back, a hand over her mouth. "Shit. Okay. Well, we really need to shift gears, then. This is still worth getting into, as taking the Council seats would be huge, but I just got word a minute ago that several major cities are burning, and we need to divert resources to dealing with those, or there's not much point trying to stop them getting bombed."

"Agreed," Angie said. "I can stay and work on getting through, just leave enough to defend us if the patricians try to take it back. I'll send out a beacon when we're through. Dawn, you marshal all the outcasts we've collected to deal with the armies and disasters in the plebeian world while the last few language Courts fall."

She turned to Daniel, her whole heart screaming at her to not leave his side, or let him leave hers. His face was worried but his eyes were full of admiration, and Angie took a deep breath, knowing what was more important than having Daniel's help with breaking the shield before them. "We have an hour before sunrise reaches the Italian Court, and the last lock breaks. Milton is the biggest single threat between us and that end. Scry, find him, and keep him distracted like only you can."

CHAPTER THIRTY-NINE

The ticking of Daniel's watch seemed to grow louder by the minute as he stared into the obsidian mirror propped on the piano in his Boston home, his hands pressing down against the keyboard cover until his many rings bit into his flesh. It was a wash of relief when the scrying magic finally clicked into place before him, and Daniel saw Cartwright stepping away from his bodyguards to duck into a back entrance for the colosseum in Rome.

He used a bit more scrying to narrow in on what part of the heavily restored theater to aim for, and Daniel arrived silently. He allowed himself a flare of satisfaction when he was greeted with the sight of Milton Cartwright's chubby backside bending into a set of lockers in the quiet basement entrance of the plebeian levels.

"Odd hiding place for a man of your stature and resources," Daniel remarked, chuckling when Milton whanged his head on the lockers. "Though, perhaps with the Senate nearly toppled, the Council hot on its tail, and patrician mansions across the globe being looted by fed-up peasants, hiding it somewhere without power and prestige was the right choice." Daniel dropped his gaze to see what the Councilor had retrieved, but the man was just holding an old cigar box. "Or are you just hiding from the front lines like the coward you are?"

Milton followed his interest, and the twisted smile he answered with made Daniel's gut clench. "Oh, so you don't know about my little backup plan?" Milton slipped two fingers beneath the lid, and Daniel braced his shields, reminding himself that the goal was to distract and derail, not end the Transvaalian right then and there. "It's honestly funny that no one's ever come looking, especially after I managed to have the Norns shorten your life for a second time. You see, I still have these."

He lifted out a handful of little bits of colored glass, and it took Daniel a long, sickening moment to realize what he was looking at. "Scraps of auras you've stolen," he whispered, frowning. "But that shouldn't be possible. Keeping loose scraps like that." Daniel's blood ran cold. "Their texture..."

"So you do recognize it?" Milton said, sifting through a handful. "Yes. The piece of magic I took from you to have the Norns cut your life thread short. And Miss Gates. And everyone else I have ever snicked a scrap from." Milton let the pieces fall back into the cigar box with a clatter, and Daniel's mind tumbled down into a spiral of every person he knew who had ever come into contact with the man.

"Did you really think you could all muscle your way in, and have your happily ever after with us? You, Dawn, Miss Forester... No no no. Ragnarök means no more consequences for illegal magic. I can use these scraps to make sure you all fall now, before you ever even have the chance." He slipped the box into an oversized pocket of his plaid jacket, and Daniel acted without thinking. His aura lashed out from him in a freezing gust, which the Councilor easily shielded against. "Is that all you've got?" Milton started to ask, but was cut short when Daniel's cane slammed into his gut, gambling that the older man was only braced for magic attacks.

Before Daniel could wind up for another blow, a dizzy ringing filled his ears, and oppressive, syrupy magic engulfed him. Daniel sensed the intentions within it—to pacify, dull, and enthrall—but his mental shields held firm. In a snap decision, Daniel let his cane fall to the floor, pretending that the magic had a grip on him as he tried to fight it.

"Good," Milton said, stepping forward as Daniel fell to one knee, wincing. "I know killing that blasted mole I could never pin anything on would throw you and your bitch off your game." Daniel frowned, trying to think of who he meant, and the answer hit him as hard as the punch to the gut that followed from Milton's fist. "Doctor Crowther should never have been made a Judge, been allowed to stay on, or invited back. I should have killed him years ago, if that's what finally brought you to your knees."

"No..."

The toe of Cartwright's oxford connected with Daniel's ribs and he pitched to one side. "I can't wait to see how much further you fall when I kill Angie Forester by tossing the scrap of aura I took from her before shoving her through the banishment Threshold into the Latin lock, and let the magic eat her away from the inside out. I'll be sure the scrap of yours I've held onto all these years, used with the Norns twice, goes in last so I can watch you suffer watching all the rest."

Daniel wheezed, scrambling to hold on to his magic and focus as the world threatened to spiral. It hadn't been an accident, like Daniel had thought. His best friend, his brother, had been killed to get to him. Angie would be next, without the chance to defend herself.

When Milton shifted for another kick, Daniel caught the man's ankle, wrenching and twisting, sending him to the floor with a heavy thump and a whoosh of air. "You killed him?" Daniel half-yelled, half-sobbed, throwing himself onto the Councilor's chest, his Air aura lashing without restraint all around the hallway of lockers, tossing heavy benches against walls and doors. He slammed a fist into Milton's face as the older man weakly tried to fight back, and the decade-old ache easing in Daniel's chest for every subtle blow Cartwright had ever dealt him finally being answered was intoxicating. "You killed Jonathan." Another strike, stealing the air from Cartwright's lungs as the man drew breath to speak. "And now you threaten to kill Angie? You're the one who someone should have stood up to and stopped a very, very long time ago."

A blast of magic threw Daniel back as he pulled back for a third, and when he'd scrambled back to his knees, he was alone with his cyclone. Milton was gone. A scream of deep, consuming rage echoed through the room, reverberating as his magic caught and carried it off a thousand surfaces. Daniel stayed on all fours, his head dropped. He had failed. He had finally stood up to Milton Cartwright, and now he felt his purpose, hope, and justification dissolving.

A Voyaging beacon touched his mind faintly, like from a half-world, and Daniel stood, grabbing his cane and pulling a hand down his face, before he realized it wasn't from Angie. He froze in place, sensing Milton's identity through the summons. He weighed his options for three breaths before rolling his shoulders, feeling the reassuring weight of his own backup plan, and gathered his intentions.

The only reason Milton would call him to wherever he'd gone was if it were a trap. And Daniel had no choice but to go.

CHAPTER FORTY

D aniel's feet landed on a black-pebbled beach he knew, and his first flitting thought was of Angie trying to break in through the Threshold that stood nearby, built from shards of obsidian the size of men. Daniel turned quickly, his shields at full strength, as he flexed his left wrist against the gold watch a scrap of Angie's aura had been bound into and the anti-possession tattoo inked beneath it.

A blast of magic hit Daniel's shield and scattered across it like fuchsia tar before he saw where it came from, and he cursed long and heartfelt as another blast hit him, the opaque, sludge-like magic sticking to and lingering on his shield, completely obstructing his sight. Daniel took a deep breath, expanding out his magic as far as it could reach, and sucked all the oxygen from the air in a five-hundred-foot radius, condensing and holding it all in a small pocket of his aura.

He heard a gasp a little way ahead, and moved forward as fast as he dared, glad that his cane gave him a little extra stability on the treacherous footing. A burble behind him made him stop and turn just in time to see the placid ocean rise like a great beast, limbs of water crashing down on Daniel. His shields mostly held as the water built around him, confident that he could pull the oxygen he needed from it with his magic, even if he hadn't just collected all he could want for hours.

Milton's choice to attack with water felt like a targeted jab at the fresh wound in Daniel's chest where Jonathan should be, and Daniel, for once, let it sting as fully as intended. He took the pain that bubbled up in him, pulling his magic in close, and let it add speed and strength when he sent it barreling back out from him, hot as a blast from a furnace, temporarily sacrificing his shields to clear them and turn every drop of water that had climbed up from the shoreline to steam.

Daniel leapt out of the way as a shard of obsidian speared at him through the steam in an instant, and Daniel only narrowly avoided getting skewered and glad of his agility as the steam cleared and his magic gathered back into him enough to shield again. A dozen paces ahead, Milton Cartwright stood beside the Focal Nucleus of the Latin language and Council. He had somehow unlocked and activated the full flow of magic by himself, as they were alone on the beach, and before Daniel could do more than reach for his power to do something, the Councilor dropped a small shard of pale yellow glass into the lock.

Daniel lunged forward with a gasp as his magic all but disappeared. His shields were gone, and he collapsed against the arm of one of the seven obsidian thrones ringing the Focal Nucleus after only a few stumbling strides, half the strength leaving his limbs with his power and breath. "Please, no," Daniel gasped, horrible memories and desperation reducing him to a long-forgotten version of himself as he let go of any attempted use of his magic to desperately cling to any scrap he could deep inside.

"Stop," Daniel begged, falling to crawl forward on the smooth black pebbles that hurt his hands and knees. He knew his face was showing all of his raw distress and didn't hide any of it. "Please, stop. I'll do anything you want. Just don't take my magic." The feeling was horrifically familiar, and Daniel did his best to breathe through the nauseous, emotionally triggering sensation.

Milton's answer was another swift kick to the ribs when Daniel had crawled close enough, and Daniel grabbed for his ankle as had worked a few minutes before, but the Councilor anticipated, and Daniel's fingers barely grazed.

Daniel curled into a small ball, black clothes and shoes on the black beach, turning all of his attention inward as Cartwright sneered, saying something about how desperately people without magic needed and wanted to be ruled by those with it, variations of which Daniel had heard a hundred times.

He uncurled an inch to peer out at Milton, doing something with the patterns of magic there, seeming to set the ball of threads holding the scrap of Daniel's magic to one side while he prepared another. Daniel sat up slowly, clutching the hand holding the scrap of fuchsia magic he'd grabbed from Cartwright's aura when the man had thought he was going for the ankles in a fist, tight against his stomach as if hurt, as he carefully got his feet under him, and securely dug into the pebbles deep enough that he wouldn't slip.

In one fluid motion, Daniel sprung forward, plunging his fist into the lock before Milton could even reach out. He quickly let go of the scrap of magic, right beside his own—which didn't budge when he tried to pull it away—and withdrew his hand before anything could go wrong. Milton Cartwright screamed with pain, falling, writhing, to the ground. The magic flowing through the lock flared and shuddered, clearly affected by the repression of Milton's magic, and Daniel stumbled back a few steps as a blinding flash forced him to cover his eyes.

When he'd blinked away the spots to clear his vision, Milton had the cigar box of auric fragments open on the ground beside him, and was gathering a handful in his stubby fist, his face contorted with pain and insane rage.

"I wouldn't mate," Daniel said in a low growl, summoning his sleek black pistol with nearly his last scrap of magic as the magic in the lock bled them both dry, and leveled it at Milton's head. The other man froze, and Daniel summoned his cane back to his other hand, limping forward three steps to stand over the Councilor, between him and the lock that promised evil to anyone who'd magic he managed to shove in. "Dissolve those. All of them." Daniel dipped his chin, indicating the box, and cocked the pistol when Milton started to object. "Now."

Slowly, resistantly, Milton waved a hand over the box, and the faintest, weakest thread of orchid-pink magic dissolved the multicolored shards of glass back into ephemeral wisps of magic. Daniel used the very last small scrap of his own magic to blow at the stolen wisps, speeding up their disintegration, only releasing the effort that strained him to his limits when the last had dissolved into nothing.

Just as Daniel was about to lower his gun, Milton started laughing. Just a low chuckle, looking past Daniel's legs toward the water, building into barking gales when Daniel heard the crunch of gravel and turned to see five magically obscured Councilors striding up the beach, all looking angry beneath the magic that hid their age, race, gender, or distinguishing features from being understood. He shifted his grip on the weapon pointed at Cartwright, and one of the Councilors put their arm out, stopping the rest.

"You have witnesses, now." Cartwright said between barks of laughter as they started to peter off, his expression almost elated. "Now everyone will know I have always been right about you. Even if, by the looks of it, the Senate has fallen."

Daniel almost laughed, disbelieving. "Is that really something you still care about after all these years? Have you found no greater desires, or purpose in your life?"

Cartwright paused, seeming to only half-register, lost beneath unguessable delusions and obsession. "You killed her. My friend, my recruit, your sponsor. All I have done since, I have done to make you pay in kind, finally see true justice. For everything to know I'm not a liar."

"Well congratulations," Daniel said with contempt. "I'm pretty sure they all know now. But you have always been a liar, and proving one conspiracy true won't change the fact that everyone will remember you as one."

More and more people were pouring through the Threshold. All of them were, as far as Daniel could tell, Senators or Supreme Justices, past or present, many with their partners, most carrying injured friends or luggage. Daniel's stomach flipped, wondering if it meant that Angie and her group had been overrun and defeated or scared off, but pushed the sickening thought aside, turning back to Cartwright, who had shifted to recline decadently on the pebbled beach at his feet.

The pain and nausea the Councilor was still feeling from having his powers restricted was clear beneath his attempt at a satisfied smile, and Daniel backed away a pace, lowering his arm. He was painfully aware of so many pairs of eyes watching him, each new arrival being shushed into quiet observance, glad that he had been able to recover quicker, having felt the horrible sensation before. Daniel looked around for someone, anyone, who might be on his side, huffing ruefully when he realized how many were his former blackmail targets now staring at him with cautious loathing.

Daniel raked fingers through his hair, buying himself a moment to think as Milton slowly stood. None of it had worked. Not joining. Not leading. Not running away completely, or hovering at the edges. Daniel leveled his gun at Cartwright once more, indicating that he should stay put. Nearby, Barbara Collins took a step forward before stopping short, and the glance Daniel could spare her wasn't enough to tell if her instinct was to defend or attack him.

Cartwright smiled as five Councilors and two hundred other patricians fanned out around the circle of thrones, spaced out nervously between the unmoving ocean and the obsidian cliff reaching toward the sky. "You will never get what you want," Milton said softly, almost believable as the kindly and magnanimous caricature he'd once liked people to see him as. "No matter what you do. Not even if you kill me."

"Then what's there to keep you alive?" Daniel saw his question make Milton pale a shade, and lifted his voice to be heard by all as his mind stilled down to a single purpose. "A year ago, you had personally, maliciously, killed hundreds for your own gain. Now, with the damage happening in the wider world to cover your retreat here, it's at least thousands through your orders. You've lied, cheated, manipulated, and stolen your whole life even from the offices you were elected to, over and over, and yet somehow you kept winning. Over and over, tearing people down along the way, corrupting everything you touched."

Daniel could sense the mood of the onlookers shift slightly and steeled himself. "You've tried to take my heart from me over and over, and took half of it when you killed my brother. Now I finally get to take from you in kind. I swear on all I love—so much more than you, any of you, could believe me capable of—that I do this for the greater good."

A single, cracking shot rang through the air as Daniel shot Milton Cartwright through the heart, the sound redoubling off the obsidian cliff. The sound shook loose more thoughts and emotions than Daniel could begin to name.

Chapter Forty-One

Angie was riding high on the triumph of finally destroying the shields that had kept them from the Threshold for nearly a full hour, and followed the tug of Daniel's aura through the membrane of magic just in time to see Milton drop heavily to his knees on the black pebbled beach as Daniel lowered his army-issue pistol, the sound of the shot still reverberating through the predawn air.

Everyone's attention was riveted forward towards the circle of obsidian thrones beneath the cliffs, their feet frozen in place as Angie walked through their ranks, followed by a stream of her companions. Angie's awareness was held less by Milton pitching face-first onto the gravel, and more by Daniel as he reached into the Focal Nucleus he stood beside, plucking out a thread of yellow aura held within.

One of the Councilors nearby moved forward and Angie gave a short, sharp shout, pulling their attention to her as she took in their disconcerting concealment. "Oi. Don't be rash, now." Her tone was light and teasing, but with an edge the Councilor caught, falling back.

Daniel heard her and turned, his face unreadable but his aura swelling with rich yellow light as it blossomed back to full strength, warming the morning considerably. "You made it through," he said, his voice full of relief as he reholstered his gun, shedding the jacket covering it and turning to toss it on a throne in an exaggerated movement Angie noticed allowed him to do a full scan of every person watching.

Angie pushed past the Senator standing in her path between two thrones, feeling the hair on her arms stand up as she passed. In the background, a general murmur of unease was building as more and more outcast adepts from a dozen languages continued streaming through the Threshold, neither side quite sure what to do, or when.

She walked up to meet Daniel just beside the center of the magical flow cycling down through the center of the circle of thrones, through the beach below, to flow back up around the outside and complete the cycle. The two of them simply looked at the other for a long moment before Angie looked down at the body on the ground beside them. For a long moment she let herself imagine the deep relief and satisfaction Daniel must be feeling at the sight, but the thought quickly soured. Just as she had taken no true pleasure in killing her abuser a lifetime of nearly a day ago, she knew Daniel too well to truly believe it had been a source of pleasure for him.

She met his gaze again with a small, sad smile, and without breaking it, snapped her fingers with a flare of her aura, reducing the body of Milton Cartwright to ash that was quickly scattered and gone by the restless wind swirling around them. As if it was the signal everyone had been waiting for, a great clamor roared to life on all sides as conflict exploded.

Angie sent up a wild beacon to Dawn, hoping she could bring reinforcements, and almost missed a flash of movement in the corner of her eye lunging for the core of power beside her. Angie moved to react, but the Councilor bounced off of her shields as a wild chunk of magic went hurtling over their heads.

"Your oligarchy is over," Angie said with bitter joy, watching the Councilor eyeing the lock of magic threads beside them within the shield. "You can no longer force your twisted, sadistic will onto the masses." Angie's fire teased up, almost lazily, and she let it as the Councilor turned away, unreadable.

Angie scanned further out over the crowd as dozens more rebels arrived, and soon overwhelmed the patricians with sheer numbers. Almost as quickly as it had started, the fighting ceased. Stragglers who refused to stand down were efficiently herded to the Threshold and tossed through by Dawn, who laid a latticework shield over it Angie suspected would prevent anyone she didn't approve of from returning from that particular destination.

The Councilor who had made a run for the Focal Nucleus sat down on one of the thrones, and one by one the others did the same, all still obscured. Other people pushed their way to the front of the crowd that once more turned to watch, many of them Senators and other people of power and influence Angie recognized. Barbara Collins, Lord and Lady Braithwaite, Noah Byrne, and a dozen others she'd spoken to at some point were among those that packed themselves into a tight ring in between the thrones, others stacked in behind them.

"What do we do now?" Daniel asked, unbuttoning his cuffs and rolling up the sleeves of his black silk shirt. "My magic's gone. Milton did something with a scrap of my magic in the lock there." He tugged off his tie and banished it as Angie's aura warmed the air around them to an uncomfortable degree, which she suspected his own added to.

Angie blew a long breath through pursed lips, doing her best to process a thousand possible pros and cons in a few seconds. She gestured to one of the two empty thrones—the one Daniel had tossed his jacket onto—and he followed her direction, settling himself with ease. As he sat, Marissa Hayward quietly slipped into the throne beside him, her full attention fixed on him, and one of the Councilors laughed, dozens of patricians copying them nervously.

"What exactly is it that you want, Miss Forester?" they asked, their voice layered with too many pitches and accents to pull apart. "Is it a seat amongst us? Because it appears yours has been taken."

Angie soothed the way the patterns of smoke in her aura swelled at the jab. "I want justice, and safety," she replied, feeling herself heat when another ripple of laughter answered. "Not just for myself, but for everyone. I want the world to be better."

"Is that all?" the Councilor mocked. "Well, I don't fancy your chances of taking on the Council in our own holy site, even if you can keep us away from our Focal Nucleus for an hour, or a day. You can't change or break us."

"That's where you're wrong," Angie snarled. "There *will* be a new counsel in power before any of you leave this place, and it *will* be one that represents the people and acts in the interest of all those who have been locked away from magic for centuries." She tried to see any of her friends and comrades over the line of sneering, jeering, angry faces ringing her, a glittering wall of fine clothes and jewels, but failed.

Angie reached for her necklace, breaking the chain with a sharp tug, curling her fingers around the silver key pendant. She saw several people watching gasp, surging forward, but Angie's magic flared out to brush them or their shields and they fell back. She felt deep inside, willing herself to shift to flames that wouldn't be dragged under by the flow of magic without losing her anchor in solidity or memory. The demons of long, hurt, mistreated anger in her heart sang, and she shifted. "Your time is over, and you can't stop a new day from dawning forever."

Angie plunged her fist into the lock, pulling all the heat away from the silver of the key in it until the demon screeched out, livid at having been disturbed from its home and dying in the half-world that was foreign to it. The moment Angie reached into the lock she dissolved the scrap of Daniel's aura held there with the first small splinter of the dying demon.

She could feel the other intentions, controls, and patterns built into the Latin Focal Nucleus, exerting their force over the wider world of Angie's earth. A bead of sweat rolled down the back of her neck.

An ancient language begging to die. Nuclear bombs on airplanes already in the sky, waiting on simple orders to drop. Oppression and exploitation of a global Empire, now made hollow but no less insistent by the loss of the language Court disseminating the goal. Massacres of innocents, for no better reason than needing to shut up those pointing out how miserable their lives were. Life magic, in its entirety, glowing and mysterious, diminished from millennia spent locked away. Unlimited resources for anyone with magic and the knack for conjuring them, just out of reach and stagnant from disuse. Fresh, young shoots of new languages desperate to see the light, carefully pruned back every time they reach for the sky.

She didn't even notice that Daniel had stopped time until the repeated, looping of the screeching demon drilled through her skull, forcing her back to her immediate reality. She looked around quickly, realizing she hadn't yet been attacked as expected, and decided that the pure shock on the faces of most of the onlookers was her saving grace.

It took her a moment to realize that the five remaining Councilors enthroned before her had been unmasked, and she smiled darkly as she took each one in. A middle-aged Hindustani man sat opposite Daniel, a beautiful young blonde woman on one side, an ancient man wearing the long robes and head coverings of the Arabian peninsula on the other. On his other side sat an oddly nondescript man with pale skin, almost no hair, and a bulbous nose, dressed in a stuffy, dusty-green uniform of some sort, and beside him sat the plump, curly, worried Jasper Rose. Angie's surprise that the patrician she'd always thought of as sweet and mild-mannered was a member of the Council only caught her for a moment before she pushed it aside.

"This is your chance," Angie called out, walking in a slow circle around her fist in the center of the splintering lock of magic, her attention split between assessing her audience, and monitoring her state of grace within the torrential magic threatening to go very, very wrong if given half a chance. "If you want to ever convince anyone that you saw the error of your ways. That you were one of those who stepped aside to make way for the new order when it reigns, then this is your last fucking chance to change with the tides and step away."

Many onlookers shifted uncomfortably. Some audibly gasped as Jasper Rose stood, stone-faced, before turning and stepping away. Dawn stepped forward to take their place, seeming to appear from thin air, and settled herself into the throne with a wide, flashy smile. Angie turned her piercing attention to Marissa, where she sat beside Daniel, and the raven-haired beauty squirmed. Casey appeared beside her, placing a hand on her shoulder, his expressive face pleading, and after another beat of hesitation, Marissa let him take her place, melting back into the crowd.

Many of the other faces Angie knew in the first row of standing patricians between the thrones dropped their heads and turned away as Angie's gaze fell across them, each one bringing her a note of relief and pride that those who knew her best believed that she was not to be fucked with.

"You don't know what you are doing," the pretty blond Councilor said in a heavy French accent, her beachy-waves shifting as she shook her head, her lips pursed. "This lock is not like the others. If you break that, you break too much. You break the system of order and of law. You break the ancient Patrician Order, and you cannot understand what that means, or you wouldn't even think of it. You would be inviting and creating even worse suffering than you now think you are stopping us from."

Angie hissed through her teeth, prepared to rebut, but Dawn cut her off. "Angie, stand down," she said. "We can bargain from this position. We can do this without tipping over that edge."

"No," Angie said, her vision clouded by more than just her flames, smoke, and glimmers of heat. "The time for negotiation and compromise ended when Jonathan was murdered."

Dawn's expression turned wooden. She swallowed several times, her gold aura shivering in close to her skin. "He's dead?" Her voice was small and tight, and Angie couldn't do more than reflect the deep pain and sorrow that flashed across Dawn's smooth face before she seemed to collapse and shrink, dropping her face and hiding it with her long, thick braids, dyed deep blue, her whole body silently shaking.

"Listen to her," the Hindustani man said, with a sideways bob of his head toward Dawn. "You've had your little victory. Now go home. You can't break this Council without breaking your own world, and you can't get what you want by taking a seat for yourself. You can never truly be one of us."

The words struck something deep in Angie, ingrained into her life since magic like a splinter that she could never quite get out. "I have never wanted to be one of you!" The world bubbled from her like lava, thick with anger, resentment, and disgust. "I have never wanted to be a selfish, mean, fascist fucking sellout. You have all been telling me that I can't truly be one of you since I was given my magic, and not once have I taken it as an insult. It is the greatest reassurance any of you have ever given me for my future, and the future of my world and loved ones.

"You are all evil fucking fascists," Angie shouted, refusing to feel anything other than powerful in owning her emotions, and finally speaking the truth to so many ears who didn't want to hear it. "You are in no position to decide who is in or out." Angie poked at the demon suspended in her fist, mid-death, and it shrieked a little louder, the first shard of its glassy, fracturing demise slicing off into the pebbles at the feet of the ancient Arab man, taking a few strands of the Latin lock with it. "I am. Now get out. Every single one of you who was appointed to this Council before today, stand up and leave. It's time

for someone more deserving, and significantly less practiced at causing harm, to take your place."

"A little girl like you can't scare me," the Hindustani
Councilor said, narrowing his eyes. "I am Ramesh. The
longest-sitting member of this Council, and the architect
of the world for the last thirty years. You don't scare me."

"No? Let's see if I can convince you." She felt
light-headed from how much power she was using, but
Angie pushed for another burst, and Ramesh brought his
shields up a moment too late to not choke on the bitter
smoke of burning plastic. He coughed harder and harder,
clearly trying to clear it with his own magic, and Angie
smiled. "Drop your shields and I'll stop." Ramesh stood,
his eyes wide, and coughed several more times before
dropping his shields, and Angie's smoke returned to her.

"You stupid bitch," he coughed, his graying mustache
quivering.

Angie's aura flared briefly, and Ramesh sank awkwardly
to one knee, his hand flying to the fresh burn on his
shoulder that had forced him down. "No," he snarled
through gritted teeth. "I sacrificed too much to get here. I
have too much to lose in stepping away" He stood shakily
using the arm of his chair. "Your man may have the balls
to kill a Councilor who targeted him for many years, but
I doubt you have the balls to kill anyone."

Angie only hesitated for a moment before snapping
her fingers, and Ramesh screamed as he burned from the
inside out, falling into a pile of ash. The intentions of the
Latin lock still pulsed through the sixth sense awareness
of her aura, and Angie felt no remorse, overwhelmed by

how much suffering she knew with certainty had come from every single person who had ever had the chance to change or fix it and chosen not to in her lifetime alone.

"You have all gone far too long without remembering what fairness even is. You were all ready to destroy a fucking planet because the people who live there aren't willing to keep kneeling before you without complaint. So now, here's what I demand from you. Leave now, and maybe you get to live."

The onlookers cheered and booed, and Angie felt the tension ratchet up. There were many, many adepts she didn't recognize from other languages, and she couldn't tell if they were booing her, or her leniency.

The ancient man stood, trembling, and held onto the back of his throne to turn away. The pale man in the uniform stood to help the old man shuffle away, looking caught between resentment and relief before they stepped through the Threshold. A half dozen rebels moved to follow, but others held them back with dark looks at Angie.

The French woman lingered longer, her hands braced on the armrests of her throne, looking around as if waiting for someone to swoop in and spare her. Angie willed a blast of flames in her direction as she pushed the demon cracking out through her fist of flame another degree, and the last Councilor stood with a squeal, half-tripping on the pebbled beach before disappearing into the crowd behind her throne.

Just as Angie took a breath, not even able to process what she'd just done and won, a great dowsing power landed on her, and she gasped. Three enforcers off to one side all had their auras trained on her, and more patricians quickly joined as they realized what was happening. Angie couldn't breathe in, and the magic pouring over her in an ever-increasing deluge threatened to extinguish her flames. Angie turned her full attention to her fist in the heart of the Focal Nucleus, willing it to stay as flame that wouldn't be harmed, and could come and go at will without help.

For a moment, Angie desperately considered backing off and Voyaging or Skipping away to escape the massive, targeted attack and try again some other day, but a single, deep breath of air, touched with pale yellow magic, broke her panic. With each breath she took after, oxygenated magic rich with a faint awareness of love and admiration fed her fire until she could easily withstand the assault.

She spotted Daniel through the blinding torrent of magic, seeing him fighting off a dozen attempts to repress his own magic which was feeding her, her heart swelling with love and pride. She caught his eyes and mouthed the words '*time-stop*'. As she did so, Angie gathered every scrap of herself she had ever held back, bending her knees, and threw it into her aura as she straightened to her full height, the moment of expansive bliss overriding all else. It roared up in her, fed and fanned by Daniel's Air magic. Milton had been right to fear their combined efforts.

A firestorm roiled over everything and everyone nearby. Angie held her intention firm that it should not burn any flesh or clothing, but let the sheer impact of the heat and light pummel against every surface, redoubling and reflecting off of the obsidian cliffs back out towards the frozen sea. As she did so, the demon in Angie's fist stopped skipping like a broken record and exploded outward with every scrap of heat, power, and intention Angie could dump into it, a hundred shards ripping apart the last patrician lock in existence from the inside out, each thread of ancient control caught and torn away.

The experience was ecstatic. Complete control and mastery over the forces within her she had struggled to control since they were first awakened, in a moment of complete, blissfully entwined melding with Daniel's magic beside her.

A lifetime of frustration, discontent, and injustice seemed to come full circle in Angie's soul, and she was barely aware of her surroundings when time restarted in more ways than she'd anticipated as the flow of magic that had been so carefully preserved by the lock at its core disintegrated.

The whole world lurched with enough force to send Angie and everyone else flying a few feet through the air, landing hard on the pebbled beach. Daniel's magic once more separated for hers, and the guttering draft she felt in its absence made her arms prickle.

"Daniel..." Angie was up to her knees again before most, pushing her hair out of her face with a hand of solid flesh, still clutched around her key pendant. Daniel was pushing himself up from the black pebbled beach nearby and seemed unharmed.

She twisted to see the cycling flow of magic through the Latin language holy site past him slow, drift apart, and bleed out into the cool morning air as the first rays of sunrise touched the top of the cliff face high overhead. Angie wasn't the only one who spotted the small glimmer of gold shining off the obsidian, and she scrambled to her feet as the distraction caught many of the onlookers, stuffing the silver key with the three interlocking rings at the handle carefully deep into her pocket.

Daniel appeared at her side, and Angie gave him a long, grateful, look of shocked triumph which he returned. Around them, most of the others had gotten back to their feet, and Angie reached for the last of her powers. She flared them in a great, showy ball of fire that expanded harmlessly passed everyone on the beach in a rainbow of red, orange, yellow, blue, white, gray, and black, before reaching its zenith and shrinking back down to encapsulate Angie in a skin of fire and smoke as she walked up the empty obsidian throne framed squarely beneath the cliff face.

Silence hung heavy in the creeping sunrise, and Angie contemplated the throne for a long moment before turning and gracefully settling into it, her hands dangling over the ends of the armrests dripping flames to the black pebbles below. She settled an easy, dark smile across her face, and looked out at the sea of faces before her, only truly seeing a few.

Once upon a time, Jonathan had been her single audience member as she'd sat on a black throne on the stage of the Globe in London, and wondered to her out loud if the sight was a prophetic one. Angie's throat tightened and her eyes stung. He'd be proud of her, right? The thought was followed closely by another that cut deep. *I'd give all of this up for another day with him in the world.*

Daniel was the nearest person to her, and Angie drank in the sight of him standing before her in the flat half-light, illuminated by his own glowing magic. His skin was lightly sheened with sweat, the cuffs of his shirt still rolled up to reveal his leanly muscled arms and the tattoos on the insides of his wrists. He'd drawn his gun again at some point in the last scuffle, and the sight of it casually in his hand thrilled and scared her. He watched her closely, unreadable, for a long minute before summoning his holster, putting it on, and slipping the weapon into it beneath his shoulder. He took three long, elegant strides, and settled himself on the throne beside her.

Dawn sat stiffly in the throne on Angie's other side, her hands in her lap, unreadable, and Casey took the throne beyond her. Mahina, Anthony Shupee, and one of Dawn's wives, Olivia, took the rest, and Angie watched, deeply moved but painfully detached, as one by one, every single lavishly dressed patrician she could see was nudged and shoved out of the way for an ordinary adept in jeans, or a hoodie, or a floral-print dress to take their place.

She slowly let the fire encasing her fade, feeling more depleted than she ever could have imagined. She watched straight ahead as the golden glow of the rising sun swelled just below the far-distant ocean horizon, centered over the obsidian Threshold, and everyone else joined her.

Her losses, wins, failures, and triumphs of the last day tumbled over each other through her heart, mind, and soul, and as the first rays of sunlight to touch the core of all patrician magic in thousands of years touched her eyes, Angie closed them, and let herself just exist for the first time in far, far too long.

CHAPTER FORTY-TWO

Angie opened her eyes when Daniel's aura caressed hers in an alert, and saw the Threshold before her ripple, expanding forward to outline the front of a person before snapping back away, revealing the newcomer. Angie recognized them as an enforcer from her first conference, a tall man with a uniquely strong jaw and dark, receding hair. He stopped short after only a few steps as more people started coming through after him, frowning at the unexpected array of people on the thrones.

Angie stood, bracing to fight another wave of patricians who'd missed the handover, but the man yielded a step, raising his palms. "Look, I clearly missed something," he said, flinching, dropping his arms to cradle one with the other. "But it doesn't matter much. The world's on fire. Cell phone communications are down across the globe, and the Imperial army is all but dissolved, since almost all auxiliaries have deserted in numbers too high for the legionnaires or centurions to keep rounded up." Daniel stood up beside her, shifting in closer, and the man sighed, glancing over his shoulder at the injured and wide-eyed patricians streaming through the Threshold. "Is Ragnarök off, then?"

"Yes," Angie and Daniel said firmly in unison.

"Well, then. We'd better all go do something about the lunatics trying to burn the world to the ground. We aren't sure who, but it definitely seems to be a magical source for some of the worst ones. Or, that might just be the media spinning it. Radio's still working, somehow."

Angie felt Daniel's aura ripple cold, and touched his bicep with a reassuring caress of warmth through her aura. "We will," she said softly. "But five minutes, or even an hour, won't make much difference." Daniel relaxed an inch. "They won't bomb a world they still have to live in, and with all of the Focal Nucleus locks broken, the orders to do so have gone silent." Angie stretched up to her tiptoes, searching for Marissa among the growing hoard of bodies, but didn't see her.

Angie's gaze slid past where the Latin lock had been, now an empty patch of air over a boring spread of dark pebbles. It didn't feel real that the Patrician Order had fallen, and with it everything it had controlled. "So the Empire?" she asked, already knowing the answer.

"Fallen," the man with the injured shoulder said as Lady Braithwaite appeared at his side, her face stern as her honey-colored aura spread like a salve over the joint. "There are rumors that the emperor is holed up in Rome, but his reach has been severed."

"The wound in the world," Angie whispered to herself, remembering how Daniel had once described her act of breaking the English Focal Nucleus to her.

Daniel overheard, watching her. "It looks ugly, but it's clean."

The words brought Angie far more comfort than she expected. A good chunk of her stress left her with a silent sigh, replaced by a creeping, avoidant numbness she knew she would pay for later but didn't have the energy left to fight.

A ripple of commotion made them both turn, and Angie saw the telltale flash of Seth's ginger hair and the coiling ropes of fire in his aura. A small woman seemed to be dragging him forward by the hand, and Angie blinked in surprise when she realized it was Léa. Her heart-shaped face beneath her mountain of hair was distorted with grief and joy, the combination making Angie uneasy.

Seth spotted Daniel, and his face lit up, eagerly grinning at his sponsor's clear place of prominence and influence in the grand setting. Angie felt Daniel shudder almost imperceptibly through his aura, and felt blissfully vindicated in her early and lasting dislike of his newest recruit.

"I'm so sorry," Léa said, her eyes glinting with her burnt-orange magic. Her voice changed, reverberating with new layers, and Angie put an arm around Daniel's back as she felt him tense.

"An angel of flame and chaos will bring an end to order. Water will stand against the Empire and fall.

Demons shall let the angel pass, leading them to the broken door.

The Angel in the Forest. Two are one, one is two, all is nothing.

Fawl's fall... Beware the Flame..."

"Stop," Daniel interrupted, and Léa closed her mouth with a snap.

"I'm so, so sorry." She giggled, picked up a stone from the beach, and disappeared with a cry of grief.

"Was that Léa?" Dawn asked, appearing from a cluster of people, her voice hoarse. Angie nodded, and Dawn swore. "I'll catch up with you both later. I have to go deal with that." She jogged to and through the Threshold, Seth hot on her tail, and Angie tried to ignore the knot of stress that formed in her gut. She couldn't begin to do anything with what had just happened, and pushed it aside to worry about how many of her rebellion friends Seth and his kind were seeing in the revealing setting until that, too, had to be pushed aside for Angie to not collapse in on herself.

She spotted a face in the crowd she hadn't noticed before, and waved for Demitria to come over, Nikolaus trailing protectively behind her. Angie tried not to see the fresh tears reddening both their eyes, or the fully unlocked terracotta-red aura swirling around the tall Hellenes man.

"Could you do me a favor?" Angie asked, looking past Demitria to beckon Dawn, Casey and the others still sitting to stand as people began moving more casually among the thrones and talking to each other, looking for loved ones, leaving through the Threshold, and such. She glanced at Daniel, needing some sign of reassurance or support from him before she went on and finding it. "I'd like you to destroy these thrones. Make sure that the Latin Language Court is dead for good."

Everyone in immediate earshot looked stunned. Demitria nodded hesitantly, replying in imperfect English. "Okay. But didn't you say you wanted there to be the new Council for the people like us?"

Angie smiled as genuinely as she could, weariness settling heavily over her. "Yes, I did say that. But I might have been wrong. The Latin lock is gone completely. That was what made the Council what it was. But even if there is a new Council someday," Angie gestured around at the empty-feeling thrones in the glowing, fresh morning light, "it shouldn't be ruled from thrones. Please."

Demitria nodded, and, with a glance at Olivia, she raised her hands, closed her eyes, and all seven thrones crumbled to piles of rubble.

"Thank you," Angie said and Demitria blushed, bobbing her head, and Nikolaos pulled her away.

For an awful moment, Angie didn't have the faintest clue what to do next. Mild panic bubbled up in her as she tried to think of any next step to take, literally or otherwise. Then Daniel shifted beside her, and her doubt and apprehension shifted to her core. "Daniel," she said softly, turning to him fully and stepping in so only he could hear. He said nothing in response, as hard to read as Angie's own emotions felt to share. As had been the case all day since her return to flesh, a thousand things that needed to be said hovered on the tip of Angie's tongue, but none passed her lips. The grief in some of them lodged in her throat, and across from her Daniel's Adam's apple bobbed.

"What comes next?" she asked, hating herself for asking the easiest question, even as she was flooded with relief at handing over the responsibility of knowing to anyone else.

Daniel scratched his beard, glanced at his hand, and summoned a pair of black leather gloves from somewhere, pulling them on. "Next, we watch the sunrise."

Angie huffed a weak laugh, but let Daniel pull her into a careful embrace. She let the world around them fall away from her awareness, breathing in the smell of him, the solid warmth of his arms, and relishing the feeling of the sunlight on her cheek. She turned to look out where the shining gold sun was just finishing rising over the iron-gray sea, sending glittering rivers of gold sparkles out across the water.

"As it should be," Daniel said, and Angie tried her best to hear the hope he clearly intended for his words to hold. "Moving forward into an unknown future. Not holding onto the stagnant moment of the present. You did good."

Chapter Forty-Three

A ngie felt the burden of her grief grow heavier with every passing day. Not just for the loss of her dearest friend, but for the world she and the rest were scrambling to salvage, and more subtle losses inside herself and in the space between her and Daniel which she wasn't ready to unpack yet.

She made her way down the ground floor hallway of the Tudor mansion on the English Conference site, picking her way around the trash and vandalism that had beaten them to there after the magical protections hiding and disguising the site had fallen in the chaos in the solstice. Thankfully, the rural sites had been spared most of the devastation that had hit the bigger cities.

Her aching, incessant sorrow deepened as she pushed open the door to Jonathan's office. A lack of sleep pressed at her eyes as much as the tears that filled her nights instead, and she instinctively tapped the front pocket of her jeans, wishing to the bottom of her heart that she still had the first, old copper sigil coin Jonathan had given her at her first conference that had been the key to her survival on so, so many occasions. She wanted a memento of him to hold on to.

She stood in the doorway, looking around vacantly, glad to see the room seemed to have been ignored by the vandals that had come through. Angie didn't see any of the books or papers usually strewn across the spindly desk, but a standing file cabinet in the far corner beside the window looked promising. As Angie crossed the room, she glanced at her reflection in the round, bronze-framed mirror behind the desk, and stumbled to a stop, her face going slack.

It felt like a dream as Jonathan's dear face looked back at her from where her own reflection should be. Reality stood respectfully suspended as Angie took in every line of his tan face, every dark hair on his head and in his trimmed beard, her chest starting to heave as her careful scan came to rest on his kind, observant ice-blue eyes. Her vision blurred, and she quickly blinked it away, afraid the sight would be gone the moment she looked away, sending tears rolling down her cheeks.

Jonathan's face in the mirror was compassionate and sad, and Angie searched for what to say, knowing she must either be dreaming or hallucinating and not wanting to mess up the last thing she might ever get to say to the only person who had ever made her feel so completely known, safe to be herself, and utterly dear while expecting nothing in return. She tried to get a dozen thoughts to form on her lips, but none could do justice to everything in her heart.

"I know," Jonathan's image said, in the exact tone of voice he'd always used in real life, and as the words touched Angie's ears, there were suddenly none other that could ever have been as perfect, or that she'd needed to hear so badly without realizing it. Angie sobbed fully, falling to a heap on the floor as grief consumed her.

She'd expected the break over into release to wake her up, but when the deepest crying eased and Angie still knelt on the floor, hunched over her knees, she sat up, bewildered, still blubbering slightly and sniffling. The mirror looked empty from the floor, but as Angie stood, the top of his head appeared exactly when she expected to see her own, his full, dear face appearing when she stood fully upright.

"I miss you," Angie said, the words tied tightly to the deep ache they pulled from, making it throb.

"I am always nearby. I will always be there with you, one way or another."

A fresh sob shook Angie's whole body, glad her memory had recalled the exact intonation of this voice with those words he'd spoken to her once before. More tears fell down her face, and Angie walked forward, pushing the desk to one side to avoid losing her line of sight. Jonathan's face grew larger as she got nearer, just like her own reflection would.

When she touched the glass, a small shock connected with her finger, making her snatch it back. Jonathan-in-the-mirror smiled, the smile lines at the sides of his eyes cracking deep, and Angie watched in astonishment as his imaged moved forward from the glass like colored mist, slowing expanding down to form shoulders, arms, a torso, legs, and feet until a life-size projection of him stood before her.

Angie didn't know what to do or say, numb shock having overridden her sorrow for a moment. "Is this real?" she eventually managed, finally acknowledging the impossible truth that she was definitely awake. He clearly wasn't solid, more the consistency of thick smoke, and he smiled.

"You're not hallucinating, if that's what you're asking." Angie just stared and Jonathan stepped aside, gesturing at the mirror. "Look at the back."

Angie stepped forward, angling herself to keep Jonathan in her line of sight as she tilted the mirror away from the wall, still afraid the vision was going to fade. A glint of copper fell away from the lower rim of the mirror frame in the back, and Angie caught it reflexively. The size, shape, and weight were instantly and intimately familiar, and Angie pressed the sigil coin that had seen her through her banishment to her chest with both hands, her face pinching with shocked, emotional relief.

Angie's mouth pulled wide and she cried again, this time with an overwhelming joy and relief she could never have expected. She held the coin to her like it would melt the moment it touched the air, and she would lose her best friend all over again. She hadn't lost all of him. She wouldn't forget what he looked like, or the sound of his voice, and that step up from utter loss sent her soul soaring.

A minute passed as Jonathan stood beside her, and Angie quieted once more, finally daring to look away from him as she pulled down one long sleeve of her dress, drying her wet face.

"Did we win?" Jonathan asked with a lopsided grin, the tilt of his dark brows betraying his hidden, worried concern beneath the question.

Angie laughed, strange and raw, the act deeply welcome in her tight chest. "I think so," she said, not willing to think about it as deeply in that moment as she did when she should be sleeping. "The Patrician Order was defeated, the Empire with it. All the people of earth are free." Angie knew it was an exaggeration, but at least she had seen enough proof that many more were free now than had been a week ago to not feel guilty in saying so. "How are you..."

Jonathan's proud, beaming grin slipped a little toward sadness. He rubbed a hand across the back of his neck. "I'm... I'm a memory. A full set of a single person's memories, beliefs, thoughts, feelings, and the rest. A backup version of the personality that was Jonathan, if you will."

"Like Léa kept going on about," Angie said without really realizing.

"Yeah. Exactly. I suspected they were directed at me, so I spent all of my free time finding a way." His almost-opaque eyes glistened. "And I'm so glad I did."

"How?" Angie asked as a dozen more questions ran into each other after the first and she tried to make a mental list to not forget any.

Jonathan's ice-blue eyes searched hers for a long moment before he answered, looking apprehensive. When he spoke, his tone was cautious and soothing. "I promise I will tell you someday, Angie, but not today. I promise I have very good reasons to hold back for now. Please trust me. Just know that this memory saved version of me is magically stored in that coin. Where it goes, I also go."

Angie pressed the coin between her palms, her mind already racing through every precaution she could possibly take to ensure she never lost it, and could never have it stolen, when her stomach lurched. "Oh," she said in a very small voice. "Do...do you want me to give you to her? Your wife? And your kids?"

Jonathan shook his head with a wince of guilt. "No. They wouldn't understand, and it would prevent them from moving on. They are cared for by my brother and his family now, I think, with lots of Dawn's people to check in on them. Let them grieve."

Relief that she didn't have to part with the precious coin she'd just gotten back flooded her with the full force of her desperate fear of losing it during her banishment, and Angie released a calming breath. "And me?"

Jonathan smiled. "I'm selfish. I'm not ready to lose you, yet, either. I trust you to let me go when you're ready."

Angie nodded, trying to remember one of the other questions she'd meant to ask. "Oh! Do you want me to call you an angel? Since that's your faith?"

Jonathan blinked, clearly surprised. "No, but thank you for asking. My soul has moved on, if I had one. That's not what's left behind here. Call me a ghost, if you must. I am just memories."

Something nagged at Angie's mind, one last note of disbelief, and she chewed the inside of her cheek, trying to name it. "Do you really know me?" she asked, and before she could rephrase the question to be clearer, Jonathan's gentle answer stilled her worries.

"I always have, and I always will. Whoever you have been, are, or will become."

It was a long moment before Angie could reply, something more than she could understand within herself hovering just out of reach. "You were my home," she said, wishing it made more sense out loud than it did in her head. "I was always safe, and seen and understood around you. No matter what was going on with me, I always knew you'd be there for me, no matter what. Being around you was safe, and..." Angie's throat tightened, and she had to swallow several times before she could finish the thought. "I like the version of me I got to be around you the best. It felt more true that who I am with anyone else, even myself. And now, even with this ghost of you, it's gone." Angie dropped her head, turning the heavy copper coin over and over in her fingers. "I don't know where home is anymore, and don't even know what direction to go looking for it in."

"I hear you," Jonathan said, and Angie was content with the comfortable silence that followed.

When Angie finally felt ready to step out of the otherworldly moment, she shifted toward the door, giving Jonathan an awkwardly apologetic look.

Jonathan chuckled. "I'm bound to the coin, like I said. As long as you have it with you, I can be anywhere nearby, and I can go dormant back down inside it when you don't want to talk to me."

Angie nodded, relieved, and tucked the coin carefully into the deep pockets of her dress. As she strode toward the door, Jonathan asked, "Do you have any news about the locked half-world key vault?" and Angie's gut dropped.

"No," she replied. "But I've been there before. If the wards around it collapsed with so much of the other Senate and Court magic, maybe I can gut-instinct my way back?"

"Please try," Jonathan said, and Angie took a long moment to just appreciate the still-unreal relief of him no longer being absent in her life after grieving him so intensely. She shook herself and set her natural Voyaging ability out into her magic and intention, concentrating hard on the tiled basement she'd visited with Daniel once, picturing and feeling it with as much detail as she could conjure.

She'd barely shifted her weight to take a step when the Voyaging magic yanked her middle, and Angie's eyes flew back open.

She stood in a familiar windowless, tiled basement filled with emptied and smashed crates, stretched out before her all the way to the dead-end wall at the far end from where she stood, Angie spun around, realizing the vault door was just behind her, and her mouth fell open. The thick door stood open wide only a foot away, and the ringing, barren emptiness on the other side scared Angie to her bones.

She stepped into the cavern and sent a long blast of flames hurtling toward the distant side of the massive cavern. In the illumination of the fire, Angie looked around at the thousands upon thousands of tiny hooks in the stone walls that had once held keys to the half-worlds locked away by the most ancient adepts and more recent agents of the Patrician Order.

Every single one was gone. Angie was certain it wasn't any of her friends who had taken them.

Angie turned to Jonathan beside her, deeply relieved to not be there alone. His dear, weathered face was drawn with dismay and concern, and he turned away from the empty vault solemnly.

"You need to tell the others right away," he said, and Angie had to fight the smile that rose at the pure sound of his voice. "This is very, very bad. One last thing," he added as Angie nodded seriously and turned away. He looked nervous when Angie quirked a brow at him. "Please don't tell anyone else about me yet. I... I think I need time to adjust."

Ange nodded, not prepared to unpack anything more that day, and pulled the sigil coin from her pocket. She watched Jonathan fold down into it, disappearing completely into the metal, and as she Voyaged away to find Daniel, she felt uncomfortably reminded of watching demons fold themselves down into the silver key pendant hanging at her throat.

She glanced one last time into the empty vault, thinking back over the last few times she'd seen a key used in a Threshold, and she shuddered. There was someone she needed to find.

CHAPTER FORTY-FOUR

"**W**e found her!"

Daniel turned, relieved. He and Mahina had been speaking quietly about moving her and her family into the mountainside home above Lahaina where they could be safer and more comfortable, and he gave her a nod that promised they'd continue the conversation later as they both turned to where Angie and Anthony had just arrived.

They stood on one of the gravel paths bordering the little village green of what Daniel still thought of as the rebellion compound, supporting a shivering column of rags between them. Angie and Anthony quickly helped her to one of the picnic benches nearby, and Daniel warmed the already sweltering summer afternoon, hoping the woman they held would stop shaking and glad he was dressed down in a white button-down and khakis.

"This is Sakshi?" Daniel asked, resting a hand on the shoulder of Angie's dark blue jacket as she sat beside her rescued refugee, her freckled face full of guilt and relief.

"Yeah. Sakshi, I know you probably recognize him from your visions, but this is Daniel."

Sakshi raised trembling hands to push back the ragged shawl wrapped over her head, and Daniel tried to hide his shock. Her face across her eyes was heavily scarred, he guessed from an acid attack, her rich brown skin fused and melted. She was, without a doubt, fully blind, and he frowned, puzzling over Angie's assumption that she'd recognize him before remembering that she was a true Seer and shifting uncomfortably.

"Oh, the thread," Angie said, turning to Daniel, and he summoned the large hank of fine silk thread Angie had asked him to find, handing it to her. Angie placed it in Sakshi's hands, and the Hindustani woman stilled, smiling.

Daniel stepped back as the hank in Sakshi's hands unraveled like it had life of its own, glowing with her turquoise magic, and snaked out faster than he could track to touch and trace every object nearby, flinching back from the feet of the people when it bumped them. People had slowed and gathered to gawk as they went about their day, and many skittered away from the threads before reading the lack of stress in the four people nearest the newcomer, and cautiously relaxing.

"Thank you," Sakshi whispered on a breath rich with gratitude. "May I?" she said, turning to Daniel, and with an encouraging smile from Angie, he nodded, releasing his shields a degree. In a few seconds, the turquoise-tinged threads scaled his body like fast, tiny snakes, clustering more densely over his face and hands than the rest of him.

Daniel swallowed, deeply uncomfortable, and the threads retreated as quickly as they'd advanced. Angie looked up toward the common house, twitching like she was going to jump up, but didn't. Daniel turned to see Casey duck his head and slip around the side of the building out of sight as quickly as he could while still appearing casual. When he turned back to Angie, her lips were pressed tight, and Daniel sensed she was trying to not look at where the young man had disappeared. Daniel hadn't asked what their falling out had been, and doubted he would before she chose to tell him.

"Thank you," Sakshi said again, and Daniel released his added heat to the air, seeing that she'd stopped shaking. "Someone said they were you before, and my Sight..." she trailed off, her face contorting. "You weren't the first to find me. Another did, a short while ago. He was blocked from my Sight, but he sounded like Fawl, and smelled like Angie, so I trusted him. He rescued me, made me think I was safe, and asked me questions."

Sakshi's aura was condensed around her head, and Daniel tugged at Angie's jacket, pulling her away from the Hindustani woman, and motioning with his head for Anthony to do the same. Both gave him questioning looks, but Daniel knew what he was doing. Any Seer who used their gift regularly fell to the madness of it, and his gut was telling him such a moment was coming.

Sure enough, when Sakshi spoke again, her voice was touched with insanity, but thankfully not the layered tones of prophecy, the threads running through her hands writhing out from her along every surface like she was caught in a thick spider web. "I told him the words of the alone one. He asked for them all. When I told him, he thanked me and took me back to where he found me. But I lied." Sakshi giggled, a deranged, helpless sound, her mouth stretched tight with a smile. "I didn't tell him everything. Even the part you didn't hear, fallen one. I didn't tell him about—"

"No," Daniel said quickly, his wind teasing up. He felt Angie's gaze on him, warm and intense, and found the words he needed to express his deep revolution at the thought of having more prophecy hanging over his future. "No one decides our fates but us."

Angie gave him a wide smile, which he returned, and Sakshi was silent. She tilted her head, her face turned toward him for a long moment. Daniel watched as she slowly became serious, and her aura released and evened out around her. "I understand. But not knowing what lies ahead on your path doesn't stop you from reaching it."

"I know," Daniel said, his jaw tight. "But if we don't know what is supposed to come next, we can't help it be a self-fulfilling one."

"As you wish. But you may ask me when you're ready to know."

"Do you think it was Seth?" someone said behind him, and Daniel jumped slightly, turning to see Nikolaos and Demitria. Both were watching Sakshi closely, and Daniel was glad that Nikolaos had been warned to avoid using his gift of Sight as much as possible to delay the effects, as the Hindustani woman clearly hadn't been given the chance to.

An image of Léa seated on a stone bench beside him flitted before his eyes, fear creasing her heart-shaped face as her aunt asked her to use her gift to aid their cause despite the damage to her young mind. Guilt soured the air of Daniel's aura, overriding his lingering bitterness toward the girl for letting him believe Angie was dead all through her banishment.

Everyone nearby turned to Daniel, and he failed to hide his shudder. Beside him, Angie shrank back, clearly not wanting the attention she was getting by standing beside him. "Maybe. He's been trying to reconnect with me since the solstice. But I've had my reasons for keeping him away." Daniel shared a loaded look with Angie. She'd read some of the letters his former recruit had been leaving at his New York mansion. One letter would go on and on about how Daniel was the only true leader Seth wanted to see on a throne and how he just wanted to make things right and give Daniel everything he wanted. The next would be a single paragraph threatening to announce a bounty on Daniel's head through his network, whatever that was.

Daniel cleared his throat, intent on changing the topic away, but Sakshi beat him to it. "What became of the Eden emigrants?" she asked, he threads retracting slightly to her. "I saw them go through the Threshold change, but then the Sight faded."

"We don't know," Daniel replied. "We don't know how many layers out that half-world is, so we don't know if those who were there would have been able to just Skip back. We haven't yet been able to sort out who went through, to track down if they made it back or not. Thresholds can only be built from our world, but the key was banished somewhere, so perhaps someone opened a new Threshold for them to return through. We don't know." Daniel's thoughts flicked across the patrician loyalists he might consider asking, like Noah, Marissa, Jasper Rose, and the other former Judges or Senators he had some report with, but dismissed the idea. Friendly communications hadn't been reestablished after the solstice coup, and the time was far from ripe to make a first attempt.

"And the ones outside of our world whose lives were once tied with yours? Once you stepped away from them, they also faded from my Sight."

The strangeness of telling a true Seer anything they didn't already know struck Daniel as he answered. "As far as I know, they are all fine for the moment." He had covertly checked up on Tonya and her family, and Angie's ex they'd bumped into in London, and knew that Hannah and Jonathan's kids had left to live with a relative, but he didn't think he could get through talking about it out loud again with Jonathan's death being an unavoidable part. "Yeah. They're fine. All of them made it out of the capital cities that took the worst damage, and are seeing the biggest lingering unrest. None were caught in the fires."

Sakshi nodded, her posture and aura sagging, and Mahina swooped in. "That's enough. You clearly need rest. Come. We'll get you situated." Daniel moved out of the way with Angie as Mahina, Anthony, and a few others who had established themselves as the outcast welcoming committee bustled the frail Sakshi away.

Angie waited until they were alone before turning to him, her voice low. "Where's Dawn? I haven't seen her since the memorial and burial." Daniel's mind tried to steer him away at the mention of Jonathan's memorial to spare him, and his aura snapped cold. "Sorry," Angie said, her elfin features drawn with sadness as her aura flared, offsetting his arctic expression.

Daniel waved a dismissive hand. "It's fine. She's trying to pursue the new resource production access, but it's off to a tiny, disappointing start. The world is a very, very big place, and for the rare folks both willing and able to produce anything, their quantities are very limited. This isn't an instant fix, but we do now have access to the potential of getting it working someday. When she's not doing that," Daniel shrugged, "you know."

Angie didn't have to reply, and Daniel sighed. They all knew. Jonathan was dead. There was a hole in the world, and the world wasn't as fixed as any of them had hoped.

They got home to their Cotswolds cottage an hour later, Voyaging right inside, their usual staunch wards still down from the small wake they'd hosted a few days ago after the larger memorial. "I'll get those back up," Daniel said, and Angie acknowledged mutely.

Both just faced each other for a long moment in the soft, tranquil silence. In the week since Angie's return at the solstice they'd barely touched at all despite living under the same roof, certainly never in front of witnesses, and Daniel's fingers flexed at his sides as he once more itched to caress her, but held back. Angie felt like chaos, and who he was inside was already in so much turmoil, feeling raw and tender in the absence of his dearest friend and the long, well-used protective masks of his years among the patricians that the thoughts of entwining himself fully with her again felt like playing with fire in a way he couldn't yet commit to.

Daniel jumped as the magically enhanced sat phone clipped to the back of his belt started ringing, already missing the full use of his sleek and silent cell. "Yeah?" he answered, and Anthony's voice cracked through the speakers.

"Turn on the radio. Seth's on. You want to hear this."

The line went dead and Daniel stepped away to the radio sitting on the kitchen counter, and set it to the local Imperial station. Angie stepped in close, and both listened tensely as Seth's voice filled the room, full of zeal and charisma.

"The Angel in the Forest. Two are one, one is two, all is nothing. This, my friends, is the prophecy that was spoken to me at the very moment the patrician Council fell. I am your angel. I have freed you from the oppression of the New Roman Empire that has oppressed you all for so long, just as the first Roman Empire oppressed and mistreated its citizens, even eradicating the true prophets of the savior. I say to you now. We have entered a new age. It is time to cleanse the earth and be reborn into a new age of mankind.

One forged through the crucible I promise of a world where heretics, sinners, and all those set against us first burn here, then in the eternal hell that awaits them."

The sound clicked over to some shitty cult song Daniel could vaguely remember Seth listening to at some point during their time in the cottage at the conference site, and he switched the radio off. Bile rose in his throat, but when he tried to reach for the will to go running off to pursue this latest shift of the world around him further out of his control or understanding, all he could find within was the deep ache of long grief. He turned to Angie, seeking her comfort, and when she spoke, he didn't have the energy to do more than let the words echo and fade in their tiny oasis of peace.

"I don't think the prophecy was about me."

Chapter Forty-Five

"Why here?"

Angie considered Jonathan's question, not sure she could explain. "Any place is as good as another. One of the ex-Councilors, Jasper Rose, has been spotted all over this part of the country."

"Have you told him the rest yet?"

"He knows the gist of it. We've talked, and I think he's coping. He'll be here soon to see me off. I'm already beaconing." Jonathan's ghost sunk back into the copper coin in her pocket and Angie touched the silver key at her throat, leaning back against the side of her new hatch-back in the bright desert sun. She already missed having a demon held inside. Maybe she could find her way back to the half-world where they lived…

She shook her head, taking a deep breath. The demons that had raged so hard and so long in her heart since escaping the depths of her abuse had finally calmed and quieted, the still, easy comfort their absence left in her chest still foreign to her. She should let herself be de-monless for a while. Especially since she had her best friend in her pocket whenever she needed companionship.

Daniel's arrival stirred up a cloud of dust, thanks to the currents in his bright yellow Air aura and Angie squinted, holding her breath, until it settled. She gave him a small, sad smile, and he returned it. "You all set? Looks like you have everything."

"Yeah. I think so. As long as Dawn got the constant refilling magic working on my gas tank, since a bunch of stations are closing."

Daniel moved nearer, his cane tapping on the packed dirt lot off the distant freeway in the empty desert valley, and Angie pushed off the car to face him, ending up closer to him than she'd intended. She felt herself flush, and her resolve faltered.

"Where will you go?" Daniel asked, his voice low.

"Reno, first. That's where Rose was spotted, and we need to find them before the mobs do. Sakshi says they are key to tracking down some of the keys to dangerous locked half-worlds that went missing." Angie shrugged, her eyes darting off to the horizon as the fresh, raw freedom of the open road tugged at her chest. "After that, anywhere I want, as always. I can drive anywhere in the Americas now that all the provincial borders have fallen. And if I want to go somewhere further, you know I can get there in a blink." She almost made a joke about seeing if she could visit half-worlds, too, in her car, but decided against it remembering how Daniel had reacted when she'd first tried it, so long ago now.

She could feel the nearness of her hometown in her bones, just a few hundred miles away, and she crossed her arms over her stomach, her fingers picking at the sleeve of the dark blue jacket that had once been her sisters, just over the faint scar above her elbow hidden beneath.

"So you'll come and visit?" Daniel's words were full of genuine, worried uncertainty, and a lump rose in Angie's throat.

"Yes. Of course." Daniel's answering smile still looked a little sad, and Angie added, "If nothing else, I'm sure that sleeping in my car again is going to get old real fast, and that soft mattress at the cottage will be too tempting to resist."

Daniel huffed a small laugh. "It will always be ready for you. Pursuing Seth and the Emperor in their hold-out in Rome, since we think they kept the nukes, won't take me far from home very often."

Daniel combed his shaggy hair straight back out of his face with one hand, and Angie's heart skipped a beat. She hadn't seen that gesture since before her banishment when he'd cut his hair shorter. The sight took her right back to who he had been in the early days. And who she had been. She missed both past versions of people she knew to her core. The strangeness of it, standing there, older and wiser, with Daniel before her made her aura leak oak and hickory smoke into the dry desert air.

"I just need to move. To be totally free for a little while," Angie whispered, second-guessing all of the long conversations she and Daniel had had about parting ways since the solstice, needing to make sure he understood her reasons one last time before it happened. "I need time alone to figure out who I am now, with everything that had been forcing me to be who I was now gone. I just need time."

"I understand," Daniel said, his gaze dropping to his shoes with a tight but gentle smile. "You know I'm feeling the same."

She did, and Angie tried her best to see the man before her as clearly and completely as she knew Jonathan would have effortlessly. The words 'I love you' formed on her lips, but she knew that if she spoke them, she wouldn't be able to do what she must. Instead, she thought it as hard as she could, letting it show in her face, eyes, and languid, silver aura, trusting that Daniel understood why she couldn't say it out loud, couldn't mean it in that way right then.

"Here," she said, twisting and leaning in through the open window of the car to grab a plastic cup from the console, holding it out to Daniel. He smiled fully, wide and genuine, at the large strawberry milkshake pearled with condensation, taking it from her happily. She grinned back, glad she'd thought to grab it at the pit stop she'd made ten minutes ago, and kept it from melting with a touch of magic.

"Do you remember the first time..." Daniel asked slyly before taking a long sip through the straw, and Angie laughed.

"Yeah, at the airport. You'd wanted one at the gas station in Nevada, but the muggers distracted you. It was the first thing I was ever able to give you. To say thank you for everything you were giving me. I'll always remember."

"Me too. And thank you." Daniel took another long sip, then stepped right up to Angie, reaching past her to set the milkshake on the roof of the car behind her, and the aroma of rosewood smoke crept into her aura before she could stop it.

"Can I ask for a favor before you go?" he asked, and Angie nodded, half-distracted by trying to cool the way she'd heated at his nearness. The smile lines around his eyes crinkled, and for the first time in a long time, Angie saw his tired age, starting to gray, and wondered how much time they had left toward the center of their shared life thread.

He pulled out his sleek black cell phone, and Angie shook her head with amusement. "That doesn't work anymore, not with the cell network down. That's why you gave me this, and hopefully got yourself a new one." She pulled the chunky satellite phone from the pocket of her jacket, wiggling it, before tossing it onto the passenger seat of her car.

"Yeah, I know," Daniel said awkwardly, his handsome face beneath his short, thick beard turning slightly pink. "I was actually wondering if it would be okay for me to take a picture of you? Please. It would mean a lot."

Emotion washed over Angie and she did her best to blink it away, shoving her hands into her pockets and nodding, since she suddenly couldn't get anything to pass her throat. Daniel stepped back a pace, unfolding a pair of reading glasses onto his nose one-handed and lifting the phone. Angie did her best to smile as he leaned back, staring at the little screen, and tapped it.

He turned the phone around to show her for a few seconds before putting his glasses back away, and Angie marveled, half dismayed and half comforted, at how easily she could mistake the Angie in the image for her exactly as she had been many years ago. In another hatchback. In the same blue jacket, her long, curly auburn hair pulled up into a braided bun. The same wide smile with sad eyes. She wished she could see all the ways she'd changed internally in the snapshot, and the wish brought up far more emotion than she expected.

"Wait," she said when her voice returned, holding out a hand as Daniel stepped forward, starting to drop the cell phone back into his pocket. She leaned forward, slipping it from his grasp, and tucked her other arm around behind Daniel's back, pulling him in close and nestling into his side. She raised the phone high in front of them, and his thumb absently rubbed along her ribcage, making her melt. Her heart swelled at the sight of the pure, open joy she saw in both of the faces on the screen, and clicked the button, capturing the moment.

She shifted away, overly aware of how much she didn't want to, and held the phone back out to him. When he reached out to take it, Angie shifted it to her other hand, grasping his with hers, their thumbs intertwined. Her eyes brimmed as Daniel gasped, his lips parting, and then smiled at her with his dark eyes. She let them just stand like that for a long, beautiful interval, certain that Daniel was remembering the first time they ever touched skin-to-skin without his curse affecting her, their hands clasped just the same, just as she was.

"I'm going to get that photo from you," Angie said when she finally let go and relinquished the phone, her voice gruff. "Off that phone, someday, when we've repaired the world enough to do so with cell reception, or internet, or something like that again."

Daniel's mouth pulled down at the corners, but his aura breathed warm and rich. "Good. I'll hold you to that." He paused, searching Angie's face. "We'll figure it out. It won't be like this for long. We'll find a way to fix it."

Angie's lips trembled as they stretched, feeling more hopeful, free, and quietly confident than she had in longer than she could remember. "I know." The words caught in her mind, but she wrapped her fingers around the heavy copper coin in her pocket, and the grief that swelled in her chest eased just as fast.

Daniel took a deep breath, standing so close Angie could have kissed him, and his full attention seemed to return to him. "Be safe. Please. This world out here wasn't safe when I met you, and I fear it's going to get worse before it gets better."

A growing shape in the corner of Angie's vision made her shift her gaze over Daniel's shoulder. On the far horizon, a plume of gray smoke stretched up slowly for the clear, wide desert skies overhead. Angie pulled her attention back before he could notice, trusting that once she got moving, she would get to anything and everything she needed to in time. Daniel raked his hair straight back off his face just like he used to when his hair was longer, before the beard. Angie realized it was the first time she'd seen him make the familiar, endearing gesture since her return from banishment nearly a year ago, and promised herself she'd see it again.

"I will be. You just do the same. And I promise—I will come home."

THE END

—◦◆◦—

Did you enjoy this book? You can make a big difference! I would be very grateful if you could scan the code below and spend just five minutes leaving a review on this book's Amazon page. Honest reviews of my books are the most powerful tool in my arsenal when it comes to getting my books in front of more readers, and it helps me write more of what you want and like!

A Mind of Smoke

Want to follow Angie and Daniel's next adventure and get updates on the next installments in the series? Or just chat? I love hearing from my readers, so scan the code below to stay connected on Facebook!

www.facebook.com/rebeccamaeve.hartwell

Also by Rebecca Maeve Hartwell

Continue the adventure with Angie and Daniel in the next book in the Unlocked series, coming in 2024!

~

Want to catch up on their story so far? Check out the earlier books in the series!

A Heart of Flame – The Unlocked series Book 1

Is magic all she's ever wanted, or one more dangerous gift?

When fire erupts within Angie, she's snatched away into a glittering new world, leaving behind her suffering and turmoil under the boots of the Empire. As beautiful facades burn away, Angie fights to fix a world even more broken than she is.

Daniel's assignment proves far more dangerous than he bargained for. Angie transforms his life in one impossible way after another, ripping away his masks. As she does, he fears for the secrets they conceal. Salvation, trap, or ruin; he's only certain of one thing—she changes every-thing.

Caught in a web of beautiful lies and painful truths, se-cret passions battle against deep wounds. Will Angie and Daniel find enough healing in each other to overcome their darkness with light? Or will they succumb to the demons in their lives and tumble beneath the deadly currents of the magical world...

A *Heart of Flame* is the first book in the dark-romantic ur-ban-fantasy series Unlocked, featuring complex charac-ters, immersive worlds, and high-stakes magic. If you like rebellious hope, dizzying luxury, and spicy connections, you'll love this dazzling new action romance! Unlock A *Heart of Flame* to start this captivating series today!

Grab it here!

A Heart of Flame Paperback

~

A Soul of Light – The Unlocked series Book 2

A lock is broken, the world is cracked, and time is running out.

Angie dreads the consequences she didn't think she'd live to face when she defied the patricians and released their ancient, hoarded magic. But the doorways she's opened are being crossed from both sides, and she may be the key to unlocking secrets long kept safe. If her flames illuminate the truth, anyone standing beside her will face a high price from those who want her dead.

Daniel's dreams of relief, belonging, and hope for everyone he loves are tantalizingly within reach. He tries to keep his balance as worlds collide, reveling in his restored magical and political power. But he must bargain what's dearest to him as disruption threatens to give way to desperation, and may lose as much as he hopes to gain.

Angie and Daniel must return to the opulent, corrupt community that nearly broke them, falling into a maze of betrayal and warping power, and treacherous encounters with malicious creatures threaten to cut the threads of their existence short. Can they prevail through their ever-changing world of political scandal and forbidden magic? Or will they lose each other—and themselves—to the currents of fate which threaten to rip them apart...

A *Soul of Light* is the second book in the dark-romantic urban-fantasy series Unlocked, featuring complex characters, immersive worlds, and high-stakes magic. If you like rebellious hope, dizzying luxury, and spicy connections, you'll love this dazzling new action romance! Unlock A *Soul of Light* to continue this captivating series today!

Grab it here!

A Soul of Light Paperback

~

Also available in the Unlocked Universe:

A Life of Stone - A prequel novella in the Unlocked series.

Frozen in stone is torture beyond imagining. Returning to life is worse.

Demitria has been sleeping in stone for two and half thousand years. The centuries pass, barely noticed, until someone touches her with a spark of familiar warmth, and her blood quickens beneath her skin of marble. Her desire to live pulls her on, even as the trials of her past—and the fears of her future—push her to stay safe, cold, and solid.

Nikolaos is forced to set aside the revenge that has driven him into the life he now leads when he sees a familiar face at an auction. Not among the sea of wealthy bidders, but on an implausibly lifelike statue. He becomes its caretaker when his employer purchases it, both men hoping it will bring their dreams to life.

When the man who holds them in his unforgiving fist demands what he cannot have, chaos tears through the beautiful facade of the isolated world he rules. Will Demitria and Nikolaos overcome their ancient wounds, finally claiming their own destinies? Or will they lose everything to the hard fate the Gods—and other magic users—have dealt them...

A *Life of Stone* is a teaser taste for the dark-romantic urban-fantasy series *Unlocked*, featuring complex characters, exciting alternate worlds, and high-stakes magic. If you like rebellious hope, dizzying luxury, and spicy connections, you'll love this captivating new action romance! Unlock A *Life of Stone* to start exploring this captivating series today!

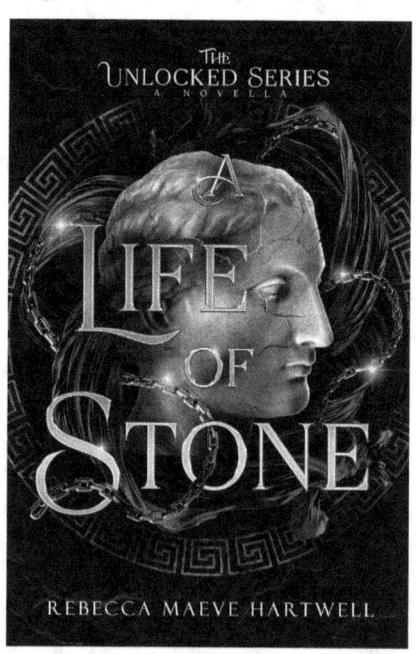

To claim your FREE ebook copy of A *Life of Stone*, scan the code below, Or visit: www.rebeccamaevehartwell.com/a-life-of-stone

A Life of Stone

About the Author

Rebecca Maeve Hartwell grew up unschooled on a horse ranch in the Nevada mountains, immersed in her own world of fantasy. Playing dress-up with elaborate backstories, building forts and inventing entire fictional wars in which to defend them, devouring library books, or even directing friends in plays and home movies she scripted, everything was a story, and everyone was a character in them.

Despite this, she never considered a career in writing until her mid-twenties, instead indulging her love for plots and magic through re-enactment, acting, and escaping bad situations through daydreams. It was in the darkest moments in her life that the seeds for the first novel she wrote were planted, and she became an author in the hopes of helping others to escape, survive, recover, and thrive, just as the stories of others helped her to.

Rebecca lives and writes in Maine with her two cats. She enjoys Lindy Hop swing dancing, sewing costumes, and long drives in the dark with just the right music playing.

Learn more about Rebecca Maeve Hartwell and her books by joining her newsletter through her website:

www.rebeccamaevehartwell.com

Or by following her page on Facebook at:

www.facebook.com/rebeccamaeve.hartwell

Many, many thanks to every singe person who encouraged and supported me in writing. I love you all dearly.

Cover By Faera Lane.

Copy Editing by Tiffany Shand of https://writenowcreative.com/

Further Editorial and feedback thanks to:

Greg Marbais

Mary Pel

Jocelyn Montana

Laura Fortier

www.ingramcontent.com/pod-product-compliance
Lightning Source LLC
Chambersburg PA
CBHW072108250626
47159CB00007B/2349